EVERE

A Collection of Contemporary Turkish Literature

AHMET ÜMİT

Born in 1960 in the city of Gaziantep in southern Turkey. He moved to Istanbul in 1978 to attend university. In 1983, he both graduated from the Public Administration Faculty of Marmara University, and wrote his very first story. An active member of the Turkish Communist Party from 1974 until 1989, Ümit took part in the underground movement for democracy while Turkey was under the rule of a military dictatorship between 1980-1990. In 1985-86, he illegally attended the Academy for Social Sciences in Moscow. He has one daughter, Gül. Since 1989, Ümit has published one volume of poetry, three volumes of short stories, a book of fairytales, one novella, and six novels. One of Turkey's most renowned contemporary authors, Ümit is especially well known for his mastery of the mystery genre, as reflected in many of his bestselling novels and short story volumes. Drawing upon the unique political and historical background of his home country, Ümit delves into the psyches of his well-wrought characters as he weaves enthralling tales of murder and political intrigue.

AMY SPANGLER

A native of Ohio, resident of Istanbul. She is the co-editor and co-translator of *Istanbul Noir* (Akashic Books, 2008) and the translator of *The City in Crimson Cloak* by Asli Erdogan (Soft Skull, 2007) as well as many other works of Turkish fiction. Spangler is currently director of the literary agency AnatoliaLit (www.anatolialit.com and lecturer in translation studies at Okan and Boğaziçi universities.

PATASANA

Ahmet Ümit

Translated by
Amy Spangler

§

Publication No. 894

Contemporary Turkish Literature 9

Patasana

Ahmet Ümit

Original Title:

Patasana

Translated by Amy Splanger

Cover Design by Utku Lomlu

Page Layout by Bahar Kuru Yerek

First English Edition: February 2011

ISBN: 978 - 975 - 289 - 800 - 4

Certifacate No: 10905

Printed by Melisa Matbaacılık

Tel: +90 (0212) 674 97 23

Fax: +90 (0212) 674 97 29

EVEREST PUBLICATIONS

Ticarethane Sokak No: 53 Cağaloğlu/ISTANBUL

Tel: +90 (212) 513 34 20-21 Fax: +90 (212) 512 33 76

Distribution: Alfa, Tel: +90 (212) 511 53 03 Fax: +90 (212) 519 33 00

e-mail: info@everestyayinlari.com

www.everestyayinlari.com

www.twitter.com/everestkitap

To Gül

“The squares of the city I filled with the bodies of those I had slaughtered. The city and its homes I pillaged and plundered, demolishing them from foundation to roof. The temple towers of brick and mud, the temples and their gods I razed to the ground. Canals I had dug from the Euphrates into the heart of the city. Thus did I drown the temples, the gods, and the city itself, that no one might find them ever again.”

From a tablet of Assyrian King Sennacherib

Samuel Noah Kramer, *Mesopotamien*, pg. 77,
Rovvohlt Verlag.

CHAPTER ONE

The first thing she saw was the light, flashing like a firefly in the darkness that had suddenly descended upon the plain. Leaning against the stone wall of the ancient city, she followed it with her eyes, the only thing visible there in the enveloping blackness. She was tired and alone, yet oddly, she did not miss the others. A light wind carried the delicately sweet fragrance of oleander. She closed her eyes to better take in the feeling of the wind upon her skin. As soon as she closed her eyes, however, the breeze stopped. A buzzing noise seemed to issue from a far off place and, curious to discover its source, she opened her eyes. The fireflies, she saw, had begun to multiply; two, five, eight... Soon, their numbers were increasing so quickly that she could no longer keep count. And as the number of fireflies increased, so did the darkness of the night. And as the night grew darker, the buzzing sound grew closer. Pulling herself away from the wall, she listened intently to the approaching sound. No, she hadn't been mistaken; it wasn't coming from the fireflies. Her eyes waited patiently, focused upon the crowd of lights that multiplied as they drew closer, her ears intent on the buzzing sound as it rose and fell in waves. She could hear the sounds better now and, although she still couldn't quite make out what was being said, the melody seemed familiar. And then she recognized that old, familiar refrain: "Allahu Ekber. Allahu Ekber."

Suddenly the fireflies disappeared, and people bearing torches emerged from within the darkness. In the light of the torches Esra could see the men's fists stretched out towards the sky, and their green flags waving against the black background of the night. She felt her entire body grow tense with fear. In a state of panic, she stepped backwards in retreat, but was stopped by the ruined walls of the ancient city. The crowd was approaching with slow but determined footsteps. "Allahu Ekber. Allahu Ekber..."

All of the townspeople stood facing her, their eyes riveted upon her. The light stirring in the shadows pulled strange masks over the faces of these people she knew, frightening her senseless and making her heart beat so madly she thought it would rip right through her chest. "Allahu Ekber. Allahu Ekber..."

She knew she had to escape, but she couldn't. She remained rooted to the ancient wall, her eyes fixed upon the approaching crowd. The mass of people before her showed no signs of anger; it was cool and measured as step by step it drew closer, crying out in a single voice: "Allahu Ekber. Allahu Ekber..."

Terrified, she lost all hope of being rescued. Covering her head with her hands, she fearfully waited for the first blow to strike, be it stone or fist. But instead of a blow came the sound of a voice which, although it seemed to come from afar, was strong enough to drown out "Allahu Ekber." She lifted her head and, staring into the darkness behind the crowd, tried to understand what the voice was saying. The person to whom the voice belonged was repeating two words, two familiar words. She could hear the words and she knew that she knew them, but she was unable to figure out exactly what they were. She just kept listening, as if mesmerized by the voice. The person behind the unearthly chant was a stubborn one, for he resolutely continued repeating those same words until finally, she was able to discern what it was he was saying.

"Esra Hanım... Esra Hanım..."

As soon as she grasped the words, the inside of the room lit up, sunlight pouring in through the window to restore to her belongings their rightful appearance. The room she occupied, a small room of the elementary school, the halls of which had been overflowing with village children just two months ago, was filled with her things. In one swift motion she sat up in her bed. Someone was beating madly upon the door to her room as that voice stubbornly continued to repeat her name.

"Esra Hanım... Esra Hanım..."

She stumbled blindly out of bed, and without a second thought as to her actions, made a beeline for the door. But when she reached the middle of the room, she stopped. She tried to calm herself down. It was at that moment that she realized she had nothing on but a T-shirt. "Just a minute, I'm coming," she called out to the person at the door, her voice still trembling from the chilling thrill of her dream. She headed for the linen pants she had left on the chair next to the head of the bed. The person at the door must have heard her, for he stopped yelling. While putting on her pants, she thought about the voice and was sure that she recognized it but, still suffering from morning grogginess, was unable to identify its owner. It wasn't until she opened the door and found herself looking into his timid dark eyes that she realized the voice belonged to Captain Eshref.

Captain Eshref was standing a step away from the door. As soon as she saw him, her lips instantly formed into a smile. She had never been fond of uniforms, but on Eshref the crude, green cloth seemed to shed its function and take on the appearance of a normal outfit. She thought of her high school days in Istanbul when she made fun of girls who went out with military school students, calling them "imbeciles" who were "just taken with those pretentious uniforms." However, she felt no shame at "stooping" to that same level herself now. In fact, although she believed that such relationships during an excavation had a negative effect upon her productivity, she nevertheless continued cultivating her interest in this tall, tough-looking yet shy military Captain.

Once she had overcome the shock of this morning surprise, Esra's thoughts anxiously turned to her appearance. She had just planted herself in front of the man without even looking into a mirror to straighten up her hair and make sure she looked presentable. In the mornings, her face would usually be swollen, her eyes bloodshot. But this morning, she was doing an injustice to herself by thinking such thoughts. The uncombed hair falling across her forehead gave her face an expression of innocence while her large hazel eyes sparkled pleasantly from beneath eyelids heavy with drowsiness.

Esra's was a beauty not so obvious at first glance; rather, it was a beauty to be discovered, gradually, over time. Although she was well into her thirties, she had a petite face that had not yet dared to show any wrinkles, large honey-colored eyes looking out from beneath brown eyebrows, and, located between her small nose and delicate, slightly asymmetrical chin, lips that were neither thick nor thin and were as adept at talking as they were at kissing. The apparent flaw of her crooked mouth, which became more obvious when she talked, only added a touch of childishness to her serious face, and hence an air of cuteness. But Esra herself was oblivious to this; she didn't think of herself as being attractive at all.

It was a rather forced smile that the Captain wore upon his face as he greeted Esra. "Sorry we had to wake you up," he said, groping for words. "I tried to reach you on your cell phone, but it was off."

"I turn it off at night," said the young woman. "But it doesn't matter that you've woken me up, I usually get up around this time anyway." It was only as she reached the end of her sentence that she became aware of the worried look on Eshref's face. "What's up with you? What happened?"

The question only caused Eshref's pupils, already in a stir, to move about more quickly as he struggled to look the young woman in the face. After some hesitation the bad news finally rolled off his tongue.

"Hadji Settar's dead."

The impact of his words struck Esra like a violent blow. Hadji Settar's white-bearded, smiling face with the pom-pom topped hat that made him look like an Aramaean religious man who had lived thousands of years ago appeared before her eyes.

"He's dead?"

Actually, she had heard quite clearly? what the Captain had said, but she wanted to be certain.

"Yes, he died this morning." The Captain felt no relief at having delivered the news. His voice was heavy with more than just the depression brought on by news of a catastrophe; its inauspicious tone gravely implied that an ominous prediction was about to come true. "He fell from the minaret. He went up into the minaret this morning like he does every Friday to make the call to prayer..."

He fell from the minaret? So that means it was an accident! Esra felt the weight of her grief become lighter.

"He shouldn't have been climbing up into the minaret at his age," she mumbled.

The Captain shook his head sorrowfully, as if he could guess what she was thinking.

"We don't think it was an accident. We think someone threw him off the minaret."

"Are you sure?" the young woman asked. The anxiety in her voice was unmistakable.

"The walls of the minaret balcony are pretty high, it would be impossible for him to just lose control and fall off. Someone must have thrown him..."

She tried to object, "But this is pure speculation?"

"If only that were the case," said the Captain apologetically. "The congregation at morning prayer saw a monk dressed in black running away from the mosque..."

Hadji Settar thrown from the mosque, a monk dressed in black fleeing from the scene... It was all downright confounding and she was having a hard time grasping just what had happened.

"Wait a minute Eshref Bey," she said interrupting him, "this is all wrong. Come inside and let's start from the beginning."

For a brief moment, a look of indecision appeared on the Captain's dark face, but it quickly gave way to compliance. He turned to the private who was waiting in front of the jeep parked out front, rifle in hand.

"Don't go anywhere!" he yelled. "We're going to leave shortly."

The soldier quickly stood at attention and roared in reply, "Yes, sir!"

Esra let the Captain inside, and before closing the door her gaze settled upon the Euphrates flowing in the distance just behind the young private. The river, assuming a purplish blue hue beneath the morning sun, silently continued to flow along the same bed as it had for thousands of years.

She regretted having asked the Captain in when she realized just how messy her room was, but then chided herself for having such a thought. Faced with a death that might just put the entire excavation in danger, there she was thinking about how messy her room was! Meanwhile Eshref, who was still in a state of shock, was in no condition to be concerned by her lack of tidiness. She cleared off the chair next to the table before asking Eshref to have a seat.

The Captain collapsed onto the chair as Esra settled into the one across from him. The photographs lying on the table immediately caught Eshref's eye. The Captain was looking with such intense interest at the various photographs of the cuneiform tablets that one would have thought he could actually read Akkadian. Esra, however, was not in any condition to satisfy his curiosity at the moment. She quickly gathered the photographs up and placed them in front of her.

"Are you sure Hadji Settar was murdered?"

"I'm afraid so," said the Captain, finally coming to himself. "The eyewitnesses' statements and the investigation we conducted at the scene of the incident indicate that this is a murder case," he concluded, his eyes timidly focused upon her face. This frightened expression of a soldier who had served in the front lines during the war in this region, who had participated in dozens of military clashes, and who had seen hundreds of dead bodies, both surprised Esra and upset her. It upset her because Captain Eshref was at the top of the list of people she felt she could trust. He had supported the excavation team from the very first day of the season and was the first to assist them whenever they were in need. But then maybe she was wrong. Maybe the Captain wasn't really scared... Perhaps it was just that, dumbfounded by this mysterious death, he was confused as to what to do next...

"Look, Eshref Bey," she said, putting up the strongest front she could, "you know how important this is. If the news spreads that Hadji Settar was thrown from the minaret, and especially that a monk dressed in black was responsible..."

"It's started to spread already," replied Eshref in a hopeless voice. "The mosque's imam, Abid, gave a sermon at the head of the dead body saying that this happened because they dug up The Black Tomb."

Esra shuddered. The scenario that had occurred to her as a mere possibility when she first came to the region and saw the holy burial place at the site was now happening for real.

"That's ridiculous! How can they possibly think such a thing?"

The Captain didn't reply, but Esra believed that he thought if the excavation were stopped, everything would get back on track, or that he at least favored such a possibility. More importantly, she knew that if he wanted to, he could indeed put an end to the excavation. The question was, would he really do such a thing?

"You have to find whoever did this," said Esra after a brief silence. She realized that her voice came out a bit louder than necessary, but if she remained silent, the indecisiveness that had captured the Captain would take her into its clutches as well. "You must find whoever did this," she repeated resolutely. "If they're found, then it'll be obvious that this has nothing to do with our excavation."

She thought she detected a certain sparkle in Captain Eshref's eyes. Taking this as a sign that she was beginning to have an effect upon him, she continued speaking in her tone of unwavering conviction.

"This is a small place, it shouldn't be that difficult to find the murderer."

Avoiding her glance, Eshref mumbled worriedly, "It won't be that easy if it's the insurgents who are behind it."

"Insurgents? You mean, you think it was they who killed Hadji Settar?"

"Absolutely. I reckon that they escaped over here, to these parts. We've searched the fields around Göven Village but haven't been able to find anybody. Since I was already in the area, I thought I'd stop by and deliver the bad news."

"Thank you for letting me know," said Esra, "but this idea that the insurgents are behind it doesn't seem very reasonable to me. What reason would they have for killing Hadji Settar?"

"To create unrest, anarchy, to shake up people's trust in the state."

These grounds didn't convince Esra either.

"With so many issues that they could readily use as a means of provocation, I really don't think they would feel the need to commit such a murder."

"You don't know the people of this region at all. You're digging at a spot that is sacred to them. And this makes the townspeople feel uneasy. Rebels don't hesitate to use any opportunity they can to create unrest. That's why they killed Hadji Settar."

"I'm not so sure, I think it's more likely others are behind this."

Even if he didn't agree with her, the Captain still looked at the young woman attentively, as if trying to grasp what she was getting at.

"I think it was religious fanatics who killed Hadji Settar," Esra continued. "You said yourself that Abid Hodja immediately started talking about us as soon as we arrived, and you know that I've been receiving threatening phone calls."

"But we don't know whether the people threatening you are religious fanatics or not."

"I think it's them. I can tell it's them, from their style. They used the word 'Allah' in every sentence. And even though they've sent numerous threats, never once have they used a swear word."

Esra paused. "But then of course, nothing can be said for certain," she added. "If only you could catch them, then everything would come out in the open. And we wouldn't have any problems with the locals anymore either."

"Yes, you would. Believe me, even if we did find the murderers, the townspeople would still blame the excavation. Before the excavation started, everything was just fine. 'These people came along and turned our tranquil life into chaos,' that's what they'll say."

"But that's just ignorance," she objected.

"Call it whatever you damn well please, but it's the way these people live," said the Captain, quickly reducing Esra to silence.

"So what are we going to do?" Esra asked in a tense voice. "Are we just going to leave the excavation half-finished?"

"I don't know, believe me, I really don't know, Esra Hanım."

This cowering state, this submissive attitude of his was starting to get on her nerves.

"Look Captain," she said, placing great emphasis upon the title 'Captain', "you may not know what *you're* going to do, but *I* have to carry out this excavation until the job is completely done. We've discovered some very important finds here and I won't leave this job half-finished because of some folk's groundless beliefs."

The look of indecision in the Captain's dark eyes was replaced by one of condemnation.

"A person has died," he said in a knowing voice.

"And that's exactly why we shouldn't leave the excavation half-finished," said Esra, firing right back. "Hadji Settar was on our side. He said that it was not disrespectful for us to excavate at the site of the holy tomb. Maybe that's why he was killed. If we leave the excavation half-finished, that would above all be an act of disrespect to the memory of Hadji Settar. We have to continue with the excavation so that the murderers don't achieve their goal."

This time, what she said made an impact. The Captain's anger was dissipated and his face assumed a more determined expression. But it could hardly be said that their conversation had put him at ease. For a while the two of them sat without speaking, until the Captain motioned towards the photographs.

"Are these finds from the excavation?" he asked.

Esra also had started looking at the photographs.

"Yes, the first tablets we found. They were written approximately two thousand seven hundred years ago."

The Captain picked up one of the photographs and carefully began studying the scrawls on it.

"Who wrote this?" he asked.

"The Hittites, or rather, the Neo-Hittites."

"Are these Neo-Hittites the ones we call 'Eti'?"

"Yes, the founders of Anatolia's first large empire. Although they were of Indo-European lineage, they resembled our own ancestors, the Ottomans. Just like the Ottomans, they too migrated to Anatolia from abroad, and just like the Turkish tribes, they lived together with the people of Anatolia for centuries, blending together with the locals before establishing a large empire. And when I say large, I really mean large. At the time, their empire was second in size only to that of the Egyptians."

"Wow, so it really was a large empire," said the Captain, impressed. "So what kind of writing is this?"

"Cuneiform. Actually, the Neo-Hittites used hieroglyphics. In this case, though, the scribe used cuneiform to make it more durable. What's more, in order for the tablets to be accessible to a wider audience, he wrote in the Akkadian language. Akkadian was like English in those days... It was the written lingua franca by which different countries in Mesopotamia and Anatolia understood one another."

"So can you understand what's written on the tablets?"

"Of course we understand... Timothy Hurley, the American who is our dead languages expert, has deciphered ten tablets so far... And it turns out that we've got an extremely interesting find on our hands, because these don't look at all like the kind of tablets we're used to uncovering."

The Captain's thick but shapely eyebrows became slightly knit.

"How's that?"

"Tablets usually have to do with some kind of royal testament, religious text, pact between countries, social law, treaty, or epic poem, but a very different story is told on these tablets."

"A story?" asked the Captain curiously.

"Well, the word 'story' just kind of slipped out, I mean, well, perhaps I should have said confessions. In any case, these tablets comprise the earliest non-official historical document ever known so far. That is to say, these tablets were not commissioned by any king."

"Who wrote them then?"

"Somebody by the name of Patasana. He was the chief scribe of the palace, a very important government position among the Hittites. These men were extremely well educated. They knew several languages. Their duty was to compose texts as dictated by the king, not to write down their own feelings, thoughts, and memories. But that didn't keep the scribe Patasana from writing down his own story. That's why the tablets are so important. We're thinking of announcing this discovery of ours to the whole world soon."

"Is it really that important?"

"Extremely important. Have you ever heard of The Epic of Gilgamesh?"

"I've heard of it, never read it though."

"Well, it's one of the earliest written epics in human history. And we think that these tablets are just as important. We believe that what we have here is the earliest documentation of humankind's non-official history. We're going to hold an international press conference sometime in the coming days. The German Archaeological Institute has even started working out the details of just how we're going to go about announcing this important find."

"So what did the man write that makes it so important?"

"We think that he's telling the story of the ancient city's final days. And together with the history of the city, his own personal history as well. The first tablet begins, 'I was a scoundrel living in the age of tyrants.'"

The Captain looked thoughtfully at the tablets a while longer before standing up and saying that it was time for him to get going. Once on his feet, however, he paused for a moment to take yet another look at the photographs on the table, then turned to Esra and with a bitter smile upon his lips mumbled, "So he says, 'I was a scoundrel living in the age of tyrants', eh?"

THE TABLET ONE

I was a scoundrel living in the age of tyrants. A scoundrel made by the gods into a coward. The most repugnant of scoundrels, and the most pitiable. A scheming palace scribe whose heart fed on sycophancy and whose mind fed on animosity.

Whereas he should have been murmuring poems under the spell that the real lords, the Storm God of the Sky Teshup and his wife the Sun Goddess Hepat together with our Goddess Kupaba, blew into his breath, he became a former poet who did not hesitate to betray even his own competence by composing treaties in the self-interest of kings.

A two-faced man of ceremonies who, hiding his deep pain behind his majestic clothes and the magnanimous hate that pervaded his body behind a mask of happiness thicker than bronze, instantly appeared before the King of Hatti at the latter's every command.

The most dishonorable man on the face of this earth who, while his beloved was dying for the sake of her love, chose to remain silent, holding his hands together at his breast with all of the dignity of his allegiance to the king. The disgrace of men. The most despicable of profligates who, rather than honorably die for love, did not hesitate to take refuge in the magnificent shadow of his own worthless existence which continued to grow amongst the stone walls of the palace.

I, Patasana, the advisor to King Pisiris, the chief scribe of the Hittite palace, a valuable member of the parliament of Panku, am the most degenerate of nobility.

I, who swim amongst the dead, I, whose fate as determined by the gods is to writhe in pain for eternity, am the chief scribe of the palace, Patasana.

Miserable Patasana who, with the treaties and letters he wrote, changed the destiny of his country, but failed to influence his own.

I say to you who will find these tablets: Beware. May the curse of the gods that has turned my life from a flowering tree into a dry branch not fall upon you as well. May they not condemn you to a life of unhappiness by the commands of a tyrant king as they have mine.

Before reading these tablets, go to the temple. Win over the hearts of the thousand gods of the Land of Hatti. Take valuable votive offerings and pay your respects to my Lord and yours, Storm God of the Sky Teshup, his wife the Sun Goddess Hepat, and the Goddess Kupaba. Offer these up that another person may not be added to the thousands who, because of me, have been crucified, flayed, burnt, and exiled from their homeland. And may this curse upon me of so many years not lead to the ruination of yet another.

If you are not going to do as I say, then by no means should you look at, touch, or read these tablets. Do not breathe in the moldy air of this underground room of stone where I have hidden them. Whether you are a youth with legs as strong as those of a filly, or an elder who can barely stand on his own two feet, run with all of your might, run far, far away from here. Do not mention these tablets to anyone, not the person closest to you, not the woman you embrace at night. Maybe then the gods will forgive you, maybe then you will escape from this curse that has collapsed like a dark wall onto this city of wisdom, onto the sparkling shores of the Euphrates.

Oh you, the sight of whom is foreign to my eyes, the voice of whom is foreign to my ears, the name of whom is foreign to my memory. I know that when you enter this room below the palace, this shelter of mine where I have hidden these tablets, I will have long ago departed into the land of the dead. I know that even after my death, the gods will not forgive me. They will make this curse, which burns and scorches my heart, my companion for eternity. And they should do so, for

I do not wish to be forgiven. I deserve this. My only wish is that those who come after me may know of my life and what I have lived. That is why I have written these tablets. And that is why I have baked them over a fire, making them hard that they may endure the test of time whose teeth are more ravenous than those of a ravenous mouse. I placed the tablets in order on the shelves I made in this room beneath the palace. These tablets are for you. These tablets are for the one who reads them.

You may doubt everything else, but you can be certain that these cuneiform tablets contain not a single falsity. I have written down my fear and my courage, my goodwill and my evil-doing, my trust and my doubt, my compassion and my treachery, my selfishness and my self-sacrifice, just as they are. Later I weighed these words in my mind. I took out those that were insipid, those that were false, and those that were exaggerated. I desired that the person who took these confessions, this grand testament of mine into his hands, not become bored, that he read it as he would the Legend of the God Telipinu, devouring it in a single sitting. However, even if I have failed to explain myself well, you can be certain that what I have written contains not a single word of untruth. My words that were not true I had carved onto the wall of the Water Gate in praise of the King Pisiris, and it was with these words that I furnished letters to the Phrygian King Midas to fool him; I strung such words together to confound the Urartian King Rusa and I expended them to provoke the Assyrian King Sargon. I used exaggerated, fancy, lying words to set kings, whose names were large but their selves small, and who swelled with pride the more they were flattered, quarreling with one another. Not even one of those lying words has made its way into the tablets you will read.

Stranger, you who are about to be partner to my secrets. Whether you are royalty or a man of piety, kind-hearted or a tyrant, intelligent or a good-for-nothing idiot, I do not know. I hope that you are a good person. I hope your heart is full of love and courage. I hope that you are intelligent enough to understand what you read, and to learn from what you understand. And I hope that you tell others of what you have read, and that they then tell others as well. I hope that my dark destiny will be whispered from ear to ear, that it will be translated into all of the languages of the Euphrates, that it will be written down on tablets and passed down from the old to the young, and that children will grow up with this legend. Maybe then people will start behaving sensibly, maybe then they will quit committing acts of tyranny, maybe then there will be less death, and maybe then there will be less pain.

CHAPTER TWO

The pain of the news she had just received cast a shadow upon Esra's face as she stood there in front of the door, watching the Captain's jeep make its jolting departure. Although the sun had not yet reached its peak, the entire plain was already enveloped in heat. In these parts, the morning coolness lasts no longer than breakfast time. After the frosty chill of the night that makes one shiver to the core, dawn approaches, turning the sky from black to ash, and from ash to orange. And as soon as the sun shows its nose at the peak of dawn, the brief coolness comes to an end and a hellish heat suddenly takes its place. The gardens over which the walnut, plum, apricot and mulberry trees cast their shadows; the fields of cotton and corn, their borders marked by large stones; the villages with their mudbrick houses; the sturdy fortress walls that continue to stand the test of time; and the ancient city—with its ruined palace, temples, reliefs, and countless secrets—which served as the Hittites' metropolis for hundreds of years begin to burn furiously.

In order to protect themselves from the heat, the excavation team begins working before sunrise, before the pleasant smelling, thin fog rising from the Euphrates melts into the vast blue of the sky. They lay down their tools before noon, in midmorning, and don't start working again until mid-afternoon, when the raging sun has finally calmed down and begins its descent back into the horizon. Only then do the archaeologists who still have work to do return to the dig. But today is Friday, that is, the day that everyone has off; a day when even the least religious of the workers goes to town to perform his Friday prayers. And so the excavation site has been turned over to the former smuggler Selo with his double breechloader rifle, and Eshref has had the chance to arouse Esra from her sleep this morning. If it had been any other day of the week, he would have had to go to the excavation site to find her.

As she watched the Captain's jeep, Esra wished he hadn't found her, hadn't delivered this news. The more she thought about it, the better she comprehended the magnitude of the disaster that might result from Hadji Settar's murder. And every detail that came to her mind lowered her spirits and increased her pessimism that much more. It was as if Captain Eshref had taken away Esra's trust in him and run off with it. The decisiveness she had shown just a few brief moments ago dissolved into a cloud of nothingness in no time, just like the cloud of dust that rose and then disappeared behind his jeep. She felt helpless, like a small girl left all alone in a country that was completely foreign to her.

Eshref was right; one couldn't rightly claim that Esra really knew the people of this area. It is true that she had been together with the locals of various parts of the Southeast for the two or three month excavation season each summer for the past ten years. During that time, she had been a guest in their homes, had supervised them as workers on the digs, had helped the women give birth, and had attended weddings. She had witnessed their ignorance, their generosity, their poverty, their small acts of cunning, their sincerity, and their merciless destruction of one another. But she still hadn't solved the mystery of the stern taciturnity that was never absent from their dark faces burnt so roughly by the sun. She couldn't understand whether it was their ignorance or their arrogance that they were hiding behind that silence of the downtrodden that they all, women and men, young and old alike, wore upon their faces like stern masks. Over the course of these ten years she had been unable to comprehend how they viewed life, the real motivations that underlie their actions, their thought system. Even though they lived in the same country, to her they were still like foreigners whose next move she could never predict. It was precisely this obscurity that had fueled her anxiety ever since they had started having problems because of the Black Tomb. Once, the matter seemed to have been settled thanks to Captain Eshref's resolute conduct and Hadji Settar's ability to calm everyone down. But now, having received news of Hadji Settar's death, that same anxiety began to swell within her once again, this time even stronger than before. For whatever reason, it was only the worst of possibilities that occurred to her. The most dreadful scenes passed before her eyes, from the villagers rebelling against the archaeologists, whom they held responsible for everything, with Hadji Settar's bloody shirt in their hands and the "Allahu Ekber" cry to God on their tongues as they come to stone the excavation site, like she had seen in her nightmare the night before, to them capturing every member of the team and burying them alive in the ancient fortress' underground storerooms which lie below the Black Tomb...

Violently swinging her right hand in the air as if trying to banish all of the negative images, she murmured, "I must remain calm, I must remain calm." Then suddenly she became frightened that someone might see her out there making strange movements and talking to herself like that and so she quickly went inside. She was overcome with a feeling of regret as soon as she stepped inside her room. Why didn't she tell the others about what was going on? If a decision was going to be made, it should be a decision reached by all of them together, in which case she would also be freed of having to accept all of the responsibility herself. It was a soothing thought, but a voice told her that it was wrong. She was the head of the excavation; the person to make the decision would be none other than Esra Beyhan. Actually, the person who had the ability to stop the excavation was the so-called authorized archaeologist. Unlike the head of the excavation, the government authorized archaeologist served as a kind of legal supervisor who inventoried the finds and oversaw the foreign archaeologists. He or she also possessed the power to terminate the excavation if deemed necessary. Fortunately, Kemal was the authorized archaeologist on this excavation. The truth of the matter, however, is that this was no coincidence. Kemal, a member of the staff at the Istanbul Archaeological Museum, had met and fallen in love with the photographer Elif the previous year on the excavation and so, with the help of some influential people at the ministry, had secured himself the position of authorized archaeologist on her dig. Frankly, it suited Esra's interests to have someone like Kemal with whom she could work in harmony, or, to be more precise, an old friend who wouldn't interfere in her work. If instead of Kemal she had been assigned one of those highly bureaucratic minded authorized archaeologists, as most of them were, what state would they be in right now? He or she probably would have stopped the excavation immediately. But then again, was it really right not to? A murder had been committed, meaning that not only the excavation but the lives of the excavation team members might be in danger as well. Naturally it was the right of each of the team members to put forward their own thoughts about whether or not the excavation should continue. However, it was she herself who, as the head of the excavation, would determine the options and present them to her colleagues. On the other hand, such an action could be perceived as weakness on her part and therefore demoralize them...

Standing there in the center of the room not knowing what to do, she noticed the pack of cigarettes on the small stand at her bedside and, without a second thought, headed straight for it. As she hurriedly pulled out a cigarette and placed it in the corner of her mouth, she noticed that her hands were trembling. At that moment, she realized just how much she despised the thoughts flying about in her head and the helplessness she felt, not to mention the trembling of her hands. She yanked the cigarette from between her lips and threw it onto the small stand, as if it were to blame for all of this. It wasn't a cigarette that she needed. She needed to get hold of herself; if she panicked, this excavation, the first excavation that she had ever headed, would end in a fiasco. Her failure to succeed would not only have a negative impact upon her career at the university, but would also mean that she would be a great disappointment to her esteemed teachers, like Behidje Hanım who had encouraged her to take on this excavation, and the President of the German Archaeological Institute's Istanbul Branch, Professor Krencker, a colleague who had always supported her. And what would she say to Elif? And Teoman? And Kemal? These young people had been working with her on this project for two years. The written correspondence, applications for permissions, efforts to find sponsors, establishing relations with foreign archaeologists, all of it had taken so many long months. And what about the foreigners on the excavation team? How would she explain the situation to them? Would she call Timothy and Bernd and tell them, "Sorry, but due to some stupid superstitious beliefs, just when we've found what may be the oldest documents of non-official history to exist on the face of this earth, we're going to pack up and move out"? Perhaps the more experienced Timothy would agree with her decision to a point, but wouldn't Bernd, who had tried so hard from the beginning to seize her own position and who, because he failed to achieve this goal, detested Esra, wouldn't he make fun of her? Wouldn't he write a letter to the German Archaeological Institute, the group covering most of the excavation expenses, telling them that she, the excavation head chosen by Istanbul University, had made a hash of the whole thing? No, no... She couldn't leave the excavation half-finished. She had to get her head together and do the right thing. The excavation crew needed to see an excavation head who was sure of herself, otherwise all of her efforts would be in vain. First of all, she had to win back the confidence she had lost; at the very least, she would have to regain the calm composure that she had had the previous day before she went to bed...

Maybe her morning grogginess was to blame for letting this sudden dose of bad news shake her up so, sending her into convulsions of doubt, wondering what to do next. It occurred to her that she hadn't even washed her face yet, but that doing so might help her to gather her thoughts together. She walked outside with an air of determination and headed for the faucet beneath the grapevine in the small garden. She turned on the water and began washing her face. Having devoured the frostiness of the night, the water was ice-cold. Indifferent to its chill, she splashed the water on her face and wet herself behind the ears and on the nape of her neck. Unfortunately, none of it did any good. Neither did the inauspicious uneasiness growing inside of her disappear, nor did the questions buzzing in her ears decrease. She tried to disregard it; "you're fine, you're fine," she said to herself, shaking her head. But she knew that she wasn't fine, what's more, she realized that her uneasiness was reflected in her face, that she looked like she would just start bawling at the slightest touch provocation. She went back to her room. Her eyes landed on the pack of cigarettes and, no longer able to resist, she took out a smoke and placed it in her mouth. She lit up impatiently and then, closing her eyes, took a few deep drags. A bitter tobacco smell filled the room. When she opened her eyes, she saw the ash-colored smoke rising to the ceiling and eagerly took several more puffs, as if the smoke would otherwise be going to waste. She looked at her hands; they were still shaking, but she felt better now. She sat down on the chair that the Captain had just gotten up from a short while before and began to think.

They must have murdered Hadji Settar in order to drive the archaeologists out of the region. She thought of Fayat, who ran errands for the Koran course, a tall man with big blue eyes and a sparse beard. Fayat was the son of Hadji Settar's sister, but he in no way resembled his uncle. Summer or winter, he walked around with a green turban on his head, a brown robe on his back, and a scepter in his hand. Fayat was as distant to the excavation team as Hadji Settar was close to it. Whenever they ran into him he would pucker his face as if it were Satan himself who stood before him. The second week of the excavation, he had walked all the way here to warn them. Esra could not forget that day.

Her assistant Teoman, the authorized archaeologist Kemal, excavation photographer Elif, and one of the students, Murat, were sitting beneath the arbor drinking tea and looking over the photographs that had been taken two days earlier, the same day that Fayat had made his appearance. Esra was the first one to see him. It was as if he were a spectre emerging from the heat. He just stood there beneath the sun, directing his blue eyes full of resentment straight at them. For a while, he stood there in complete silence, looking them up and down with his wild eyes as if they had come from another planet. Unable to discern what it was he wanted, the group just stared back at the strange man. Esra's eyes moved to Fayat's thin, dark ankles visible between his dust-covered plastic shoes and black, full-gathered knee breeches. The weakness of those ankles, which looked so brittle it seemed they might snap at any moment, strangely contradicted the strong looks emanating from his blue eyes. Unable to stand the tension, Esra finally told Fayat not to stand under the sun and asked him to come under the arbor. Her voice was friendly, with not a hint of belittlement. But Fayat's lips curved slightly upwards as a look of condemnation appeared on his face and he said, in his broken Turkish with his Kurdish accent, that it was a great sin to dig around the Black Tomb and that if they didn't stop this, they would be in big trouble. As the team members sat there looking at one another, lost as to how they should respond, Halaf, who served as both their driver and their cook and happened to be washing dishes in the kitchen at that moment, burst out of the kitchen, still in his apron.

"Hey, who do you think you're threatening, man?" he said, badgering Fayat. By the time Esra and her friends intervened, Halaf had already landed two whopping slaps that laid Fayat flat on the ground. By the time strapping Teoman and nimble Murat came to Fayat's rescue, Halaf had roughed him up thoroughly. Fayat lay on the ground with a busted lip, blood oozing out, painting his teeth a deep red. Fayat refused the hand that Teoman extended to him and stood up by himself. "Allah will punish all of you," he said as he shook the dust off of his breeches, his voice filled with hate, "Just wait, God Almighty will deliver your punishment."

Then he disappeared into the heat just as quickly as he had emerged from it. As soon as Fayat was gone, Esra called Halaf and told him that his job was to prepare their food, not to go beating up on people. Halaf, whose only intention had been to protect the archaeologists, and maybe show off a bit, was both surprised and saddened by Esra's attitude and apologized profusely.

Although she had been upset by the incident, Esra decided not to tell the Captain about it because she didn't want to get the gendarme involved, and she definitely did not want the matter to be blown out of proportion. She decided to talk with Hadji Settar instead. Hadji Settar was furious when he heard about what Fayat had done, and so he found him that night and gave him a sound scolding. Fayat never bothered the excavation crew again, but he still continued to scowl whenever he saw them, as if they were filth before his eyes.

Could Fayat have been the one who committed the murder? She didn't think so. Even if he did despise the excavation team, Fayat held his uncle Hadji Settar in high esteem. It was said that he had received his earliest religious education from him. But what if Fayat had more fanatical hodjas who were willing to run the risks of killing, of being killed? Even the mosque imam Abid had immediately begun talking of the curse on the excavation. There was talk about the secret activities of the radical group Hezbollah, especially in those areas where the Kurdish population was particularly large. What if they had murdered Hadji Settar because he was helping out the archaeologists? Why not? It's true that everybody in the area loved Hadji Settar. He was a man of tremendous influence in the region. Maybe Hezbollah had killed him for precisely that reason, because they saw him as an obstruction to their efforts to spread their own fundamentalist views amongst the people. And by knocking him off, they could more easily deal with the infidel archaeologists as well.

For centuries it had been the holy Black Tomb that the local people had taken refuge in and reached out to for help when there were droughts or floods, when they became ill or were barren, or when their daughters remained at home as spinsters. Esra and her team were going to excavate the Black Tomb, the holy burial place that assisted the villagers in this world and the hereafter. It was natural for them to view this as an attack upon their beliefs or, to use Fayat's words, a kind of blasphemy. And after the death of Hadji Settar, there was nothing to stop Hezbollah or whoever was responsible for the murder from provoking the people, as Abid Hodja had done this morning.

On the other hand, religious strife hadn't been the cause of any deaths in this region for years now. Although people did oppose things they found to be contrary to their beliefs and had been known to violently hurl threats at one another upon occasion, they had never killed anyone because of a religious dispute. So perhaps she was wrong. Perhaps it wasn't the religious fanatics who had committed the murders. But then who else could possibly want to murder Hadji Settar?

The thought occurred to her like a thunderbolt as her eyes slid to the tablet photographs lying on the table. "Treasure hunters," she murmured. Yes, treasure hunters... Why hadn't she thought of them before? They might be after the treasure the city's last Hittite king Pisiris was said to have hidden from the Assyrians. They probably believed that it was the treasure that the archaeologists were digging up and so, in order to stop the excavation and get their own hands on the treasure first, they murdered the excavation's most respected local supporter. Who could these incredibly merciless and cunning men be? Memili the Cripple, who had been caught earlier while trying to sell the reliefs from the King's Gate, appeared before her eyes. No, it couldn't be Memili the Cripple. It made no sense at all that that short, misshapen man, who talked about them behind their backs but who did nothing more than wheedle them whenever their paths actually crossed, could organize such a thoroughly planned conspiracy that included murder. But nobody else came to mind.

The Captain had said that it was a monk dressed in black who had pushed Hadji Settar from the minaret. The murderer must have worn black to disguise himself. Or perhaps he had specifically worn black in order to show the connection to the Black Tomb. This made more sense. That way the people, believing that a curse had been brought upon them, would exact more pressure to get the excavation stopped. Stopping the excavation suited the interests of both the fanatics as well as the treasure hunters. Yet the question remained: Who murdered Hadji Settar?

THE TABLET TWO

I, who am responsible for all murders, suspect of all crimes, both murderer and victim; I, the wretched servant cursed by the thousand gods of Hatti; I, the former poet, the hapless lover, the king's chief henchman and executioner; I, who betrays the bread he eats, the water he drinks, the air he breathes, and the land he lives upon; I, the scribe Patasana.

I say to him who will read these tablets: I hope that the cursed shadow of the gods stays away from you; I hope that you will have a life as sweet as honey and as long as the Euphrates.

I, too, once had just such a beautiful life. Many people in the country of the Hittites considered the Patasana family fortunate. My forefathers and their forefathers were neither slaves nor common people. They always resided in the palace. Ever since the time of the deified, great hero King Suppiluliuma they have been palace scribes. Our forefathers continued in this occupation even after our large country was divided into small kingdoms by the attacks of barbarians who arrived from the sea by ship and from land by their ox-driven carts hundreds of years ago, because the kings needed men like us who had received proper education and knew the rules of government. Therefore, my forefathers were always nearest to the king and each remained a valuable member of the Panku Assembly of Nobles. Just as kingship is passed down from father to son by the bond of blood, so, too, in our family is scribesmanship passed down from father to son. That is to say, I did not choose this occupation myself; it was forced upon me by virtue of blood, like an ill-omened brother.

Of my scribe forefathers, I know only my Grandfather Mitannuwa and my father Araras. And I love my grandfather Mitannuwa more than I do my father Araras. To me Mitannuwa is not just a grandfather; he is my teacher, my friend, the man who made Patasana Patasana. My grandfather Mitannuwa is every bit as friendly, warm, and jovial as my Father Araras is cold and insensitive. It is strange just to think that two creatures who are such opposites of one another could be father and son. As for me, I resemble both my grandfather and my father. With regard to my feelings, I resemble my grandfather, and with regard to my mind, my father. Can you possibly imagine what a horrible thing that is? What my heart tells me to do, my mind tells me not to. What my mind finds to be noble, my heart considers sycophancy; what my heart considers to be right, my mind deems criminal. One half of me is wild and zealous like the spring wind, the other half, insensitive and lethargic like the winter cold. One half of me listens to my inner voice, the other to knowledge and the learning imposed upon me.

For years I embodied two separate people who looked in the same direction and saw two entirely different things. Although I tried to simultaneously fulfill the wishes of both, unfortunately, I failed to be completely one or the other. Instead, I constantly wavered between the two. Had I been able, I would have expelled the half that was my father and become completely like my grandfather, but alas, I could not. What misfortune that the gods made me embody these two opposites! Having been denied the will to resist, I tried instead to suppress them. And though I sometimes believed I had achieved this, in the end, I understood that I had always been mistaken.

When my grandfather looked at the Euphrates, he saw the secret of our joy; my father saw in the Euphrates the strength that made us superior to our enemies; he saw olives, chickpeas, wheat, apricots, and grapes. When you asked my grandfather what the Euphrates meant to him, he would say, "In the daytime, it is the light that is reflected in the beloved's eyes; at night, the beloved's flowing black hair." If you asked my father, the answer was obvious: "The Euphrates is a body of water that must be protected from the enemy."

CHAPTER THREE

Sunrays stretched down like fingers to touch down upon the dark waters of the Euphrates. Along the river, all of the trees, from the oldest walnut to the youngest fig; all of the villages, from the most ancient to the youngest; all of the herbs, from the most medicinal to the most poisonous; all of the animals, from the most docile to the wildest; and all of the people, from the richest to the poorest; began to brighten up, warm up, and wake up.

Esra stepped out of her room with an air of determination. She intended to speak with her friends immediately, before she was struck by another panic attack, and without losing any more time. When she got to the door, her eyes were dazzled by the glaring brightness of the sun. She realized then that she had forgotten to put on the straw hat that was otherwise never absent from her head, but she didn't turn back to get it; instead, she began walking to the classrooms at the front of the school.

Teoman, Kemal, and Murat were staying in a large classroom where they also housed the computers. Actually, Kemal wanted to stay in the same room with his girlfriend Elif, but Esra said that it wouldn't be appropriate in this conservative community, and since Elif supported Esra in her view, he had no choice but to share this space with his male colleagues. Elif was staying in the small room next to theirs. Bernd had settled into the classroom directly across from them, while

Timothy had chosen the sunny classroom that looked onto the garden.

Esra decided to speak with her own crew first. No matter how much his authority seemed more showpiece than real, as the excavation authority, Kemal had the right to know about this situation. Only after they had discussed it amongst themselves would she explain the situation to Timothy Hurley and Bernd Burns. But just as she was turning the corner of the school, she ran into the rather imposing Timothy. He was wearing black pants made of thin, shalvar-like cloth and a faded t-shirt. He looked quite robust, in spite of his fifty-one years.

"Good morning," he said in nearly accent-free Turkish. In his right hand he held a thick branch full of dangling fish. "*Shapıt*," he said holding the branch up in the air to show Esra, "the most delicious fish of the Euphrates. A gift from the Antep fishermen..."

Esra glanced at the fish, their scales turning a fiery red under the sun, in complete disinterest, unable to hide the anxiety so clearly reflected in her face. Timothy put down the branch full of fish.

"What is it? What's wrong?" he asked in a concerned voice.

The tone of his voice was so friendly, so sincere, that Esra forgot all about the decision she had made to tell her own crew first and broke down right there.

"Hadji Settar's been murdered," she said.

Timothy's large, velvety black eyes opened wide with surprise.

"He's been murdered?"

"Yes, we need to get everyone together and talk. Would you wake up Bernd? I'll wake up the others."

Timothy didn't ask any more questions, but just walked silently with Esra to the front of the school building.

They had chosen as their meeting room the large room that Teoman and the two other guys were staying in. They had lined the benches up to make three beds next to the windows and spaced just a few meters apart from one another. Four other benches had been placed directly in the center of the room where they now served as computer desks. The remaining desks were stacked up by the back wall.

The team gathered together in no time, but then had to wait fifteen minutes before starting the meeting because Bernd was nowhere to be found. When the German archaeologist finally appeared at the door, he said that he had gone for a bike ride along the Euphrates. Timothy was surprised.

"Why didn't I run into you then?"

"It's normal that you wouldn't," said Bernd. "The Euphrates is a long river."

Timothy didn't dwell on the matter. When none of the other team members asked any questions Esra, trying to appear strong, told them about Hadji Settar's death. At first they couldn't believe their ears, and so they bombarded her with questions until they were finally convinced that it was indeed true. Every one of them was overcome by a deep sadness. There wasn't anyone among them who had not been fond of Hadji Settar. The old man had known how to win all of them over, even Bernd. Teoman was the first to break the silence holding sway over the classroom:

"Maybe Hadji Settar had a heart attack and just fell from the minaret."

"Perhaps it was an old blood feud?" suggested Kemal.

"But the Hadji didn't have any enemies," retorted Murat. "Who would want to kill him?"

"Murat's right," said Elif. "I haven't met anybody around here who isn't fond of him..."

Esra listened to all of the others discussing what had happened, and was just about to say herself that she thought the murder had been committed by someone hoping to stop the excavation, when Halaf entered the room. The young cook had heard what they were talking about through the open door.

"No reason to wear yourselves out over the matter; I know who killed him," he blurted out, forgetting his original intention of asking them whether or not he should fix breakfast now.

All eyes were instantly on Halaf. What was this man saying? Feeling everyone's eyes on him, Halaf took a step backwards. He thought of Esra's reaction when he had beaten up Fayat.

"I'm sorry Esra Hanım," he said, "but I heard what you were talking about and so it just kind of, you know, slipped out."

"How did you know that Hadji Settar's been murdered?" Esra asked, her face serious, her voice tense.

Halaf's response came reluctantly yet swiftly.

"The soldier from Ankara standing by the jeep told me while Captain Eshref was inside talking to you."

The grave look on Esra's face changed into one of curiosity.

"So the soldier told you he knows who killed Hadji Settar?"

"No, he doesn't know, but I do."

Now Esra was confused.

"How do you know?"

"The murderer told me," said Halaf. His face displayed the innocence of a man unable to comprehend the gravity of his own words.

"So, you mean the murderer came and told you about it after he'd killed Hadji Settar?" said Kemal with a sarcastic smile, thinking Halaf was talking a bunch of nonsense.

Halaf looked daggers at him. Somehow he just couldn't bring himself to like this tall, lanky boy from Istanbul.

"C'mon, do you really think that's possible?" he said shaking his head. "Of course he told me before it happened."

This time it was Murat, the youngest and most impatient of the crew members, who spoke up.

"So then who is the murderer?"

"Shehmuz. Rojin's uncle Shehmuz," responded Halaf without a moment's hesitation.

Esra was beginning to get annoyed at the way Halaf related the incident in bits and pieces.

"And who the dickens is Rojin?"

"Rojin is Hadji Settar's last wife..."

Before Esra's eyes appeared the image of a pleasantly plump young woman with a smiling face, red henna designs painted on her hands, and a tattoo of three dots on her temple. They had met when Hadji Settar had invited Esra and the other crew members to his house. Rojin was almost young enough to be his granddaughter and if Hadji Settar hadn't announced to them, "And this is our third lady of the house," they would never in a million years have guessed that this young woman was his wife. The strange thing was that the young woman didn't look at all unhappy. She had eagerly kneaded the ingredients of a delicious meat ball dish while the other women busied themselves preparing the floor where the meal would be eaten.

"Shehmuz was passionately in love with Rojin, but her uncle gave her to Hadji Settar instead of to him."

Esra's anger had subsided and the tone of her voice was much calmer as she asked, "And how do you know all of this?"

"During trips to Antep and back I ended up in their minibus a few times. Shehmuz told me."

"So Shehmuz is a minibus driver?"

"He's the helper in Memili's minibus. They don't tell me about it, but I know they have some other jobs, dirty jobs, on the side as well. They kept asking about the excavation. Like, 'We heard you found some gold, eh?' Or 'Have you found any treasures?' Last year he spent a few months in the slammer for growing weed in his backyard."

"Weed?" the young woman asked curiously.

"Hashish," explained Timothy, "Indian marijuana - you know."

Bernd silently laughed at Timothy's words, and Murat soon joined in. Esra shot a hostile glance at Murat, but the prospective archaeologist was quick to avert his own eyes. Actually though, she was more annoyed at Bernd's laughing than she was at Murat's.

"Yes, marijuana," Halaf continued to explain. "The guy's as filthy as they come. I think that bastard Shehmuz's the one who murdered Hadji Settar."

"What exactly did Shehmuz tell you?" This time it is was Esra who spoke up. Seeing her moss green eyes directed right at him, Halaf's face turned beet red. He answered the question, but couldn't bring himself to look her in the face as he did so.

"He kept saying that he was going to bump off the old priest as soon as he got the chance."

"Interesting," said Esra. She felt a sense of relief. If this hypothesis was correct, then the excavation wasn't in any danger. Maybe it was Memili who had provoked Shehmuz to do it. In this way, not only would Shehmuz succeed in getting the woman he loved, but the rumor that the excavation was cursed would spread quickly amongst the people and gain credibility. "Very interesting," she mumbled again, the slightest glimmer of hope detectable in her eyes.

"We should tell the Captain about this," she said, turning to face the others.

"You're right," Teoman said, seconding her. "They should catch that Shehmuz right away."

Everyone except Bernd concurred. The German archaeologist stirred on the bench where he was sitting. "Why are we getting involved in this anyway?" he asked in a distressed voice. "Isn't this a job for the police?"

"But it's our business, too," replied Esra sternly. "The townspeople who have learned of Hadji Settar's being thrown from the minaret have already started talking about the curse of the Black Tomb."

"But that's ridiculous..." Bernd said.

"It's not ridiculous at all," interjected Timothy, his tone of voice reflecting the confidence of a man grown wise with the rich experience of his years. "That's the way their beliefs are. And seeing as we are their guests, we should respect their beliefs, even if we think they're ridiculous."

Bernd laughed bitterly.

"These kinds of rumors go round wherever there's an excavation," he murmured. "When Howard Carter found Tutenkh-amun's burial in the Valley of Kings, everyone talked about some curse of the Pharaoh, but the rumors didn't keep the archaeologists from getting on with their work."

Esra was just about to tell them that they just didn't understand when Murat ventured to put in his two cents worth, making a royal mess of the whole situation in the process.

"But what you say isn't even the half of it. After the tomb was opened, one of the men responsible for the excavation, Lord Carnavon, died and then one by one the other members of the excavation team met their own deaths as well. And the incident still hasn't been properly explained. Back then it was all over the headlines in London for a very long time."

Listening to this assertion of Murat's, who believed in the existence of supernatural powers and fostered an interest in parapsychology, Esra let out a deep sigh, while Tim twisted his lips derisively. Teoman and Elif were following the discussion with great interest and Kemal was silently shaking his head as if to say, "What a fine predicament we've gotten into," while Halaf just seemed frightened by what he was hearing.

"That was resolved long ago," said Bernd, giving the young student the once over, a deprecating look in his eyes. "In 1933 Professor Steindorff declared that there was absolutely no truth to those rumors. And so the newspapers moved on to other subjects that would likewise entertain their ignorant readers. It's very strange that a bright student like yourself should continue to believe such nonsense!"

Murat was just about to fire back when Esra jumped in.

"We'll discuss this another time. The important thing right now is that this murder be solved without the incident doing any harm to the excavation work... I think what Halaf has said is very important. It could be that Shehmuz is the one who murdered Hadji Settar. It would be a good idea to inform the Captain of this. But we also need to be careful."

"Why should we be careful?" Again it was Bernd who protested. "We're doing a dig here. It's the Neo-Hittites that concern us, not the solving of Hadji Settar's murder."

With a determined look on her face, Esra turned her attentions to the German.

"Look here, Herr Burns," she said, "I don't know how you foster relations with the locals when you head an excavation, but I'm in favor of getting on well with them. And I know this country *and* its people better than you do. Please listen to what I have to say without interrupting me; this is for the safety of us all, including your own."

"Our safety?" asked Timothy. "Have you heard something?"

Rather than respond to Timothy, Esra turned to the young cook who continued to stand there before them.

"Thank you, Halaf," she said. "What you have told us is very important; you are going to be a lot of help to us in solving this case. But now you need to go to the police station and explain all of this to the Captain."

Halaf's face grew long.

"Do we have to go over there? Couldn't we just tell them on the phone..."

"We'll call them before we head over, otherwise Shehmuz could get away. But they are going to want you to give a deposition," explained Esra. Then, realizing just how nervous the young cook had become upon hearing these words, she tried to calm him down. "Don't worry," she said reassuringly, "we'll go together to the Captain."

His nervousness was not quelled, but he bowed his head like a man prepared to accept his fate.

"In that case, let me go get breakfast ready," he said, before dragging his feet out of the room at a funereal pace.

Once the young cook had put enough distance between himself and the others, Esra resumed.

"Actually, we're in no concrete danger," she said. Her eyes were directed at Timothy, but she seemed to be speaking to all of them. "But still that 'Curse of the Black Tomb' rumor has really got me worried. Religious beliefs are very strong in this area. We need to explain to the people that the excavation is not disrespectful to their beliefs and that it will not cause some curse to be unleashed. And we definitely need to do this without using the gendarme as a middleman. Hadji Settar's presence was very important for us. He was one of the townspeople and they listened to him. But now there is no Hadji Settar. We've lost the one person who had the ability to stop the fanatics who oppose the excavation. Now we need to take on more responsibility ourselves."

"You're right," said Timothy, scratching the whiskers of his one-week copper-colored beard. "We had a similar experience at a dig near Ninova. We wanted to take these cuneiform tablets that were sacred to the locals, but the people there refused to give them to us because they believed that the tablets protected them from misfortune. The head of the excavation, the French Professor Andre, turned to the government for help. Some unpleasant things happened then, like we were fired upon, and in the end we had to abandon the excavation and flee the area. What's more, we had to do so without a single tablet in hand. A falling out with the locals is the worst thing that can happen to you in this line of work. As soon as you have a falling out, you might as well start packing up your stuff because it means the end of the dig."

Bernd scowled at Timothy's words, and Esra picked up where she had left off.

"But," she said, "that doesn't mean that we up and leave the excavation half-finished. We mustn't let the workers at the dig know that we are worried. Our work must continue. Nobody should even think about leaving the dig."

"What do you mean 'leave the dig'?" asked Bernd. "The German Archaeological Institute is going to great lengths to set up the press conference. I talked with Herr Krencker yesterday. He said all preliminary preparations have been made."

Esra felt a sense of relief.

"Bernd is right," she said, "from now on let's forget all about any mention of stopping or abandoning the dig."

"We have no other choice," said Timothy, continuing to rally behind her. "We can't leave the excavation now that we've got our hands on such an important find. I don't know about the rest of you, but I can hardly wait to read the other tablets Patasana wrote."

THE TABLET THREE

O, you who shall read these words. Perhaps will find what you read here insufficient, perhaps you will want to know yet more. You will want to absorb, consume the information all at once, like the bottomless wells in the Euphrates that swallow up rafts, cattle, sheep, people. But learning is not easy; you must be patient like a turtle and as stubborn as the wind that grinds lofty rock cliffs to a powder.

Or perhaps you will find my words exaggerated, you will think that what I tell is full of mysterious traps intended only to mislead the reader. Or perhaps you will say, "I've heard many such stories before." But believe me, what you have heard is only a small shore of the fog-covered Euphrates, whereas the truth, like the bulging river that the dark fog envelops, in all of its mercilessness and magnificence, is hidden in the lines of these tablets.

First I am going to tell you about my noble-hearted grandfather, the poet Mitannuwa. I call him a poet because, although he rose to the position of chief palace scribe, he would want to be remembered as a poet. As he had me read from tablets filled with lines of words from foreign languages, he would tell me:

"Akkadian, Luwian, Hurrian, Aramaean; don't learn these foreign languages just for state correspondence. Treaties, laws, and contracts don't tell a person anything. They only protect the petty interests of gods, kings, and noblemen, whereas epics, legends, and poems, they broaden your horizon. What's behind the mountain, what is the sea like that into which the Euphrates empties, what do the trees beyond the plains look like – they teach a person all of this. More importantly, they teach us that we are a part of the world. They teach us that the dark-shadowed walnut tree, the squat stump of the grapevine, the plump ears of grain, the dry herbs, the ant on the ground, the snake in the hollow, the wolf in the mountain, and the sparrow hawk in the sky are our brothers and sisters. These writings teach us about us. The reason why one learns Akkadian should be to read the Epic of Gilgamesh and the poems of the Sumerian poet Ludingirra; the reason why one learns Hurrian should be to read the Legend of Gurparanzah in its original language. And of course you should learn the other epics, legends, and songs, too. You should know by memory in the languages in which they were written the epics of Kumarbi, Keshishi and Good and Evil, the Legend of the Moon That Fell Out of the Sky, and the Legend of Telepinu. Otherwise you will fail to understand the secret of life and you will be no different from the brown donkeys that carry water from the Euphrates from morning to night; you will turn out to be a man like your father Araras, who spends all of his time in the service of the king's interests, a man who never laughs nor weeps nor becomes angry."

I would listen to him and do as he said. By the age of fifteen, I had already memorized all of the legends he had told me to. My father was not pleased that I dedicated most of my time to epics and legends, but he refrained from interfering, most likely in order to avoid arguing with my grandfather. As for me, I would do my best to keep from vexing him, for in reality, I was not rebellious like my grandfather. I was docile, not fond of quarreling, and was in favor of conciliation, even if it meant making concessions.

My father would warn me that we should be very wary of the Assyrian Empire, the preeminent power of the region; it was a kingdom so treacherous and savage that it would not hesitate to kill thousands of men in a single swipe. Nor were the Urartians to our Northeast to be disregarded either, for they were eagerly awaiting the opportunity to destroy us. As for the Phrygians to our Northeast, however, they were concerned only with stopping the Assyrians, who were expanding the reaches of their empire by the day.

My father spoke not only of politics; he would also explain in a simple but very cold manner how a text was to be translated into our language. In addition, he would take me to the palace library whenever he could and, after reminding me that administering the library was one of the chief scribe's duties, he would carefully explain everything, from preservation of the tablets to the shelving system. And as soon as he was done explaining, he would make me repeat everything down to the last detail just to make certain that I had understood.

So, my grandfather Mitannuwa and my father Araras taught me about different things, using different methods. I would listen with interest to what my father told me, but I much preferred the lessons with my grandfather in his house that looked out upon the Euphrates.

CHAPTER FOUR

The police station was situated on a high hill next to the Euphrates. It was a quaint, one-story building, with a small, well-kept garden which lay in the shade of apricot, plum, and mulberry trees. The garden was surrounded by a stone wall, large and square in shape, and the police station building stood directly in its center. There were sentry points at each corner of the wall, plus two soldiers standing guard at the entrance door. Day and night the soldiers kept watch at these points, impervious to the summer heat or winter chill. Between the river and the police station was a two story building containing apartments that housed the soldiers and their families. The garden of the apartment building was more nicely kempt, and more grandiose, than that belonging to the police station. An asphalt road, which had not been repaired since the last elections and was riddled with pot holes, connected the town to the villages and ran right by the police station. Not once did the villagers ever see the sentry points unoccupied, as they made their way along this road and into town. Yet the conflict that had been going on in this region for the last sixteen years hadn't really affected these parts much. Five years earlier Kurdish guerillas had attacked a military convoy, but most of them had been captured dead. Except for a few minor incidents that occurred later, there had been no armed activity in the area. The late Hadji Settar thought that this was because of the area's wealth. Everyone had a garden to look after, a field to plant. Given this situation, who would abandon their work to head off to the mountains? The Captain, however, believed that the reason for this relative peace lay elsewhere; he thought that it was because the army had successfully countered the guerillas' initial attacks. Nevertheless, it could hardly be said that the current state of affairs really put the Captain at ease. Despite the lack of any armed struggle on their part at the moment, the Captain thought that the insurgents were still active in the region. And although he didn't automatically assume everyone in town to be a member of the insurgent organization, he knew that there were people who were sympathetic to it and those who supported it in the town as well as the nearby villages. He was especially suspicious of the Gencelis. Mahmut, the youngest son of the Gencelis, who comprised one of the two largest tribes in the region, had gone off to the mountains to join the insurgents, a fact which only served to increase the Captain's suspicion that this large family had ties to the organization. Meanwhile, the other large tribe, which, though Kurdish, had taken the Turkish surname Türkoghlu - Son of the Turk - had always sided with the government. To tell the truth, the Captain wasn't particularly fond of them either. He thought that the Türkoghlu tribe only appeared to side with the government because of the easy money that they got out of being village guards; if the balances were to shift, there was no guarantee that they wouldn't turn their guns on the soldiers.

Esra noticed this uneasiness about Eshref when she and her team first came to the region. When the Captain suggested during their very first days of excavating that he assign soldiers to guard them, she didn't hesitate for a second before turning him down.

"I don't think they'll attack us," she said. "We're scientists and academics."

The Captain had looked at her as if she were a gullible babe utterly ignorant of the ways of the world.

"You don't know them at all. For them, the important thing is stirring up trouble. They don't hesitate to do whatever it takes to raise a ruckus. They don't care one bit about the fact that you're working for science."

But Esra did know them. Two years earlier, they had raided an excavation she had been working on at the ancient city of Milidia near Malatya. In the darkness, it wasn't clear how many of them there were. Only one of them approached the excavation crew. A thin, tall, thickly bearded man with piercing eyes, he had asked for food supplies in pristine Turkish. When head of the excavation Ertem Bey took a little too long to respond, Azad used his rifle to point to the cabin that they used as a kitchen.

"If you don't give it to us, then we'll just take it ourselves," he said. The fact that someone whom they didn't know at all was so familiar with their camp that he knew exactly where they kept their supplies gave the head of the excavation a scare, and so he immediately told the others to prepare the requested supplies. As he waited for the supplies, Azad turned his attention to the finds from the excavation. His interest piqued, he took a closer look at the stones with hieroglyphic writing on them, and the statues of gods and goddesses.

"So is all of this really all that important?" he asked.

"Yes, very important," said Esra. "It tells us about life thousands of years ago. By uncovering these artifacts, in a way, we're rescuing the past from darkness."

"It's a fine occupation," he mumbled, passing his gun from one hand to the other. Then directing his eyes at Esra, he added: "But it's today that really needs to be rescued from the darkness. It's not enough to try and rescue just the past from darkness, when today an entire people is still living under tyranny, and in darkness, too."

Esra wanted to tell him that she didn't agree, that science and politics were two different matters, and what's more, that terror would not get anybody anywhere, but she was afraid of Azad, whose silence became all the more frightening as he stood there before her, gun in hand, and so she chose to remain silent. "If you tell the gendarme, you will pay," warned Azad as he took off with the supplies the excavation crew packed up for him. Then together with his friends, he disappeared back into the darkness.

They didn't inform the gendarme. There was no use in stirring up trouble for themselves like that.

Esra hadn't told Eshref about this incident. No matter how much she trusted the Captain, she considered him to be a part of this war, and so she was reluctant to tell him because she thought that he would try and connect any and every incident back to the conflict in the region.

All of this flashed through Esra's mind as the van pulled up in front of the police station.

Captain Eshref was waiting for them at a table beneath an old apricot tree. A blue and black checkered cloth covered the table, upon which a bulky walkie-talkie was buzzing away. Eshref stood up with a smile when he saw his guests come through the front door of the police station. He didn't have a cap on, and his short hair clearly revealed his broad forehead. His strong chin completed the harmony between his prominent cheekbones and dark eyes, and his sun burnt skin added a particularly masculine attractiveness to him.

What a sweet smile he has, thought Esra. She had heard that he, like herself, had been married and divorced, and that he had a daughter.

She pulled herself together when she heard Eshref's voice welcoming them. Watching as he politely asked them to have a seat in the empty chairs next to the table, it seemed to her that he had regained his composure, that he wasn't ruffled as he had been that morning. Noticing his new mood, Esra asked hopefully as she took her seat:

"You've caught Shehmuz perhaps?"

The Captain grew serious. "No, not yet," he replied. "I sent a team to his house after talking with you, but he wasn't at home, so they went to the bus station. We hope to find him there."

Esra listened to the Captain, angry at her own rashness. There was a moment of silence as she took off her straw hat and sunglasses and placed them on the table next to the buzzing walkie-talkie.

"Was he really the one who killed Hadji Settar?" asked the Captain.

She understood from his tone of voice that he was skeptical of this possibility, but instead of asking him why, she just said, "That's what he told Halaf." Then she turned to look at the young cook, who was still standing up.

"Why don't you sit down," she said. "Sit down and tell the Captain."

As Halaf meekly took his seat, the Captain called out for tea to be brought to them, which a private provided in no time.

"What village are you from?" asked the Captain, after taking a sip from his tea.

"Alagöz," said Halaf, pointing to a hill in the distance, "behind that. A good ten kilometers from here."

"Are you Kurdish?"

Halaf was unnerved by the question and hesitated to respond. Esra also found it to be a rather odd question.

"Let me put it this way," said the Captain, "do you speak Kurdish?"

Halaf's sun burnt face relaxed.

"I do, Captain," he said. "Everyone in our village does."

The suspicious look on the Captain's face didn't change any.

"So how long have you known this Shehmuz?"

"I've known him for a long time. I've always seen him on trips from the village into town."

"Does he know Kurdish too?"

"He does, Captain. Most people around here do."

"How well do you get along with Shehmuz?"

"I don't really know him, just exchange greetings, that's all."

"So if you don't know him, why did he tell you that he was going to kill Hadji Settar?"

Halaf went pale in the face, feeling that he himself was being accused of wrongdoing.

"I don't know, Captain. We were in the van, we'd just taken off. I was sitting in the back. The seat next to me was empty, so that Shehmuz came and sat next to me. He'd been trying to keep on good terms with me ever since the excavation started anyway. We saw Hadji Settar in front of the garage. Shehmuz swore when he saw him. And so I said, 'Why are you swearing at the holy man?' So then all the way into town he told me about how much he loved Rojin. He said that one day he would kill Hadji Settar."

The Captain listened to the young cook intently, as if afraid of missing a single gesture, or the slightest quiver in his voice.

"Okay," he said once the questioning was over, "thank you for your help. Go on and drink your tea now. You haven't touched it since you came. Go on and drink up now so that our boys can get your written deposition."

"Um, Captain," said Halaf after drinking his by then ice cold tea, "Shehmuz won't know that I've informed against him, will he?"

"So what if he does?" asked Eshref, directing a harsh glance at Halaf's worried face.

"Nothing, Captain," said Halaf. He swallowed nervously. "But these fellas are like vicious dogs, they'll bite a man in thc back when he least expects it."

The Captain's eyebrows arched suspiciously.

"Who do you mean by 'they'?"

"The Cripple Memili's men. Shehmuz is their jackal."

"The Cripple Memili also smuggles antiques," said Esra, feeling the need to offer an explanation. Seemingly irritated by how the Captain was pressing Halaf, she added: "He might have provoked Shehmuz."

"Could be," said the Captain, shaking his head. Then, looking at Halaf with a fatherly smile he added: "Don't get worked up over nothing. Nobody will know about your deposition."

The Captain took Halaf, who had downed his tea in one gulp, inside. Left alone at the table, Esra turned her eyes toward the Euphrates. Though she'd been here for so many days and seen it so many times before, for the first time it struck her just how much the Euphrates looked like the Bosphorus. It was as if she had gone back thousands of years in time to perch upon a hill and look down on that strait in Istanbul. The old wooden shore houses, concrete villas, restaurants, cafes, asphalt road always packed full of automobiles... None of them were there. There was only a blue river flowing between two strips of green trees. And the civilizations that had been established and demolished, demolished and reestablished for thousands of years within this green area...

"Hello? You still here?" She came to at the sound of Eshref's voice. "What are you thinking about?"

"Nothing," said Esra, gathering herself back together. "For a moment there, the Euphrates looked like the Bosphorus to me."

"The Bosphorus?"

Eshref, too, had begun looking at the river.

"Like the Bosphorus hundreds, thousands of years ago, of course."

"It seems you miss Istanbul. So do I."

Then he realized that Esra's glass was empty.

"One more?"

"Yes, please," said Esra, her lips forming a sincere smile.

The Captain motioned to the private standing a few meters away for him to bring two more cups of tea. The private shot off like an arrow.

"Do you have anybody back in Istanbul?"

"My mother and my daughter," said Eshref. He became lost in thought. "My mother lives alone in Üsküdar. She's rather up there in age now, and I'm afraid something will happen to her. My daughter lives with my wife."

"Don't you ever consider moving back to Istanbul?"

Eshref turned his eyes towards Esra. He looked at her in a way that he'd never looked at her before, deeply, as if he were about to tell her a secret. Feeling that he was about to say something important, Esra became all ears, but Eshref averted his eyes, like a child afraid that his guilt might be revealed.

"No, I don't," he said evasively. "So who do you have back in Istanbul?"

"My parents."

"Do you live with them?"

Esra laughed. "Come on Captain, you must have mistaken me for a young woman fresh out of university. It's been years since I left my parents' home. I got married and moved into my own place the year I finished university, which was ten years ago. I've been living in an apartment in Küchük Chamlıca ever since."

A look of embarrassment shot over Eshref's face, but, trying not to show it, he indicated Esra's left hand with his head.

"I assumed you were single since you're not wearing a wedding ring."

"I'm divorced... We separated two years ago."

Just then the soldier came with their fresh cups of tea and gathered up the used glasses. Esra pulled a pack of cigarettes out of her bag and held them out to Eshref. The Captain gave the pack a quick glance. Esra thought he wasn't going to, but then he reached over and pulled one out.

"Probably won't be the end of the world if I smoke just one," he said as he placed the cigarette between his lips.

"Haven't you ever smoked?" asked Esra as she took a cigarette from the packet for herself, too.

Eshref gave her a meaningful smile.

"I was a serious addict until a year ago. Then the doctors forbade me to smoke anymore."

"Doctors? You don't have any serious illness or anything, I hope?" said Esra as she lit their cigarettes.

"No, no," he said, "you know how doctors are."

Realizing that Esra was looking at him with a certain affection, he quickly changed the subject.

"Actually, it wasn't the first time I'd quit smoking. I first started smoking when I enrolled in the Kuleli Military High School. You know, that urge to look grown up. But then one day—I don't know whether to call it a stroke of good or bad luck—I was caught by our school commander, Colonel Salih Sorgun, of whom all the students were in complete awe. To us, Colonel Salih was a real legend. He was tall, blonde with blue eyes like Mustafa Kemal, a very imposing man. There was nothing contrived about him at all; his austerity was honest and true. He was a soldier through and through, in the way he looked at things, his behavior, his words, his uniform. We'd instantly stand at attention, and even hold our breath, whenever he walked by. Think about it, I was caught by *that* man. Actually, you can't even really call it getting caught, he just saw me. He didn't get angry, he just gave me this condemning look and in a harsh voice said to me, 'Throw that away.' I threw it away immediately. I was so embarrassed. I was afraid I'd be disciplined. I wasn't, and nobody told me not to smoke, but I never touched another cigarette again. Not until much later, until '91, when I went to Shirnak."

The Captain grew silent once again. He was staring, lost in thought, at the burning end of his cigarette.

"You started up again after Shirnak?" asked Esra, as if wanting to remind him of her presence.

"In the mountains," said Eshref. He spoke as if in a dream. "Actually, we called it the field, the terrorists called it the mountains."

He began laughing quietly, shaking his head as he continued to speak:

"When a war lasts for such a long time, you start to become more like the enemy. You talk like them, think like them, act like them."

But then he suddenly grew anxious and, throwing his not yet half-smoked cigarette onto the ground, mumbled, "Excuse me, I must be boring you, going on about my memories like that."

"No you aren't, not at all. Please go on," said Esra, but it was too late, a silence had already begun to settle between them again. Esra directed her eyes, full of questions, at Eshref, but when she failed to draw a reaction, she shifted her gaze once again to the Euphrates. It was the Captain who broke the silence.

"Let me tell you something Esra," he said in a serious voice, devoid of any feeling whatsoever. "I don't think it's at all likely that Shehmuz is responsible for the murder."

The Captain's strange mood, these actions of his that she had such difficulty understanding, had begun to annoy Esra.

"Why?"

She tried to make her voice devoid of any feelings, too, like the Captain's.

"Why don't you believe Halaf?"

"I believe Halaf," said the Captain. "But these are just things Shehmuz said in a moment of anger. Neither Shehmuz nor Memili has the courage to kill Hadji Settar. These are little men. They're not the types that could handle the consequences of committing murder."

"Jealousy is a very powerful emotion, Captain," Esra objected. She had crossed her arms and directed a self-assured look at the Captain. "A jealous person generally acts without thinking about the consequences."

"You might be right, but I don't think someone like Shehmuz is capable of feeling such intense jealousy either. The intensity of any jealousy he might feel would only be enough to make him swear at Hadji Settar behind his back."

Esra felt herself growing enraged at Eshref's pedantic talk, and was about to ask, "So you know Shehmuz that well, do you?" when the walkie-talkie began buzzing more loudly.

"Could be our boys," said Eshref as he picked it up.

"This is the police station, roger."

A high pitched male voice broke through the buzzing.

"This is Sergeant Major Ihsan, sir."

"Yes Ihsan, have you caught the suspect?"

"Yes we have, Sir. We're on the road to Antep right now."

"What are you doing on the road to Antep?"

"We caught the suspect as he was making his escape to Antep, Sir. We're on our way back."

For a brief moment Eshref's eyes drifted over to Esra; the young woman's smile reflected pride at having been proven right.

"Okay Ihsan, I'm waiting for you," said the Captain before putting the walkie-talkie back on the table.

"You see," said Esra in an insinuating voice. "You didn't believe it, but the man was making his get-away."

"We'll see," said Eshref, forcing a smile.

Just then, Esra saw Halaf emerge from the police station and approach the table. She began gathering her stuff and getting ready to go.

"Are you leaving?" asked Eshref, by all appearances saddened at the prospect.

"There's work to do," said Esra as she placed her glasses in her hat. "And if I stayed, you wouldn't let me in to listen to the questioning anyway."

"Unfortunately not, but I'll let you know what comes of it."

"I would appreciate that," said Esra. Then she turned to face Halaf. "Everything okay? Shall we go?"

"All good, Esra Hanım," said Halaf. As he said this, he crisply stood at attention, just like the soldier who had brought the teas.

"Then we can go home now."

Esra, too, had stood up.

"We have to stop by town and pick up some supplies," said Halaf.

"It would be better if you didn't go into town today," interrupted Eshref. He, too, was now on his feet. "It hasn't been long since the murder happened. Some idiot with the wrong idea could try to harm you."

A determined expression came over Halaf's docile face.

"Don't you worry, Sir. With God's help, no harm will come Esra Hanım's way, not as long as I'm with her."

Esra looked with a sweetly amused smile at Halaf standing there, all puffed up with self-importance like the tough guys of yore. "Is it really necessary for us to go into town?" she asked.

"We don't have to, but since we've already come all this way..."

"If we don't have to, then let's not. There's no use making the atmosphere any more tense than it already is." Then she turned to Eshref: "So when will all this be over?" she asked, a deeply concerned look on her face.

"I wish I knew," said Eshref. "We'll see once the funeral's over."

Esra had completely forgotten about the funeral.

"Right. So when exactly is the funeral?"

"I doubt it will happen before tomorrow. The public prosecutor sent the body to Antep for an autopsy."

"I'd like to come to the funeral, too."

"I'm sorry, but that's impossible. They don't look fondly upon women participating in funerals. You can go to offer your condolences later. Mourning lasts a long time around here."

THE TABLET FOUR

O you who are witness to my mourning of so many years! O patient reader who endeavors to unravel the secrets that underlie these incidents! I shall tell you of the deep hatred felt for one another by two people with the same blood running through their veins. I shall tell you of the two utterly dissimilar souls of two related bodies. I shall tell you of the unwavering hostility between a father and a son. I shall speak of the deep malaise within my family which led to the Storm God's curse upon me.

My grandfather Mitannuwa disliked his own son Araras more than he did his worst enemy. Yet my father had reached the highest position that one could in this country, second only to king. Though lacking seniority, he was the most revered person in the assembly of nobles. None of this, however, meant anything to my grandfather Mitannuwa. He did not love his son. And he did not hesitate to say so. He constantly berated him, both when alone with him and in front of others. And though he was not one to openly reveal his feelings, my father Araras, too, did not care for old Mitannuwa.

According to my father, my grandfather had considered him no less than an enemy from the time of his birth, because my grandfather's first wife, Tunnawi, had died while giving birth to him.

Tunnawi was my grandfather's beloved, his greatest passion. He used to call her "the love of my heart." And Tunnawi loved my grandfather, too; he never had to ask her for anything twice. Around the time that Tunnawi became pregnant with my grandfather's child, he caught a large carp in the Euphrates. When he spliced the carp's stomach open, from it emerged a black fish of a sort that they had never before encountered in the river. Considering this to be an ill-omen, my grandfather headed straight for the fortuneteller. And the fortuneteller, too, told him it was an ill-omen, and instructed him to throw it back into the Euphrates. My grandfather immediately did as the fortuneteller said. But it was no use, for the Storm God Teshup must have loved the beautiful Tunnawi more than he did, for he took her for himself.

When he heard that Tunnawi had died, my grandfather swore off all food and drink; he was unable to go to the palace for days; and most importantly, he wouldn't even look at the face of his new born son. It was only days later that he took his son into his arms, yet he continued to hold my father responsible for his wife's death. "He never forgave me," my father would explain. "Not once did I see him look at me lovingly, not once did I feel him take my hand compassionately. For him I wasn't a son, but the person responsible for his wife's death. He treated me as such throughout my childhood and up into my adulthood. Thank the gods that our king's father, Kamanas, took me under his own protection and treated me like his own son. And so my father's maliciousness couldn't hurt me anymore. If it had been left up to my father, he would have raised me not as a scribe, but as a shepherd. However, the former great king and now deity Kamanas took responsibility for my education just as he did for his own son, Astarus. He protected me from Mitannuwa. Because he was unable to avenge his wife's death, for which he held me responsible, my father's animosity towards me continued for the duration of his life on this earth. As a son, I will never forgive him."

As he related this I would see the blood drain from my father's long face and I would become frightened at the deep hatred that would flame up in his narrowed eyes. But then sometimes I would notice my father grow sorrowful, too. The dejection of an orphaned child unloved by his own father would descend upon the face of this confident man who was always capable of carrying out even the most important of duties in the palace. At times like these, although I loved my grandfather Mitannuwa very much, I could not help but become angry at him. I could not understand how the wisest man along all the shores of the Euphrates could be so ruthless towards his own son.

CHAPTER FIVE

It was already noon by the time the van pulled up to the camp after completing its bumpy ride over the asphalt road along the Euphrates. The weather was sizzling hot, and a warm silence prevailed—that is, if you don't count the stubborn songs of the field crickets as they chirped away in the small grove in front of the school, their songs emerging from the poplar trees which were in a veritable race to the sky, their long, slender branches stretching forth and dainty leaves atwitter.

When Esra walked into the classroom, its windows agape in the hope that they might channel a little coolness, Esra was pleased to see Kemal and Teoman hard at work in front of their computers. Teoman was working on drawings of the ancient city, while Kemal was entering data about excavation finds. Upon seeing her friends plugging away like that as if nothing had happened, she couldn't help but wonder if she weren't perhaps overreacting. A murder had been committed, true, but then so many people were being killed in this region as it were. Hadji Settar's face appeared before her eyes once again. Yes, his death saddened her, but like Bernd had said, what did it have to do with them anyway? Why did it upset her so much? She blamed the Captain for it. The way he had delivered the news, so early in the morning and with his frightened behavior, had inevitably influenced her own reaction to it. She was angry at herself for letting the Captain's behavior rub off on her like that. She might be fond of him, but she shouldn't have allowed him to influence her thoughts so easily.

"Hello Esra," said Teoman as soon as he noticed her arrival. "How did it go?"

"Fine," said Esra as she took off her hat and sunglasses. "Really well, Shehmuz was caught on the run. Now if he just admits to having committed the murder, we'll be free of this whole mess."

Taking his eyes off the computer for a brief moment, Kemal waved a hand at Esra in greeting, and then mumbled: "So I guess things are looking up, huh?"

Esra didn't respond, instead she asked, "So where are the others?"

A frown appeared on Kemal's face, and it was Teoman who answered the question.

"Tim, Elif, and Murat went off to Yazır village. Tim's going to talk with them about his book. Elif said she was going to take photos. And Murat just went along for the ride."

"I thought Tim was translating tablets," said Esra. She seemed disappointed. They had three more tablets that needed to be transliterated and translated.

Picking up on the implication in Esra's tone of voice, Kemal took a break from the computer.

"I really don't get this Tim anyway," he said, feeling no need to disguise his animosity. "Is he an archaeologist, a sociologist, what? Who knows! He never sticks around the excavation site. He's always traipsing about. There's not a village left along the Euphrates that he doesn't know, and not a villager that he hasn't become buddies with."

"Well, the man's been here for five years," offered Teoman in explanation. "If we'd been coming back here that long, we'd know the area as well as he does, too."

"I don't understand Elif either," said Kemal, continuing his rant. "Why is she always trailing him everywhere?"

Fully aware of Kemal's jealousy of the American, Teoman provoked his friend further, laughing under his breath all the while.

"Well, he's a good-looking man, and what's more, he's a foreigner. Our gals are just crazy about foreign men."

"Just crazy about them, right," said Kemal, virtually foaming at the mouth. "Dude, the man is Elif's Dad's age."

"Man, you think Freud—may he rest in peace—strained his brain so hard over the Elektra complex for nothing?"

"Don't get me started dude. I'll show your Freud, and your Elektra complex..."

"C'mon now boys, that's enough," said Esra. Having successfully made it through the stress of the morning and regained her peace of mind, she was laughing now as well. "There's nothing going on between Tim and Elif."

Temoan let loose with a roar of laughter, and then gave Kemal a friendly pat on the head. "I don't think there is either, but this idiot thinks so, because he's so madly in love with the girl."

"You're the idiot," said Kemal, pulling his head away from Teoman's hand. "I wonder what you'd do if you were in my place?"

"All jokes aside, we're very lucky to have Tim working with us," said Esra, growing serious. "Just think about it, if it weren't for Tim, the tablets would have to be sent to the university, where they'd be deciphered by someone there who knows Akkadian... It's a great privilege to be able to learn right on the spot what the texts mean. We can't expect him to come to the excavation site every day. He's a specialist." After a short pause, she shook her head, as if an important opportunity were passing them by. "But it would've been nice if he'd deciphered those tablets today..." she added. "I guess he wanted to work on his book on his day off. Anyway, I suppose the man should be allowed at least that luxury."

"Of course he should," grumbled Kemal with biting sarcasm. "Just let him jump in the jeep and go village hopping while we bust our asses here on these computers, with not even the slightest mention of the concept of a day off."

"That's enough already. C'mon now, stop complaining and get back to work," said Esra, trying to calm Kemal down. "So where's Bernd?"

"How should we know?" said Teoman. "If he's not in his room, then he's gone for a bike ride... He doesn't lower himself by talking with the likes of us... What do you want from that pompous guy anyway?"

Actually, Esra's feelings for Bernd weren't any different from those harbored by Teoman. She preferred, however, to conceal that fact.

"Well now, it seems the excavation team has a case of xenophobia."

"C'mon now Esra," objected Teoman. "You don't like that Nazi-faced guy either."

"You shouldn't talk like that... He's not a bad person, he's just got a different way about him."

"Sure would be nice if he changed his way," grumbled Teoman. "The whole team can't be expected to follow his lead."

"I think it would be best if you'd just calm down," reprimanded Esra. "The excavation is taking place in our country, and we're the ones in charge of it."

"And what's more, it's the Germans who are funding it," said Teoman sarcastically.

"There's that too. Yes, the Germans are providing funding, but that's not why we put up with Bernd. He's part of the team. And I don't want any member of the team to be ostracized by the others."

Teoman looked at Esra with a distressed expression, but he didn't say anything. Taking their silence to mean that they agreed with her, Esra felt no need to continue their discussion and gathered up her stuff to leave.

"Well, if you don't need me for anything then I think I'll just go check in on him." Before she got to the door, though, she turned around to face the boys. "See you at dinner," she said in a soft voice that made it clear she was trying to endear herself to her friends once again. "Halaf is making a delicious *mücver*, with bulghur rice in *halis* butter and plenty of salad on the side."

As she made her way down the corridor, its walls riveted with thin cracks, its plaster crumbling, she was thinking that Teoman was right. Of all the excavations she had ever been on, on none of them had she ever encountered anyone as dislikeable as Bernd. Cold, overly ambitious, difficult... If it weren't for his passion for bike riding, it would be fair to say that he was completely removed from everyday life. In his free time he never joined the excavation team, but either withdrew to his room to work or hopped on his bike to take a tour of the nearby villages. But no matter how much he tried to distance himself from everyone else, it was Esra's duty to win him over, to break through his frigidity. Unlike other scientists who had to deal solely in their subject of study, archaeologists also had the added pressure of being expert organizers and psychologists capable of fostering good relationships with others. She had no choice but to get along with Bernd. So, she should at least do her best...

It was in the midst of these feelings that she knocked on the German archaeologist's partially open door. When she heard him say, "Come in," she poked her head in and gave him a smile.

"Do you have a moment?"

Bernd had lifted his head up to look at the door. He was sitting at his desk in this extremely tidy room, pen in hand and several sheets of papers in front of him.

"Please, come in, come in," he in his heavily accented Turkish.

"Were you working?" asked Esra, still standing in front of the door.

"I was writing a letter," said Bernd, pushing back his round lens glasses, and thereby accentuating the steel blue color of his eyes.

"I'm sorry, I'll come back later then."

"No, don't go. Please, come in. I'm done writing the letter." Bernd motioned towards the bench next to him. "Come, have a seat."

He seemed to have forgotten all about the quarrel that morning. Esra sat down on the bench to which he had pointed. Her eyes drifted to the papers in front of him. "Could it be that he's sending a report to the German Archaeology Institute?" thought Esra worriedly.

"A letter," he said, as if he had read Esra's mind. The sharp lines on his long, thin face had relaxed, and the harsh look in his steel blue eyes had softened. "I'm writing to my wife Vartuhi. To Germany."

Esra found that to be a rather peculiar name.

"Vartuhi?"

"Yes, it means 'rose' in Armenian," explained Bernd in a sweet voice.

He must love his wife very much, Esra thought. And then for some reason, her ex-husband Orhan came to mind.

"Hachik, I mean my father-in-law, was born in Turkey," said Bernd; though it took a while, Esra eventually grasped the meaning of what he was saying. "It was from them that I first learned Turkish."

"Really?" she asked curiously. "When did they leave Turkey?"

"A long time ago," said Bernd. The shine left his blue eyes. "Long ago... During the war. It was a horrible time... The Turks were so cruel to them. They killed their men, raped their women, sent an entire people into exile, even the elderly and the children."

The pleasantly friendly Bernd of a just a moment ago was gone now, replaced by the too familiar peevish German.

"Unfortunately every country has these kinds of incidents in its history," Esra said, feeling the need to defend herself.

"But it's awful," said Bernd puckering up his face. "My father-in-law's father died, and so he took his mother and with great difficulty escaped to France. But he never managed to adapt, he just goes on and on about 'my homeland, my homeland...' At the same time, he rains down curses upon the Turks."

"It's not easy of course," said Esra, trying to be gentle in the face of Bernd's harsh words. "But these are very controversial matters."

"There's nothing controversial about it," said Bernd, completely sure of himself. "It was genocide. The world accepts it as such. It's only the Turkish government that denies it."

Esra was trying to contain herself:

"Like you said this morning, this issue isn't ours to deal with. So why don't we leave it to historians to research the facts and let us get back to our excavation."

Bernd turned a deaf ear to Esra and went on talking.

"Despite all that savagery, they still love this country," he said. "Until last year, Vartuhi and I always used to come over here together. My grandfather, too, is always super curious about these parts. He asks us a ton of questions every time we come back from Turkey."

"So your wife didn't come this year?"

"No, she didn't. She's pregnant."

"Too bad she didn't come along," Esra said, thinking that this was an open door to compromise. "How many months along is she?"

"Six," said the German. His voice had grown soft again, and the dullness in his blue eyes had given way to a sweet twinkle, like the color of the Euphrates beneath the early afternoon sun.

"We're expecting the baby in early September."

"Do you know if it's a boy or a girl yet?"

"A girl," said Bernd, "which is what I wanted. I adore girls."

"Me, too. They're so adorable, so beautiful."

"Do you have any kids?"

Esra quickly averted her eyes.

"No," she said. She wanted to tell him about the baby girl she lost when she was five months pregnant, but then changed her mind. "No, I don't."

It was obvious to Bernd that Esra was grieving.

"Don't be sad, you're still young, one day you will."

"No, never," said Esra to herself, but not to Bernd.

"Enough about me," mumbled Esra smilingly. "What are you going to name your daughter?"

"Mayreni," said Bernd. "That's what Vartuhi wants to name her. It was her grandmother's name, on her father's side."

"I hope Mayreni has a long and healthy life."

"I hope so. Thank you for your good wishes."

Esra figured this was as good an opportunity as any to broach the topic she'd come here to talk about. "This morning I was a little crass with you," she said in a humble yet confident tone. "I'm sorry if I hurt you."

Bernd looked at her carefully. Then he shook his head.

"No, no. There's no need to apologize. It's your job. I said what I thought, and you did the same. So there's no problem."

Esra was relieved. She thought that the German archaeologist would be looking to get back at her for what had happened that morning, that he would cop an attitude, and that this would keep them from getting along. If it had been Timothy that she was dealing with, then getting along would be simple. Timothy had common sense, and he was well-educated and experienced. He'd been translating the tablets that emerged from the sand-covered tumuli of Mesopotamia long before the idea of being an archaeologist had even crossed Esra's mind. However, he had never used his experience to claim any kind of superiority. Touching the tablets, deciphering the writing upon them, and standing side-by-side, shoulder-to-shoulder with the other members of the team was enough for him. Though Esra sometimes got the feeling that he was hiding something, she'd never once witnessed any negative behavior on his part. He wasn't interested in showing off, or flaunting his knowledge or experience. Perhaps that's why everyone on the excavation, except for Kemal, was so fond of him. The same was not true of the German archaeologist, however. He, too, had received a good education and mastered his own field of training, but he had been unnecessarily fussy from the very beginning of the excavation and never missed a chance to stir up trouble. He always seemed to be on the lookout for flaws. Esra couldn't be certain of his sincerity. How many times had she thought to herself, "I wish we hadn't taken Bernd on as part of the team"? But German archaeologists had an undeniable influence over the universities in Turkey. It was German academics fleeing Hitler who had established the Hittitology Department, and Turks had adopted German working methods in the field. Considering the situation, it wouldn't have been easy not to take someone like Bernd onto the team. Esra thought that the only solution was to do her best to put up with him and his unpleasantries and go on with the excavation, avoiding conflict by any means. But Bernd's behavior at that moment surprised her. She couldn't help but think that she had been wrong about the German. Perhaps it was the distance between him and his beloved Vartuhi that made him so disagreeable. She should be more understanding towards him. With a grateful glance she said to Bernd, "I'm glad you feel that way."

"How could it possibly be otherwise?" said Bernd, feeling no need to disguise the fact that he found Esra's behavior at that moment to be unnecessarily emotional. "We're doing the world's hardest job here. Of course there will be arguments, but the most important thing is that there be discipline. As you said this morning, it is you who is responsible for this excavation."

Esra sensed the disdain in these words, but she chose to ignore it. For the first time since the excavation began, she had established positive dialogue with Bernd. She knew that they were two very different people, but today's talk had broken the ice between them and brought them closer.

THE TABLET FIVE

I never saw my grandfather Mitannuwa and my father Araras act in any way intimate with one another. And each of them had a different explanation for the animosity between them. According to my grandfather, my father was more cunning and a greater liar than an Assyrian merchant. He said of my father that, not only was he an inauspicious seed and a disloyal child, but he was the best educated scoundrel along all of the Euphrates shores.

My grandfather himself vouched for the first part of what my father had to say of him. "When the gods took Tunnawi, the beloved of my heart, away from me, I was like a sheatfish washed ashore; I was at a loss, with no idea what to do," my grandfather would explain. "I forgot not only that I was a father, but I forgot even my very self. Tunnawi was my childhood love; we had grown up together. She was everything to me. When she died, everything ceased to have any meaning. I didn't feel like seeing or talking to anyone, not even our kind-hearted king Kamanas. With the permission of the earthly beloved of the Storm God, our hero king, our lord Kamanas, I took two of my loyal slaves and went to a small island in the middle of the Euphrates. My slaves dropped me off on the island with a raft and returned.

"For three days and three nights I ran about that island like a mad man; for three days and three nights I howled in pain like a dog; for three days and three nights I wept like an old woman. By the end of the first day, I had nearly lost my voice; by the end of the second day, my tear ducts had dried out; by the end of the third day, I had depleted myself of all strength; and on the dawn of the fourth day, I became blind to the light. When I saw the light again, I was at home in my bed. It was in vain that my hands searched amongst the fragrant, cool sheets for my beautiful Tunnawi, love of my heart, she who made my bed a place of joy. Then just as the black tulle of mourning was about to enshroud my heart, something wholly unexpected happened. The merciful king Kamanas came to my home. Can you imagine, that great person, that hero king, representative of the gods on earth, King Kamanas himself, came to my home, which was built upon his command, on land that he himself had bestowed upon me? He took the baby onto his lap. 'Look,' he said, 'this is your son. Look at what a beautiful child he is. I'm going to name him after my father. Henceforth, he shall be known as Araras.' Then he held the baby out to me. Confused and ashamed, I took him onto my lap. With pain, with love I pressed to my breast my child, himself so unaware of his innocence, of his orphanhood.

"The more my son grew, the more I came to love him. I took him with me everywhere I went, my chest swelled with pride as I witnessed his skills. Whenever I had the chance, I would take my son to be in the presence of our lord, the hero king Kamanas.

"The great king Kamanas was so fond of little Araras that he bestowed upon us the honor of allowing him to be educated together with his own son, Astarus. When I received word of this news, I was overjoyed, and tears of happiness poured forth from my eyes like waterfalls. For days I ran about intoxicated with this honor that our king had bestowed upon our family. But the dark betrayal that I was to encounter would show me what a foolish mistake I had made.

"The more my son grew, the more he came to look like me; his physical similarities, however, were not reflected in his behavior. He was as respectful as a priest, as industrious as a slave, as intelligent as a fine scribe. The Storm God Teshub had given him all of the fine qualities that a father could want in a child. Not once did he oppose me, no matter how harsh my words. He always heard me out, but there was such a shadow cast in his eyes, such cunning in his actions, and that's what frightened me. Never once did I see a childish look in his eyes, or a naïve smile cross his lips. Even in those days, his actions, his words, his smile were all controlled and measured, much like those of a scribe constantly tailing the king. My friends spoke of my son's qualities with praise. I, however, felt concern. And it wouldn't be long before I found out that I was not wrong to feel so.

"When our powerful king Kamanas met his death after falling from his horse during a lion hunt, fortune smiled upon my son and the young king Astarus, who never went against my son's word. After the end of the 14-day funeral for the hero king Kamanas, before his ashes had even settled into the vessel into which they had been placed, they began realizing their plot of intrigue. My blood son Araras convinced the young king Astarus that he should get rid of the elderly members of council. They removed me from my office and attempted to cast a shadow upon my honor. But they were not powerful enough. They only took from me the name, power, and authority that the kingdom had given to me. But my freedom and dignity they could not touch."

As I listened to the events that my grandfather Mitannuwa narrated to me with such rage, I would wonder how much of what he said was real, and how much was exaggeration. My grandfather was like a haystack on fire; he was quick to flame, but his anger was always short-lived. Once ignited, however, he would lose himself, not hesitating to speak the first words that came to his lips. That's why, while listening to what he said about my father, I would listen intently as if the man before me were a young man fallen prey to his anger, and I would contemplate his words long and hard before believing him.

CHAPTER SIX

After dinner, Esra sat in the shade of the arbor and tried to while away the time by thinking about all that had happened. But her thoughts always floundered at a certain point, always got stuck on wondering just what Shehmuz would have to say. Had he confessed to the crime? And if he was responsible, who was backing him? It was impossible to interpret what had happened without knowing what he'd said. So they had no other choice but to wait for the results of the interrogation. But it had been hours since they had last heard anything from Eshref. The more Esra waited, the less optimistic she became, and the more she found herself getting caught back up in that morning's anxious mood .

"I wish I'd gone with Halaf to take dinner to the site watchman, Selo," she thought, despite the sizzling heat. Perhaps time would have passed more quickly at the site. She was out of luck though, for Halaf must have reached the excavation site a long time ago. In fact, it was even likely that Selo had already finished his meal and rolled two cigarettes from his smuggled tobacco, and that they were by now puffing away at them, stretched out across from one another in the shadow of the fig tree at the King's Gate. She wanted to be with them at that moment, to listen to them talk about the upcoming harvest this year or the changing climate due to the artificial lakes forming because of the dams built along the Euphrates. She finally withdrew to her room, where in a state of distress she lay down on her bed and did her best to focus her attention on the historical novel she'd been trying for so long to finish. But she was unable to focus, and so she put the book down and got back up, and then headed for the front of the building, to the room with the computers.

Kemal was alone in the room; Teoman had left to take a nap in the hammock beneath the dark shade of the walnut tree in Grandma Hattuch's pomegranate garden. Trying to reduce the suspense as she waited, she sat down in front of one of the computers and got to work. She was compiling an inventory of the uncovered pottery, shards, numerous seals, two copper and one silver statuette showing Assyrian influence, an Aramaean style necklace, a vase, and the tablets.

So far, they had uncovered twenty-four tablets from the small room of the library below the palace. Ten of the tablets were pieces of a text about the epic of Gilgamesh, while fourteen of them were Patasana's writings. Unlike the texts about the epic of Gilgamesh, Patasana's tablets were only slightly damaged. When the palace collapsed, the room where the scribe stored the tablets was buried beneath a thick pile of rubble and stone. But the Patasana tablets were durable because they had been baked, and so they didn't crumble when exposed to the sunlight. Nevertheless, the excavation team immediately copied the texts onto paper and took photographs of them. There were cracks in the third, fourth, and seventh tablets, but they were still in one piece.

As she recorded the information about the finds, Esra listened expectantly for her mobile phone to ring, but for some reason, it just wouldn't. Did an interrogation last this long? Perhaps the questioning was long over but the Captain saw no need to let her know. Maybe I should call, she thought for a brief moment. But then she quickly changed her mind—what if they were still questioning him? She should leave them alone. After all, the Captain was sure to call her. Or would he? Seeing as he'd come to tell her about the murder at the crack of dawn, it was unlikely that he'd wait to tell her whether or not the murderer had confessed... Really now, what did the Captain think of her, she wondered. Several times she had caught the passion in his eyes when he looked at her, but it was difficult to correctly interpret those evasive glances of his. Those glances revealed the hunger of a man who had been without a woman for a long time. Hey, that's an aspect of a relationship that certainly shouldn't be belittled; however, Esra wanted more than that. She, too, hadn't had a serious relationship since she broke up with Orhan. For a while she had gone out with Haluk from the university's Prehistory Department. He was a handsome man, but he was such a windbag that she could only put up with him for a month. So what did she see in the Captain? She didn't know the answer to this herself. The only thing that they had in common was that both were from Istanbul. They were so different with respect to their education, how they viewed life... She recalled the talk they had had in the garden of the police station. Once again she thought how silly it was that the Captain suspected that the terrorists were behind any and every incident that occurred in the region. What really upset Esra, however, was how the Captain would seem so sincere and try to get so close to her one moment, and then suddenly withdraw the next. "He doesn't know what he wants," she mumbled.

"Sorry," said Kemal, who was at least as ill at ease as Esra, "did you say something?"

"No, not to you." She had turned to look at Kemal, who was standing in front of the window. "I was talking to myself." Then, in order to change the subject, she quickly added, "They're still not back, are they?"

"No, they aren't," complained a distressed Kemal. "And I doubt they will be until this evening."

When Timothy and Elif failed to come to dinner that evening, Kemal lost all ability to focus. At first he tried to continue with his sketches, and then when he was unable to do that, he played a little Tetris, then wandered about the room aimlessly, then, after becoming bored of that, too, he went back to playing Tetris, before finally standing there before the window waiting for the return of the girl he loved. He'd been standing there for at least an hour.

"Why don't we take a walk," said Esra in a gesture of friendliness. "The sun's let up now."

Kemal sighed. "We were going to go swimming in the Euphrates. What if she comes and I'm not here..."

"But she's already late."

The young man hung his head hopelessly.

"That's true," he said, "but I still have to wait for her."

Esra was annoyed by Kemal's indecisiveness.

"It's up to you," she said as she turned the computer off. "But I'm bored, and I'm going for a walk."

When she reached the corridor, she heard the sound of music. It was the deep moan of a cello, accompanied by the barely perceptible sound of a piano in the background. The sound was coming from Bernd's room. Esra slowed down as she passed by his closed door. It was a sentimental melody; she recalled the music but couldn't come up with the name of the composer. She thought that Bernd must be rereading, with longing and a sweet sprain in his heart, the letter he had written to his wife, to the sound of this music. Wasn't she, too, like this when she had gone off on an excavation during her marriage to Orhan? Back then, she, too, would get infected by the thousands of years of loneliness of these ancient cities and an odd melancholy would overcome her. Especially during her free time, when work was winding down, not to mention the nights when the stars flickered in the sky like sparks from flint... The flint bit was Halaf's. And now how did her mind get stuck on that? What was wrong with her? As if they didn't have enough trouble to deal with it as it were, now she was getting all sentimental. "Pull yourself together, Esra," she said as she exited the school.

As she approached the arbor, she saw that Halaf had returned from the excavation site. With a hose in one hand, he was wetting down the dry, cracked earth, and watering the purple four-o'clocks and red geraniums. "Don't work too hard," said Esra, inhaling the sharp scent of the geraniums.

"Yeah, just thought I'd cool the place off a bit here."

"That's a good idea. It smells wonderful. So what's going on at the excavation?"

"It's just like always," he said, and then after a short pause, "But Uncle Selo didn't look well to me."

"I hope it's nothing serious. He's not sick or anything, is he?"

"Oh no, he's not sick or anything. It's just, I don't know, here's this man who used to look me in the eye, but now he looks at my feet."

"What are you trying to say?" Esra asked carefully, giving the cook a stern look.

"No, nothing for now, just that you should be wary of this Uncle Selo. He and his brother, those fellas used to be smugglers before they installed all those landmines at the border. They're used to easy money..."

"What do you mean 'they're used to easy money'?" said Esra harshly. "Don't speak in riddles. If you know something, say it outright."

"I don't," said Halaf. "God's my witness, I've never seen Uncle Selo do anything bad or steal or anything, but, well, I don't know, he was acting oddly today. He asked about you guys, and he never does that. When I told him the Captain came to the school this morning, his face went white as chalk."

"So what's wrong with that? So the poor fella was worried about us, is that so hard to believe? Besides, whenever there's mention of the Captain, don't you go all pale yourself? I trust Selo. Hadji Settar found him for us. So far, he's done a great job. He's an honest man."

"You're probably right," said Halaf, retreating a bit from his previous statement. Still, he couldn't help but add, "Marry garlic and it takes forty days before you catch a whiff."

"Don't you worry, Selo wouldn't do anything to hurt us. Enough of your groundless fears. Just tell me now, what's for dinner this evening?"

"I'm fixing the fish Timothy brought," said Halaf. Then with a sour face he grumbled, "Kemal says 'don't use tomato paste or garlic,' but these fish are tasteless without them. The only thing he knows is sea fish."

Esra, who had witnessed these debates before, was sick of Kemal's whining. Esra had thought that using tomato paste was rather odd at first herself, but after eating the fish and realizing just how delicious it really was, she came to agree with Halaf. But Kemal still kept insisting that Halaf cook it without the tomato sauce.

"Fix ours with tomato sauce and set his aside. He can cook his own fish however he likes."

Pleased at her response, Halaf headed for the kitchen. Just then, she heard the news come on the radio that was hanging from the arbor. The deep voice of the newsreader was announcing that five security officers had been martyred and thirty-two terrorists killed in a conflict in Van, and that military operations were continuing non-stop. Esra was so used to such news that it had absolutely no impact upon her anymore. Still, she couldn't help but mumble, "Pity, what a pity," as she walked away from the arbor.

The heat had begun to wane, and it cooled down within a few hours. These were Esra's favorite hours of the day. She hadn't put her hat on, or her sunglasses. She squinted into the horizon. The brightness of the sun had dimmed, and then slowly gone out, turning from a golden yellow to the color of honey.

In order to reach the river, she first had to walk the length of a pomegranate grove to a path that was lined on one side with thorny purple flowers, and on the other with dried weeds. She looked into the pomegranate grove to see if she could see Teoman, who had gone there to sleep in the hammock. She noticed apricot and plum trees here and there amongst the blooming pomegranates. The apricots hadn't yet ripened, but the ripened plums had already begun falling onto the ground. Instead of Teoman, though, she found the owner of the grove. Despite her wrinkled face, Grandma Hattuch was still the cutest old lady in the world. "My dear girl, can I help you with anything?" she asked in her usual hospitable tone, thinking that Esra was looking for her.

"Thanks, Grandma. I was just going for a stroll and thought I'd see if our Teoman had woken up yet."

The old woman had been a little leery of them when they first came to the area. She was afraid they'd plunder her grove or hurt her in some way, and so she tried to keep her distance from them. But then seeing that they meant her no harm, she let her guard down, and within no time had become chummy with them, due in large part to her inability to resist the sweet talk and charm of Teoman, who never failed to ask her how she was doing every time he passed by the grove. Now whenever she saw anyone from the team, she immediately went up to them and started chattering away, complaining about her son who lived in Antep or about her crazy daughter-in-law in the village.

"My boy Teoman's at the other end of the grove," said the old woman, with a smile that was very becoming to her toothless face. "I sent him to sit beneath the apricot tree. It's not good to sleep in the shade of a walnut tree. It'll make you sick."

"He'll get sick anyway if he keeps sleeping so much," said Esra disapprovingly, yet compassionately.

"He'll be just fine, just fine. I woke him up a little while ago. You come along now, catch your breath. I'll make some tea for us."

"Thank you. Perhaps another time. The others are waiting for me now."

"As you like," said Grandma Hattuch. "Open your hands." The old woman grabbed a handful of the plums she had gathered in her skirt and handed them to Esra.

"These are too much," said Esra, sweetly surprised.

"Go on and take them now, girlie, go on, take 'em. What are you worried about? It's not like you don't have any teeth, like me. When I was your age, I couldn't get my fill of these."

Esra loaded the bottom of her blouse with the plums. She couldn't go down to the river anymore, not with all these plums. She bid Grandma Hattuch farewell and had just started walking back to the school when she heard the sound of a motor. Her heart fluttered with joy. Could it be the Captain? She stopped by the side of the road and waited, wondering if it was him. The sound of the motor grew louder, and before long an old model Land Rover appeared as it climbed the small hill. Murat was driving the jeep. Timothy and Elif were seated in the back. The girl was merrily telling the American something. She looked so happy that Esra couldn't help but wonder if Kemal were right, that Elif really was in love with Timothy. The folks in the jeep had seen Esra as well, and pulled up next to her.

"Where've you been?" Esra asked. She had her eyes fixed on Murat and had posed her question in a voice that was a bit louder than necessary.

Murat was taken aback.

"We were with Timothy," he stuttered.

Not realizing that Esra was upset with them, Elif broke in excitedly:

"The villages are so interesting. They just love having guests."

Her voice was spirited, smooth, and ecstatic, like that of a child unaware of her responsibilities.

"I hear you're going swimming with Kemal?" Esra asked.

An annoyed look came over Elif's face.

"I don't feel like swimming at all."

Esra thought Elif was acting like a brat. She wondered why any of this should matter to her, but still she couldn't help but have a word: "If only you'd said so this morning, the poor boy's worried to death."

"What's there to be worried about! We stopped by the photographers in town."

"What? You went into town?"

"Yes," said Elif, unable to comprehend Esra's stunned reaction. "What's wrong with going into town?"

"It's complicated. I wish you hadn't gone into town."

"The village was very calm," said Timothy. He was leaning down to look at Esra through the window. "The people that we talked with were very kind to us."

"Nobody thinks we've brought on any disaster or anything," said Elif. "I think Bernd's right, we're exaggerating this whole a thing a bit too much."

"We're not exaggerating anything," said Esra angrily. "A person has died. Every day I get threatening messages on my mobile phone... Besides, it isn't me, but the Captain who says we shouldn't go into town."

"You mean Eshref Bey?" said Timothy. "We saw him, too."

"You did?"

"Yes, he stopped us on our way back as we were driving by the police station."

"Did he say anything about Shehmuz? Has he confessed?"

"I don't know. He didn't mention Shehmuz, just said that he would be stopping by for a visit this evening."

"So we invited him for dinner," said Elif.

"For this evening?"

"Yes, he didn't play hard to get when he heard there was *shapit* for dinner," said Elif, with an innocent blink of her green eyes.

A bit stunned by this piece of news, Esra just stood there next to the jeep for a while.

"Hop on in, let's go," said Murat.

"You go on, I'm going to walk. After all, it's just a hop, skip, and jump from here."

Murat didn't insist. He drove on in the jeep, which left a thin cloud of dust in its trail. Esra took a step back away from the rising dust. So Eshref hadn't called because he was coming over. Should she interpret this to mean that the murderer had been caught and that the issue resolved, or that the questioning had left them empty-handed? In any case, she would learn the truth of the matter in just a few hours.

THE TABLET SIX

How can a child torn between his grandfather and his father possibly understand the truth; what can he do but listen to one and then the other, like a wretched servant torn between two sparring gods?

Whenever he would begin to tell me about his quarrel with my father, my grandfather would lose his head and talk incessantly.

"How is it even possible," he would roar, "that a person to whom you gave life, who shares your blood, who is the perpetuator of your lineage, should betray you!"

According to Mitannuwa, my father had been consumed by such an uncontrollable ambition that he did not hesitate to use even the young king Astarus in his ploys to become chief scribe.

Mitannuwa did not marry for a long time after the death of his wife Tunnawi, not until the goddess Kupaba granted him the opportunity to fall in love once again, just as he had crossed the threshold into old age. His hair was graying, his posture slightly stooped, and he found himself growing winded at the mere task of climbing the palace stairs, when he became captivated by the curly-haired, doe-eyed slave girl Mashtigga, herself as agile as a mare, and as beautiful as one, too.

If he had wanted, my grandfather could have warmed his bed together with her every night, but then that would have gone against his noble character. He wanted to marry Mashtigga. There was nothing in the Hittite laws that forbade a free person from marrying a slave. But for some reason, perceptions changed when the person in question was the chief palace scribe. Many noblemen in the Assembly condemned my grandfather for this act of his. However, my grandfather was able to gain the support of our powerful king Kamanas, who was still in good health, and with the king backing him, like the formidable buttress of a snow-capped mountain, he succeeded in making all of his critics ineffectual. The wishes of the Storm God Teshub, however, he could not oppose. And so just after my grandfather was married, Kamanas fell off of his horse and died.

According to my grandfather, my father jumped at this chance, initiating a silent coup d'état whereby he had my grandfather removed from his position and himself chosen to replace him. Upon learning of this decree, my grandfather put forth no protestations, but simply withdrew, infuriated, to his home. Of the family, he talked only with me. He avoided my mother, and did not want to hear even the slightest mention of my father's name. His sole comfort was his wife Mashtigga. He had been removed from his scribal position, one that he had respectfully filled for so many long years, but it meant naught to him, for now, after so many years devoid of passion, he had Mashtigga, his new beloved. Every day he wrote the young woman a poem. Mashtigga's wavy hair like a rebellious ivy, Mashtigga's dark, grape colored eyes, Mashtigga's crimson cheeks, Mashtigga's slender gracefulness... Mashtigga Mashtigga... Nothing but Mashtigga.

He withdrew to his house where he lived with the woman who had been his slave just a year before, and was now his wife. But then, an unexpected disaster befell him. His beautiful wife Mashtigga, for whom he had forfeited his career, and to whom he had written tablets and tablets full of poems, ran off with a young Aramaean poet who had been my grandfather's guest. Like a wounded lion, my grandfather was overcome with a mad rage. He kicked out all of the women in the house and threw all of the poems he had written for Mashtigga together with all of her belongings into the Euphrates.

He locked himself up in his house and would accept no one. He wouldn't even let me come over for a visit. It was only after several days of self-confinement that my grandfather, finally calmed down, emerged. Yet he seemed to have lost his former enthusiasm, glee, rage. He looked into people's faces with eyes that were dead like the Euphrates at the end of summer.

His close friend, the Chief Priest Valvaziti, recommended that he get a "clean sleep." Perhaps the gods had something to tell him. My grandfather took the Chief Priest Valvaziti's advice. He ritually prepared for the clean sleep and lay down in his bed. Alas, the Storm God Teshub truly did come to him in his dream. Suddenly emerging from the darkness to appear before him with his cap of pointed horns, a spear in his right hand, a sword hanging from his belt, and a bunch of three lightning rods in his left hand, Teshub told my grandfather that he should take an interest in his grandson rather than poisoning his days with longing for an unfaithful woman.

The clean sleep transformed my grandfather. He called me to his side and told me, "From now on, it is I who shall take care of you. I am now responsible for your education."

My father's response to this news was one of caution. He did not trust my grandfather one bit and feared that he would do something evil to me. But I was not of the same opinion. Despite all of his irrational behavior, my grandfather was hardly capable of evil towards his enemies even, let alone his own grandson. After all, he had already proven his benevolence by forgiving Mashtigga and her lover after they were captured several months later. So when my mother, too, gave her consent, I began taking lessons from my grandfather.

From then on I stayed with my grandfather from sunup until sundown. He took me to see clergymen, minstrels, sculptors. He involved me in their conversations. Meanwhile, I showed him the quatrains I had written. He was delighted to learn that I was writing poetry. After that, we began working on my poems. I derived great pleasure from the time that I spent with him; I only wished he would cease to speak so badly of my father. But he didn't; he continued to rain curses down upon my father until one day, once he was certain that he had provided me with a thorough education, without a word to anyone he took leave of our city on the river shore.

One morning I arrived at his two-story house to find the doors open. There was nobody inside. He had left me a tablet in the spacious room where we held our lessons. On the tablet it was written:

"Me dear son Patasana, my time is now up. I feel that the gods will soon beckon me to their side. In any case, I myself have grown tired of this city, of these people. And seeing as you are a grown man now, there is nothing left for me to do. I do not want to die here. I do not want a lot of frauds to shed fake tears and sing words of false praise for me at my funeral ceremony. My heart will not consent to letting a bunch of scoundrels sully my death with their insincere sorrow.

"You are a fine young man. You have received a fine education. The only thing you have to do now is observe your father and make sure that you do not become like him. Believe me, son, in order to be happy, it is enough that you refrain from doing as your father has done. And that is easier than learning cuneiform. However, I am not certain that you will be able to do this. Because sometimes, I think I glimpse in your eyes that same dim expression of your father's. I hope that this is but a trick of the gods. I hope that it is not as I suspect. I hope that you are intelligent enough not to waste your life on the meaningless self-interests of kings. I hope that you find endeavors that will make your days meaningful. Goodbye, my beloved son. May the Storm God Teshub, his wife the Sun Goddess Hepat, and their children the God Sharruma and the Goddess Kupaba bless you with goodness and beauty. May they bestow upon you a long and happy life."

After I had finished reading the tablet, I just stood there, not knowing what to do with myself. It was true that my grandfather had always surprised us with his unexpected behavior, but this was really too much. He was already old, so why drag himself into some meaningless adventure when he could spend his last days in comfort as a respected man of society? I took the tablet and left the house. I ran into my grandfather's slaves at the bazaar. They said that their master had freed them and left the city. I hurried to the palace and appeared before my father. I told him what had happened. He wasn't the least bit concerned. "Don't worry, he'll come back," he said. As the gods are my witness, these were my own thoughts as well. But my grandfather did not return.

CHAPTER SEVEN

Despite his promise, the Captain didn't show up. The excavation team had gathered under the arbor, as they did every evening for dinner, and had been waiting for him for nearly an hour. Halaf had set the long wooden table, illuminated by a yellow lamp hung from the very top of the arbor, for eight people. The young cook had prepared vegetable rice to go along with the fish and a salad comprising mostly of the thick romaine lettuce that grew along the edge of the Euphrates. But he was waiting for the guest to arrive before cooking the fish.

"We might as well go ahead and eat now," said Esra finally. "It doesn't look like the Captain's going to make it. Something important probably came up."

"A phone call would have been nice!" complained Kemal angrily. "With so many people waiting for him..."

"I think the Captain's had a busy day," said Timothy, rising to his defense. "He was on his way somewhere when we ran into him today."

But Timothy's words failed to calm Kemal down.

"Well, he still could have called." Then, looking at Elif out of the corner of his eye, he added in a needling voice, "But then it seems that making people wait has become a habit of ours these days!"

An icy chill descended on the table. When Elif and the others had returned from their excursion, Kemal had taken Elif aside and begun berating her, but the young woman had been quick to snap right back at him: "I can do whatever I want, you have no business interfering in my life." Now, it seemed that Kemal was set on provoking yet another argument. Realizing this, Elif ignored her boyfriend's words and headed for the kitchen, supposedly to help Halaf.

"We went to see an old woman called Infidel Nadide today," said Murat, hoping to clear the air.

"Infidel Nadide?" asked Teoman curiously. "why 'infidel'?"

"The woman's both Christian and Muslim. She believes in both Jesus and Mohammed. She's got not one holy book, but two—the Bible and the Koran."

This all seemed very odd to Teoman. "Is there some kind of sect like that here?"

"Nadide's actually Christian," Timothy explained. "Her parents are part of the Gregorian Church."

"Then she must be Armenian," said Bernd. "My wife's Gregorian, too."

"That's right," Timothy said, nodding his head up and down. "When the Armenians fled after the war, they left their youngest daughters with their neighbors."

"Oh no, now Bernd's going to give us one of his interminable lectures," thought Esra, but she didn't interrupt the conversation. Instead, it was Teoman's turn to speak up. His interest was obviously piqued by the dialogue, and so, leaning on the huge elbows he had placed upon the table, he asked, "So there were Armenians in this region?"

"Oh, geez, Teoman!" complained Murat. "Haven't you seen the mosque in town?"

"Yeah, I've seen it, so what about it?"

"I'll tell you what about it, that mosque used to be a church."

"How was I supposed to know that?"

"If you'd paid attention to the architecture, you'd have known," said the German. "Do its arches, its beams look like the ones in the mosques here?"

"So, you mean our people put that minaret, the one that Hadji Settar was thrown off of, on it afterwards?"

"Yes," Bernd jumped in. "The Turks made a habit of doing that. There's a huge church in Gaziantep that was converted into a mosque. The church was designed by Sarkis Balyan, the famous architect from Istanbul, in 1876. Then for years the Turkish Government used it as a prison before emptying it out, sticking a minaret on it, and opening it up for worship as a mosque."

Esra was eager to change the subject, but then Murat stepped up with a question that only served to deepen the discussion:

"There weren't any religious wars in ancient Mespotamia, were there?"

"The Armenian deportation didn't have anything to do with religion," said Bernd, responding to the question in his own unique manner. "The heads of the Party of Union and Progress exiled the Armenians so that they could turkify Anatolia."

"You have some interesting viewpoints," said Timothy. "Where does your interest in this topic stem from?" Timothy asked, and everyone's eyes focussed on Bernd.

"I'm writing a thesis entitled 'The Destruction Wrought By Civilization'," he explained, now looking rather ill at ease. "So of course I have to analyze all of the great massacres of history, as part of my research."

"None of the massacres on earth could have been as organized and widespread as Hitler's," said Teoman. There wasn't a hint of reproach in his facial expression or his voice. The words just poured naturally out of his mouth .

"And one shouldn't forget the atomic bombs that the Americans dropped on Hiroshima and Nagasaki," added Kemal, who had been looking to take a swipe at Timothy since the onset of the discussion. "You can hardly claim that the instantaneous destruction of hundreds of thousands of innocent people was less than Hitler's barbarity."

"I think every massacre should be analyzed within its own context," said Esra, trying to effect a compromise. "Just because one massacre's worse than another doesn't mean that we should disregard any of them."

"No objections to that," said Timothy, before turning to look at Murat and, finally, addressing the issue of Mesopotamia.

"A little while ago you asked a very relevant question," he said. "Back when there was polytheism, I mean, back before our Hittites had been wiped off the face of the earth, there had never been a war caused by religion. In fact, when a tribe took over a country, it took the statues of the gods in that country to its own temples, because it thought that in this way, it could get more gods, more powerful gods, on its side. Conflict stemming from a clash of beliefs only began with the rise of monotheism."

Bernd was just getting ready to deliver his comeback when Teoman interjected. "So what happened to Infidel Nadide, Tim? You were telling us about that."

"Right, Infidel Nadide," said Timothy, smiling. "The woman's real name is Nadya. She was ten years old back then. Her neighbors raised her, and changed her name to Nadide. They began to bring her up like a proper Muslim, but Nadide never forgot the things she had learned as a young child. So on the one hand she learned about Islam, but all the while she secretly continued to pray to Jesus. Years went by and she married, had kids. One day her daughter-in-law found a cross next to the Koran that was never absent from Nadide's bedside. The daughter-in-law, who wasn't all too fond of her mother-in-law, spread this bit of news throughout the village. That's how Nadide's secret that she'd kept for so many years was finally revealed. And ever since then they've called her 'Infidel Nadide.'"

"So you're saying that they've been insulting her all this time," said Bernd with an accusatory look in his blue eyes.

"I don't think you can really call it an insult," said Timothy, scoring even more points with Esra. "So they called her an infidel, but you shouldn't take it so seriously. After all, the village accepted her for who she was. Except for the occasional impertinent jerk, nobody ever stuck their nose in her religion. And she continued to believe, with utmost sincerity, in both Jesus and Mohammed. 'Aren't both of them prophets of God? Aren't they both guardians of people? I believe in God and pray for both of them.' That's what she told us."

"She was such an adorable woman," said Murat, throwing himself into the conversation once again. "She has eight children and twenty-four grandchildren. She's at least eighty years old, but she still dyes her hair with henna and her velvety black eyes still beam when she looks at you."

Kemal was annoyed by Murat's enthusiasm, by how excitedly he talked about all of this, and so he just couldn't help taking a verbal punch at the other young man.

"Looks like you chose a wrong occupation, my boy. You should have been a sociologist, then you could've spent more time with the wonderful people of our homeland."

"There's no need to be a sociologist. Archaeologists have enough human contact as it is."

It was the first time since the beginning of the excavation that Murat's voice came out so full, so sharp, as if he were challenging Kemal. The sharpness was not lost upon Esra. She looked at Murat out of the corner of her eye. He had swung his long, curly hair over his shoulder so that it flowed down his back, and he was stroking his thick, moustacheless beard—the spitting image of an Assyrian clergyman—as he stared Kemal down. "It seems our boy is finally coming into his own," thought Esra with a feeling very much like pride.

Murat was one of her better students. He wasn't just hardworking, but intelligent, too, and more importantly, he was crazy about archaeology. His only fault was that he was a little too caught up in all that parapsychology. But Esra, thinking that even the best of us have our faults, had seen nothing wrong with letting him join the excavation.

When Esra, as his professor, first suggested to Murat that he join the excavation team, he couldn't believe his ears and was on cloud nine for the rest of the day. But the more he thought about it, the more worried he became that he might not have what it takes. He imagined that the rest of the excavation team members would be smarter than him, more experienced than him, not to mention that they would have two foreigners with them as well. So basically, in his own head he had blown the whole matter way out of proportion. But then the past two weeks had taught the clever boy that nobody was perfect. He saw that everyone, including Esra, for whom he had the utmost respect, had their faults, and at times even acted in ways that he found to be foolish. When on an excavation, there are two points that one has to pay attention to: the first is to do the best job possible, and the second is to adapt oneself to the conditions of living and working together as a team. His days on the excavation had shown him that the latter was the hardest part of all. Everyone was doing his or her best. But when it came to living together, differing personalities immediately made themselves apparent, so that arguments broke out when it came to even the most trivial of matters, from deciding what to have for dinner to whose turn it was to use the shower. Since it was impossible to put a stop to the arguing, the important thing was to see to it that the arguments didn't hurt anyone's feelings. Despite all of this, Murat still found excavation life to be much more exciting than he had thought it would be; in fact, he was more than excited, he was absolutely captivated by it. After all, touching, swallowing the dust of the earth here, permeated as it is by that unique scent, those pale yet permanent colors and fluctuant yet deep lines of a history going back thousands of years inevitably leads your mind, your entire body to be consumed by a profound curiosity. And even if you want to, you can't possibly break free of this effect; and so in the end, you spend a lifetime hopping from excavation to excavation, a veritable detective on the hunt for the tiny traces and deformed clues that will lead you to the truth buried there, somewhere, beneath the centuries.

Kemal had looked daggers at Murat after the latter's response, but had refrained from pursuing the matter any further.

The irksome silence at the table was broken by Timothy's deep voice: "Isn't there any alcohol to go with the fish?"

"I think it'd be better if we didn't drink tonight," said Esra, the expression on her face indicating that she expected the others to be understanding of her request. "Tomorrow's a workday. I don't want to see anybody hung over at the site."

"One little glass never hurt anybody," said Teoman, seconding Timothy.

"I know about your one 'little glasses,'" said Esra, before pleading, "I really think we shouldn't drink tonight."

Any other time Teoman would have sweet talked the head of the excavation into going along with their request, but seeing that she was in rather low spirits tonight, he couldn't bring himself to launch on an argument with the unpredictable Esra this time around.

"Okay, we'll just have our drinks another time then," he said with the fortitude of a man bowing down to his fate. "Pass me that bread so I can slice it."

Elif emerged from the kitchen holding a glass of lemon juice and approached the table, with the smell of fried fish in tow. Teoman, who was cutting the bread into thin slices, persisted in his whining: "The fish *still* isn't ready yet?"

"Hold your horses," said the young woman, smiling to reveal her perfect, pearly white teeth. "We just now put them in the skillet."

Kemal's scathing eyes were directed right at the young woman. Elif, however, paid no attention to him and casually set her glass on the table.

"And now on top of everything else, we have to deal with this, too," thought an annoyed Esra. "This idiot Kemal's sure to get all depressed now. I hope he's wrong, I hope Elif's not really interested in Timothy."

As these thoughts passed through her mind she heard the sound of an aproaching car. Everybody at the table looked towards the road. Only a pair of headlights was visible .

"The Captain's jeep?" Timothy conjectured.

The jeep pulled up to just twenty meters to the right side of the arbor. First the Captain got out, followed by a sergeant and two soldiers.

"Oh man!" said Teoman in a fit of exaggerated anger. "There's four of them! There goes our supper."

Esra gave Teoman a disapproving look and then stood up and walked over to the jeep. She had a solemn expression on her face, and there were hints of hurt in her eyes.

"Sorry I'm late," said the Captain. He was apologizing, but his actions belied the mischievous joy of a clever kid who's just scored an unexpected victory. "But I didn't want to come empty-handed," he continued, with that same impish attitude. "I've got something for you in the jeep,".

A dumbfounded expression came over Esra's face. She had no idea what he could possibly be talking about.

"Come here," he said, shaking her hand. "I think we have some of your royal scribe's tablets here; what was his name?"

"You mean Patasana?" Esra mumbled, still trying to grasp exactly what was going on.

"Yeah, yeah, his tablets. Or rather, I think they're his tablets. We also got a goblet made of gold, a silver deer figurine, a bronze statue of a woman, and a necklace."

Her curiousity piqued, Esra walked with the Captain towards the jeep. "So where did you find all of this?" she asked.

"In Memili the Cripple's vineyard house," explained the Captain. By this time they had arrived at the open middle door of the jeep. "See, here they are," he said, motioning towards the items on the floor of the jeep.

The first thing to catch Esra's eye was the statuette of the woman, followed by the deer, the goblet, and the necklace. Right next to them lay two tablets, one of which was broken. She picked up the tablet on top, the one that was still in one piece, and began examining it in the dim light of the van. These were just like Patasana's—18 by 27 cm clay tablets, with writing on front and back in six columns on each side and a colophon containing a summary of the tablet's contents on the back. When she looked down to the bottom of the tablet she saw the seals and knew the Captain was indeed right—these were Patasana's tablets.

"I don't understand! When did they steal these?"

"Last night," the Captain explained, obviously proud at having given the young woman a real surprise. "I'll tell you everything in a bit. I just brought these over to show you, but I'll have to take them back to the station now because they're evidence."

"But we have to translate the tablets," Esra murmured anxiously. "Taking photos of the other finds is sufficient, but you have to let us make copies of the tablets."

"How long will that take?"

"A day at the most."

"Okay, but make sure it doesn't take any longer, because the public prosecutor's going to want all of the evidence."

"Okay," Esra agreed, breathing a deep sigh of relief. "I'll turn these over to you myself in a day."

Timothy, Murat, and Teoman, curious as to what was going on, approached Esra and the Captain. All three had their eyes on the tablet in Esra's hands.

"Patasana's tablets," explained an exasperated Esra. "And four more important finds that were stolen from right under our noses."

"Where do you want the soldiers to put these?" asked the Captain, as the archaeologists stared at the finds in bewilderment.

"Oh no, we'll carry them ourselves," said Esra. The Captain couldn't tell if she had said this in order to spare the soldiers the bother, or because she was afraid the soldiers would damage the finds. But he didn't insist. Murat and Teoman had already taken hold of the tablets anyway. Murat's eyes meanwhile were fixed upon a bag that was also in the van.

"Should we take this bag, too?"

"That one doesn't belong to you," said the Captain. "It's got hashish in it."

"Hashish?" Esra asked in surprise.

"Yes, we found it at the Cripple's house, too."

Ten minutes later Captain Eshref was sitting at the table telling the excavation team the whole story. Teoman's fears had been in vain, as the sergeant and the other soldiers didn't stay for dinner. Everyone at the table—including Halaf, who was anxious because dinner was late, and Teoman, who was suffering from severe hunger pangs—hung on the Captain's every word.

"When we first began questioning Shehmuz, he said that he wasn't on the run, but just making his regular rounds in the van. Sergeant Ihsan, the man who had caught him, corroborated his statement, saying that there was nothing in his actions to indicate that he was fleeing. I asked him about Hadji Settar, and as soon as I said the name, all the blood drained out of his pock-marked face.

"'I didn't kill him,' he said.

"'You did kill him,' I said. 'There are eye-witnesses.'

"'Then they're lying!' he howled, 'I swear they're lying, sir.'

"'It's not a lie,' I said. 'Don't even try to deny it, we know you're the one who murdered Hadji Settar.'

"'Oh, Captain please, no,' he said and prostrated himself before me. But one of the soldiers thought that he was trying to attack me, and so he struck Shehmuz on the head with the butt of his rifle. Shehmuz collapsed to the ground, and was a little shaken up, but still managed to get back up on his knees. 'I'll do whatever it takes, sir, just don't do this to me!' he begged, paying no mind to the blood running down his forehead. But he was careful not to try and approach me again.

"'Alright, so where were you last night?'

"'At home,' he said, putting on an innocent face.

"'I see,' I said. 'Obviously you have no intention of telling us the truth.'

"'I swear I'm telling the truth, sir. I swear by the love of God I'm telling the truth.'

"'Don't swear!' I screamed. 'You're looking me straight in the eye and lying. We talked with your brother and he told us that you were nowhere to be found until the morning call to prayer.'

"His face grew dark for a moment, but then he pulled himself together and attempted an explanation.

"'I went fishing, sir,' he said in a quivering voice. 'The Captain before you banned fishing, that's why I didn't want to tell you.'

"'And just who do you think you're trying to fool here?' I asked, walking right up to him.

"Shehmuz tried to scoot back on his knees, but the soldier standing next to him lowered his rifle butt down on Shehmuz's left side.

"'Stay put, man!'

"He lay down on his left, crippled with pain. I leaned over him and said in a calm yet firm tone, 'I'm warning you for the last time. We know that you didn't go fishing. No one comes back from a fishing trip before sunrise. You went home this morning right after the call to prayer, while it was still dark outside. And you didn't bring any fish with you either. And you couldn't have anyways because you hadn't been waiting for fish to swim into your net in the Euphrates; you'd been waiting for Hadji Settar so that you could push him off the minaret.'

"Shehmuz lifted his head just a bit, and looked helplessly first at the two soldiers standing next to him, and then at me.

"'Okay, sir,' he said. 'I'm going to tell you everything, but it's not what you think. I wasn't anywhere near the mosque last night. I was out of town.'

"'Look, there he goes, lying to us again,' I said angrily. 'Give me that cartridge belt.'

"'Please sir, don't,' he said, crouching in fear. 'I swear this time I'm telling the truth. We were at the Black Tomb last night.'

"This time it was my turn to be surprised.

"'You were at the Black Tomb?

"'Yes, we were at the Black Tomb. Treasure hunting, as you've probably guessed.'

"'You're lying again...'

"'I swear it's the truth, I swear on the life of my family it's the truth.'

"'Was anyone else with you?'

"Shehmuz paused.

"'Look,' I said, waving a stern finger in his face. 'If you can't prove to me that you were at the Black Tomb, I'll have you locked you up for the murder of Hadji Settar.'

"His eyes gleamed wild yet full of fear, like a jackal who's been cornered. Finally, he confessed: 'Cripple Memili's son Bekir was with me.'

"'And just what did you find at the excavation?'

"'Everything we found is at Memili's vineyard house,' he said in a weary voice.

"'We'll see about that. So where was old Selo, the excavation watchman, while you were digging up your treasure?'

"'Old Selo's daughter-in-law had given birth to a son. He'd been wanting to go see the baby for several days. So Memili told him, 'Go on to the village, Selo, and I'll send my boy Bekir over to watch the excavation. Isn't that what friends are for?' Selo's a naive man. He trusted Memili. So he was in the village when we were there. He has nothing to do with any of this.'

"'After Shehmuz's confession, we caught Cripple Memili's son Bekir at the garage. We searched the vineyard house where we confiscated all of the finds that he told us about, plus a sack of hashish. At first Bekir denied everything, but it didn't take much pressure from us before he admitted that what Shehmuz had told us was true.'"

The entire excavation team had been enthralled by the Captain's story, and now that it was over, they just sat there motionless, dumbstruck. Halaf was the first to emerge from his captivated state.

"I had this feeling that there was something up with that Uncle Selo. He probably understood that there was something wrong at the excavation when he arrived in the morning, but the deed had already been done. And then he couldn't tell anyone because he was afraid."

"We should fire him," said Kemal. "We hire him to keep watch over the excavation, and he goes and turns it over to thieves."

"More importantly, the excavation may not be safe tonight either," mumbled Esra worriedly. "Maybe Uncle Selo got scared and deserted it."

"He hasn't deserted the excavation," said the Captain self-assuredly. "We took Selo in for questioning. And I put two men on duty to guard the excavation."

Esra gave the Captain a grateful look.

"Thank you. We'll take care of the watchman issue tomorrow," she said. But she was still pondering the questioning. "So in this case, Shehmuz didn't murder Hadji Settar, right?"

"So it seems," said the Captain. This seemed to dampen the joyful expression he'd been wearing since his arrival.

"I think you're wrong," objected Kemal. "What you've told us doesn't prove that Shehmzuz didn't murder Hadji Settar. He could have gone and killed Hadji Settar after stashing the stolen goods at the vineyard house."

"It's hard to be sure," said the Captain calmly. "A technical crew is coming in from Gaziantep tomorrow. They're going to gather fingerprints. Only then will we be able to tell anything for certain."

"In that case, we can get on with our meal now," said Teoman, who was on the verge of starvation. "After all, going hungry isn't going to help us figure this out any faster."

TABLET SEVEN

We never were able to find out what happened to my grandfather Mitannuwa. The messengers we dispatched to find him all returned empty-handed. Once we had given up all hope of ever finding him again, my father Araras began to take a greater interest in me. I can't say that he was pleased about Mitannuwa's disappearance, but he did want to benefit from the opportunity that arose out of his absence. He began spending most of his time outside of the palace with me. He didn't approve of me writing poetry and pressured me to work more on official tablets. I did as my father told me, but I also secretly continued writing poetry. It's odd, but I never grew angry at my father; to the contrary, I came to understand him better with each passing day.

Mitannuwa used to call my father the king's stooge. With experience I learned that this wasn't true, that he was just a dedicated official of the government.

That year, during the harvest season, our king became ill. What began with leg cramps turned into agonizing pain, and finally ended in our king's death within the span of only a week. Offerings and votives were presented to the Storm God Teshub, his wife the Sun Goddess Hepat, their son Sharruma, and the Goddess Kupaba. The best soothsayers of the land between the rivers were brought to tell us how to do away with the evil clouds hovering above the king's head.

The soothsayers looked at the liver of a slaughtered sheep. They studied whether the thick part of the liver was at the top or the bottom and shook their heads hopelessly.

The soothsayers set a female eagle and a male eagle aflight over a plain below the Euphrates. But the birds did not meet in the sky; they flew in opposite directions.

The soothsayers placed two eels in a pool, but the eels, too, swam in opposite directions, signalling that the time had come for our king to depart from this earth.

The soothsayers were proven correct, for King Astarus withered away in seven days time, ascending to heaven at the end of the seventh day. A ceremony lasting fourteen days and fourteen nights followed, just as it had following the death of his father, Kamanas. His body was cremated, its flames dispersed to the winds, to the gods. His ashes were then placed in an earthen vessel.

King Astarus was replaced by our new master, the new beloved of the gods, Pisiris. When Pisiris ascended the throne, he was young like Astarus had been when he became king. However, he was nothing at all like Astarus. Astarus was a king who lacked self-confidence. That's partially the reason why he couldn't do anything without first consulting the Council of Elders. Pisiris, on the other hand, was extremely ambitious, cruel, and exceedingly self-confident. In the third month of his reign, he completely destabilized the Council of Elders. He began ignoring the Council's decisions, and implementing none of their decrees. My father sought to oppose him, but the king openly threatened him, saying "Either you are on my side, or I terminate the tradition of the post of palace scribe, a post which your family has held for so many generations." My father was aware of the error of the king's ways, but he did not have the fortitude to stand up to him. I can't say that he was a coward, just that he was constitutionally incapable of opposing Pisiris. He was capable of carrying out unimaginably intricate schemes against foreign rulers, and even against the elders on the council, in order to protect the king's interests, but he could never do that to Pisiris.

Pisiris' mind was occupied with much more dangerous thoughts, to say nothing of his despotism within his own administration. He desired to see himself as a Hittite emperor, like in the days of the great empire. He furtively began contriving plans against the Assyrian Empire under whose sovereignty we lived, completely disregarding the puny strength of our tiny kingdom. My father tactfully cautioned the king against this as well, and constantly implored him to abandon this dangerous goal. But Pisiris was too young, too ignorant, too ruthlessly ambitious to see the truth. He paid no heed to my father's warnings. And in the end, my father bowed down to the king's excesses, which would eventually lead to both their deaths, and began to live in harmony with him. After all, Pisiris was his king, the representative of the gods on earth. To oppose him would mean arousing the fury of the gods, and inviting great misfortune.

CHAPTER EIGHT

Throughout dinner, Esra thought about the air of misfortune that seemed to hang like a pall over them. While everyone hungrily went about stripping the fish clean on their plates; while Teoman quickly gulped down his food and chatted with Murat; while Kemal continued to sulk and Elif to laugh loudly in affected joy; while Timothy, always a sucker for conversation, asked the Captain questions about the military and Bernd smiled to himself while listening to all the babble at the table; while Halaf, standing just two steps behind the table, accepted words full of praise for the delicious meal, and Esra herself felt Eshref sneaking glances at her more frequently as he grew increasingly weary of the American's questions, Esra pondered Hadji Settar's death, but failed to reach any conclusions. She didn't think it at all likely anymore that Shehmuz was the murderer. Yet she couldn't help but hope that perhaps it would turn out to be him after all. If Shehmuz ended up being the murderer, it would solve everything, rescuing them from the ominous shadow of this murder that had descended upon the excavation like a living nightmare. But why would Shehmuz have committed two crimes like this, one after the other, both in the same night? Moreover, the manner in which the crime was carried out just didn't mesh with Shehmuz's character. To go up into the minaret in the pre-dawn darkness and wait, to push Hadji Settar off, above all to wear black in order to hide his identity... for some reason, she just didn't think that this behavior fit with Shehmuz's personality at all. Would someone capable of committing these acts traipse about town declaring, "I'm gonna murder Hadji Settar"?

"You seem rather lost in thought," said the Captain as everyone was drinking their tea. "I thought you'd be pleased that we found the tablets."

Esra quickly gathered herself together.

"I'm grateful to you for that," she said. "If you hadn't confiscated the tablets, Patasana's story would have remained incomplete... But..."

She paused as if she just couldn't seem to find the right words.

"But..." the Captain said, coaxing her to continue.

Out of the corner of her eye Esra glanced at the others sitting there at the table. Everyone was off into their own little worlds.

"Finish your tea and let's go for a walk," she said.

The Captain understood that the young woman didn't want to talk there in front of the others. He finished off his tea in two quick gulps.

"We're going for a stroll," she told the others. Seeing that the Captain, too, was getting up to leave, Halaf rushed up to them.

"You're going to come back, right? I haven't served the fruit yet."

"Thank you," said the Captain with a sincere smile. "The meal was delicious. I've eaten so much, I really don't think I'll be able to eat anymore."

A few moments later the Captain and Esra were walking together along the dirt path. They'd gone just a few meters when Esra asked, "Shall we go down to the river shore? There's a full moon tonight, it's bright out."

"As you wish, Ms. Esra," said the Capain. He was doing his best to conceal his feelings, but the joy in his voice clearly revealed how pleased he was at her suggestion.

Esra grinned mischeviously.

"I say we put a stop to the formalities now."

"Okay," said the Captain bashfully, but obviously very pleased.

"You were right," Esra said as they walked past Grandma Hattuch's pomegranate garden. Lowering her head to avoid a branch that hung over the fence, she continued: "We suspected the wrong guy."

"Well, you can hardly say that it was all for nought. Thanks to your suspicions, we were able to catch some smugglers."

"But we didn't catch the murderer," Esra said unhappily. "I'm wondering if we shouldn't question Fayat."

"I know that you're suspicious of the fundamentalists, but it doesn't seem like a very realistic scenario to me," said the Captain. He fixed his eyes upon the dirt path illuminated by the faint light of the full moon, as if whatever it was they were searching for might be lying out there in front of them. "There aren't any religious organizations in the region powerful enough to commit such a murder."

"The people associated with the Kuran course, Abid Hodja, Fayat?"

"Them?" the Captain said, making a face. "C'mon now, committing a murder, *them*? They may look tough, but it's all show. They're such cowards, they're frightened of their own shadows. If it hadn't been for Hadji Settar, they would've had a hard enough time even opening the Kuran course."

"Have you heard of an organization called Hezbollah?"

"There aren't any Hezbollah here. The Hezbollah are more around the Batman area. If you ask me, it has to be the separatists who are behind this murder."

"Okay, so are they active in this region?"

"They aren't involved in armed conflict, but I'm sure they're doing some agitation-propaganda."

"Agitation-propaganda?"

"That's what they call it," the Captain explained. "It means actions carried out to get more people to join the organization, and to fire up opposition between the people and the state."

Esra disagreed. "I've seen neither a terrorist nor any evidence of such actions here."

The Captain stopped and turned to face her. "So you don't think Hadji Settar's murder could be part of such efforts?" he asked.

Esra stopped, too. She looked at the Captain. The cool breeze blowing in from the Euphrates carried with it the strong scent of oleander, its color invisible in the darkness. The pale moonlight accentuated the sharp contours of the Captain's face. Esra felt her heart skip a beat as she looked at him. "There's no proof of any such thing," she said. "But you must know something or you wouldn't be talking like that."

"No, I don't," said the Captain in an unnecessarily harsh tone of voice. "Why don't we change the subject now?"

Esra was annoyed by this attitude of his, but she didn't press him. They walked silently along the path for a while. And they continued walking in silence until they reached the old river bathed in moonlight.

"Extraordinary," murmured Esra upon seeing the Euprates, which extended before them like a silver streak between the dark shores. She gazed for a moment with awe at the river, then removed a pack of cigarettes from her shirt pocket and took one out. About to put the pack back in her pocket, she turned to the Captain, as if suddenly recalling his presence there beside her.

"Would you like one?"

The Captain didn't feign any reluctance.

"The doctors won't be happy about it, but what the heck, I might as well light up my second smoke of the day."

Esra lit their cigarettes. The amorphous smoke slivered up into the air and mixed with the scent of oleander.

"That's right," said Esra, recalling their conversation that morning. "Today in the police station garden you started to tell me how you began smoking in Shirnak, but then you just dropped the subject."

The Captain turned and looked at the young woman for several moments.

"It's not a very nice story."

"You should've thought of that before you started talking in the first place," Esra responded in a reproachful voice. "What's really not nice is leaving a person wondering."

The Captain wasn't offended by the reproach; to the contrary, he liked that she was behaving as if they were friends who went way back.

"If you really want to know, I'll tell you," said the Captain. "Look, there's a rock over there," he said, motioning toward the left where the reeds came to an end. "Let's go sit over there."

They sat down next to each other. The rock, having absorbed the heat of the sun all day long, was still warm. With each slight movement that he made, the Captain's right arm touched Esra's left shoulder. But neither considered moving away.

"It was in the sixth month after I'd moved to Shirnak," began the Captain. "I was still an officer then. We were in the mountains, carrying out military operations one right after the other. On the night that I referred to, I'd fallen asleep near dawn. I heard these sounds. It was the sound of voices, broken by intermittent silence. I opened my eyes. I'd forgotten where I was. My eyes turned to look at the slowly brightening sky. A series of black clouds rolled through the ash gray sky. I suddenly remembered that we were in the mountains. With an effort I finally got my body, numb from the humidity, moving and sat up in my sleeping bag. I saw two people arguing just a few feet in front of me. The bulky body of Sergeant Reshit I could easily make out, but I couldn't tell who it was that he was talking with.

"'What's going on over there?" I yelled out angrily.

"Sergeant Reshit instantly stood at attention.

"'Seyithan would like to speak with you, lieutenant," he said, his voice deep as if submitting an oral report. 'I told him you were sleeping, but he didn't listen...'"

"My eyes moved to look at Seyithan, who was standing next to Reshit. Though I couldn't quite make out his face, I could sense the derisive grin on his lips. He approached me, completely disregarding the sergeant.

"'Get up, sir,' he said. 'It's time.'

"As Reshit looked at us, trying to figure out what was going on, Seyithan continued.

"'I've found them. They're in a shelter. Bedirhan, and a few others... They're half an hour from here."

"When I failed to respond right away, his reckless boldness turned into downright impertinence:

"'Are you not coming? But you promised..."

"'Alright, I'm coming,' I said, harshly interrupting him as I emerged from my sleeping bag.

"Unable to comprehend exactly what was going on, Reshit asked, 'Shall I wake up the rest of the team, sir?'

"'No,' I said as I put on my parka. 'Seytithan and I are taking this one alone.'

"'But sir...' Reshit began.

"'No buts about it,' I said sharply. "'You'll be in charge while I'm gone, okay?'

"'Yes, sir,' he said, still standing at attention.

"Five minutes later we were on the road. We made our way along a path, steep rock cliffs on one side, the other thick with shrubs. Despite the parka I was wearing, the morning chill worked its way into my bones, and my rifle kept getting heavier and heavier. I looked at Seyithan out of the corner of my eye. He was equally impervious to the darkness and the cold as he skipped along nimbly like a goat over the small stones. A short while later the road became very narrow. I didn't want Seyithan to walk in front of me. He noticed my hesitation, and without a word took the lead. He didn't say anything, but that foul smile on his lips said plenty.

"Seyithan wasn't a soldier, he was a village guard. He was one of the Zerkul tribe's shooters. He'd participated in nearly every major conflict that had taken place in the region and rescued soldiers from ambush more than once. Though he wasn't officially registered, he was considered part of the army. He'd wander about in the mountains all by himself, and everyone was always worried that he was certain to get himself killed, but to that day he hadn't suffered even a single injury.

"This perhaps innate militancy of his inspired in me more fear than respect. I think this fear arose from the fact that in my first conflict, I myself had panicked and stayed back, and Seyithan had recognized this. That day he came up to me immediately after the conflict, and didn't hesitiate in the least to take a dig at me. 'What was that, sir, were you staying back to clear up the rear zone there in the heat of battle, huh?' he said. He had humiliated me in front of my men, but he was right, I'd chickened out and stayed behind. The other commanders and the soldiers didn't criticize me for this. Like me, they, too, had received excellent commando training and taken part in plenty of rigorous maneuvers. But maneuvers were one thing; real life, that was something else altogether. No matter how good their training had been, they'd all had an experience similar to the one I had that day. They'd had the same reaction upon their first encounter with heated conflict; they'd hesitated, and they'd stayed back. Those who weren't shot grew accustomed to the harsh conditions and began to learn the ways of war. A few operations later I, too, had overcome my fear. But Seyithan never stopped hinting at my cowardice and messing with me right there in front of everyone every chance he got.

"When I arrived back at the police station two months later following a successful operation, Seyithan began needling me again—'Coming back from sweeping the rear zone again are you, sir?'—and I lost it. I turned around and gave him a good, hard punch in the face. He fell to the ground, onto his back, and I jumped on top of him. The soldiers had a hard time getting me off of him. For a moment, through the crowd I caught a glimpse of his bloody face, but there wasn't a hint of pain in his eyes, and he just continued looking at me with that same insulting grin on his lips. That evening, the Captain called for me. He said that Seyithan was ignorant, but that he was useful to us, that we couldn't do without him, and that I should make my peace with him. I wasn't at all happy about this, but there was no overriding a superior's command.

"It was two weeks after that incident when I saw Seyithan leaning against the bent trunk of a mulberry tree in the garden behind the police station. I walked up to him. When he saw me, he just raised his eyebrows and gave me this look.

"'Why can't we be friends, Seyithan?' I asked.

"'We just can't, sir,' he said.

"'Why not?' I asked.

"'Because you're a coward,' he said calmly.

"Blood rushed to my head. This man was looking me right in the eye and insulting my honor; but I kept my cool.

"'I'm not a coward,' I said, at least as cold-blooded in my response as he had been in his. 'It's true that I hesitated during my first conflict, but you saw in the operations after that just what kind of a person I am.'

"He said nothing, just stuck his hand in his pocket, that nasty grin plastered all over his face, and took out a silver tobacco case with an embroidered lid. There were thick hand-rolled cigarettes of contraband tobacco in it. I'd seen them before. Seyithan always rolled cigarettes in his free time. I thought he was going to offer me one, but instead he just lit his own and began smoking. After inhaling deeply, seemingly oblivious to my presence, he continued.

"'I've seen how you fight,' he said. 'But I still can't trust you. What if one day, you just don't know what to do? What if you just desert us in the middle of battle?'

"'I would never desert you like that, and you know it.'

"'I don't know it,' he said. 'How can I?'

"'Alright then Seyithan, how can I win your trust?'

He looked at my face carefully, and for the first time I saw genuine sincerity in his eyes.

"'There is a way,' he said. 'But you wouldn't want to do it.'

"'Why wouldn't I? Tell me what it is.'

"'Will you come with me when I find Bedirhan?'

"'Of course I will. The whole crew'll come.'

"'I don't want the others to come. Just the two of us...'

"'Just the two of us? Okay, but why?'

"'I have to kill my brother.'

"'But what if there are a lot of them?'

"'Don't you worry, I'll catch him when he's alone.'

"I hesitated. Could I trust him?

"'You're not gonna come, are ya?' he asked hopelessly.

"'No, I'm going to come,' I said. 'But on one condition. You have to tell me why it is that you want to kill him.'

"'All right,' he said, and began telling his story:

"'Bedirhan and I are twins. We looked exactly alike, like two halves of the same apple. Our pa is a blood relative to the tribal chief. That's why he killed a man and ended up in prison. And so as children we were taken in by the chief. Bedirhan's smarter than I am. He's a reader. Our tribal chief sent him to the city. 'Bedirhan's going to study and look after our legal matters, and you're going to stay here and protect us,' he said. We were all happy that Bedirhan was going to study and become a lawyer. But when Bedirhan got to the city, he forgot all about his tribe and went and joined the insurgents. He snubbed tradition; it meant nothing to him anymore. And as if that weren't enough, he came back here and began shooting at his own tribe, at his own state. That's why it's my duty to kill him.'

"I studied his facial expression as he talked. His thick eyebrows arched in anger, his eyes shone like fiery pieces of charcoal. What he said was quite convincing, but still it seemed to me that he was hiding something.

"'That's it?' I asked.

"'What do you mean, 'That's it?'' he said, looking me straight in the face. Then he shook his head. 'I get it, you ain't comin' with me.'

"'No, I am.'

"'Really?' he asked, flashing his nicotine stained teeth.

"'Really,' I said. 'But from now on, no more picking on me all the time.'

"'Alright, no more of that,' he said. 'No more teasing, but don't expect friendship from me until we've taken care of this.'

"That's what Seyithan said to me. And that's why we went off together to hunt down Bedirhan. The path we were following ended at an oak grove. There we began walking side by side again.

"'Their lair's at the other end of this grove,' said Seytihan.

"'Let's be careful,' I said, my finger automatically heading for the trigger of my rifle. 'They've probably got someone on watch.'

"'They did, but I took care of him,' he said, taking something out of his pocket and holding it out to me. I looked at his hand; in his palm lay a large ear, still damp with blood.

"'When did you kill him?'

"'An hour ago.'

"'What if his buddies have noticed?'

"'Impossible,' he said, looking at the ear he held in his hand. 'The unlucky fella had just taken over patrol.'

"It became cooler as we made our way into the oak grove, so much so that I was nearly shivering from the cold. But I had to maintain my composure, otherwise Seyithan might mistake it for fear. In a short time we reached the mouth of the shelter. The entrance was covered with thick shrubbery, so that you could hardly tell there was a lair underneath.

"'Let's toss a grenade in and pick 'em off as they come out,' I whispered.

"'There's another entrance to the shelter,' he said, now whispering himself. 'You throw the grenade in from below the shrubs, and I'll keep watch over the rear exit.'

"'No way,' I said decisively. 'You'll go and call me a coward again, say I fled from the conflict.'

"'No sir, no I won't, I swear it,' he said earnestly.

"'Yes, you will too,' I said, pressing him. 'I can't trust you anymore.'

"'Trust me. You know that it's me who has to kill Bedirhan. It's no good if I'm not the one who does the deed.'

"My eyes wandered over to the shrub-covered shelter and I changed my mind, suddenly aware of just how dangerous and silly this whole discussion was.

"'Alright,' I said. 'I'm going to silently count to a hundred, then I'm tossing the grenade into the shelter.'

"'Okay,' he said, then in the blink of an eye he made his way over to the other side of the shelter, stealthy as a shadow. I drew closer to the shelter and gently parted the shrubbery. I took the grenade out of my belt and began counting to a hundred. Then I pulled the pin and threw the grenade into the shelter. I dashed backwards, away from the shelter, and threw myself behind a small mound. As soon as I lay down on the ground the grenade went off in a thunderous explosion. Thick clouds of smoke drifted out of the mouth of the shelter, and I immediately heard the sound of Seyithan's kalishnikov. I heard a man, shot, screaming in pain. But I still continued to be cautious and stayed put for a while longer. A deadly silence settled upon the oak grove. Just as I was thinking about calling out to Seyithan, I heard the sound of his kalshnikov once again, and the sound of a pistol in response. The sounds were muffled, which meant that Seyithan must have entered the shelter. Then it became quiet again. My eyes were locked upon the shelter entrance as I waited expectantly for Seytihan to emerge, bellowing out a victory cry. But seconds passed and he was still nowhere to be seen. Finally, I couldn't stand it any longer, and crawled over to the entrance of the shelter. All ears, I perked my ears for any sounds coming from inside. I thought I could hear someone moaning. But then I thought no, that isn't moaning, it sounds more like someone's crying. Curious, I slid in through the entrance. I thought it odd that the shelter was so bright, but then I saw that the grenade had blasted a hole in the ceiling, letting the early morning light seep in through the dry branches above. I moved along, my back to the wall, my hand on my rifle's trigger; in front of me stood a rock that virtually divided the shelter into two. I looked into the other section of the shelter through an opening just wide enough for a single person. Two people lay on the ground, motionless, near the entrance of the cave. I could make out Seyithan there in the shadows behind the rock; he was kneeling next to the head of the third person, who I assumed was his brother, weeping. I could tell he was crying from the way his body was shaking. 'It seems our stone-hearted warrior has softened up,' I thought. I gently approached him. Within a few steps he became aware of my presence and leapt to his feet, pointing his pistol straight at me. That's when I realized that he wasn't Seyithan. I pointed my rifle back at him. I might have considered myself at an advantage because I was armed with a rifle, but I didn't have much confidence in my superiority in this respect as I'd heard that Bedirhan was every bit as good a shooter as his brother. Like me, my enemy also hesitated, looking me in the face, unsure of what to do next. I tried to draw a few steps closer.

"'Stay where you are,' he said. Not only did he resemble Seyithan with his posture and curly hair, but his voice was a lot like his brother's, too.

"'You're already done for,' I said. 'You're surrounded.'

"'I highly doubt that,' he said in a weary voice. 'Seyithan would've wanted to kill me himself. He wouldn't have brought others with him.'

"He was completely right, and I was rather taken aback by that.

"'So you think you know your brother that well, do you?'

"'I don't think so; I know that I know him very well,' he said in a tearful voice. 'Not only are we alike physically, but our feelings, our actions are a lot alike, too.'

"'Tell me if I'm wrong, but it sure looks like you're grieving for him,' I remarked in a derisive tone.

"'I am,' he said.

"'Why did you kill him then?' I asked.

"'It was dark, I didn't recognize him,' he explained.

"'So you wouldn't have killed him if you'd recognized him?'

"'No, I wouldn't,' he said sharply.

"'But he was going to kill you,' I said, just to rub it in, and distract him. 'He lived for the day he would kill you.'

"'I know,' he said. 'He had to.'

"'He didn't have to; he was a man of strong will, so strong that he'd go so far as to take the life of his own brother out of love for his country, his people.'

"'Do you truly believe that?' he asked, his voiced tinged with sarcasm.

"'Of course I believe it. I've been with him in the mountains for months. He's told me everything,' I said.

"'I'm sure he didn't tell you everything,' he said.

"'What do you mean?' I asked curiously.

"'Seyithan had no choice but to murder me because otherwise our family would become outcasts. Maybe they'd even be killed by the tribe. We have seven other siblings. Seyithan had to kill me to protect our mother, our father, and our brothers and sisters.'

"'You're lying!' I screamed, surprising even myself at the extent of my anger. 'He vowed to kill you so that his country would not be divided, so that his people would remain strong.'

"'I'm the person you're talking about. I'm the one who rejected his family and rebelled against his tribe so that his own people might be free. And the price that his family might live, Seyithan...'

"Out of the corner of my eyes I looked at Seyithan lying there on the ground, two dark stains on the breast of his parka, burbling like tiny springs.

"'He wasn't my enemy,' Bedirhan continued. 'He was my brother. If only he'd shot me instead.'

"'You're lying,' I repeated.

"'I'm not lying,' he responded, cool-headed and confident. 'I'm trapped. If they don't kill me today, they're sure to kill me tomorrow. It doesn't matter to me who does, my brother or someone else, it's all the same to me. But if Seyithan had killed me, then my family, my siblings would be saved. And Seyithan would still be alive, too.'

"I recalled Seyithan's odd behavior, and the words coming out of this terrorist's mouth began to make sense to me. I looked at Bedirhan's face. There was sincerity in his eyes, just like there had been in Seyithan's eyes the day we made our pact. A strange idea occurred to me. For a second, just one second, I thought about disguising him as Seyithan; nobody would be the wiser. Bedirhan seemed to have read my mind.

"'If only I had another chance...' he mumbled hopefully.

"'That just now occur to you, did it?' I said, interrupting him.

"'Some things you gotta experience yourself to understand.'

"A voice inside told me that I couldn't trust him, that he might go and murder the tribal chief the moment I set him free. And then I would be the one to bear the heavy burden of responsibility for what had happened.

"'If I die, too, my family will have lost two sons at once...' he murmured. 'We have to put a stop to this bloodshed.'

"'Stop it!' I screamed in desperation. 'I don't trust you.'

"'You should,' he said in a voice of surrender. 'We should trust one another. I trust you. Here, take my pistol if you want.'

"'No,' I said. 'No, I can't let you go.'

"'He silently looked me in the face, with the hopelessness of someone awaiting his imminent death. I was so confused. If I let him go, nobody would understand that he was Bedirhan, nobody but his mother perhaps. And he wouldn't tell anyone... And at least one person, but not just one person, an entire family would... I realized that I had begun to lower the barrel of my rifle. I must have lost my head. Why did I want to let him go? Why was my shell so soft all of a sudden, after so many long months of bloody conflict? I don't know, but for some reason, I just couldn't help myself... If I let him go, then maybe his siblings, his children wouldn't look upon soldiers with such enmity. I couldn't be sure, I just couldn't, but... At that moment, the sound of gunfire reverberated in the shelter; I held tightly onto the rifle trigger and instantly threw myself to the ground. Bedirhan's body lay beneath my bullets, shaking like a leaf in a storm.

"Then I heard a voice say, 'I shot him, I shot him.' I turned my head and saw Seyithan, who with his last ounce of strength had managed to fire his gun one last time from where he lay. 'I shot him sir. Don't forget, it was me who shot him,' he said, and then his head collapsed back to the ground. I walked over to him. His eyes were rolled back in his head. I felt for his pulse; it was still. This time he really was dead. I left him and turned to his brother. He was looking at me with such a peaceful expression, as if he had just sat down against the wall to take a breather. His chest was ripped to shreds. Each time he opened his mouth blood streamed out of it, but he nevertheless persisted in trying to tell me something. I put my ear next to his mouth.

"'Tell them that Seyithan killed me,' he said. 'Do it, tell them that Seyithan killed me.'

"I said nothing. As his body began to convulse, I got up and made my way to the shelter entrance.

It was quite bright outside by then, and as I turned on my walkie-talkie, a nasty rain started to fall. After reporting to Sargeant Reshit to tell him my whereabouts, I went in the shelter and took Seyithan's tobacco from out of his pocket. I was lucky, the blood hadn't reached the tobacco case. I lit a cigarette and began smoking. And that's how I became addicted the second time around."

Esra was impressed by the story, but tried not to show it. Still she couldn't help but ask, "So were you the one who turned Bedirhan and Seyithan's bodies over to their family?"

"Yes. They received Seyithan's body with the utmost respect, as if it were that of a holy person. But they didn't even want Bedirhan's body. Seyithan was buried with military honors, with a flag wrapped around his coffin. Bedirhan was buried in a mountain, no hodja, no ceremony, nothing."

"How sad."

"Yes, it is," said the Captain with a deep sigh. "Unfortunately, there are thousands of cases just like it. But only those directly affected by it have any idea what it's like. There are lots of people completely unaware of the war that's being waged here. Only those who've lost their sons, husbands, or brothers, and those still fighting, are aware of all that's happening. Those that walk about the mountains, the plains, along the streams, each cavity an ambush waiting to happen, impervious to snow and rain and winter cold. Those who end up crippled or who lose their minds, and those who make it back in one piece, but also with a heavy heart. It's they who will never forget what they have lived through. And even if they try to forget, those experiences will seep out of from some part of their memory and remind them of that past. Those who watch what's happening from their TV sets, who read about it in newspaper columns, who spout on and on about the war from their comfortable vantage points, they don't, they can't possibly fathom this."

Esra was oblivious to the reproach in the Captain's voice.

"It's odd," she said. "I noticed that when you told me that story, you didn't differentiate between Seyithan and Bedirhan. Yet one was on your side, and the other was the enemy."

"Give me another cigarette," said the Captain. After lighting the cigarette and taking two deep drags, he tried to explain.

"You're right. I didn't hate Bedirhan. And I didn't hate Seyithan either. I just felt sorry for the both of them."

"Seems like you might have had some respect for the two of them too, huh?"

"Yes, the respect that a hunter has for his prey."

"Hunter?"

"Don't misunderstand me, I don't mean to say that it's a one-sided deal. Sometimes, maybe even most of the time, it's we who are the prey. No matter how cruel, awful, and unbearable the deeds that we do, they're the people that we're up against. And we're the ones that they're up against. And both sides are putting their lives on the line. Sometimes I'd talk with their leader on the walkie-talkies."

"You mean to call them to surrender or something?"

"No, no, we'd chat. Without cussing or insulting or threatening one another. We'd just chit chat, talk about football matches, stuff like that. It may sound like nonsense to you, but I could tell from the sound of the man's voice that he felt a kind of closeness to me, and I think I felt an affinity for him, too. At such moments, that terrorist that I was out on the prowl for, and who was out on the prowl for me, he'd seem much closer to me than anyone else far away from the war."

"I see," murmured Esra.

All of a sudden the Captain turned to face Esra. He looked at her as he would a stranger, as if she were someone completely alien to him. Esra, unable to decipher the meaning in the Captain's eyes there in the darkness, smiled innocently. The Captain didn't even notice that she was smiling. He wanted to ask Esra, "Do you really truly understand?" The question reached the tip of his tongue, but then he changed his mind. Inside, deep inside he felt that familiar chill. In a while, his hands would start to shake. He tried to hide his hands, afraid that Esra might see. It was time he got back to his apartment.

"Shall we head back now?" he asked, barely able to control his voice. "It's gotten late."

Esra felt that as the Captain was telling her about all that had happened, in is own mind he relived each moment, and felt once again the same pain, the same fear, the same anxiety, the same regret. A warm feeling, a combination of compassion, pity, and love for the Captain welled up inside of her. If she could have, she would have taken this soldier, sitting their in his uniform, gun at his waist, and held him to her breast as if he were a young boy woken up from a bad dream, and she would have comforted him by telling him that it was all over now, that it was all in the past now. But instead, she brought herself to do nothing but agree. "Yes, let's head back now." Because the Captain did not want to make her partner to his worries, his fears, his anxiety.

TABLET EIGHT

At the time that Pisiris first ascended the throne, I was occupied with the initial concerns of youth, trying to deal wih the unrelenting tension of my awakening body. Although my father had tried to isolate me from any other topics, taking my reins firmly into his hands, women became my sole interest, and became I like a young stallion drawn to the scent of mares. I had seen with my very own eyes the great passion that my grandfather Mitannuwa felt for Mashtigga. May the gods forgive me, but I must confess that I was deeply affected by the sight of beautiful Mashtigga's youthful body, her contours further accentuated by her expensive clothes. Although completely aware that my actions were a sin that would not go unpunished, and terribly disrespectful, when I lay alone in bed, I could not help but think of Mashtigga.

One night, I dreamed that I myself was Mitannuwa. It was an odd dream. My body was still my body, but I had become Mitannuwa. I was in the cool bedroom on the lower floor of his two-story home. I was mumbling an Aramaic song, lying on my back in the spacious bed where my grandfather took his mid-day naps. At that moment, I noticed that someone was watching me. I turned my head to find Mashtigga's kohl-blackened eyes bearing right into me. My heart began to beat madly, but I still managed to smile at the beautiful woman. Mashtigga did not smile back though; she slid next to me, like gently flowing water, like a light wind. She sat up in the bed and began running her hands over my body. The heat of her hands penetrated my body, setting the blood beneath my skin on fire. I tried to sit up to kiss her, but she stopped, pushing my body back onto the bed. She was so sure of herself, it was as if she were my mother, as if, no offense to the great goddess Kupaba, as if she were my creator. The surprising thing was that I derived so much pleasure from this situation. She had me spellbound with her eyes, her touch. In a state of ecstasy, from the corner of my eye I watched what she was doing to me. She carefully removed my clothing. I was too ashamed to look at my own body, but the pressure between my legs was so great, I knew that my organ was as hard and taut as the spears of the palace guards. At one point I saw Mashtigga's eyes look at me there, and I saw the desire burning hungrily, voraciously, in her cheeks. I tried to sit up to caress her, but with a commanding touch she pinned me back onto the bed. Then she pulled her gown up to her waist and sat down on me, as if mounting a horse. At that moment I noticed that there was liquid running down my legs. When I opened my eyes in bewilderment, I was relieved to find that it had all been a dream. But the wetness between my legs was still there. I sat up quickly and looked down to find that, yes, I was indeed wet there. I felt so ashamed. I immediately got up and washed myself. The next day I went to the temple and begged the gods to forgive me for this awful dream. After that day, I took care never to look at Mashtigga or be alone with her unless absolutely necessary. But I could not help but blush whenever I saw her. And the young woman realized this. Several times I saw her looking at me thoughtfully with her kohl-blackened eyes. This both excited and frightened me. It excited me, because a beautiful woman was looking at me with interest; and it frightened me, because that woman was my grandfather's wife.

After Mashtigga ran away, I began to take an even greater interest in women and girls. I couldn't help but stare at them. One day, when I was swimming in the Euphrates with Pirva, my blood brother who was the son of our neighbor and three years older than myself, and with whom I often went hunting, he asked me, "Does your organ get hard like mine does?"

I tried to change the subject, but my friend persisted. He told me that it was normal and that we had to find women for ourselves now. I asked him how, and he told me that he paid one of his family's own slaves a quarter shekel for her services. He had been with the woman several times himself. I refused. Priva tried to convince me, telling me how young and beautiful the woman was, but I could not possibly bring myself to make love with a woman who slept with anyone for money, and who was, moreover, a mere slave. "Then you'll just have to wait for the New Year's Celebrations," Pirva said. "The New Year's Celebrations? What do you mean?" I asked. And so Pirva proceeded to ridicule me, saying, "You really don't know anything, do you?" he said. "At the New Year's Celebrations the temple prostitutes make love voluntarily for the Goddess Kupaba. Everyone who has the right to enter the temple has the right to make love to them as well. But it is they who choose with whom they will make love. You're young, strong, a noble... Who would they choose if not you?"

I, too, knew that the temple prostitutes made love voluntarily on holidays for the goddess, but I had never thought that the day would come when I would benefit from this service. Perhaps because of my education – I had been conditioned to use what I learned for the benefit of the gods and their beloveds here on earth, the kings. According to what I had been taught, ceremonies were necessary only for the purpose of appeasing the gods, for placating their anger, and not for satisfying my body's hunger. But it was difficult to explain this to the desire awakening in my very skin. And so, consumed by the desperation of a man unable to hold sway over his own body, I began to wait for the New Year's Celebrations.

CHAPTER NINE

Esra looked on helplessly as events unfolded. Although she detested having to take on such a passive role, she failed not only in her attempt to influence the investigation into Hadji Settar's murder, but also to get the man to whom she was attracted to open up to her. Tonight, she had thought that the thick wall between them had crumbled when the Captain shared his experiences with her. But then suddenly, before she even had a chance to realize it was happening, he had re-erected the wall between them. The worst part, however, was that she just couldn't bring herself to get angry at him for this. By sharing those stories with her, he had stripped her of the final weapon of defense she had had left at her disposal: her anger. A person who had lived through such harsh experiences was a person who needed to be helped, not made into the object of someone's anger. But the man wouldn't allow it. Esra had wanted to get to know the Captain, to become closer to him, but even the very first bits of information that she learned about him had resulted in nothing but deadlock. Maybe he didn't trust Esra well enough. He saw her as one of those people who pontificate about war from an all too comfortable distance. And he wasn't exactly wrong in that respect. But did one really have to take up arms and head off to the mountains to do battle in order to even broach the topic of war? Didn't she, too, feel the negative effects of this damnable war, which had cost thousands of lives and settled over this country like a dark shadow? "Of course I do," she murmured to herself decisively. "I have just as much right to talk about this issue as he does." However, this was something she could explain to a normal person, not to a man whose mood changes by the hour, and who flees from a conversation just when it has reached its most intense moment.

She was sitting beneath the arbor as these thoughts ran through her mind. Halaf, who had taken the Captain back to his apartment, had left the kitchen light on. Any other time Esra would've turned it off immediately, but now she didn't feel like budging one bit. None of her friends were anywhere in sight. Timothy was working on the tablets, Kemal was in Elif's room discussing their relationship, Murat and Teoman were long asleep, and Bernd's light was on in his room where he was diligently at work, as he was every night, on his master's thesis entitled "The Devastating Effects of the Development of Civilization in Mesopotamia." "I should be working with Tim," thought Esra. Perhaps grappling with her own work would keep her mind from getting caught up in such complex, difficult topics. Her father, Salim Bey, a doctor of philosophy, always spoke of "right-thinking." But was there really such a method of thought? Right-thinking, that's something that can only be imparted to an advanced computer. In daily life, with each resolved issue immediately being replaced by another, what's "right" can be arrived at only by passing though a process involving a series of thoughts and conduct, and this process has to repeated for each question or problem; what's more, success is never one hundred percent guaranteed. Esra's father Salim Bey knew this to be true, but he nevertheless continued to emphasize time and again the importance of right-thinking. Another oft-repeated phrase of his was, "Don't put yourself in the center of the action, my girl. You can't solve all problems, and you can't be everywhere at once." Her father was never one for empty talk, but was there really any indication that he knew what he was talking about? If he'd been able to think right himself, then he wouldn't have left Esra's mother to live with a woman his daughter's age. "What does that have to do with right-thinking?" she mumbled to herself. "The poor guy was just in love."

As her father, too, had admitted, love had nothing to do with right-thinking or logic. Or rather, love has a logic all its own, and this logic has nothing to do with right-thinking. This was a logic ruled by passions; an entirely different, complex process constantly tripping up, dragging down, and misdirecting the mind. Her father loved her mother, and he couldn't stand being away from Esra, but everything changed when Nilgün entered his life. "Arrgh, all of this is ancient history now," a distressed Esra grumbled to herself. She'd do better to look after her own affairs instead of chastising her father. After all, she'd gotten separated, too. What's more, she'd separated without any consideration for the concessions that Orhan had made, or the effort he'd put forth towards their reconciliation. "But it wasn't because of love that I ended my marriage," she thought. They just couldn't keep it up any longer, and it had gotten to the point that everything Orhan did only annoyed her, because his love wasn't sincere. And isn't such insincerity itself actually a kind of lovelessness? And then there was the whole Captain affair...

As her thoughts drifted towards uncertainty, like an oleaster branch caught up in the flow of the Euphrates, she heard the sound of Halaf's arrival. He emerged from the van, a surprised smile spread across his lips at the sight of the excavation director still sitting there beneath the arbor.

"Something wrong, Esra Hanım? Any other time you'd have withdrawn to your room by now."

Esra looked gratefully at him, this carefree, easy-going young blood of Barak, who managed to take care of pretty much all the team's legwork.

"No, no. I just thought I'd sit out here in the cool weather a bit."

"Good idea. Shall I brew you some tea?"

"No thanks."

"Then why don't I fix you a coffee."

"Alright then," said Esra. She really wasn't in the mood for coffee, but she didn't want to hurt Halaf's feelings. "But only if you have some with me."

Esra watched Halaf as he walked towards the kitchen. Both the head of the Archaeology Museum in Antep as well as Kemal's friend Rüstem Bey had recommended him. He had done the cooking, driving, and other jobs at an excavation in Adıyaman conducted by archaeologists from Ankara. And the team from Ankara was extremely pleased with his performance. He was a cook by profession, and had worked at İmam Çaghdash, one of Antep's most famous restaurants, before leaving to do his military service. Once he had completed the service, he went to Istanbul and carried on with his profession at a restaurant in Samatya called Bedir. In addition to his knowledge of the rich Antep cuisine, consisting of a synthesis of Turkish, Kurdish, and Arabic dishes, he had also had the opportunity to learn the foods of nearly all the different regions of Turkey, from Bolu to Izmir. But when one day his colleague, chef Kara Nuri of Urfa, tried to sully his honor, he drew the knife he'd been using to separate meat from bones and instantly stabbed the old bugger in three places. He got out of prison after serving a year long sentence, but he didn't want to remain in Istanbul any longer and so returned to Antep. Unfortunately, he didn't find what he was looking for in his hometown either, as the chefs he used to work with learned that he'd been in prison and therefore didn't want to hire him, thinking that he'd become nothing but bad news. So then he ended up working a little here and there, and then began going to the excavations in the summer, thanks to Rüstem Bey. They paid well, and more importantly, the people he worked with were understanding, and treated him like a person.

Esra, too, was pleased with Halaf. He was respectful, clean, and honest. Most importantly, he was hard-working. Although his eagerness sometimes reached the point of meddling, he never hesitated to carry out any tasks at the camp, and he always ran to help those in need.

Ten minutes later Halaf was pouring the bubbly Turkish coffee from the *cezve* into the tiny coffee cups. By the time he'd taken in the empty *cezve* and brought back two glasses of water, Esra had already taken her first sip of the brew.

"Health to your hands, it's delicious."

"Bon appetit," replied the young cook. "It doesn't match the coffee made in our rooms, but it'll do."

"What do you mean, 'the coffee made in our rooms'?"

"In our villages in Barak there are these rooms. Those who can afford it hold room soirees. The rooms are places where men gather for conversation and entertainment. Guests arriving in the village are also entertained in these rooms. New meals are cooked every day, and everyone chats about what's going on in the village."

"A kind of assembly," murmured Esra. "Like the agoras of Roman cities."

Halaf didn't get the reference, so he just gave her an odd look and went on with his story.

"Adolescent boys are taken there, too, and taught customs and proper behavior. I was educated in such rooms myself. The coffee brewed in the rooms is much stronger than this here; it has a very different taste. One drink and you're done for. It's the equivalent of five of of these."

"Interesting. We should go to your village sometime."

"Whenever you'd like, Esra Hanım," said Halaf eagerly. "It would be my pleasure. But the things I've told you about were true ten years ago. There are still rooms today, but they're not like they used to be. Houses have televisions now. Instead of going to the rooms, villagers just sit around and watch TV."

"So there goes our coffee," said Esra regretfully, and half jokingly.

"Oh no, there are still folks who make the bitter coffee. We'll go to Kurdish Reshit, he's a master when it comes to making that coffee."

"Really Halaf, this morning you told the Captain that you were Kurdish, but as far as I know, the folks in Barak are of Turcoman origin."

"You're right, Esra Hanım. The people in the Barak region are Turcoman. But there's been a lot of mingling. There's been a lot of exchange of daughters in marriage, so they've all become relatives. Turcomen mixed with Arabs, Arabs with Kurds. But the traditions of Barak haven't disappeared."

"Like the Hittites thousands of years ago," thought Esra. Didn't they mix with the Aramaeans, and the Luwians? So it seems some things never change in these parts.

"My great-great grandfather Shaban Agha was from Urfa," continued Halaf. "Shaban Agha was Kurdish. He murdered two people in Siverek and fled to these parts. That was in Ottoman times. Shaban Agha was a swashbuckler, a real tough guy. First he was a soldier, and then an officer for the Ottomans. And anyway he couldn't have lived here if he hadn't been an officer. Everyone belongs to a tribe, and they don't readily accept strangers. But with him being an Ottoman officer, that changed everything. The tribes were intimidated by him, and so they respected him. Shaban Agha married four women of Barak. And he had children by all four. He bought land from the Ottomans, and continued his line. That's how Alagoz Village came to be."

Recalling the Captain's doubts, Esra asked: "Was there anybody in your village who joined the separatists?"

"There was one," said Halaf in an annoyed tone of voice. It was obvious that he wasn't at all fond of this topic. "Ayyush's son Cemil. He went to the mountains two years ago, and his body came back this winter. But two soldiers from our village were also shot and killed. Crazy Done's son Ferit and Haco's son Mahmut." He became lost in thought, but then raised his head to ask, "Are you and the Captain thinking that the separatists are behind this?"

"I don't think so. But I also understand where the Captain's coming from. He's been through a lot."

"He's been through a lot, but he's not thinking right. There's no separatists or anything here. And even if there was, they'd take out the police station and shoot the village guards. They wouldn't go near a holy man like Hadji Settar."

"How do you know?"

"The Gencecis' youngest boy Mahmut is in the mountains. They say he's a commander. This Mahmut was as close as could be to Hadji Settar when he was little. He was really caught up in his religion, until he ended up in Diyarbakir. That's where he changed. But still he retained full respect for Hadji Settar. Before he left for the mountains, whenever he'd come to town, the first thing he'd do was stop by the old hadji's house, kiss his hand, and ask for his blessing. What I mean to say is that there's no reason at all for the separatists to target Hadji Settar."

"I just don't know," said Esra, sighing in indecision. "Okay, so what about Fayat?"

"You mean that Fayat that I beat up?"

"Maybe not him, but those backing him, Abid Hodja for example."

"If Abid Hodja were any kind of real man, he'd first look to restore his own honor," said Halaf, his voice heavy with disdain. "His older sister Belkis living in the village of Göven has been Reshat Agha's mistress for how many years now. Reshat Agha is at her house whenever he gets the urge."

"Doesn't this Belkis have a husband?"

"He's in Germany. He never calls or asks how she's doing. So, the woman's been abandoned you see. If Abid Hodja were any kind of man, he wouldn't have let his sister take up with that Reshat Agha..."

Esra had seen Reshat Agha just once. He was in his thirties, dark skinned, short, with a square shaped face and a thin moustache. He always carefully looked others up and down, as if measuring them up to tell if they were friend or foe.

"No, Esra Hanım," Halaf continued, "those guys couldn't pull off a job like that either. They're nothing but greedy men of the cloth. Where there's a funeral with a feast, or a *mevlud* with sherbet, they're there. Hardly the types capable of murder."

"But Fayat didn't hesitate to come all the way out here to threaten us."

"Cripple Memili put him up to it. Otherwise, Fayat's not the type of guy to come out here by himself."

"Well then who killed Hadji Settar?"

"Shehmuz, who else?"

"You heard what the Captain had to say."

"I did. And I think it happened just like Kemal Bey said. First they stashed the antiquities in the vineyard house, then Shehmuz sent Bekir on his way and headed to the mosque."

"Isn't two crimes in one night rather risky?"

"Shehmuz doesn't give two cents about the risk. When he saw that nothing happened when he stole the antiquities, he just thought, 'Why don't I go and knock off Hadji Settar this evening while I'm at it.'"

"So who do you think the folks in town will hold responsible?" Esra asked.

"If we'd gone into town during the day today, we'd know."

"I've heard there are some who say that this has only happened because we came and started digging at the Black Tomb."

"That's Cripple Memili and Fayat's pack. Nobody else would say something like that. But our folks wouldn't believe it anyway, because everyone knows what kind of cloth Cripple Memeli and the whole Koran course circle are cut from."

"Don't you think they'll pressure us to stop the excavation?"

"Who'd do that? They don't have the guts. Besides, you're not digging up the Black Tomb. You're digging some twenty meters beyond it. And anways, nobody'd have anything to say even if you did excavate the Black Tomb."

"Are you sure about that?" Esra asked with a stunned expression on her face.

"Of course I'm sure. All that stuff about respecting and fearing the Black Tomb is a thing of the past. Now everybody's just worried about the quickest way to make a pretty penny. Here the land is plentiful, there's hardly anyone who doesn't own a field. You know, that's the reason why we had so much trouble finding workers to help out at the excavation. Nobody wants to get into trouble getting mixed up with the state."

"Are we the state?"

"You're the state. Aren't you in cohorts with Captain Eshref? Don't you worry one bit, nobody's going to touch the excavation."

"That's not what the Captain says though..."

"The Captain is an odd man, Esra Hanım. Just between you and me, he's already been nicknamed Crazy Eshref by the soldiers."

"Now that's hardly fair to the Captain," Esra said, suddenly growing harsh. "Eshref Bey has been a great help to us."

Realizing his blunder, Halaf rereated back a step back.

"Don't get upset now, Esra Hanım, it's just second hand information; I'm just telling you what I heard from the soldiers."

"Well looky here, I wasn't aware that it was coffee hour!" said a voice, interrupting their conversation.

Timothy stood just a few steps behind them, shaking his head in mock anger.

"I thought you'd gone to bed," said Halaf standing up. "Please, let me make you one, too, straight away."

The American, a head taller than Halaf, walked up and gave the cook a friendly pat on the back.

"Just a joke. Turkish coffee's fine after dinner. But if you drink it before bedtime, you won't be able to get any sleep."

Halaf turned and gave Esra a shy look.

"If you've nothing else to say to me, then I'll go and wash the dishes."

The dejected expression upon Halaf's face made Esra realize that she'd been a little harsh.

"Thank you, Halaf dear. The coffee was delicious. And thank you for the conversation as well."

Halaf's white teeth sparkled happily in his sun burnt face. He gathered up the empty coffee cups and headed for the kitchen.

The American had taken a seat across from Esra. He'd had his straight, brown hair cut very short, and with his large, velvety black eyes below his eyebrows, shapely like those of a woman, he looked about with a carefree, cynical, yet altogether agreeable expression on his face. His short copper colored beard, with glints of grey here and there, extended from his temple to his chin, lending his sharp facial features a more mature air, and complementing the cynical look in his eyes. "A handsome man," thought Esra. It wasn't difficult to understand Elif, but what was strange was Esra's attraction to Captain Eshref rather than Timothy. Esra always believed that love was born out of need. She had sensed at their very first encounter that Timothy didn't need anyone. But was that really true? Doesn't a person need others, no matter how strong he or she is? Perhaps, but Timothy sure didn't seem to. You could have a good time with Timothy, but not a serious relationship of any depth. But Captain Eshref... Oh yes, Captain Eshref... She didn't know why she was so fond of him. What she did know was that this weary souled soldier who'd suffered the trials and tribulations of war had a distinctive effect upon her, that he excited her. Yet she had no time for romance. She'd been presented with a fabulous opportunity in her career, having uncovered an important find on the first excavation under her supervision. This should be more important to her than everything else. And it was important, but it didn't stop her from finding herself interested in Captain Eshref. "Don't put yourself in the center of things," the sound of her father's voice echoed in her ears. "You can't solve everything, and you can't be everywhere at once." Perhaps her problem was that, despite her apparently decisive behavior and strong appearance, she suffered from a profound lack of self-confidence. That's why she sought to prove herself, and to make everyone accept just how tough, and just how good, she was.

"It seems you've got something on your mind, huh?" said Timothy, his hyper curious voice breaking Esra's concentration. "It's not like you to sit out here at this hour of night."

"No, it's nothing. I'm just fond of the cool night air."

"Sometimes it can be a little too much though. Take care that you don't catch cold."

"You seem like a real local. You know the region even better than I do, even though you're American."

"I had a professor at Yale, Mr. Weiss. He used to say that archaeologists don't have a homeland. 'Your home is wherever you happen to be working,' was his motto. I was in Iraq ten years ago, and that was my homeland then. Now I'm here, and so this is my homeland."

"Still, there must be times when you miss your own country, things back home."

"Of course there are. Some nights I think about New Haven, and how I miss those summer nights I used to spend there with my family. Where I come from, summer nights are extremely hot. There's this humid heat that's just suffocating. Sometimes the cool breeze from the ocean would blow by Long Island Sound to our two-story house and garden and make the wind chimes my father hung out on the balcony play out a sweet jingle. On some nights, even when I'm here, I still hear that sweet jingle."

"Your family's in New Haven?"

Timothy shook his head sadly.

"Unfortunately, both my mother and my father have passed away."

"I'm sorry."

"I was sorry, too," said the now pensive Timothy. "But once I thought about it, I understood that it was wrong of me to feel sorry. They lived long and happy lives. My father could have died in the Second World War, my mother could have fallen victim to any one of the rising number of attacks by street punks. Thank goodness none of that happened. My mother and father lived together in a loving relationship until my mother was seventy-one, and my father was seventy-five. And they died together, too, in a plane wreck. The only wish they never saw come true was that they be able to hold their grandchildren."

"You don't have any kids either, do you?"

"Nope, never happened," said Timothy. After a moment's silence, he changed the subject, adopting now a more serious tone:

"I looked over the tablets that Captain Eshref brought in."

"Are they damaged?"

"Not seriously. They're cracked and chipped here and there, but the writing is legible. At least, we can figure out what's written on them."

"I'm glad to hear that. I was scared silly that Patasana's story was going to remain only half complete."

"I doubt it'll remain incomplete. The rest is sure to come."

"There's something else that has me worried, too—that the tablets aren't safe enough in the school basement."

"Are you afraid they'll be stolen?"

"There's that, too, but actually I'm more afraid of the conditions damaging them."

"There's nothing to be afraid of. The door's solid and locked. Besides, I doubt that after holding up like they have for two thousand seven hundred years the tablets are going to go bad in just a few weeks. But then this basement is hardly our Beinecke Library, though it is plenty dark and cool enough."

"The Beinecke Library?"

"What? You mean you've never heard of it?" Timothy asked, his voice at least as shocked as Esra's had been.

"No, I haven't," she said. Her voice came out harsh, as if questioning what was so imperative about this bit of knowledge.

Timothy realized that the young woman felt insulted by his response.

"Excuse me. I didn't mean to be a know-it-all. Beinecke Library is rather famous, so I figured you'd probably heard of it."

"And so just where is this famous Beinecke Library?"

"At my university, Yale. It houses many of the world's most valuable books and handwritten documents. It's also a wonder of modern architecture, and really stands out amongst the gothic style buildings at the school. In the windows, they use very thin marble instead of glass to keep the books and documents from being damaged by the sunlight. Plus there are special panels inside that maintain the humidity and temperature level."

"Interesting," murmured Esra, impressed by the description.

"I'll take you on a tour if you come to the U.S. some day."

"I'd love to... Maybe the Patasana tablets will make a real splash and Yale will invite us themselves, so you won't have to."

"Why not?" said Timothy in a dreamy voice, as if imagining the fantasy of it then and there. "The tablets are certain to make a splash. When will the definite date for the press conference be set?"

"I don't know. That's up to the German Archaeological Institute. I think we should know within a day or two. But first we need to translate the tablets."

Timothy hung his head sheepishly.

"You're right, I've neglected the translation work a bit. But I promise to sit myself down and decipher tablets all day tomorrow."

TABLET NINE

O stubborn reader of these tablets. I shall tell you of the greatest shame, the most exhilarating joy of my early youth. I shall tell you of the ruthless love trap into which a young man, falling prey to his own body, fell, and how a fatal passion first began to bloom.

With no sign of better days to come, and everyone believing that the dark, winter nights would never cease, a wind heavy with the new year's rains suddenly began knocking upon our city gate. Once its step made of sunshine fell upon our doorstep, the ash gray clouds deserted the sky, the sun made its generous debut, the Euphrates grew lush and abundant, the crops sprung forth, and the trees bloomed rich with flowers. By the pattering rains our city was rinsed, cleansed, prepared for life anew, like a princess waiting to be crowned.

The New Year's Celebration did not take place in the great temple like the other celebrations, but in the small, one story temple within the bountiful fields outside the King's Gate.

When the New Year's Celebration finally came around, I was restless and anxious. On that night, I didn't get a wink of sleep. The next day, I was to have relations of a sort I had never experienced, for I was to have intercourse with a woman. I tossed around in my bed until, at last, it was morning. My father, upon seeing that I had awoken early and roused everyone else from their sleep, thought my haste due to the excitement I felt because of the New Year. We bathed and put on our finest clothes. This year I would once again stand by my father's side, as I had these past three years.

Upon reaching the palace, we saw that everyone was consumed with preparations for the approaching celebration. The king and queen had risen long beforehand. The members of the Panku Council of Nobles, my father and I among them, together with the palace attendants, waited as the king and queen donned their magnificent apparel in the rooms which had been specially laid out for the celebration. But our highnesses' primping went on and on.

Finally, our king and queen emerged from their rooms, having dressed in the gowns that befit them so perfectly. With two attendants and a guard in front of them, they walked out of the palace, and we followed them. When they emerged at the gate, the red-gowned musicians took their places at their sides. Thus did the parade begin. As we set off, the musicians began to play their instruments, and the divine chanters began to pray and dance. A confident smile on his face, our King Pisiris watched the dancers as he marched along slowly. We members of the nobility followed behind him. Behind us came the palace attendants carrying cattle, sheep, wine, and food to be sacrificed to the gods. And at the very end came the people. Our colorful, merry parade continued through the King's Gate to the small temple amongst the bountiful fields.

At the temple, the king and queen were met by the Chief Priest Valvaziti. After the welcoming prayers, the chief priest entered the temple together with the other priests and the musicians. Meanwhile, those who remained in the garden paraded before the king and queen once more, chanting. Just then, two court attendants approached our king and queen with ewers in hand. After washing their hands with the water that was brought to them, our king and queen entered the temple. A few of the nobles, including my father and myself, followed them inside. As soon as we set foot in the temple, Chief Priest Valvaziti signaled for the priests to resume chanting. The king and queen curtsied and bowed in respect before the gods. And after them we likewise curtsied and bowed before the gods. As the king and queen took their places on the throne, we stood on their left side, our heads hung low.

Once the chanting concluded, the palace's head cook entered with a finely cooked offering of meat. He placed the meat in the holy areas of the temple: on its hearth, at the window, and at the gate lock. Then he took up the lion-shaped holy vessel and presented the wine inside to the king. Our king touched the wine with his hand, and then the head cook offered the wine to the gods.

A new phase of the ceremony was now under way. The king and queen stood up from the throne and bowed in respect before the gods. The musicians and chanters were escorted out of the temple. The symbol of the king, a staff curved at one end, and a golden spear were brought into the temple. The king took the staff, and then he and the queen sat upon the throne again. The hands of the now seated king and queen were washed once again. Meanwhile, the holy table was also brought into the temple. The table was adorned with food. A loaf of bread was passed from hand to hand until it reached the head of the line of palace attendants. The chief attendant divided the bread into half. The broken bread was passed from hand to hand and then sent outside.

Then the musicians began playing music, but they no longer sang or chanted. They only played melodies on their instruments. The food and drink was passed around. When our king and queen stood and toasted the gods, the holy meal commenced. Our holy table overflowed with an array of scrumptious food and drink—fruit gathered from the shores of the Euphrates, mutton, beef, game, fish, the finest wines, beers, white bread, and every edible item one could think of. Once everyone had eaten and drunk to his heart's content, the Chief Priest Valvaziti signaled for all present to stand.

King Pisiris came to the head of table, and raising his glass, said the following:

"At this celebration, we have eaten to our fill, and quenched our thirst for the Storm God. A thousand thanks be to them. May they never allow us to suffer the loss of their protective wings, may they grant us health and drive our enemies to defeat. With their help, may the country of Hatti be restored to its former greatness and glory. May we reign supreme at the four corners, may our sovereignty spread throughout the land, may our name be on the tongues of all who live along the shores of the Euphrates, and may our fame extend throughout the world..."

I paid close attention and saw how Pisiris' eyes burned with desire, how his voice quivered with ambition. My father noticed the same, and with a deep sigh before the insatiable ambition of this young king, he bowed his head hopelessly.

As soon as the king had finished his speech, the chants resumed. Once the songs had ended, the mass of people bowed to pay their respects to the king and queen before dispersing. The king and queen were the last to depart from the temple. Unfortunately, both my father and I were to return with them. It was a long-held tradition for the palace officials, every one of them, to follow the king and queen until the very end of the ceremony.

CHAPTER TEN

That morning, the members of the excavation team, every one of them, awoke before sunrise. The distant sound of the call to prayer emerging from the village down the way added a melancholic, mystic feel to the atmosphere. Halaf, having woken earlier than the rest, had already brewed the tea, boiled water for coffee for the foreigners, and set the breakfast table. Bernd and Timothy were the first to arrive. Timothy, who would not be going to the excavation site, still had on his clothes from the day before, while Bernd had shaved and had his khaki colonial hat with him. Bernd, paying no heed to the taunts of his colleagues—"That's the same hat Hugo Winckler wore when he carried out the first Hittite excavation at Bogazkoy back in 1906"—never took his place in the field without donning this hat, which he believed to be very effective in shielding him from the heat. Esra was the next to arrive after Timothy and Bernd. The two foreigners smiled politely at the young woman. Before the three of them had even had a chance to strike up a conversation, Kemal, Murat, and Elif made their appearances as well. Teoman was no where to be seen.

"Hasn't Teoman woken up yet?" asked Esra.

Kemal couldn't have cared less; it seemed he hadn't had a good night with Elif.

It was Murat who answered her question. "He's in the toilet," he said. "He headed straight there without even washing his face."

A mocking smile spread across Timothy's lips. "I'm not at all surprised, considering how much he ate last night," he said.

Everyone at the table smiled, except for Kemal and Elif. This fact did not escape Esra's observation. "We've got our hands full with these two," she thought to herself.

"Eggs anyone?"

It was Halaf who asked the question, as he approached the table with a cheese plate in hand.

"What the heck do you mean eggs?" chided Kemal. "This place is going to be on fire in just an hour. Eggs'll give us all allergies. You want to make us sick do you?"

Halaf immediately went on the defensive. "But Mr. Bernd says that he simply won't have breakfast without eggs."

Bernd turned ever so slowly to direct a self-confident look at Kemal. "It's true," he said, "I need to eat eggs in the morning, otherwise I feel hungry. But not like this. Fried eggs with ham."

"Eggs and ham?" Kemal said with a grimace. He motioned towards the food on the table. "Two kinds of cheese, black olives, green olive salad, butter, honey, grape molasses, tomatoes, cucumbers, green peppers... You mean to tell me this isn't enough for you Bernd?"

"Every country has its own breakfast culture," replied Bernd. "And we don't eat olives or cheese of the type that you do."

"You don't eat cheese?" Murat exclaimed in a shocked voice.

"We do, but sliced swiss cheese. And with it, jam and croissants. I prefer eggs and ham though."

"But that's so unhealthy," said Kemal, continuing with his protestations.

"I think it's very healthy," responded Bernd emphatically. "There's a Russian proverb that says, 'Have breakfast alone, lunch with friends, and dinner with enemies.'"

Murat's eyes had glided over to land upon Timothy.

"Timothy my man," he said, as if the two of them were old buddies going way back. "Why aren't you picky about your breakfast? From what I hear, cornflakes are the only thing that satisfy the American appetite."

"You're misinformed. We also eat eggs and ham. But I eat whatever I can find these days."

"You'd have a hard time finding ham in the Iraqi desert," teased Murat.

"That's true. But as you see, it's impossible to find it in Turkey too."

"And it's a good thing," said a stern-faced Kemal. "Otherwise the majority of the crew would spend most of their time in the loo, like Teoman does."

"Anyway, since there isn't any eggs and ham, I guess that means there isn't any problem either," said Timothy, putting an end to the discussion.

This retort, combined with the grogginess everyone felt at this early morning hour, put a temporary end to the conversation—until Teoman got back from the bathroom.

"You've got a flat tire," he said. "It's dangerous around here, I wouldn't advise you to go riding your bike around here at night."

"But I didn't take a ride last night!" said Bernd, flabbergasted.

"Things like that happen," said Timothy. "Sometimes your tube loses air by itself."

"Forget about the bike and take a look at yourself, brother Teoman," said Murat kiddingly. "We thought you'd fallen into the toilet."

Teoman had had his fill of this young student's teasing, but he didn't give his emotions away. "You see, that just goes to prove, when a wolf grows old, he becomes the butt of dogs' jokes," was all he had to say.

His comment was met with a silent laugh. And when Murat refrained from pushing him on the point, the topic came to a prompt close.

Esra was lost in thought. Ever since the previous night, she'd been thinking about what Halaf had told her. Could the young cook be right? Had the prospering locals ceased to believe in prophesies and sophistries? Or was Halaf just trying to keep the crew around, afraid himself of losing his job if they should leave? They'd have to see how the local workers behaved at the excavation in order to understand if Halaf was right or not. However, Esra wasn't at all that sure that the workers would even show up today. If they thought the excavation was responsible for what had happened, they would never again have anything to do with this crew. While she generally took the jeep to the excavation, this time around she decided to take the van that picked up the workers. If she saw any signs of uncertainty amongst the workers, she would try to convince them that the excavation had nothing to do with the unfortunate events.

After the rather short breakfast, Teoman and Kemal gathered up the excavation equipment and everyone crowded into the jeep. Kemal was going to be driving the jeep, and Elif, who didn't want to be in the same vehicle as him, chose together with Esra to take the van that Murat would be driving. Kemal responded to this unusual behavior on the part of his girlfriend with obvious tension yet remained silent, revving up the jeep engine and hitting the road to the old Hittite city without a word. Those in the van waited for Halaf, who was preparing the meal they would eat at mid-morning, and would take off only once all of the food and cutlery had been loaded up.

The van made its way swiftly down the slowly dawning road. It would still be a while before sunrise, but the nip in the air had already begun to subside, and the heavy fog covering the Euphrates to disperse, as the darkness made its exit. They would pick the workers up from Stone Bridge, which lay above a dried out stream bed at the turn just a kilometer away. The workers waited there patiently every morning, beneath the large wild pear tree just beyond the bridge. They'd been able to gather together ten workers from two different villages, but only thanks to Hadji Settar. These were poor villagers, but still each of them had his own field, albeit small. But then four of them had let it be known from the get-go that they would quit their work at the excavation once the cotton picking season began. Esra had figured that their workload would be lightened by then, and anyway, they could bring day workers from town if necessary. But now with Hadji Settar's death, forget about finding men from the town, they were in danger of losing all of their workers as it were.

Sitting in the passenger's seat next to Murat, Esra had her eyes fixed on the road, and she inhaled deeply from her cigarette as she pondered whether or not they would find the workers waiting beneath the wild pear tree. And continued to worry, until they made their final turn and she saw the portly Maho, head of the workers, waiting.

"They've come," she murmured. "Halaf was right. They've come."

"Why? Weren't they going to come?" asked Elif, bewildered by Esra's response to the sight of the workers. A vacuous expression appeared in her sleepy eyes. Instead of answering her, Esra just motioned with her head towards the group of workers: "They're all here, all ten of them."

Maho was standing up with his eyes fixed on the road, waiting for them, while the other workers were squatting down, with only Şıhlı leaning back upon the bulky trunk of the wild pear tree. They were all smoking. The smoke emerging from the group glided up through the dark branches of the wild pear tree to disappear into its large bosom.

"They look like a flock of geese," said Murat. "And Maho's like their chief, a step ahead of the pack, scanning the area as he tries to figure out where they can get their next meal."

Elif laughed silently, but Esra didn't even smile.

"That's a poor analogy. Those aren't geese, they're people."

Murat didn't try to defend himself, but just made do with a silent laugh, as Elif had.

The workers started moving as soon as the spotted the van. Those who had been sitting stood up and made their way to the bridge. Once the van had parked along the side of the road, they took one last drag from their cigarettes and then tossed the butts into the dried out stream bed lined on either side with pink and yellow oleander. Two of the young men, one dark complected, the other with brown hair and fairer skin, looked at the women in the van, and did their best to conceal the burning hunger in their eyes. Except for the hint of curiosity upon seeing Elif and Esra in the van, a sight they weren't used to, the other workers looked at them like they always did, naturally and with respect. As soon as the van door opened, although Maho was at the front, they all started to cram in at once.

"Selamaleykum," said Maho as he tried to squeeze his bulky frame through the door.

"Aleykumselam Maho Usta," said Esra. She was used to exchanging greetings like this with them now. As Maho took a seat next to Esra, the other workers jostled each other, half jokingly, as they settled into the back of the van. As the van took off, Maho turned to the excavation director:

"Is something up, Esra Hanım, that you've come to pick us up?"

Esra tried to appear calm.

"Oh no, there's nothing the matter, Maho Usta. I'd been taking the jeep every day, and so I thought I'd take the van today for a change. What's up with you all? How are you?"

"How do you think," said Maho, his leathery sunburnt face puckering in a sorrowful expression. "We heard about Hadji Settar; we're all devastated by what happened."

Esra sighed deeply.

"Yes, we were very saddened by the news, too. He was such a good man."

"He was like a saint," said one of the workers. "Like Robin Hood."

"He was a very righteous man," interjected another. "No one ever heard of him telling another what to do."

"So who do you think is behind this?" asked Esra in an attempt to understand what the workers thought about the crime.

"Whoever did this isn't from around these parts," said Maho decisively. "Nobody from these lands could possibly kill Hadji Settar."

Esra, who felt that they blamed the crew themselves for what happened, was getting ready to ask what they meant by "a stranger did it," when SHırhlı spoke up. "The person who killed him is a cursed devil," he said. "No human being could possibly do such a thing."

"If I find the person who killed Hadji Emmi, I'll strangle him with my own hands," grumbled another of the young workers.

"The person who murders him will go to heaven," said another.

"That's what Abid Hodja said in his sermon yesterday, too. The killing of Hadji Settar's murderer is a holy duty."

"The gendarmes caught SHehmuz," said Esra, trying to sound out the workers' views on that aspect of the matter.

"That ass SHehmuz couldn't pull of a stunt like this," said Maho. "They've got the wrong man. Someone from outside is responsible."

"Who from outside could have done this?"

"Casim said that Syria's behind this."

"Who's Casim?"

"Smuggler Casim. He owns the glass-paned coffeehouse at the bazaar. He used to cross the border twice a day before they laid the mines. He gave up that line of work after they put all those mines there, but he still knows the other side of the border real well. There's nobody in Halep that he doesn't know. And he's gained the love and respect of folks on either side of the border."

"He's a renowned man, red-blooded, a real swashbuckler," murmured one of the awestruck young villagers.

"Robin Hood," said the worker who'd used those same words to describe Hadji Settar just a while before. "When he was a smuggler, for every five lira he made, he'd give three to the poor."

"He's still like that," said the puny worker scrunched up in the corner of the back seat. "He gives *iftar* dinner every day during Ramazan."

"Why is Casim suspicious of the Syrians?"

"Why do you think?" grumbled Maho. "Cause we cut off their water. Used to be ten times as much water flowing down there before the dam was built. Cutting off their water is as good as slitting their jugular."

"That's all good and well, but it's the state that built the dam. What does Hadji Settar have to do with it?" Esra grumbled back with a scowl.

"Syria don't differentiate between the state and the people. They just think, 'So you've done evil upon me, well I'll just push the finest, holiest man you've got from off the minaret, as a lesson to others.' I mean, it's kinda like they wanted to intimidate our government."

Though she could hardly glimpse any truth in these childish thoughts of theirs, she did manage to find some comfort in them, because it meant that no one was thinking the incident was due to any Black Tomb curse or anything of the sort. She had just decided not to broach the topic at all when Şıhlı spoke up to prove her wrong.

"At the sermon yesterday," he said uneasily, "Abid Hodja also said, 'This incident is also due in part to the digging at the Black Tomb.' He said, 'It is not right to disturb the graves of holy men.'"

Maho turned around and glared. At first Şıhlı just tried to avert his eyes, but then finally he gave in and hung his head. The van became dead silent. Not a soul spoke. After a while, as she listened to the sound of the motor and the din of the equipment rattling as they made their way along the dirt road, Esra understood that the workers had already discussed this matter amongst themselves. They must have decided to continue their work on the excavation, despite opposition from Şıhlı. She wondered: Were there any other workers who shared Şıhlı's thoughts? Even if there were, it was obvious that they were not in the majority. In fact, even Şıhlı, under the influence of Abid Hodja, didn't seem too resolute about the matter. After all, here he was; he wasn't skipping out on the excavation. And so Esra decided that the best defence was a good offence.

"Look here my friends," she said, "I don't know what Abid Hodja thinks, but Hadji Settar's death had nothing to do with any kind of curse. You're a part of this excavation. You know that we haven't removed one single stone from the Black Tomb. To the contrary, we've cleaned up its surroundings and taken care of it. You've seen this with your own eyes."

Voices of agreement arose within the van.

"Yes, by God that is the truth. Even that Timothy and that German with the cold eyes, the ones they call infidels, even they painted the outside of the Black Tomb with their very own hands."

"The Black Tomb's never been so well taken care of," said another eagerly.

"Just you forget about these sophistries, Esra Hanım," said Maho. "Abid Hodja's words were based upon what some ignorant folk had to say. If he came and saw the Black Tomb for himself, he'd understand the truth too."

"That's not what you said to the Hodja though," said Şıhlı, immediately regretting it.

Maho turned around and glared furiously at Şıhlı, who was sitting two rows behind.

"Why you trying to raise a ruckus, huh?" he said in Kurdish. "If you don't want to come, then don't come. It's not like we begged you to come or anything. If you want I can stop the van and you can get out right now."

SHırhlı didn't say anything, just hung his head, but Maho still had steam to let off.

"If you're gonna come, then come. But keep quiet. Don't get everybody riled up. We're all here cause we're trying to scrape by. Your dear Abid Hodja doesn't have to worry about that, cause he gets his paycheck from the state each month, and he wiles away the hours in his own lodgings. If we don't work, we go hungry. 'Working is the greatest form of worship.' That's what our master the Prophet, and the saint buried at the Black Tomb, said. So where's the curse in that?..."

Although the only part of the head worker's speech she really understood were the words "Black Tomb," Esra could pretty much guess the content from the way he said it. Maho continued his grumbling in Kurdish all the way to the excavation site, stopping once in a while to turn to Esra and say in Turkish, "Excuse us, we're ignorant folk."

Maho's words were a relief to Esra. When Esra saw through the front window of the van, which Halaf had polished to a fine shine the night before, the ruined walls of the ancient city, her heart leapt in sweet excitement, much like it did upon returning to her home in Istanbul after a long journey.

TABLET TEN

Once the ceremony was over and the king and queen had entered the palace, my heart was overcome by a sweet excitement. I appeared before my father and asked for permission to leave, and as soon as I had gotten permission, I swiftly made my way to the temple. As I passed before the long walls decorated with reliefs, for a moment my eyes fixed upon the carving of the Naked Goddess, holding her breasts in her hands. Of their own accord did the pace of my feet slow. All sorts of lewd thoughts besieged my mind, a series of obscene images passed before my eyes. I felt my face grow warm, and I quickly distanced myself from that relief, angry at myself for having looked at the Naked Goddess in such an improper manner. Before climbing the broad stairway to the temple, flanked on either side by double-headed sphinxes, I bowed my head and touched my face to the ground. I was breathing heavily by the time I reached the magnificent door to the temple. I had no intention of waiting, however, and immediately made my entrance. I was overcome by this feeling that I was a complete stranger there in that temple I had visited so many times before, as if I were in a place completely foreign to me, amongst people utterly unknown to me. I hid behind one of the large columns so that the temple officials would not see me in this state, and waited for my excitement to pass. At that moment I saw that the reliefs of the Storm God Teshub, his wife the Sun Goddess Hepat, and the Goddess Kupaba, were all looking at me. It was as if they were alive; the sunlight drifting through the windows illuminated the faces of all three, and it seemed as if the exalted masters were trying to tell me something with their eyes, bathed as they were in the light. Perhaps they did not approve of what I was doing. Perhaps I should wait for my father to find a favorable mate for me in order to satisfy this burning curiosity that made my every day and my every night a travail of great longing, to slake this incessant desire consuming my body. Is that what my masters, the true owners of my being, were trying to tell me with their frozen expressions? I mean, there was no law in this city stating that all young men were to sleep with the temple prostitutes. The more I looked at the faces of our creators, the more my courage dwindled. I was just beginning to think that returning home would be a good idea when I felt a hand touch my shoulder. I turned around to find myself facing Chief Priest Valvaziti, still in his ceremonial garb.

"What are you doing here, young Patasana?" he asked. My hesitation to respond, combined with the look on my face, made it clear to the chief priest exactly why I was there.

"You came here to have sex with the temple prostitutes, didn't you?" he asked with a scowl.

I didn't know what to say. I lowered my head so as to avoid looking into his furious eyes. The chief priest continued to scold me.

"And you are ashamed of this holy rite. So it shames you to accept the gifts of these self-sacrificing women, who worship our goddess by offering their bodies, is that it?"

The more he spoke, the more I wished for the earth to swallow me up right then and there.

"This behavior of yours is nothing but ignorance, but because you are young, I will forgive you. This is nothing to be ashamed about, no cause for condemnation. The Goddess Kupaba also wishes for you to make love with one of these holy women. Dispel the shame from your face, the fear from your heart, and follow me, young Patasana," he said, and began walking.

I followed Valvaziti in silence. We passed before our gods and then at the end of the large room turned into a dimly lit corridor with high ceilings. The corridor was lit with oil lamps hung before each of the rooms. The light music emerging from an unknown source and the pleasant scent of incense summoned one into a dream world. But I was filled with such great anxiety that I could not bring myself to set foot into that dream world. The chief priest stopped in front of the third of the doors lined up along either side of the corridor.

"Go in there and wait," he said motioning towards the door with his hand. "You shall be chosen."

Without a word, and without even looking him in the face, I bowed in reverence and then entered the room.

There was no one inside. The sound of the music from outside could be heard inside the room also, and the air inside was also heavy with the scent of the burning incense. I then noticed the large bed against the right side wall. The bed was covered with an embroidered blanket. The embroiderers had taken great pains to decorate it with images of the reeds along the Euphrates, the birds that flew above the river's waters, and the fish swimming in it. Once inside the room, I just stood there, uncertain of what to do with myself. Then I heard footsteps approaching from outside. In a state of panic I sat down on the edge of the bed. A short while later, the door opened. Two women walked in. Their faces were exposed, but their bodies were covered in snow white dresses from head to toe. The women smiled respectfully and welcomed me. They were at such ease that it was immediately apparent that they were senior temple prostitutes, well trained in the games of love. As they approached, I noticed that there was someone else behind them. This third woman seemed hesitant to show herself. When the two women in front drew apart, I got a better look at her. But before I even got a good look at her, whether due to the gracefulness in her timidity, the light that she radiated in the room, or her appearance which warmed the beholder to his very depths, I was already aware of her ethereal beauty. She had her head bowed low. Her black hair spread over the white gowns covering her elegant body. She gently lifted her head, and directed her dark brown eyes at me timidly, hesitantly, like a doe. Upon first sight of her warm eyes that bore right through me, I understood that before me stood my first love, the woman who would change my life. Filled with excitement, fear, and joy, I sat upright.

CHAPTER ELEVEN

Two soldiers happily stood up and approached Esra. Fearful and shivering from the cold, they had stood watch all night amongst the city ruins, which had become frightening phantoms in the darkness. When the wind began to blow harder towards midnight, emitting a moaning-like sound as it coursed through the branches of the sweet smelling oleaster tree at the head of the Black Tomb, they had retreated farther back, towards the palace ruins, and begun to pray for the speedy onset of dawn, all the while cursing their commander, Crazy Eshref. Fortunately the wind died down, the darkness withdrew, and the jeep carrying the archaeologists down the narrow road shrouded in the ash gray light of the wee hours appeared. When they spotted the jeep, thinking that their rescue was near, the soldiers quickly made their way down the slope, but then when they learned from the sour faced man named Kemal who stepped out of the jeep that the excavation director was in another vehicle, they began to wait once again, cursing under their breaths. If it had been up to them, they would have taken off right then and there, paying no mind to Esra Hanım or anyone else. But the commander's orders were very strict; they were not to leave the site before talking with Esra Hanım. There was someone else on watch with them; the excavation watchman Selo. Arriving at the excavation site almost simultaneously with the jeep, Selo too awaited Esra, humiliated by the embarassment of his failure to perform his duty. When the van carrying Esra arrived half an hour later, Selo and the two soldiers met the excavation director at the vehicle's door. The two soldiers beat Selo to the punch, addressing the young woman first and telling her in a single breath that they wanted to return to the police station. Esra suggested that they stay for breakfast, but when they refused, she told Murat to take them back to the station. Although not exactly pleased with this assignment, the young student did as he was told and headed off to deliver the two soldiers, who were in a wretched state due to their tense night on watch and lack of sleep.

Seeing that the excavation director had taken care of her business with the soldiers, Selo walked up to her. "Please forgive me, Esra Hanım."

Seeing the old man standing there before her, Esra grew very serious.

"This just won't due, Selo. We keep you at the site so you can guard it, and you go and turn it over to thieves."

"I swear I didn't have the slightest clue," Selo said, trying to explain. "It's that wretched Cripple that's to blame for the whole damn mess. He fooled me, too."

"So what if someone else comes and fools you?"

"Oh no, nothing like that will ever happen again. I was done ignorant once. Never ever will I do something like that again."

Esra couldn't stand to see this man, aged well ahead of his years, pleading with her any longer.

"What you did was a huge mistake," said a distraught Esra, "but I'm not going to fire you..."

With a show of the few teeth he still had, all of them stained yellow with tobacco, Selo smiled gratefully.

"God bless you."

"But if you ever leave the excavation unattended or let anyone else in here again..."

"I swear to God, I swear on the life of my newborn grandson, it will never happen again. Forget about Cripple Memili's men, from now on not even the sheep of a deaf shepherd will be allowed in here..."

He was set to continue with his speech when Esra cut him off. "Alright Selo," she said. "From now on, be more careful."

Selo grew quiet, a grateful smile planted across his lips. Thinking that they'd lost enough time already, Esra made her way straight to the ancient library. She wanted to find out just how much damage Shehmuz and his friends had done to the excavation site. With the excavation crew in tow, she made her way over the rough ground and through the ruined walls to the remains of the library. Stooping down upon the floor of the palace, which was comprised of gravel and pieces of mud brick, Esra began to inspect the damage.

She could tell that Shehmuz and Bekir had dug up square 5D, which the crew itself had already begun excavating. Done with their deed, they had expertly covered up the area they had dug up. However, it wasn't easy to fool a trained eye, and so the more experienced diggers could tell upon first glance just where the smugglers had dug, because the floor at that particular spot was darker and softer. Still, there didn't seem to be too much damage done. The thieves, failing to find anything but tablets here, abandoned the library to go digging in other areas of the site. It must have been these other areas where they uncovered the statuettes of the woman and the stag, the necklace, and the goblet. Esra wondered where they might have uncovered those finds. "Most likely the temple..." she thought. But this thought didn't have much of an impact upon her; to her, Patasana's tablets were more valuable than all of the undiscovered temples, all of the untouched ancient treasures in the whole world.

"These guys are more careful when it comes to digging than we are!" exclaimed an awe-struck Kemal, standing beside Esra as she knelt inspecting the floor.

"Good for them," responded Esra, "that way they did less damage to the site."

"What I don't get is how these guys learned to excavate so systematically, just like us."

"They learned from archaeologists, how else," said Esra as she stood up. "Halaf says that Cripple Memili has his men work as diggers on the excavations, and so that's how they learn proper excavation techniques."

Kemal's astonishment did not abate.

"Well I'll be," he mumbled. "What a sly pack of foxes." He had his eyes on Elif as he said this, but the young woman didn't respond in the least.

"Anyway, let's get to work now," said Esra. She took note of the gradually reddening sky. "In a little bit this place is going to be burning up." Looking at Bernd, she continued: "You all continue excavating the library. Teoman and I will check on the temple."

Bernd gathered up his own crew, while the other workers headed off towards the temple together with Teoman, Esra, and Kemal. A few meters later Esra looked back and yelled out to Elif, who was still with Bernd.

"Aren't you coming?"

"I want to take a few shots," the young girl said, struggling to remove her camera from its bag. "For the lawsuit."

"Alright, but don't be dilly dallying around there too long. We're going to need photos of the other places the thieves dug into, too."

Bernd's crew had already gotten down to work as Esra and the others made their way to the temple.

The remains of the ancient city were spread over a circular area of a few kilometers. The eastern and southern parts of this circle were bordered by the Euphrates, while on the north was a stream bed, which used to carry pristine water all the way to the river, but which had meanwhile turned into a marsh, and on the west by an asphalt road which formed an artificial border. Unlike the surrounding fields, the area where the remains were located was covered by dried weeds. The capitals of columns, basalt stones with hieroglyphics carved into them, the unburied remains of a collapsed arch, countless mud bricks, and pieces of marble among the yellow grass swaying in the wind continued to resist time as the stubborn witnesses of the city's past life. But the real proof that undeniably revealed the existence of the city were the remains of the palace, library, and temple in the fortress perched atop this hill along the Euphrates.

The crew had begun excavation work starting with the library and the temple. The "head digger" at the library was Bernd, and at the temple, Teoman. Kemal acted as the field director. Murat was their all-purpose man, performing all sorts of tasks, while Elif took notes when she wasn't taking photos, and Esra was the overall supervisor, determining insufficiencies and needs, and making sure that the excavation kept on track and in step with the general plan. But once they began uncovering Patasana's tablets, Esra began to concentrate all of her attention upon the library excavation. She knew from both the Hittite tablets uncovered at Hattusha as well as the Assyrian sources obtained at excavations at Ninova that an important library had been located in this city. But to tell the truth, not in a million years would she have guessed that they would turn up texts like the ones Patasana had written. If they could uncover all of Patasana's writings, not only would they have found the earliest non-official historical documents ever to be uncovered, but they also would have made a significant contribution to both history and archaeology by having seized the opportunity to learn in detail just what happened to this city, which had been Assyrianized in 705 B.C.E. and had been known as a Hittite metropolis. That's why, even as she made her way to the temple to determine the damage done in that area, her mind remained on the Patasana tablets yet to be uncovered.

Leading around one hundred meters downhill from the palace to the temple was the main road that the Hittite kings would have used for processions during festival ceremonies. Once decorated with magnificent reliefs, the wall and other remains along this route had become a playing field for green lizards. Once Esra and the members of the excavation crew arrived at the temple, they found that, unlike the library, the temple wasn't so quick to give away the location from which the thieves had smuggled their goods. They ended up having to scour every inch of the temple, of which only the stairway remained intact, its columns and thick stone walls broken and buried. And after about an hour of looking, it was at a totally unexpected location that they finally found the spot that the treasure hunters had dug into—at the foot of a collapsed wall ten meters beyond the sphinx, only its rear end remaining, in the garden of the temple.

Shehmuz and Bekir had done a fine job here, too, as they had in the library, at successfully covered up their tracks after exhuming their goods. If the excavation crew members hadn't known that the site had been pillaged, they never would have noticed that this spot had been dug into.

Esra and Teoman got down on their hands and knees where the thieves had dug and ran their hands over the ground, as if it would somehow reveal to them what was underneath, and tried to figure out what had happened. Kemal, five of the workers, and Elif, who had just joined them, stood around the other two, silently waiting to see what would happen. Rolling the dirt in her hand, Esra raised her head and looked at Teoman.

"Are you thinking what I'm thinking?"

"I think so, yes."

Kemal, who understood nothing of what they were saying, grumbled:

"Why don't you share those thoughts of yours and let us in on the secret, too."

"I think we are standing right above the room where votive offerings were accepted," said Esra gleefully.

But Kemal, whose mind was still on Elif, found this explanation insufficient.

"May I ask just how you came to that conclusion?"

"It's simple," said Esra. "If you uncover three finds at the same spot, then that means there's more to come."

As soon as Esra had finished, Elif pointed her camera at the spot they were referring to and began clicking away.

"But couldn't this just be the home of a wealthy person?" Kemal objected.

"At the bottom of the temple stairs?"

"I agree with Esra," said Teoman. "The room where the votive offerings were accepted couldn't be upstairs, because heavy items were being brought here—animals that are hard to carry, like deer and pigs, as well as large jars of wine and olive oil. The room would've had to have been somewhere easily accessible."

His friend's words were logical, but Kemal nevertheless continued to put up a fight.

"We can't be sure without excavating."

"What, so we should just leave the center of the temple and start digging here?" grumbled Teoman.

"Let's not get in a rush," said Esra as she stood up and brushed the dirt from her hands. "Let's assess the situation at this evening's meeting and reach a decision that way. It's not right to go about changing our plans just like that."

Teoman took a relaxed breath.

"You're absolutely right," he said. "We can't just go changing where we excavate on a whim."

Kemal had no objections to this.

"Okay then," said Esra. "C'mon now and let's go to work. We've already lost enough time as it is."

As Teoman gathered together the workers and headed for the temple, Kemal turned and looked at Elif before walking after them. Esra noticed the look, and the mixed expression of anger and hurt on his face. Esra thought that he would call for Elif to come along, but the young man just followed the rest of the excavation team without a word. Elif, too, noticed that Kemal trailed after the others without pause, but she paid no heed. Esra, resentful of the other woman's behavior, couldn't help herself.

"So just how much longer is this going to go on?" she asked.

"Just about done," said Elif, thinking that she was referring to her photographing.

"That's not what I mean. I mean this spat between you and Kemal."

Elif lowered her camera. Out of the corner of her eye she looked at Kemal, who was at quite a distance by now.

"The man's totally lost it. He's so possessive; he's jealous of anyone I spend time with."

"But you're doing just about all you can to make him jealous."

Elif was caught off guard by Esra's reaction and looked at the other woman, both her friend and her superior, with a stupefied expression.

"You don't really know what's happened," she said by way of explanation.

"What I saw last night was enough for me. You stood the guy up, even though you'd promised to come. He waited for you for hours."

"Okay, so yesterday I made a mistake," said Elif, annoyed by Esra's take on the situation. "And I apologized. But he's just gotten carried away with the whole thing."

"I wonder what you would do if you were in his place?"

Elif thought that Esra was taking sides with Kemal. Yet she had thought that Esra would support her in this matter.

"He treats me like some kind of registered real estate, his property, and his alone. But I have my own life."

"I'm not saying that I approve of Kemal's behavior, but you should be careful, too."

"I am careful, but it's not enough," Elif replied in a tense voice that was gradually growing louder. "It doesn't matter where I go, where I look, what I wear, I'm guilty of something. What else do I have to do?"

Seeing that Elif had grown very tense, Elif softened the tone of her voice.

"You shouldn't hurt one another. This only does harm to you and..." she was about to say, "those around you" when Elif interjected:

"And the excavation, right?" she snarled.

The two women's eyes met. For the first time since they had met, Elif looked at Esra defiantly.

"You don't think about anything but the excavation anyway. Nothing else at all. What about the people you live with, your friends, huh? Their troubles, their worries?..."

Esra stood frozen, stupefied as she listened to Elif's hyper rebellious entreaties.

"You used to say that an archaeologist should be like a psychologist, too, but you didn't even take the time to come talk with me face to face. You say that we're friends, pals, but it's all just so many words..."

The young girl's words were sharp as a knife, and they hurt. More importantly, what she said was true. Esra had never sat down with her to listen to her grievances, and share her own; she had criticized Elif, had given her guidance, had congratulated her, but all of this only had to do with work. She remembered when she and Elif first met. She had sat down in the old armchair in front of Esra's unassuming desk in her small office, and told her that she was studying photography, but that she was also interested in archaeology. She wanted to go on excavations with Esra and her crew. She had graduated from a good high school, and her English was good, she said. Esra, who for a long time had been in need of a reliable photographer, listened intently to what the young girl had to say. Encouraged by the smile on Esra's face, Elif excitedly began showing Esra the green album of photographs she had taken. The photographs weren't bad at all. And so Elif became part of the excavation crew. Esra became even fonder of Elif following their first dig together, but now it seemed that she hadn't done enough to prove this fondness to Elif.

"When I first started going out with Kemal, I came to you for advice," said Elif, continuing her jeremiad. "Do you remember? I asked you what kind of a person he was. 'Oh he's a good guy,' you said, just trying to get the whole matter over with as quick as you could. For you I have no value as a person..."

"You're wrong," interjected Esra. "I love you like a sister."

"Well I've never seen any sign of such compassion."

"I've been trying to treat everyone equally."

"Equality is not treating everyone the same, it's treating everyone with the same care," Elif said in rebuke. "You haven't treated us with even a tenth of the care you take when it comes to the excavation..."

Esra thought that Elif was right, and her insides twisted up in a sad frustration. But there was so much to deal with, she didn't know herself just which problems she should be taking care of first. Besides, they weren't here on vacation, so of course for her the most important thing was her work, the excavation. "No, no, Elif's hypersensitivity has nothing to do with me. I think this girl's really in love with Tim. Plus the pressure from Kemal has gotten her extremely wound up. I've picked the worst possible time to talk with her," Esra thought. "And now the poor thing's just lost it completely." She should be more understanding towards Elif. She smiled as she stepped closer to the young girl.

"Look, Elif," she said, laying her right hand on the young woman's shoulder. Elif quickly turned around as if in an effort to make a quick escape. Esra didn't let her go. "Perhaps I have neglected you. But we're going through some very hard times right now."

Esra realized that the girl was shaking. After so many tense moments since the night before, Elif was finally letting it all out, and she was crying. Unsure whether to hug her or wait for her to stop crying, Esra just stood there amateurishly by her side for a while. Then she walked over and stood across from the girl, and with her hands tried to dry Elif's eyes. At first Elif turned her head to avoid Esra, but then she suddenly embraced her. "I'm such an idiot, aren't I?" she said, sobbing. At first Esra found this behavior to be rather odd, but then she found it endearing, and so she hugged Elif back, lovingly like a sister. She was moved, and was afraid that if she opened her mouth to say anything, she, too, would start crying.

"We should help each other out more," was all she could say as she tenderly stroked Elif's hair. For a while they just remained like that. Once the girl's crying ceased, Esra spoke up once again.

"C'mon, let's get ourselves together now," she said. "If anyone sees us like this they'll have a good laugh at the state we're in."

"Okay," said the young girl, sniffling as she walked away from Esra.

"Don't you worry, everything's going to work out."

Watching the young girl as she began to ascend the temple stairs, Esra recalled that Orhan had put her through plenty of hell himself. Especially during the period right after they were married, it was the same stuff that Elif was complaining about: "No, that's too tight. No, that's too revealing," he'd say, sticking his nose into every aspect of her wardrobe. And if she were to talk with a male friend from the university, he'd pout and start having jealous fits. Just why is it that people act like this anyway? Because they're afraid of losing their loved ones? That's all good and well, but what can you do anyhow if that person doesn't love you? Maybe Elif didn't love Kemal. Nobody could blame her for that. The only solution would be for Kemal to suck it up and forget about his ex. As these thoughts passed through her mind, Esra saw Murat coming from the direction of the palace. He was in a hurry, his pace so brisk he was almost running. Curious as to what had happened, Esra headed towards him.

"I've been looking for you," the young man yelled as he approached, now just a few meters away.

"What's happened?"

"The head village guard's been killed."

"What?" said Esra. "What the hell are you talking about?"

"The chief of the Türkoghlu tribe's been murdered!"

"Reshat Agha?"

"The man himself. At the exit of Göven village. He was decapitated. And they placed his head in his lap."

"Oh my God!" said Esra, horrified. Reshat Türkoglu was a frail man of average height. He was forty years of age at the most, but looked older. He had a thin moustache, and he always wore a suit. His highly animated, grayish blue eyes sparkled mischievously from beneath his thin eyebrows. Esra thought he looked much more like a well-honed, small town business man than one of those cruel, fear inspiring aghas. They said that he didn't carry a gun, but whenever she saw him, he always had his men in tow.

"Didn't he have his men with him?"

"No. They'd gone skirt chasing in Göven, so he was alone."

"Who told you about this?"

"First the soldiers, then the shepherd who found his body... He was at the police station to give his deposition, so I talked to him, too. He says he left home at midnight. He drives the herds of the Göven villagers in addition to those of his own village. He saw some sort of spectre on his way to Göven, just as he was approaching the village. There was a full moon, but it was behind him, so the light was coming from behind and he couldn't make out what the figure was. Just then the dogs started barking like mad, and so he sensed that something was awry. He drew closer and that's when he saw it—a headless body. He was scared and stepped away from the body, and it was then that he noticed the head in its lap..."

The entire scene flashed before Esra's eyes. A body sitting in the middle of a deserted road, in its lap a head with its bewildered eyes protruding from it, the full moon looming in the background. And a few meters ahead, a shepherd frightened out of his wits at the macabre sight before him.

"The shepherd ran like mad back to his village," Murat continued. "He began banging on doors and tried to yell out, but he was so petrified he couldn't make a sound. The people in the village woke up, but they had a hell of a time calming the shepherd down. He was so worked up he was still shaking even when I talked with him."

"So did he see anyone in the area where the murder happened?"

"He says he saw a man flying in the darkness."

"What is that supposed to mean, 'A man flying in the darkness'?"

"That's what the shepherd says. 'A man fled the scene, flying on the wind.'"

"So he means he was running?"

"He didn't say 'running, he said 'flying.' The Captain thinks the same as you. He says the shepherd was in a panic, and thought that the fleeing man he saw was flying."

"Nobody knows yet who the murderer is of course."

"Captain Eshref thinks it's the terrorists. He told me, 'Tell Esra Hanım to be careful.'"

Esra knew what the real meaning of this message was, "See, everything I said is turning out to be right." She felt a slight stirring of anger within her. But then she wondered to herself why she was angry at him. Perhaps the Captain was right, and it really was the separatists who were behind the murders.

"What's going on?" asked Murat, now timid in the face of Esra's enigmatic silence. "First Hadji Settar, now the head village guard Reshat... Do you think the same person is behind both murders?"

"I don't know," said Esra. Although it was still very early in the day, her voice was weary and hopeless. "I hope not. And that the locals don't think so. Otherwise they'll go connecting the murders to the curse of the Black Tomb again."

Murat's eyes had taken on a strange look, and he drew closer to Esra.

"Perhaps the locals are right," he said. "Perhaps we really are cursed."

Up until now, Esra hadn't ever said a word about Murat's fascination with the mystical world, but seeing as this time they were talking about the excavation, she couldn't hold back any longer.

"Don't be ridiculous!" she yelled.

"I'm not being ridiculous. In his tablets, didn't Patasana mention a curse that descended upon the shores of the Euphrates like a wall of darkness? Didn't he warn that the tablets weren't to be touched without first appeasing the gods, otherwise those who touched them would be cursed?"

The connection that Murat made between Patasana's tablets and the murders was meaningless, yet it still gave Esra goosebumps.

"Are you slow in the head or something?" she roared, perhaps yelling at herself as well for shivering at the idea. "You're interpreting what's happening right now based upon the beliefs of a culture that lived two thousand seven hundred years ago..."

"And today, too..." said Murat, but he was immediately cut off by Esra.

"Would you please just cut it out now?" she said to shut the young man up. "We've got enough problems to deal with as it is without having to put up with you and your superstitious beliefs."

"But..."

"No buts about it. You're going to forget all about this nonsense. And if you don't intend to do just that, then you can leave the excavation right now."

She hesitated, and then with a suspicious look in her eyes asked Murat: "Have you told anybody else about Reshat Agha's murder?"

"N.n.n...no," stuttered the young man in response. "I thought you should be the first to know."

"Good thinking. I'll tell them about it. And if I hear about these thoughts of yours about the so-called curse from anybody else, especially the workers, then just know that you will never be allowed to come to the excavation with me ever again."

Esra then turned and left Murat standing there, looking on helplessly at her, his teacher. She made her way to the fortress at a brisk pace, as if getting away from Murat would rescue her from all of her problems as well. She didn't want to think about who had committed the murders and why, she didn't want to do any reasoning by deduction, she didn't want to be suspicious of anyone, she didn't want to debate with herself. Her mind paid no heed, however, and so even the most improbable of hypotheses wormed their way into her head and took residence there. Given the amount of pondering she did, it would have been nice if she could have reached a conclusion. But she always ended up back at the same old place: that dark, slippery uncertainty. Perhaps the best thing to do would be to stop the excavation. First Hadji Settar, now the head village guard Reshat... Death was dancing all around them. Hadji Settar was closer to them than any other person in the region, and the village where head village guard Reshat was murdered was just a few kilometers from where they were staying. Maybe it was their turn next. So was the excavation really worth endangering peoples' lives?

She paused once she reached the fortress ruins; the sky had turned red, and in a little while the sun would appear from behind the orange clouds. She walked all the way to the very farthest of the ruined citadel towers until she could see the blue waters of the Euphrates. The river flowed sinuously, like a giant snake, through the earth colored plain.

She leaned against the ruined tower and lowered herself to the ground. She took out a cigarette and lit it. She inhaled deeply. "There's no use insisting," she thought as she exhaled the smoke. She took another puff off her cigarette. Or was she exaggerating? Nah! There really truly was some kind of hex hovering over them. Two murders had been committed; the excavation crew members were uneasy, and so were the locals. The Captain was uneasy, and she herself was on the verge of losing it. It was just one setback after another. No, she couldn't risk whatever was coming next. She'd feel the pangs of her conscience for the rest of her mortal life if anything were to happen to any of the excavation crew members. And waiting a little longer before uncovering the rest of Patasana's tablets would hardly be the end of the world!

TABLET ELEVEN

I, Patasana, grandson of the wise man Mitannuwa, son of the Scribe Araras. I, callow Patasana, of destiny, hope, and love so dark, who broke the shell of childhood only to drown his mind in the mad maelstrom of youth.

The name of the black-haired, doe-eyed girl dressed in white that I encountered in the Goddess Kupaba's bedroom was Ashmunikal; this I would learn.

She had a narrow waist, was tall and slender, had skin of ivory, and the voice of a nightingale; this I would learn.

She was meek, warm, soft, her lips sweet, her eyes bright; this I would learn.

She would shame me, elate me, drown me in sorrow, die for me, abandon me to wallow in my own fear and pain; this I would learn.

She would make me into a scoundrel, a coward, a traitor, a man of cunningness; this I would learn.

I did not know that the gods had hidden my cursed fate in the dark brown eyes of Ashmunikal, the most beautiful of girls on the Euphrates shores; this I would learn.

The gods had wanted me to face my fate. They were emphatic in their commands; this I would learn.

And I began to learn at the very first moment that I encountered Ashmunikal in the temple. When the two temple prostitutes walking towards me saw that I couldn't take my eyes off of Ashmunikal, they turned and looked at her, too.

When they noticed the evasive glances Ashmunikal sent my way from behind her long lashes, they exited the room with a knowing, heartfelt smile upon their lips. This left no other obstacle except for the space between Ashmunikal and myself; if you don't count the silence. The silence, however, was like a vast gulf between us that gradually grew wider. At that moment, she showed herself to be braver than I. "I am Ashmunikal, prostitute of the Goddess Kupaba. I have chosen you as my partner to worship the goddess Kupaba, in her presence," she managed to say, though in a quivering voice. But the more she spoke, the more confident she became. "I, the youngest of the temple prostitutes, who has never been touched, offer myself to you. I entreat you to join with me in blessing this bed," she said, drawing closer to me. With her long, thin fingers she touched my hands, which I held folded before me. My awe at the beauty that stood before me compounded with my timidity to transform me into an utter fool. It was as if all the blood in my veins had frozen, and I stood as motionless as the sphinx at the temple gate. It was as though twas not a female that stood before me, but a goddess. I could not recall even the most innocent of the images of love-making that I envisioned in my dreams. It was not long before Ashmunikal realized that I was just as timid as she. When she realized my own timidity, she became much more relaxed. Perhaps she was afraid of encountering someone who would hurt her, who would humiliate her because of her inexperience. But seeing before her someone just as timid as, and even shyer than, herself, dispelled her fear. And she had to dispense with this fear, for this ceremony belonged to her. It was she who directed the ceremony, and who was thus accountable to the goddess Kupaba. No matter how afraid she was, no matter how excited, it was imperative that she carry out her duty, successfully and in full. If I had wanted, I could have dashed out of the temple then and there, but for her there was no escape. But then she did not have any intention of escaping. Especially once she had come to realize my own nervousness, for then she became quite self-confident. She walked towards the bed, commanding me to follow her. This action of hers frightened me even further. I thought that

I was going to undress before her. I imagined her own thin body. I thought of my own pointy shoulders and weak arms, so unworthy of this beautiful girl. But still I could not help but follow her to the bed. She sat down upon the bed, and called for me to sit next to her. I did as I was told. We sat side by side. She took my hand in hers and turned her face towards mine, but I averted my eyes, unable to look at her, as if I were facing a leper. My eyes swept down her long body, and below her white gown, I saw her pink nipples resembling two buds not yet come into blossom. I felt my mouth grow dry and the palm of my hands grow wet with perspiration. I hoped that she would not notice my sweaty hands. Ashmunikal moved her long, thin fingers from my hands to my chest, as if she had heard my wish. She was trying to caress me. She feigned experience, but her actions belied her amateurishness to such a degree that even I, despite my own inexperience, could clearly see through it. Still she continued to touch me. But as for me, I could not even give her a grateful look, let alone touch her. Then, how it happened I do not know, but our eyes met. I wanted to avert my glance, but I couldn't. I was shaken by the dizzying hum of a dark well. Those two drops of brown captured my mind, my heart, my body. Meanwhile Ashmunikal, oblivious to my state, sat smiling before me in an attempt to relieve my tension. Her smile gave me just the slightest bit of courage. I managed to smile back at her. Ashmunikal reached for my hands again, and as she did so, I quickly wiped off the sweat of my palms onto my dress. She took my right hand and raised it to her left cheek. Her cheek was burning hot. Finally I managed to move my fingers and ran them ever so gently over her face. Feeling this, Ashmunikal pushed my hand more forcefully against her face. Her eyes bored into mine. Not a trace of her former timidity remained. Her face shone with the determination of a female who knows what she wants. She let go of my hand and stood up. Standing before me, she began to undress. As she offered to me those most valuable treasures of this world, I, an idiot, the disgrace of all men, lowered my head. And it was at exactly that moment that I realized the great disaster that would befall me. My sexual organ, which became hard as a sword whenever I thought of any woman, let alone one so beautiful as Ashmunikal, failed to manifest itself, as if it had disappeared, as if it had melted between my legs. I sighed in fear, and in shame. I considered standing up and running off right then. But my pride would not allow it. Twas the Chief Priest Valvaziti who had brought me here, and besides, I could not just leave the beautiful Ashmunikal like that. I should wait until the end. Now relieved of her clothing, Ashmunikal lay down upon the bed, a coy expression upon her face as she covered her breasts with her hands in mock shame. Then she asked me to lie down next to her. I silently obeyed her request. He legs, like her lips, were parted. The most beautiful girl of the Euphrates shores was waiting with open legs for me to plow her bountiful field, but all I could do was stare at her hopelessly, like a villager with a broken plow. Ashmunikal, failing to fully comprehend my state, tried to remove my clothing. I tried to take it slowly, but she was insistent. Finally, she succeeded in stripping me. Now my feeble frame lay next to her incomparable body, adorned with the fruits of the gardens of the gods. I was so embarrassed, and made a final effort to reach for my clothes to get dressed, but Ashmunikal stopped me.

"Don't be afraid, just touch me," she said. "Take my tongue in your mouth, warm my skin with yours, place your hand between my legs."

With the shame of a commander who has long lost the battle, I did as she said. I began to kiss her, I tasted the sweet honey of her lips, felt the warmth of her skin in my blood, wet my fingers with the dew drops of her sex organ. I heard her moan deeply, and felt her gently rub her body against mine, felt her body convulse. I also rubbed my body against hers, but it was no use. It was obvious now that the gods had forbidden me from making love on that day. Ashmunikal lay down next to me again, and after wiping the beads from my brow, sweat borne out of my distress, she placed a kiss upon my lips.

"My man," she said, "you're my first man."

When she said that, I began to cry. First quietly, and then in great sobs. Ashmunikal wrapped her body around mine, pressed me to her bosom, wiped my eyes with her hands, and kissed my tears. She stroked my hair and soothed me until I calmed down and fell asleep in her lap. With me she, too, slept.

But when I woke up, she was no longer by my side. She had deserted me—left me alone with my helplessness, my shame, my fear.

CHAPTER TWELVE

Esra kept her fears to herself. She didn't say anything to anyone; not when they took a break at mid-morning so that the workers could have their breakfast, and not at noon when the work day wound up. If nothing else, she wanted for at least this day of excavating to carry on uninterrupted. Plus, considering the conversation she had had with them that morning, she definitely didn't want the workers to hear this piece of news from her. She felt that she just couldn't take another discussion like that, not with Şıhlı or any of the other workers. For the rest of the work day she paced back and forth between the library and the temple, appearing to be at work, but in reality pondering whether or not to stop the excavation. She looked over each stone, each ruin of the ancient city with mournful eyes, as if she would never see any of it ever again. Even the three tablets uncovered in the library failed to cheer her up. Yet what she wouldn't have given to share Bernd's emotions when he joyfully pronounced, "If this keeps up, we'll have uncovered all of Patasana's writings in no time," as he brushed the dust off of the cuneiform writing on the tablets. But the incidents that were descending upon them like dark clouds cast a shadow on her heart, and drowned her joy. The first excavation under her direction was to be abandoned before completion, and Patasana's tablets, perhaps the most important find in decades, would fail to reach the light of day, even though they were so close to being fully uncovered. This was a great injustice. No, a great stroke of bad luck... They would also have to cancel the press conference. The Germans would be furious. So what if they were. After all, Patasana's tablets weren't more important than human lives. And maybe she would never see Eshref again. Really, she hadn't thought of that before. "For God's sake, look at what I'm worrying about now. So what if I never see him again. As if the man really means anything to me," she said, trying to banish the image of his dark-complected face from her mind. But she couldn't. She recalled the incident that the Captain had told her about the day before, and then how he had dashed off as if trying to run away from her. Distressed, she pulled herself together. "Slow down," she said, reprimanding a young worker busy digging. "You hear that hollow sound? There could be something under there."

The worker blushed crimson red. To be reprimanded in broad daylight by a woman was torment for him, but he looked at the other workers from out of the corner of his eye and, seeing that nobody was paying attention to them, relaxed. He began lowering his pick more carefully. Besides, Esra didn't stick around for long, but headed towards the workers digging in the lower part of the library.

Murat was the only person on the excavation who recognized how tense Esra was. But then he was busy kneeling next to Bernd and quietly helping him to clean the tablets in an effort to remain as inconspicuous as possible after the brow beating he'd received earlier that day.

They quit work just as the sun began to shine straight down upon them. This time around Esra didn't take the van, but headed instead for the jeep that Bernd and Teoman were taking, with Kemal at the helm; Elif watched them like a meek cat. Murat climbed in the van with the workers again. Now alone in the jeep with her friends, as they made their way along the route flanked by fields of cotton and corn, Esra still didn't tell them about the murder of Reshat Agha. "I'll tell them once we're back at the school," she thought. The reason she didn't rush to give them the news was that, despite her belief that she had to put an end to the excavation, still in her heart of hearts she hoped that the excavation would continue. As they approached the school, she changed her mind yet again. She decided to talk with Tim before meeting with the rest of the crew. The man had a good decade of experience under his belt; she shouldn't terminate the excavation without consulting him first.

When they reached the school, they found Halaf chatting with a village kid underneath the arbor. As soon as he saw them Halaf stood up and quickly made his way to meet them before they had even had a chance to pull up into the shade. Esra was surprised to see Elif head straight for the kid under the arbor.

"Hello Hanefi," said the young girl.

"Hello," said the child with shining, kohl-lined eyes. "You get the photos yet?"

Elif rubbed the boy's shorn head.

"They'll be ready today," she said. "Did you come for the photos?"

"No. I brought my grandma."

"Oh, your grandma's here?"

"Yeah, she's here."

"Where is she?"

"Inside," he said, motioning with his head towards the school building.

"C'mon, let's go say hello to her, too."

Seeing Elif head towards the school together with the young boy, Esra turned her inquisitive eyes towards Halaf, who was reaching out to take her bag.

"Infidel Nadide's grandson," Halaf said in explanation as he took the bag. "Aunt Nadide. She came to see Tim, and she brought a pail of yoghurt and a basket of black mulberries."

"What's she have to do with Tim?"

"Nothing, the poor ignorant soul. She thinks America's the size of our little township here. You know that older brother of hers who escaped to America during the Armenian migration?"

Esra didn't recall.

"You know, he was talking about it last night," said Halaf. "She's Pastor Kirkor's daughter. They killed him. Her older brother Dikran tried to escape with his mother and Nadya, who was a young girl at the time. But the poor girl couldn't walk, she was so young. And so her brother left her with their Turkish neighbors. Then the brother and mother ran off to America."

"Alright, yes, I remember."

"Years later Nadide got a letter from her brother in America. And there was an address with the letter. And so Nadide sat her son down and began to write a letter to her brother. But then the letters from America stopped coming. For a full fifty years—easier said than endured—she never received another letter from her brother. And so then you know, the queer old lady found our Tim. Now she's here asking for help because she thinks he must have some news about her brother."

Esra shook her head, laughing.

"Oh my, and how's our Tim supposed to find her brother? Have they been talking for a long time now?"

"It's been a good hour," said Halaf, then with an anxious look in his eyes he added: "You haven't heard the real news yet."

"One minute," she said, realizing what the cook was about to tell her. She didn't want Teoman and Bernd, who were carrying the tablets, to hear them. The two men approached, transporting the tablets with the utmost care.

"Shall we put these in the basement or in Tim's room?" asked Bernd.

Kemal also ran up to offer his assistance.

"In the basement," said Esra, taking the key out of her pocket. "Here's the key," she said, giving it to empty-handed Kemal.

Kemal took the key and set off ahead of the others. Esra watched the three men quickly head off, eager to drop their heavy load off in the basement and then take a warm bath to rid themselves of the dust that covered their bodies, before turning to face Halaf.

"So tell me, what is it?"

"What else, Abid Hodja finally restored his honor," said Halaf. "This morning he cut off Reshat Agha's head and handed it to him."

"How do you know that it was Abid Hodja who killed the head village guard?"

"Who else could it possibly be? Messing with the Türkoghlu tribe is as good as inviting death itself. And around here, sullying someone's honor's the most efficient way to summon your own death. And whose honor did Reshat Agha sully? Abid Hodja's. And they've got issues going way back, too. So..."

"But you were saying what a coward Abid Hodja is?"

"Not just me, everybody and his brother says that the man's a lily-liver. But I guess we've been proven wrong. Besides, like they say, you should always beware of slow running water and a man who walks with his eyes to the ground. So it seems while he was walking about all mousy looking, he was actually busy devising plans to murder that guy. The man's worth his salt."

"Do you realize that you're praising a murderer?"

"Reshat Agha was a bigger murderer," said Halaf decisively. "He caused suffering to countless people, seized their land, and their women. If you gathered together all of the people that he and his men killed, you'd have one jolly graveyard. The bastard had two young guys, just eighteen years old, fed to the dogs because they'd been militants five years earlier. Then a year later he had some poor fella from Mardin thrown into a grain mill and ground out like so much hamburger. The people that died at his hand didn't have anything to do with anything. He knocked off the innocents in order to say he'd killed terrorists, and so that the state would keep employing him as a guard."

Esra didn't want to believe what she was hearing. "So have they arrested Abid Hodja?" she asked in an attempt to change the subject.

"I don't know. If it were up to me, I'd arrest him. If you want, we can tell the Captain..."

"We told him once, but we turned out to be wrong."

Halaf's good mood was immediately dampened.

"Why do you say that, Esra Hanım?" he asked in a hurt voice. "Weren't Shehmuz and Bekir arrested?"

"They were arrested, yes, but for stealing historical artifacts, not for murdering Hadji Settar."

"They murdered Hadji Settar. And it was Abid Hodja that killed Reshat Agha," said Halaf stubbornly. "You'll see, slowly but surely everything I've said will turn out to be true."

Esra gave him a once over before departing.

"I hope you turn out to be right," she said. "If anyone asks, I'm with Tim. We have some things to talk about."

"Dinner's almost ready. I made *alinazik* and *firik* rice. With sour sumac and tomatoes on the side. And Infidel Nadide's honey-sweet dates to top it all off."

Esra smiled and shook her head. Talking with this meddlesome young man of Barak, who was always so up on the latest news of the Euphrates shores, never failed to boost her morale and lift her spirits. Even when her head was so full of uncertain thoughts about the excavation's future, Halaf managed yet again to make her laugh. She headed off for Timothy's room, her anxiety a little more subdued, her heart a little more buoyant.

When she got to Timothy's room, she saw that Infidel Nadide was about to leave. Timothy, Elif, Hanefi, and the old woman were already on their feet. The woman had a black headscarf decorated with a hand-printed flower pattern. Some of her henna dyed hair stuck out from beneath the headscarf. She was wearing a pale blue calico dress. Her large feet were virtually busting out of her crude black shoes. Her posture was weighed down a bit from the years, but overall, she looked pretty healthy. Her face was darker and had more wrinkles than that of Hattuch Nine, but her eyes were full of life, just as Murat had described them. She was the first to notice Esra's entrance into the room, but when their eyes met, she averted her glance and smiled abashedly.

"Welcome," said Esra from just inside the door.

"Thank you, my girl," Nadide replied. "I hope that you are well."

"Thank you, we're doing our best to be as well as we can."

"May God bless you," she said, and then turned to the American. "I should get going now," she said. "I'll stop by in a few days to see if you've gotten any news."

Esra walked up to the school desk Timothy used as his work desk, while Elif accompanied the old woman and her grandson out.

"How's it going? Will you be able to find her little brother?"

"Her big brother," Timothy corrected her. In his hand he held a letter that was virtually worn to shreds with age. "This letter was sent from New York fifty years ago. The home at the address written on it may be long gone. But the poor woman is quite desperate. I have some close friends in that area. I'm going to get a hold of them and ask them to research the address. I doubt it, but maybe they can come up with something."

Esra looked at the letter that Timothy was holding out to her; it was torn from being folded over and over again, and the black ink had grown pale, turning a brownish color. She took the letter from him, afraid that it would disintegrate right there in her hands.

"Fifty years old, eh..." she said, unable to conceal her amazement. "How did she keep it for so long?"

"She says she kept it in her Kuran, but I bet she kept it in her Bible."

"If that were the case she would've told you now. She probably guesses that you're Christian."

"I doubt it. Or maybe she just didn't say so because she's suspicious because I'm working with you guys."

Esra handed the letter back to the American "Did you do good deeds like this in Iraq, too?" she asked, a mixed expression of jealousy and admiration on her face.

"When I was in Iraq, I didn't run into anybody with relatives in America," answered Timothy. He carefully took hold of the letter, as if its protection were his holy charge, and placed it in the notebook lying on his desk.

Esra found the extreme care he took to be exaggerated, but she didn't dwell upon it.

"I came here to talk about the excavation," she said, getting straight to the point. "Have you heard the news?"

"About the head village guard's murder?"

"Yes... This is the second murder in two days," said Esra. "What are we going to do, Tim? I'm really truly starting to get frightened."

The American listened to the excavation director with a serene expression upon his face, and then motioned to an empty chair for Esra to sit down.

"C'mon, have a seat here and let's talk."

Esra continued to voice her anxieties as she took a seat.

"I really don't know what to do. I'm afraid that a member of the excavation crew will get hurt. The murderer, or murderers, keeping hovering about us. I'm wondering if we shouldn't stop the excavation."

"Horrible things are happening," said Timothy. He'd begun to run his right hand through his copper colored beard, like he always did when he began addressing important topics. "I got pretty worked up, too, when I first heard about the incident. But then I began to think that these murders really have nothing to do with us. In fact, it's not even certain that the two murders are connected at all. Halaf says its due to honor issues, and that may be the case, or it may not."

Esra was relieved that Timothy didn't appear to be taking the incident all that seriously, but still she couldn't help but ask:

"What about the rumors though? That the locals think we're responsible for the murders?"

"I think we're rather exaggerating this whole rumor bit. With the exception of a couple of fanatics and a couple of old grave robbers, nobody in town is talking about any curse. So why should we stop the excavation?"

"For the reason I just told you–I'm afraid something will happen to the excavation crew."

"Nobody has the nerve to attack us. They know we have the Captain looking out for us."

"But that doesn't mean anything to the separatists," she said anxiously. "They've killed teachers, and abducted engineers."

"But the separatists aren't active in this region at all!"

"The Captain says that they're carrying out secret operations here, and that they get support from the Genceli tribe in particular. He says the Gencelis' youngest boy, Mahmut, is in the mountains now. The Captain also says that Müslim, the leader of the tribe, is sympathetic towards the separatists and that, at the very least, he would be willing to aid and abet them."

Timothy leaned back in his chair and shook his head:

"The Captain doesn't have an objective eye for what's going on. That's what happens when one actively participates in a war for so long. It's better if you don't take his ideas too seriously."

"Aren't you being a little unfair?" said Esra, as if offended by his words. "The Captain has been an enormous help to us. If it weren't for him, we might not even be continuing the excavation right now as it is."

"You've misunderstood me," he explained. "I'm very fond of the Captain, too. I have no doubt that he is nothing but an honest soldier. But he's experiencing a kind of illness. It's called war syndrome. This emotion makes a person mad, paranoid."

"You sound like someone speaking from experience," said Esra with an inquisitive smile.

"Because I've been to war," said the American. "I was a naval officer in the Vietnam War."

The smile on Esra's face froze in place.

"You're kidding, right?"

"Why? Don't I seem like the type to take part in a war?"

Esra's eyes slid over his muscular, athletic body.

"No, no," she said, shaking her head, "that's not what I meant to say. What I meant was, I mean, what business did someone like you have fighting in a war, let alone a war thousands of miles away from your homeland?"

"What I said is true, I fought in Vietnam. Right at the heart of the conflict, too. And I stayed there until the United States was defeated."

The surprised expression in Esra's eyes was replaced by a look of suspicion. She'd always thought now and then that there was something missing, something wrong, something concealed behind Timothy's profound knowledge, vast amount of experience, and mature personality. It seemed so out of the ordinary for someone to be so good and behave so perfectly. On the other hand, there was no reason for her to be suspicious of him. But now here she was finding out for the first time that the colleague she trusted most had been at war.

"You don't work for the CIA, do you, Tim?" she said, half-jokingly.

The American burst out in laughter.

"You've hit the nail on the head," he said, once his laughing spell was over. "Right now you are speaking with none other than CIA Middle East specialist Timothy Hurley. I'm conducting intelligence for our operative activities. And I'm using archaeology as my cover."

"Don't make light of my question," said Esra. She was trying to disguise her suspicions with her joking demeanor. "Don't forget, one of the first people to excavate in this region was the famous English spy Lawrence."

"Of course, yes, you're right. It is precisely Lawrence's example that I'm following," said Timothy, really getting carried away with the joke. "I'm a big fan of his. In fact, my code name at the CIA is Lawrence. But mine isn't Lawrence of Arabia, it's Lawrence of Barak."

Esra, too, began to laugh.

"Paranoia's contagious," said Timothy, once he'd calmed down. "All that running around with the Captain, and now you've caught it, too."

"For real, did you fight in Vietnam?"

"I just told you I did."

"Why did you fight?"

She wasn't smiling anymore, but looking now at her colleague with eyes full of questions.

"I studied at Yale with a military scholarship. My father was a foreman at a television factory. So, as you might guess, he didn't make enough money to put me through Yale. I could only start school once I'd gotten the scholarship. And those who study with military scholarships pay back their loans by serving in the military."

"So you didn't join because you wanted to?"

Timothy got lost in thought, and after pondering the question for a while, replied:

"Actually, I wanted to go to war. I was so young. And I wasn't a particularly enterprising youngster anyway. I didn't yet have a goal in life. I wanted to show off. Those days, the anti-Vietnam War protests had just gotten started, but I didn't take part in them, maybe because I was shy, or maybe because I didn't like the guys who led it. I thought they were long-haired, irresponsible good-for-nothings who smoked pot and had orgies all the time. So it was partially a reaction against them that I willingly went off to war, to prove my patriotism. It may seem ignorant or foolish to you, but if you think of it in terms of the quest of a young man in search of an identity, and without a lot of options to choose from, then you'll understand it better. It didn't end well, of course..."

Timothy became lost even deeper in thought.

"You didn't end up having to kill anybody, did you?" asked Esra. She was trying to understand what Timothy had experienced, and what he had felt. But most importantly, she was trying to figure out what really lay beneath that apparently perfect personality of his.

Timothy seemed not to have heard the question; his facial expression remained grave, and the expression in his eyes didn't change.

"It must have been awful," Esra persisted.

Timothy nodded his head up and down, as if to confirm what she had said.

"But I also learned a lot. Though its price may be a high one, war is one of the best schools in the world."

"If only such a school didn't exist at all."

"That's impossible," said Timothy, returning from the recesses of his mind. "Can you imagine history without war? Sociology, economics, psychology? Even medicine—the period during which medicine experienced its greatest advancement was the period when the Nazis used the Jews as their own personal lab rats. War is one of humankind's forms of existence. This is true both socially, as well as individually. There's no better game when it comes to drawing out the evil inside of us. Humankind has never given up on this game, and I really don't know if it ever will."

Esra looked at her colleague, taken aback by this response:

"It seems to me that you're defending war."

"No! Absolutely not, I am not defending war. I'm trying to comprehend those enigmatic creatures known as human beings."

"Human beings?" faltered Esra. "But it's the interests of states, countries, classes that cause war. How right is it to blame the common person for it?"

"You're right about the first part. Wars have been and continue to be carried out in order to furher the interests of classes and states. But in the end, it's the common people who draw the knives, pull the triggers, throw the bombs, and drive the tanks. I mean, it's the common people in uniform. So far very few soldiers have stood up to this. How many times in history have the soldiers of two warring armies joined forces to say, 'Enough already, we don't want to fight anymore,' and tossed their weapons aside? But I could give you thousands of examples of people who enjoy killing, and who have made a profession of it."

"Well that's all good and well," Esra said in protest, "but it's criminal for them to give up their weapons. In fact, they could even be executed for being traitors to their nation."

"Aren't they likely to die at war anyway? Wouldn't it be more meaningful if they were to die for a just cause, for peace?"

"That's a matter of consciousness raising," said Esra, with nowhere else to turn. "If a strong culture of peace can be cultivated..."

"And that's exactly what I was getting at. Peace isn't innate for humans. Humans don't go to the same trouble, take the same care *not* to kill as they do *to* kill. Providing for peace requires an influx of consciousness from the outside."

"Isn't that true of war, too?" Esra said, firing back. "Governments can't run the risk of war without prepping the people in advance."

"Maybe, but it's been proven time and again that war is a bad, awful thing. How is it that people can so easily be drawn into a source of destruction with such harsh consequences... And if they are being drawn into it, then the source of this needs to be sought in the human mind frame as much as it does in the draconian politics of states and the interests of greedy classes."

No matter how much she might have disagreed with her colleague, Esra couldn't help but be intrigued by his opinions. "Interesting," she said. And she didn't say this just to be saying something, for Timothy had truly surprised her. She always thought he was someone with a positive outlook on life. And not just her, but everyone on the excavation thought so, too, because that's what his actions indicated to them. Yet what he was saying right now indicated just the opposite.

"You don't believe that people are good."

"Do you?" Timothy responded. "Look at the last five thousand years of history. They're full of destruction, massacres, and war."

"But it's also a history full of magnificent cities, scientific discoveries, immortal works of art. Perhaps humans aren't one hundred percent good, that's true, but they aren't completely evil either. I think there's an equal amount of both sentiments."

"I think the evil outweighs the good. Evil is always more attractive than good."

Timothy spoke these words decisively, as if to inform her that they were immutable truths for him, making Esra feel that it was time to put an end to this conversation.

"Anyways," she said. "I don't know how we got onto this topic, but I think we should get back to work now. So what do you think, should we talk with the Captain about the excavation matter?"

Timothy sighed, and his hands headed for his beard again.

"If you ask me, I don't think we should even broach the topic with him. Let's just ask them to look out for us, I think that's enough."

"And what if he tells us to stop the excavation, that he can't protect us?"

"I don't think he'll do that," said Timothy, with a naughty sparkle in his black eyes. "He's more concerned about what you have to say."

Esra blushed. So Timothy had also sensed the increasing closeness between herself and the Captain.

"He's worried that something might happen to us," Esra said, in an attempt to make light of the matter. "And he's not all that wrong."

"I think he's exaggerating. And even if what he says is true, then he needs to protect us."

Esra was still uncertain.

"So you're saying that we should continue with the excavation, no matter what?"

The American looked at her as if he could hardly believe his ears.

"I don't understand you," he said. His voice was rebellious, angry even. "Your attitude, like you could run away at any moment, surprises me even more than the murders themselves."

"But I also bear responsibility for the other members of the crew."

"You think the others would want you to stop the excavation?"

"Murat does."

"He's still a kid. Bernd, Kemal, Elif, even Teoman, they're all proud to be working on this excavation. Don't you see the excitement on their faces every time we uncover another tablet?"

"Actually, you're right. We found three more tablets today. Some are broken, but they're not in such bad shape that they can't be deciphered."

"Now *that's* exactly what I like to hear. With a little luck, we'll soon have uncovered all of Patasana's tablets." He paused, and then smiling at Esra, continued.

"You've gone and gotten all messed up in these problems that have nothing to do with us. These problems were here before we came, and they'll be here after we've left, too. But you can't find Patasana's tablets just anywhere. If we can uncover them, the whole world will get to know Patasana and have the chance to read the earliest known non-official documents ever written. As the director of this excavation, you're wrapped up in murder cases, worrying about issues that are the responsibility of the gendarme, rather than thinking about how you're going to announce this extraordinary event to the world. Don't you think it's time now that you start focussing on the excavation, and the excavation alone?"

TABLET TWELVE

When I saw Ashmunikal in that temple room, I thought the time had come. I was now going to wash my soul in that mad river, satisfy my flesh in that divine cookhouse, slake my thirst with that divine wine. But I was wrong. Love is proof, secret, cause. I understood this when I woke up in the holy bed of the goddess in the temple room and found that Ashmunikal was not with me. I searched all over the room with the nervous eyes of a lamb that's lost its mother, but she was not there. I got up and dressed my scrawny body in my elaborate clothing. I walked out, with the hope of finding her in the corridor, as if it were my right to do so, but she was not there. The music was no longer playing, and the flames in the lamps lighting the long corridor were dimly flickering and about to go out. I unabashedly stood before the doors along the corridor and listened for sounds coming from inside, but there was no sound to be heard. It was as if everyone had departed, as if there were no one else left in the temple, except for me and my attending shame. Of course there were the all-knowing, all-seeing gods as well, those beings who dictate our every move. I fearfully made my way towards the large hall. When I reached the end of the corridor, I heard the sound of whispering. This sound put me at ease a little. When I walked into the hall, which was lit with the weary light of the evening sun, I saw no one except for Valvaziti and another priest whom he was scolding. "What if I ask Valvaziti about

Ashmunikal ..." I thought for a moment. But when I sensed the chief priest's eyes upon me, I grew afraid. Greeting him, I made my way for the exit. But just a few steps later I was stopped by Valvaziti's deep voice: "Wait, young Patasana."

I froze in my tracks. Valvaziti walked up to me. I waited, ashamed, confused, and curious as to what he was going to say. Perhaps Ashmunikal had told everybody about what happened. No, she seemed too noble to do something like that. But what if she had? What if, as soon as she left the room, she went and told the other temple prostitutes about my ineptness, my lack of manhood? I would never forgive her if she had done such a thing. The chief priest came and stood directly across from me. "You have offended the gods," he said. I was devastated by his words. So the girl that I loved, that I revered as a goddess, had cruelly derided me, had heedlessly gone and told others about my ineptitude. With these thoughts running through my head, I heard Valvaziti continue to speak:

"When you came here, you were ashamed to make love with the temple prostitutes, with these holy women. You look as if you feel better now. So it seems your worshipping has pleased you. But that does not mean that the gods forgive you. Tomorrow you are to bring a votive to the Goddess Kupaba and beseech her to forgive you. That is the only way you can achieve forgiveness."

I realized that I had falsely accused Ashmunikal. She had not revealed anything to anyone. The chief priest as well as the other temple prostitutes thought that everything had gone as it should have. While I was telling Valvaziti that I would bring the votives to the goddess first thing tomorrow, inside I was thanking Ashmunikal, and thinking that I was right, after all, to love her. In the end, I, too, had found the beloved of my heart. But who was Ashmunikal really? For a moment, I lost control of myself yet again and felt the desire to pose this question to the chief priest. I was just getting ready to ask when the young priest approached us and told Valvaziti that the temple wardens had arrived. And so I postponed asking him about Ashmunikal and bid farewell. After all, I was going to be coming back to the temple the following day to bring the valuable votives. That way, the chief priest would also be more accepting of me. If the chief priest didn't tell me who Ashmunikal was, I would find a way myself, and I would marry her. Who would they give the girl's hand in marriage to, if not to the son of the king's right hand man, the future palace scribe? As I approached the temple door with these thoughts running through my head, a horrible thought suddenly weighed heavy on my heart, darkening it like an ominous cloud on the horizon. What if I still couldn't make love to Ashmunikal, even after I had married her? What if I had completely lost my manhood? I continued to struggle with this inauspicious thought as I descended the stairs. "If that were the case, my manhood would not awaken in my own room, my own bed," I said, soothing myself. I should discard the bad thoughts in my mind; I had gotten too excited, and that's why my manhood had failed me. That was all. My mind told me that this was the case, but I still could not shake off the uneasy feeling that I felt inside. What if I failed again? No, no, I wouldn't. In a room belonging to us, just the two of us, everything would be different, and I would prove my manhood. Tomorrow, yes, tomorrow I would find out who Ashmunikal was, where she lived, and to what lineage she belonged. How could I have known that this information would prove to be my calamity? If I had been able to tell on that day that this love would usher forth such a huge disaster, and the ruin of the people of this city; if I had been able to understand that my inability to make love to her was a sign from the gods, perhaps I never would have sought Ashmunikal out again... Or would I? Would I really have refrained from seeking her out? I don't know. The desire I felt for her was so intense, so torrid, that even with full knowledge of the impending disasters, perhaps I would have sought her out, and found her, nevertheless. I would not have hesitated to commit with her those great sins that would unsettle the gods so, and to have tossed, with my very own hands, everyone—from moon-faced babies and comely women, to the hunchbacked elderly and daring warriors—into the fire, and lived arm-in-arm with death.

CHAPTER THIRTEEN

How can you enjoy your successes when the days have been darkened by news of death? When two people have been killed virtually in your midst, just one day apart, how can you possibly remain impervious to the impact of such tragedy? These were the thoughts running through Esra's head as she lay on her bed, having withdrawn to her room immediately after dinner. She had opened the window all the way, and a warm breeze carrying the languid scent of dried grass and flowers scorched by the sun drifted into her room. But Esra was in no state to appreciate the aroma. She wiped off the beads of sweat that had gathered on her brow with the back of her hand and rolled over onto her side in sheer frustration. A bit of sleep would do her a world of good, but no, her mind was preoccupied with the murders yet again, allowing her no rest. Yet Timothy's words before dinner, the relatively calm reaction of the other excavation team members to the news of Reshat Agha's murder, and the fact that none of them except for Murat and Kemal thought that the incident had anything to do with the excavation had put her worries and her mind to rest. In fact, she had begun to blame herself, feeling ashamed that she had panicked so and had even considered stopping the excavation. But once she was alone in her room, the suspicions began to eat away at her yet again, and so she had begun to obsess all over again, thinking that there must be some meaning behind these two successive murders. Yes, perhaps the murders didn't have anything to do with the excavation, but certainly the acts themselves were connected. Really though, there were virtually no similarities between the two incidents to speak of. Hadji Settar and Reshat Agha's paths had never once crossed. And the men had absolutely nothing in common. Hadji Settar was as peaceful, trustworthy, and respectable as Reshat Agha was cruel, untrustworthy, and boorish. Nor did the ways in which the two were killed bear any similarities to one another whatsoever. The only aspect that the two murders shared was that both were shrouded in mystery, a characteristic rarely seen in this region. Most of the murders that had been committed on these lands over thousands of years had been carried out according to a vengeance mentality calling for "an eye for an eye," and therefore they had been carried out in the open. Since murder was considered a means to salvage one's honor or teach a potential enemy a lesson, the greater the number of people who heard about the murder, or even better, the more people who witnessed it, the better. The farther word of the incident carried, the greater the respect gained by the tribe or family that carried it out, and the more they were feared, for they had restored their sullied honor with their own intrepidness. The fact that the person who committed the murder could be imprisoned for many long years or be killed in return by the enemy was of little consequence compared to the social respect that would be gained. Yet the murders of both Hadji Settar and Reshat Agha were shrouded in mystery. Rather than spelling out the reasons behind the murders for, the murderer had simply vanished. And this was precisely the point that perplexed Esra and made her suspect that the murders somehow had to do with the excavation. "Perhaps the real problem here is me," she mumbled as she flopped over yet again in frustration in her damp bed; maybe, just maybe the murders have nothing to do with the excavation, and nothing to do with one another. Perhaps all of her speculation was groundless. But then again, this uneasiness had not emerged out of nowhere. After all, she had received threatening phone calls warning her to stay away from the Black Tomb, although they had ceased recently, and the excavation site had been plundered. Captain Eshref kept saying that the separatists were on the lookout for an opportunity to pounce; and most importantly, two people had been murdered. As the person responsible for the excavation, she was concerned about the safety of her friends, and what could be more natural than that? If all of this hadn't happened, of course she would be devoting all of her attention to the Patasana tablets, rather than wearing herself out brooding over a couple of murders. Or would she? She asked herself this question as if uncertain whether or not she could truly trust herself to give an honest answer. "Honestly, wouldn't you be worried?" she mumbled. She recalled the feeling of trepidation that overcame her when she heard the good news that she had been appointed head of the excavation. Yet she had been waiting for this opportunity for years. After all, on all of the excavations she had participated in, she had never hesitated to assume responsibility, and had always found herself thinking for all of the other excavation team members as well. And now the opportunity she had been waiting for had finally arrived. But she was afraid. She was no more likely to be unsuccessful than any other excavation director. She was knowledgeable, and more importantly, she had plenty of experience, but still she was afraid of taking on this excavation, the first to be carried out under her own leadership. And so she called up her father. At first, Salim Bey was taken back on hearing his daughter's hesitant voice,, thinking that something bad had happened, but then he sounded jubilant on hearing the good news. "That's my girl," he said. "Always strong, always knowing what she wants, always determined. You've always done me proud. We have to celebrate this. Tomorrow we're going out to dinner. To the Bosphorus, for fish." Esra had not called her father for this kind of response. She had wanted to tell him that she was afraid, and that she needed his help. But she was too embarrassed to explain her problem after he had lavished so much praise upon her, and so she made do by simply thanking him. But then after hanging up to the phone, she felt the tears begin to flow. She had experienced the same feeling when her father had fallen in love with Nilgün. Salim Bey wanted to move out. And though

Esra's mother, unable to bring herself to separate from the man with whom she had shared so many years, did refrain from bluntly telling Salim Bey that she just couldn't let him go, she didn't resist stirring up as much trouble and drawing the process out as much as possible. Although Esra wanted her father to stay just as much as her mother did, perhaps even more so, she did her best not to reveal her sentiments regarding the matter. In fact, she actively supported her father and criticized her mother. She had always had a good relationship with her father; they had gotten on fabulously throughout her childhood and had become more like buddies once she hit puberty. Her father was handsome, wise, tolerant, and had a fine sense of humor. He bore nothing like her mother's constant delusions, anxieties, or worries. Although her mother sometimes accused him of being irresponsible, Esra realized that her father simply approached life in an entirely different manner. To Esra, her father was nothing less than a master of life. They'd talk philosophy for hours, and then don their red and yellow scarves and head off for a Galatasaray match, or to the cinema. No, he hadn't treated her like a son, but neither had he treated her in the way girls were accustomed to being treated by their fathers. It was her mother who was so intent upon being conventional when it came to raising their daughter. When she was together with her father, Esra felt more mature, more developed than others, and this difference made her happy. And that's why, even though she was distraught to hear that he would be moving out of the house, Esra chose to support her father when he fell in love with someone else. She was not like other girls, not like her friends. Although she felt very angry with her father on the inside, on the outside she told her mother to be more reasonable, and not to make the process any more trying than necessary. In the name of being mature, she met and behaved nicely towards Nilgün, even though she was actually madly jealous of this woman who was only seven years older than herself, because she was taking her father away from her. And in response to her maturity, her father sang her praises as always, constantly repeating his refrain about how special his daughter was. "Esra was different. She was smart, logical, mature, skilled, enterprising, and had complete confidence in herself."

"Was I really so self-confident? Maybe I've actually lacked self-confidence since the very beginning," she muttered. "I just appeared that way because my father wanted me to. I was trying to be that way. Just so my father would love me, be fond of me, value me. So didn't my father realize this? Or when he told me, 'You're putting yourself in the center of the world,' maybe he was actually trying to point out my lack of self-confidence? Really, could that be it? Could it be that it's my *lack* of self-confidence that underlies my aggressiveness, my urge to intervene? Maybe my constant suspicion, my effort to take everything under my own control stems from my father's leaving us. It's the only way that I can feel safe. No, now I'm getting carried away; not only that, I'm doing myself an injustice. The problems we encounter on the excavation are certainly worrisome. Anybody in my place would be upset, concerned... Maybe Bernd wouldn't be worried. There isn't a bad event that could excite those spine-chilling, steely blue eyes of his. Oh c'mon, I can imagine just how cold-blooded he'd be if his wife Vartuhi were on the excavation..."

A now fully agitated Esra sat up in bed. There wasn't much use in racking her brains with such meaningless thoughts. There was work to be done, and it was the work that she should be concentrating upon. Her eyes drifted to the telephone lying next to the pack of cigarettes on the bed stand. She picked it up and dialed the number of the gendarme police station. The soldier who answered the phone recognized her voice immediately, and got excited. Could it be that the soldiers had an inkling that something was going on between her and the captain? "Even if they haven't actually sensed it, it hasn't taken their little womanless community long at all to decide that we're a good match," she thought, blushing. "Would you put me through to the Captain?" she said to the soldier on the other end of the line.

"Right away, sir."

She found the soldier's slip of the tongue amusing. It was only a few short moments before she heard the Captain's voice.

"Hi Esra..."

"Hi Eshref. How are you?"

"I'm fine," said the Captain. Esra was surprised at the perkiness in his voice. "How are you?"

"I'm a little worried. They've killed Reshat Türkoghlu. I'm beginning to think that we really aren't safe here."

"Don't worry, everything's going just fine."

The Captain's self-assured tone only heightened Esra's sense of surprise.

"What do you mean everything's going just fine! There've been two murders in just three days!"

"Trust me, we've got the situation under control."

Now Esra's surprise turned into curiosity.

"So it seems there have been some new developments," she said, hoping that the Captain would volunteer an explanation.

"Yes, we just need to be a little patient."

"Being patient's easy, but God forbid something should happen to us."

"Trust me. Nobody's going to be able to hurt you now."

"What, you mean to say you've caught the murderer or something?"

"Please, I beg you, don't ask me any questions," he said, clearly growing uneasy. "But I promise you that you won't have anything to worry about after tomorrow."

By this point it was clear to Esra that she wasn't going to be able to drag any more information out of the Captain.

"I hope so," she said, her voice reflecting her indecision about whether to believe him or not.

"You will be. Bye for now, talk to you tomorrow."

"Bye," said Esra, but then added before hanging up.

"Be careful."

"Don't worry, by now I'm quite impervious to any more pain."

"What did he mean by that?" Esra thought. She hadn't really meant anything with her "Be careful". But the Captain was serious. He had spoken like someone about to go into battle. "I think they really have found the killer," Esra thought to herself merrily. That would mean the end of all her worries. She felt an overwhelming desire to tell her friends the news. But after giving it a few moments thought, she decided against it. What if he's wrong, or what if they end up empty-handed, like when they caught Shehmuz? It was best to not say anything to anyone. If the Captain turned out to be right, he'd be telling everyone himself the next day anyway, and if he turned out to be wrong, he wouldn't have gotten everyone's hopes up for no reason.

At that moment there was a knock on her door. She quickly gathered herself together and stood up. Standing at the door was lanky Kemal.

"Do you have a moment?"

"Come in," she said. She knew as soon as she saw him why he was here.

Kemal entered her room, heading for the table in the center, his shoulders sagging and his feet dragging.

"What am I going to do with this girl?" he said as he took a seat in one of the empty chairs.

"Which girl?"

Kemal gave Esra a reproachful look.

"I can leave now if you don't want to listen," he said.

"I'm sorry," she said, walking over to stand next to her friend. "I wasn't trying to hurt you. But you really are blowing things out of proportion."

"Blowing things out of proportion? But I'm in love with her. She's everything to me..."

"This fella's really lost it," Esra thought as she sat down in the chair next to Kemal's.

"Then you should be more understanding towards her," said Esra, now sounding a little harsh. "You can't win her affections by suffocating her."

"So you think I suffocate her?"

"You always have your eye on her, and you're constantly sticking your nose in her business."

"Because I love her."

"Too much love can also stifle a person. Elif has her own desires, her own feelings, just like everyone does. She can't live according to your wishes. Just leave her be. Let her get to know herself. Respect her wishes."

Kemal shook his head in disappointment. "Nobody has ever respected her as much as I do. But she's never shown me any respect, never considered my wishes."

Kemal raised his head, and Esra felt a sense of relief once she saw that he wasn't crying.

"You're such a good friend," he said gratefully. "And such a strong person, too. I wish I could be like you."

A bitter smile formed on Esra's lips.

"You're wrong, I'm not as a strong as I look. If I went through what you're going through right now, I'd be out of sorts myself."

"But even if you were for a while, you'd know how to pull yourself right back together, get right back on your feet. I'm not like you."

"People have the wrong idea about me," thought Esra. She fooled them, acting all brave, decisive, and wise. She wasn't the person they thought she was. But then, who was she, really? A coward lacking in self-confidence? She was confused now. When she raised her head, she found Kemal's light brown eyes on her . She gave Kemal a friendly shove, messing up his light brown hair.

"Don't get all worked up. All of this will pass."

"I doubt it. I can feel it, this is going to end badly, and I'm going to lose Elif. Maybe I already have."

"That's what you think right now, but we're going through some rough times here, and that's having a negative impact upon your mood, too." She paused, and then added hopefully, "Trust me, soon you'll be having happier thoughts," hoping, too, that the murderer would be caught the following day.

TABLET THIRTEEN

As I returned home from the temple, I tried to suppress my pessimism and think good, hopeful thoughts. The next day I would take votives to the temple and track down Ashmunikal.

I eagerly awaited my father's return home. As soon as he arrived, I went and stood before him. I told him that I had seen the Goddess Kupaba in my dreams and that she had summoned me to the temple. My father Araras looked me up and down, and then murmured, "The gods desire a gift."

Thank the Storm God, my father had believed my words.

"If the Goddess Kupaba desires a gift, then we must present her with the most valuable of our gifts," he added.

When I woke up the following morning, a jar of the finest wine, well baked white bread, a crock of honey, and a fattened lamb awaited me. My father had interpreted the dream that I had described to him as a sign having to do with my destiny. He was afraid of angering the gods and incurring their wrath towards me. And so he had acted with great generosity. In short, my lie had done the trick. It would have been difficult not to win Valvaziti over with these gifts. I had the gifts that I would be presenting to the gods loaded onto a mule driven wagon and set off for the temple, taking two of our slaves with me. When I reached the temple, I entered the large room where votive offerings were received. I had my name written onto the tablets used for record keeping and handed the gifts over to the officials on duty. I sent the slaves home with the mule wagon and headed upstairs to see Valvaziti. After entering the hall and paying my respects to the gods, I went into the holy chamber of the chief priest. Valvaziti smiled sweetly upon seeing me.

"Young Patasana, grandson of the wise Mitannuva, son of the noble Araras, you have done well to come to the temple as your first task of the morning. In this way you have won the love and trust of the gods," he said "by showing them that you fear and revere them. I hope you have not forgotten to bring the Goddess Kupaba gifts as well."

At that I handed him the tablets that I had received from the officials, saying, "I did not forget, great chief priest."

Valvaziti feigned disinterest, taking a quick glance at the tablets listing the gifts that I had brought, and then said, "The gods will forgive you, Patasana. But be certain not to make the same mistake again, not to commit the same sin."

"The gods are almighty, they are forgiving," I said in response. "They are our lords. I am a young, inexperienced, ignorant young man. I promise that I shall not commit the same sin again, great Valvaziti."

Valvaziti was pleased with my speech. He walked up to me and touched me on the head.

"It bodes well for you, young Patasana," he said. "If you bow down before the gods like this, approach them like this, please them with valuable gifts, then they will protect you and please you in return."

These fine words of Valvaziti's gave me courage. There couldn't be a better time to ask about Ashmunikal.

"Sir," I said, throwing myself at his feet. "My great lord, please forgive me, but I have a request of you. Sir, when I was here yesterday in this temple performing the holy rites, I met the woman with whom I would unite for life. It was you, my great lord, the official of the gods here on earth, who made our encounter possible. We became one for the gods. I would like to get to know that woman and take her as my spouse, if you and the gods grant me permission to do as such."

Valvaziti took hold of my hand and lifted me to my feet. And that's when I noticed the disconsolate look that appeared on the old priest's face.

"Oh my poor boy, it is best that we pretend you never asked me this question, that we never had this conversation."

Nevertheless, even upon hearing this response, I insisted on an answer.

"Please oh please my great lord, do not send me away like this. I entreat you, tell me what has happened.

Valvaziti approached me once again, grabbing me firmly by the shoulders.

"Oh young Patasana, you've fallen for the most impossible of women. She now belongs to King Pisiris."

Upon hearing Valvaziti's words, my heart began to beat with fear like that of the young shepherd who was swept away by the waters of the Euphrates the year before. Just as that shepherd sought to resist the flow, grabbing on to any scrub or brush on the wayside, so too did I make one last attempt. "But Pisiris has a queen," I mumbled.

Valvaziti shook his head hopelessly.

"Pisiris didn't take Ashmunikal as his queen. He's going to use her for a variety of services, and include her in his harem."

I had difficulty comprehending just what was transpiring.

"Alright, but then why was Ashmunikal a temple prostitute at the ceremony yesterday?"

"Because Ahmunikal didn't want Pisiris. But she also knew very well that she would not be able to resist the king's command. That's why the poor girl sought refuge with the gods. She wanted to give up her virginity to someone chosen by the gods, rather than a king whom she does not want. And that's how you two came to meet. She entered the palace this morning, as a concubine in the king's harem."

Each word that I heard was like a harsh blow hastening my demise. Poor Ashmunikal had ended up in the hands of a fumbling idiot like myself, unable to bridle his passion, and thus unable to offer her virginity to the gods. As these thoughts ran through my head, Valvaziti took advantage of my silence to continue with his warnings.

"Look, Patasana, I love you like my own son. Your grandfather Mittanuwa was a hellion, but he was my closest friend, and as for your father Araras, never in my many years have

I seen such a virtuous government official. You are of their line, of their blood. You need to extinguish the fire that Ashmunikal lit and bow down to the fate that has been ordained for you. Don't forget that our king is the representative of the gods here on earth, and their beloved. Opposing the king would mean rebelling against the gods..."

Valvaziti was right. If our king desired Ashmunikal, then this should be considered a mandate for me as well. I should obey the command and forget about my first love, Ashmunikal, she who is as noble as a goddess, as beautiful as a goddess, and as pure as a goddess, and I should endure this pain by myself, without revealing my love to anyone.

CHAPTER FOURTEEN

There was nobody with her. For a moment, Esra could not remember where she was; she felt as if she had fallen into some vast emptiness. She'd felt this way the first few days after separating from Orhan as well. For days she just couldn't get used to waking up in bed alone. Yet it was she herself who had wanted the separation. But it had been years since her divorce, so what was going on now, after so long? Frustrated, she sat up in bed. She recalled her talk with Kemal, and how she had crawled back into bed once her friend had left. She looked at the window; the soft light of the mid-afternoon sun was drifting into the room through the cheap cloth that served as a curtain. She must have slept for quite a while. And no one had come to wake her up. She was rather vexed at having dozed off for so long, for she had wanted to review her excavation notes. With a yawn she got up from bed. She looked at her face in the small mirror hanging on the wall; she looked tired, and the clumps of hair that stuck to her forehead, glued with sweat, made her look particularly disheveled. She didn't like what she saw in the mirror, but she didn't worry about it, and after using her hand to straighten out her hair a bit, she headed out.

Esra's nose was greeted by the delicious whiff of stuffed eggplant emerging from the room that Halaf, already busy preparing the evening meal, used as the kitchen. In response to a special request from everyone, tonight Halaf would be serving stuffed eggplant and pilaf, rather than the local cuisine. And on the side, there would be chopped cucumber in yoghurt with an abundant sprinkling of spearmint on top, and a bit of garlic mixed in.

Afraid of being trapped into conversation by the talkative cook, Esra let out a short "More power to your elbow" and then headed for the classroom where Teoman and the other men were staying. She ran into Bernd as she went through the school door. "I was just on my way to see you," said the German smilingly. "Herr Krencker called a little while ago. They want to hold the press conference next Wednesday. He's asking if that's a good day for you, too."

Esra panicked.

"Wednesday? So soon?"

"There are four days yet until Wednesday," said the German, clearly expressing his own approval of this particular date.

"I don't know," said Esra. She was afraid of being caught unprepared. "Let's talk with the others, too."

"Okay, let's ask them too, but there's something else you should know."

Fearing yet another problem to be tackled, Esra looked at Bernd's face.

"What's that?"

"Let's take a walk and chat a little, if you have the time."

"I was going to have a look in the computer room. I didn't stop by in the afternoon."

"They've gone swimming. Tim's the only one there. He's in his room deciphering the tablets, as promised."

"Have Elif and Kemal gone with them too?"

"Yep, they all went."

Esra was pleased by this news, and smiled spontaneously.

"Perhaps you want to go swimming as well?" Bernd asked politely.

For a brief moment Esra thought, "Why not?" but then changed her mind.

"No, forget it, I'm in no condition to take a dip right now. Let me just say hi to Tim and then we can go."

They entered the American's room together. Tim was making clean copies of his tablet translations. He stood up at once, bade them come in, and then turned to face Esra:

"I'm doing my best to have the tablets ready on time, like I promised."

"Is there any new information?"

"No, no new information, but it's definitely true that these are the earliest non-official historical documents ever to be uncovered. Each word, each line that I translate proves this to be true."

"Excellent," mumbled Esra.

"Why don't you have a seat?"

"We don't want to disturb you. We just stopped by, no special reason. Professor Krencker called from the German Institute. They're asking if we want to hold the press conference on Wednesday."

Bernd pulled a long face. He was upset that Esra had told Timothy about the conference without first hearing what he had to say.

"Fine with me," said Timothy.

Esra, thinking that the American would find the date to be too premature, was rather taken aback by his reply.

"It seems a little early to me."

"We've got four long days until then," said Timothy, blatantly expressing that he did not agree with Esra on this point. "Didn't we say we'd do it next week anyway?"

"Yes, we did," said Bernd, jumping into the conversation, pleased by Timothy's words. "It's the institute that carries the bulk of the responsibility, and they say they're ready."

"Anyway," said Esra as she made her way to the door, "we'll discuss it at the meeting this evening. Let's leave you alone now so you can get back to your work."

"Okay, see you at dinner then," said Timothy as he saw them out.

After leaving the school, they didn't go to the arbor, but walked instead along the poplar-lined road leading to the next village. The heat of the day had just begun to give way to the cool of the evening hours.

"You know," said Bernd, kicking off the conversation. "The institute's Istanbul branch had a hard time getting funding for the excavation. The folks back in Germany weren't very hopeful that any important finds would be uncovered at this site, seeing as it's already been excavated several times. And so there was a general tendency to divert resources to more important excavations."

Esra got the impression from the course of the conversation that the German was looking to pat his own back, and so she was quick to cut him off. "But in the end they did provide funding."

"They did, but thanks to Herr Krencker. If he hadn't gone to such lengths to convince them, we wouldn't have gotten a Pfennig out of them."

Esra shook her head in agreement.

"You're right. We are greatly indebted to Herr Krencker."

"He helped us. And so we should help him."

Esra paused for a moment and looked up at her German colleague, who stood at least 15 centimeters taller than herself.

"The debate at the institute headquarters continues," Bernd explained. "There are some who think too much money has been invested in this excavation. They're thinking of bringing this up again at the next meeting fifteen days from now."

Esra was pleased that the conversation was taking a course other than the one she had assumed it would.

"I get it. That's why the professor wants to hold this conference as soon as possible, so that he can shut the opposition up."

"Yes, that's exactly what I'm getting at."

"In that case, we've no other choice but to hold the press conference on Wednesday."

"That's right, we don't."

"Well then, it's agreed. Nobody wants to see our funding cut off."

"But," Bernd began, giving Esra a meek look, "it would be better if the excavation team members didn't know about this division within the institute."

"Don't you worry one bit," said Esra, giving Bernd a wink. "Nobody will find out about it. But we need to start getting ready for the press conference right away."

"I don't think the preparations will take much time. Timothy knows this territory very well. He'll guide us through it."

"You're right, Timothy's got a lot of work to shoulder. Let's address that, too, at the meeting this evening."

They walked along the road in the shade of the poplars until they could see the village mosque.

"Let's go back if you like," said Esra, seeing that they were getting close to the village. "Maybe the youngsters are back now."

Bernd offered no resistance, and so they turned around and headed back. There was another period of silence between them. The German didn't seem to mind, as he sprung down the path on the tips of his toes, but the silence disturbed Esra.

"I want to ask you something," she said. She'd been curious about the matter ever since she'd seen Bernd writing his letter the day before. Actually, she hesitated for a moment, wondering if she would be sticking her nose into his private life by asking, but then, knowing full well that Bernd enjoyed talking about his wife, she decided that it would be better to lighten the atmosphere with some chit-chat rather than continue walking in silence like this.

"Why do you write letters when you could talk to your wife on the phone?"

A hint of a blush spread over Bernd's face, and it did not escape Esra's attention.

"I'm sorry," she said politely. "You don't have to answer if you don't want to. I'm just curious, is all."

"No reason why I shouldn't answer," said Bernd. There was no sign on his face to indicate that he was offended. "Actually, we do speak on the phone, too. But I can express what I want to say better in letters, and Vartuhi likes it like that as well."

"Does she write to you, too?"

"Unfortunately, no. She hates writing. So she calls whenever she gets a letter from me."

Esra began to laugh.

"And that's when you talk on the telephone?"

Bernd joined in her laughter.

"I mean, yeah, we talk on the phone when she calls, but our talks on the phone are, how do you say it, they're..."

"Cold?"

"Yes, cold... I can't say what I want to... Maybe the fault lies with me, other people can have perfectly fine conversations on the telephone."

"I don't think there's any fault in that. I'd want the man I love to write me letters, too. But there are so few loves like yours. Your wife's a lucky woman."

Bernd's blush took on a more obvious shade of red.

"My wife says so, too. But I'm the one who's lucky."

He turned and looked at his colleague, and then excitedly continued talking, as if he were afraid that she didn't believe him.

"Her beauty struck me the very first time I saw her, sitting in the garden at Heidelberg University. She was truly beautiful, with her curly black hair, dark skin, and shiny black eyes, but I didn't know that she was the person I was looking for."

"The person you were looking for?"

"You know how they say, 'one seeks someone similar to one's self,' like that. I mean, someone you can agree with on most things, someone whose presence makes you feel at peace, someone you know you'll love, unwaveringly, forever."

"Does such a thing truly exist?" Esra wondered to herself.

"As it turned out, for me, Vartuhi was that person," the German continued. "I mean, my other half."

"Is your wife an archaeologist too?"

"Yes, we studied at the same university. She'd come from France. Like I said, at first, I was attracted to her looks, as a beautiful, dark girl. But then once I got to know her, I realized that I couldn't live without her."

Esra gazed at Bernd with unbelieving eyes.

"How long have you known each other?" she asked. And now she wasn't asking out of small talk, but out of genuine curiosity.

"Seven years," the German said. His eyes shone brightly, as if he were recalling a sweet memory. "And we've been married for three."

"Forgive my boldness in asking this, but seven years is a long time; haven't you ever felt bored of her?"

"No, absolutely not," said Bernd, shaking his head. "It's impossible for me to get bored when I'm with her."

"Maybe because you're apart so often, off on excavations."

"This is the first time we've been apart. We always go to excavations together."

Esra looked her colleague over in awe.

"The two of you are truly from a breed of extinct lovers. I started getting bored during the second year of my marriage."

"Then you didn't find the right person."

"To tell you the truth, I really don't think there is such a thing. I was in love with Orhan, I mean, my former husband. But with time, the magic of love wears away."

She paused. She was about to say, "Perhaps I'm just not ready for marriage," but then changed her mind. When she told him that she wanted a divorce, Orhan had accused her of being irresponsible and immature, saying that the reason for this was that she followed in her father's footsteps. Orhan's accusatory remarks about Esra's father only sparked another fierce argument between the two. They didn't speak to one another for days, but in a way, that was good, because it helped Orhan get used to the idea of divorce. Orhan was like Bernd. He used to say, "I feel complete when I'm with you" or "I feel like half a person without you." She had learned about the roots of this thought from her father. In his work The Banquet, based upon a talk given by Aristophanes, Plato tells about how a species of humans was created in the form of a being called Androgynos, with four arms, four legs, and two heads, and how Zeus, jealous of this perfect creature, had divided them, and that that was the reason why people spent their entire lives seeking out their other halves. It didn't matter who spoke of this kind of love, whether it was important thinkers like Socrates and Plato, or faithful lovers like Orhan and Bernd, Esra just didn't get it. How could someone possibly find him- or herself in another? Or limit "finding oneself" to just a person? What about other spheres of life, archaeology, friends, family...? The possibilities of relationships in this world, the great variety available to people to realize their greatest potential... They were speaking of two beings uniting to complete a whole, a perfect harmony. And yes, this could happen at certain moments; you could experience the same feelings with another, feel the same joy, the same sorrow, the same excitement in your heart while making love, thinking, discussing, working, listening to music, but the persistence of this feeling would be possible only through some kind of miracle or by two people successfully fooling themselves into believing it to be true. Always being in harmony means nothing other than destroying the beauty of that harmony, emptying it of all meaning. For Esra, what Bernd and Orhan described as "long term harmony" meant endless, boring minutes together, unceasing repetition, each falling into the same mode of thought and action as the other.

Contrary to what Orhan thought, Esra did not share her father's opinion in this regard. Her father was saying that he was in love with Nilgün, but once upon a time he had had the same feelings for Esra's mother. The love that he felt for Nilgün would one day disappear, just like his passion for Esra's mother had withered away over time. Was it really necessary for him to leave his wife, whom he may not have been in love with any longer, but whom he still respected, and moreover with whom he could still get along, and the daughter that he claimed to love so greatly, for a passing sentiment like this? And as it turned out, Esra saw that she had been right. The lover that he had praised to high heaven for their first few years together with time had turned into an object of constant derision. Although she knew from the start that things would end this way, Esra had refrained from telling her father this. And she didn't now either.

"Seems like you're somewhere else," said Bernd. "What are you thinking about?"

"That I'm not a complete person," said Esra. She had a mocking smile on her face. "I don't think I have the ability to love someone for a long time. I'm unable to stay that connected to someone."

As she said this, she expected Bernd to give a polite response, like, "Oh no dear, how could you possibly think that?" but Bernd showed no hesitation in quickly revealing his true thoughts on the subject.

"I can't say whether you're an incomplete person or not, but it's certain that you're an unlucky one, because you've been unable to find true love."

"And why should I be considered unlucky?" Esra thought to herself. Maybe it was actually they who were the unlucky ones. Theirs seemed a severely limiting choice, one that was far from true happiness, ridden with all of these imposed forbidden acts. Where was the beauty in placing a lover in the center of your life, and then having him wreak havoc with your life when he left, or even like Kemal did to Elif, making life a prison for the other? She didn't share these thoughts with Bernd though.

Instead, she merely responded, "What can I do, this is the way God made me."

"You'll change, too, once you've found the right person."

And now this dude had the nerve to try and console her!

"Okay then," said Esra, who had decided to turn their little conversation into a game. "So how much do you love your wife?"

"A lot, so much that I would do anything for her."

Bernd's resolute expression as he offered up this childish assertion made Esra laugh.

"What you're saying is so broad that it's meaningless. For example, what if she told you to give up your career?"

"She wouldn't do that."

"Let's say she did."

"She would never ask that of me, but if she did, then I would give up my career. There's nothing I wouldn't do for her."

"Really?"

"Of course! Once I took part in an Armenian genocide protest for her. I'm scared to death of the police, but when the police attacked three women, Vartuhi among them, I pounced on them good. I got roughed up pretty badly myself, was taken into the police station, and almost got kicked out of school. But I never regretted having done it, because it made me a hero in Vartuhi's eyes. She began to love me even more after that day."

Seeing the resolute expression in Bernd's blue eyes, Esra realized that he was telling the truth. But she couldn't help but express her own reservations about the matter.

"Being the object of such love is wonderful, but it's also frightening."

"What's frightening about it?"

"What if Vartuhi decides to leave you one day?"

"She won't. She'll keep on loving me as long as I love her."

"C'mon now. Even Siamese twins aren't that synchronic."

"This doesn't have anything to do with physical harmony, it has to do with the soul."

"Probably so," said Esra, staring at him blankly. "But I have to admit that I just can't understand it."

Bernd looked his colleague over curiously.

"That's really quite surprising. Women don't generally think like you. Love, in the romantic sense, is one of the few magical words in their lives."

"You're right, love is very important for women. And some truly believe in it. But they end up deriving more pain than pleasure from it, and some use it to push a man around at their will... Anyway, that's another topic... Actually, I should tell you that your attitude in this regard surprised me as well."

"Why?"

"I never would have expected such a grand love story from the Germans," said Esra, now making light of the matter. "Are you sure you don't have a French grandfather or something? Or maybe Latin? Or maybe some of your relatives were amongst the migrants to Brazil?"

Bernd joined her in her laughter.

"You obviously haven't read Goethe's The Sorrows of Young Werther," he said, jokingly yet a bit reproachfully. "Goethe was an incurable lover, too. For him, love is a mad river that cleanses and purifies the soul."

TABLET FOURTEEN

Having lost Ashmunikal, my very first love, the moment I had found her, I wandered aimlessly. The temple was behind me, Valvaziti's words were behind me, and now Ashmunikal, too, should be behind me. I would have to erase her image, her scent, her taste, and the sound of her voice from my mind and forget all about her.

I entered the marketplace and drifting amongst the dealers, slaves, and shoppers like a veritable ghost I made my way to the Messengers Wall, and from there to the Water Gate. I exited the gate and walked down to the Euphrates. The water of the old river was muddy, and flowed in the color of blood. I walked along the river. It was as if my feet were advancing of their own accord, as if they were carrying my body there along the river. And I continued to be carried along in this manner until I reached the spot across from the small island where my grandfather Mitannuwa had hidden for three days and three nights following the death of his wife Tunnawi. Then I fell onto my knees across from the tiny island and began to weep. I had been taught that it was improper for a man to cry. But my pain and my rage were so great that I did not care, and great sobs escaped my throat. I was angry at the gods, I was angry at the king, I was angry at Ashmunikal though she was at no fault, and most of all, I was angry at myself. I wept until I had regained myself, until I had purged myself of my rage, until the dark sorrow in my heart had dissipated. At one point I found myself staring at the small island. It was just standing there in the center of the river, calling me to distance myself from my own destiny, like the ark that rescued the Sumerian Ur-Napishti with his families and animals during the Great Flood, while all the other living creatures were doomed to death. Perhaps I, like my grandfather, should have run away to live on that island for a few days. But then the secret of my love would be revealed. Only the God Teshub knew what my end would have been should the cruel King Pisiris have learned that I was in love with Ashmunikal, his own young beloved. As I lamented the lover I had lost, so too did I fear the king's revenge should he learn of it. How I longed for my grandfather Mitannuwa to be at my side at that moment. Certainly he would have told me what to do and given me courage. Yet I, the foolish, cowardly, pathetic lover Patasana, could do nothing but silently weep and soothe the storm in my heart with my tears. This dangerous love would remain a secret between me and the chief priest. I trusted him; he would never reveal my secret to the king. He never failed to show respect during the ceremonies, but I did not think that he was especially fond of the king. And as for Ashmunikal, I was certain that by then she had already completely forgotten me, being the utterly incompetent man that I was. I sat on the shore of the Euphrates until night fell, and the wolves and the birds all returned to their nests, and then after wiping the tears from my eyes, I headed back to the city.

The dim light of the lanterns provided cover for my swollen eyes, and so my mother did not notice the state I was in. As for my father, the ominous clouds descending upon him blinded him so that he could not see the tip of his nose, let alone the sorrow of his young son.

CHAPTER FIFTEEN

It was already dark as the excavation crew sat down for dinner with the monotonous music of crickets playing in the background.

"Ah yes, the meal I've been looking forward to for days," said Teoman. He hungrily gobbled up the eggplant stuffed with ground beef as he talked. "I love this dish."

Murat, the effects of the tongue-lashing he'd received from Esra that morning now hazy in his mind, was the first one to start heckling Teoman.

"C'mon now, Teoman, just the other day you were saying that *chılbır* was your favorite dish."

Teoman, a native of Izmir, was quick with his rebuttal, "Do not even go there, dude." Murat never knew when to stop, and his teasing sometimes got on Teoman's nerves. "I love *chılbır*, too, but this belongs in a different category altogether. Do you know what I fear more than anything else? That the doctors will put me on an eggplant free diet when I get old."

"In America, eggplant's horse fodder." This time it was Timothy who tried to rattle the other archaeologist's cage.

But it was Halaf, who was just approaching the table with a pot of pilaf in hand, who responded to the American's words.

"Oh no, c'mon now, Tim," he said. "Eggplant is the king of vegetables. I really don't think it befits you to go putting it down like that. Where I come from, we make fifteen different eggplant dishes."

Murat didn't believe the cook.

"Now if that isn't a bunch of quack, Halaf! Like you could really make fifteen different dishes using eggplant."

"Why should I make something like that up..." Halaf responded as he placed the pot of pilaf on the table. He then placed his hands on his hips and looked at Murat. "If you don't believe me, I'll name them all, and you can count: fried eggplant, *karnıyarık*, eggplant kabob, stuffed eggplant, chopped eggplant, *Alinazik*, baba ghanoush, *mıcırık ashı*, *türlü*, *imambayıldı*, *sakız* kabob, pickled eggplant, eggplant jam, and Jewish guest. Does that add up to fifteen?"

"It does, but I don't really get that 'Jewish guest' thing."

"What's there not to get. It's a dish of course."

Teoman looked at the cook in disbelief.

"No offense, Halaf," he said, "but this Jewish guest doesn't sound very convincing to me either."

"Well if you don't believe me, let me just tell you the recipe," he said, and began doing just that.

"First you chop the eggplant up. Then you brown your onions and ground beef in a pan, add tomato paste, and then the eggplant. You let it cook for while and then add cracked wheat, and cook it just like pilaf. And that's how you make Jewish guest."

Murat couldn't come up with a response to this. But Teoman, who was happily swallowing another bite of his meal, did.

"I don't know about Jewish guest, but I haven't been able to live without this *karnıyarık* since the very first time I tasted it. And when my mother makes it, it's finger licking good."

"What," retorted Halaf instantly, "so our *karnıyarık*'s not good enough for you, huh?"

"No no, bro," said Teoman before lifting his fork to place another big morsel into his mouth. "Who said anything of the sort? Yours is delicious, too."

"It really is excellent," said Kemal, who was never on good terms with the cook. "Health to your hands, Halaf."

It was the first time the young man had said anything truly nice to Halaf since the excavation began, and so Halaf just looked at him with unbelieving eyes. But he didn't forget to respond: "Bon appétit."

Kemal's reaction did not escape Esra either. Perhaps their talk had done the young man some good? It wasn't just she who thought that it had – Elif had also noticed that afternoon that Kemal wasn't behaving so crankily towards her anymore, though she had been anxious about how he would act when they set out for a swim. She figured he'd give her another of those damning looks, as if to say, "Why'd you wear that swimsuit, huh?" But Kemal was altogether different from what she had expected, joking with Murat and Teoman, and paying no attention to her at all. "Hopefully he'll leave me alone from now on," the young woman thought to herself, looking at Timothy out of the corner of her eye. Kemal noticed that Elif was looking Timothy's way, but chose to ignore it.

"How was the water?" Timothy asked.

"Wonderful," Murat responded immediately. "Well, except Teoman Abi still hasn't been able to learn how to swim the *chüt depik* yet."

It was Halaf who had taught them how to swim using what they called the *chüt depik* method. The village children of the area swam that way; as they pulled their hands towards their stomachs, they swiftly beat at the surface of the water with their feet, producing a flurry of bubbles like those that trail paddle steamers. But despite all of Halaf's efforts, the excavation team members still hadn't managed to learn the technique.

"Take a look at yourselves," said Teoman, reaching out for the pot of pilaf. "At least I can manage to go for a few meters. You and Kemal can't even stay above water."

"Didn't you try?" Bernd said, turning to Elif.

"No," said the young woman. "I'm not much of a swimmer anyway. I'd probably drown if I even tried that *chüt depik* thing."

"I don't think you should try it either," said Halaf in support, as he stood next to the table. "Girls can't do the *chüt depik*."

Seeing the team back at its old antics put Esra in a good mood.

"But I swim the *chüt depik* all right," she said, jumping into the conversation.

"Excuse me for saying so, but you're no different from Teoman Bey. You can make it a meter if you're lucky, then you start swimming the old way again."

"You're joking about it now, but Aunt Hattuch saw Esra and Elif swimming. She complained to me, saying something like, 'Teoman my boy, isn't it a sin for those girls to be going in the water naked like that?'"

"Ah man," said Esra. This bit of news lowered her spirits. "We should be more careful."

Halaf tried to console them, as always.

"Now, let's not get carried away. I think she was just trying to see how you would react. She has a television at home. She watches Brazilian soap operas every day."

"Still, it's better if we keep out of sight when we're swimming," Esra reiterated. And when Esra grew serious, everyone else at the table grew quiet. For a while, the clang of forks on plates was the only sound to be heard. Esra only resumed talking as Halaf picked up the now empty pan of *karnıyarık* to take back to the kitchen.

"There are two things we need to talk about this evening."

Her voice remained solemn. This was also a sign that the meeting had begun. Except on holidays, a meeting was held every evening, either during dinner or after, in which they assessed that day's work and spoke a little about the work to be done the following day.

"The first topic is a particularly important one," she continued, looking intently at each of her friends as they finished up their dinners. "As you know, the German Archaeological Institute is asking that we hold an international press conference to announce the discovery of the Patasana tablets. This request has received a positive response, both from the university as well as all of us working on the excavation. The press conference will be held on Wednesday."

"Isn't that rather early?"

It was Kemal who voiced the objection.

"I don't think it is," said Bernd. "After all, it's not like we're going to talk about each of the tablets that we have uncovered. We'll just show the journalists a few of the tablets and explain their significance."

Esra supported Bernd in this.

"We simply cannot postpone it. We have no other choice but to get ready for Wednesday."

The silence at the table meant that everyone approved.

"Tim, Bernd, and I will speak at the press conference," Esra continued. "Since this is going to be an international press conference, I especially want Bernd and Tim to speak. That way we'll be able to emphasize the international nature of our excavation, and we'll be able to respond to questions posed by journalists in English or German in those respective languages."

"A very apt decision," said Teoman. "Where's the press conference going to be held?"

Murat interjected with his usual hastiness.

"Let's hold it at the site, in the center of the temple."

Timothy looked at Murat and smiled understandingly.

"I know that you want to impress them, but I really don't think we should do that. My previous experiences have taught me that when you hold a press conference outdoors, the journalists quickly lose their concentration, and focus more on the ruins than the speakers themselves. So the press conference really should be held indoors."

"The location for the press conference has already been decided," said Bernd. "It will be held at the five star hotel in Antep. They have air conditioning and all that good stuff. In this heat, it's the only way to keep the journalists in the meeting hall."

"You're right, but won't the journalists want to take a tour of the site?"

"That's been considered as well. Everyone's going to take rented busses back here after the press conference. There's going to be a tour of the site so that the journalists will have an opportunity to take photos or film it."

"We have to be the perfect hosts," said Esra thoughtfully. "Would the mayor help, I wonder?"

"Sure he will," came the response from Halaf, who had just returned from the kitchen. "Mayor Edip Bey will be glad to help, if you want him to."

"Are you sure? When we first came here, he said that they were short on resources and wouldn't be able to help us out."

“That’s just because he was afraid you’d dump all the work on the municipality. He’s relaxed now that he knows you don’t intend to anything of the sort. He tells everyone about what an exemplary woman, and how Kemalist and modern you are. Besides, the press is coming, and Edip Bey certainly wouldn’t let an opportunity like that pass him by.”

Esra shook her head in surprise.

“Well then! Good, it’s set. I’ll go and have a talk with Edip Bey.”

“For real, what party is this Edip from anyway?” asked Teoman as if it had anything to do with the matter at hand.

A malicious smile spread over Halaf’s broad face.

“He doesn’t have a party. He sides with whatever party happens to come to power,” he said. “I mean, he plants his tent wherever the rain falls.”

“What’s it to us what party the man is with,” said Esra, cutting short what she found to be a meaningless discussion. “Moving on to the second topic... Today we discovered a place in the temple area that we believe to be the offering chamber. Thieves have removed statues from the area, so we want to focus the excavation over there for a while.”

“That makes sense,” said Bernd. “Maybe we’ll turn up some interesting finds there.”

However, Teoman, who thought that too little attention had been paid to the temple excavation since the discovery of the Patasana tablets, was upset at this decision.

“I think we should continue to excavate inside the temple,” he said. “Let’s not change the location of the excavation just for a couple of finds.”

Kemal didn’t understand why his friend was so insistent.

“Seeing as thieves have already uncovered important finds at that spot, why shouldn’t we focus our own attention on the area for a while?” he asked.

“You talk like someone who’s never been on an excavation before,” said Teoman. “If we start excavating the offering chamber now, God only knows how long it will last.”

“But,” said Murat quite naturally, “the temple excavation could go on for months, too.”

Murat’s words were the straw that broke the camel’s back.

"Of course you have to put in your two cents worth, too!" Teoman burst out, "The new kid on the block and you're already acting like the expert."

Murat wouldn't have gotten so upset if anyone other than Teoman had spoken these words, but Teoman was one of the team members that Murat got on with best. Not knowing what to say, he looked at Teoman with a hurt look in his eyes, and then suddenly got up from the table and quickly walked away.

"Look what you've done," Elif said and then stood up to go after Murat.

A pall of silence settled over the table. It was Esra who felt the worst about Murat's predicament. That morning she had spoken harshly with him, and now before the effects of their talk had even had a chance to wear off, Teoman had gone and stomped all over the boy's pride. There was only so much scolding one could take in a single day. Esra was just about to turn and tell Teoman that he had come on too strong with Murat when they heard Elif scream out:

"Ah, something's stung me on the foot!"

Everyone gave the young woman, who had made it only a few meters from the table, a stunned look. They were unable to see exactly what had happened. Kemal was the first to jump into action.

"What happened?" he asked, springing from the table.

Elif was holding onto her right foot and hopping in place.

"My big toe's burning, it's so hot..."

The others quickly caught up with Kemal.

"Did you see what stung you?"

"I don't know," the young woman said. "I didn't see it."

As her friends gathered around Elif leaned against Kemal and began moaning, "My foot's on fire." Halaf was the last one to catch up with the group. He began scanning the area with a flashlight and found what it was that had stung Elif—a yellow scorpion that was quickly making its escape into the grass.

"Ha, there it is!" he yelled. "Oh no, it's yellow! It's very poisonous!"

The other curious onlookers had begun to gather around the frightened scorpion as it tried to make its escape when

Halaf's heavy right foot slammed down on the creature. Once he was sure that the scorpion had been thoroughly squished, he lifted his foot to reveal its mutilated body.

"Look, look, its tail's still moving," said Halaf and then he began pounding on the scorpion again. Once he had successfully carried out the execution, he walked over to Elif with flashlight in hand. The swollen red spot on her big toe was visible even in the dim light of the lantern.

Like a veteran doctor, Halaf immediately announced what they had to do. "We need to cut off the spot where the scorpion stung her and suck the poison out."

"Don't be ridiculous," said Esra, totally deflating Halaf. "We need to get her to the hospital right away."

"Halaf's right," said Tim.

"No, we're taking her to the hospital," said Kemal in reproach. The old antagonism between the two flared up once again. "Let's get the jeep and go right now." Then he turned to Elif. "Are you able to walk, or shall I carry you to the jeep?" he asked.

Elif shook her head to indicate that she could still walk. Timothy, however, still felt uneasy about the situation.

"Shall I come with you?" he asked.

"There's no need," said Kemal, cutting him off sharply. "I'll take her."

"The head doctor at the American Hospital is a friend of mine," Timothy persisted.

"I told you there's no need," Kemal yelled.

"Don't yell," said Timothy, grabbing Kemal by the collar. With his strong hands, he lifted the young man off the ground. Kemal, not expecting such a reaction, was caught off guard. And he wasn't the only one. Everyone, even Elif, who had suddenly forgotten all about the pain she was in, was looking at Timothy. Seeing that all eyes were upon him, Timothy dropped Kemal's collar like a hot potato.

"I'm very sorry," he mumbled, "I guess I lost it there for a moment."

"Well, I'd show you what for if I didn't have to get Elif to the hospital," said Kemal angrily.

"I'm sorry," Timothy said, apologizing again, "I didn't mean to do that."

Timothy's reaction had come as a shock to Esra as well. What had come over this man, who was otherwise always so measured in his demeanor? Anyway, there was no time to ponder that now. They had to get Elif to the hospital right away. She walked up to Kemal as he and Elif made their way to the jeep.

"I'm coming with you, too. You can't handle this all by yourself."

Kemal did not object. Timothy walked up to Esra as she was making her way to the jeep.

"Take her to the American Hospital," he said in a bashful voice. "I know the head doctor, David. Give him my name and he'll help you out."

It was blatantly obvious that he deeply regretted his earlier actions. He'd probably just lost control for a moment. Esra touched Timothy's hand gratefully.

"Thank you."

First they got Elif into the jeep. With great difficulty, and some help from Esra, Elif was able to lie down on the back seat. Her face was puckered in pain, and she was holding on to her right foot with both hands. "It hurts so badly," she repeated over and over as she wailed in pain.

"We'll let you know what's happening as soon as we can," Esra yelled out to the others through the window of the jeep as Kemal started the engine.

The jeep swiftly disappeared into the darkness as the others looked on with concern.

"My foot's on fire," Elif complained. "Maybe it'll cool off if I stick it out the window."

"I don't think that's a good idea," said Esra.

"Please, it hurts so badly."

Kemal couldn't stand it any longer.

"Stick it out the window. Maybe it'll help."

"Alright, come on, stick you're foot out, like that. But not too far, God forbid it got stuck on something."

The young woman eagerly pushed her foot out of the window, as if it would relieve her of all her pain.

"That's better," she mumbled when she felt the wind.

Esra was trying to find something soft to place under Elif's foot when the silence of the night was broken by the sound of a round of gunfire.

"What the hell's that?" said Kemal.

"Gunfire," replied Esra, finally placing her arm under Elif's leg to support it. "Maybe there's a wedding or something."

"Doesn't sound much like a wedding to me," said Kemal. "Sounds more like a battle."

Esra recalled the Captain's words from earlier that day. "Don't worry, by now I'm quite impervious to any more pain." Perhaps they'd cornered the murderer?

"You're right, sounds like a conflict," mumbled Esra. "Let's not get caught in the middle of it!"

"I doubt it," said Kemal. "If it's anything like that, then they've certainly blocked off the road already, and we'd notice beforehand."

Nevertheless, Kemal proceeded to put the pedal to the metal and turn up the speedometer. They quickly ate away at the asphalt in the light of the rising full moon, as trees, empty fields, and an occasional glimpse of the river rolled past. The sound of the gunfire was closer now. The conflict was obviously taking place in Göven village, which they were passing just then. "The village where Reshat Agha was murdered," thought Esra. The village was about five hundred meters to the other side of the asphalt road. The sound of gunfire became fainter as they distanced themselves from the village.

So it seemed that when he said they'd know everything the next day, the Captain was referring to the attack happening that night. They were obviously hoping to catch the murderer during the raid. Maybe they hadn't thought the murderer would put up any kind of fight. Esra suddenly felt herself overcome with a sense of dread. What if Eshref were shot during the conflict? But no, he's an experienced soldier, surely that wouldn't happen.

It seemed that the sound of gunfire had made Elif forget all about her pain. With the stunned reaction of a person in shock, she stared out of the window and tried to figure out what was going on. But as soon as the shock was over, she once again began to feel the red hot burning sensation that spread from her foot all over her body. Esra tried to calm her down, but at the same time she couldn't help worrying. "What if Eshref's killed..." But come on, how likely was that? Who knows how many conflicts like this he's been in already? Besides, they'd already trapped the man, and she was certain they wouldn't proceed to attack without taking the necessary precautions. Yet despite these soothing thoughts, she still couldn't manage to calm herself down, and so with her eyes on the moaning young woman, and her mind on Eshref, she waited for the gunfire to cease. But the sound did not stop, and neither did the anxious feeling that was gnawing away at her.

TABLET FIFTEEN

King Pisiris had my father worried. He was nothing like the kings who had preceded him. He was neither cowardly and devoid of self-confidence like Astarus, nor brave and wise like Kamanas. Pisiris was ambitious, cunning, and rude. And with these characteristics, he quickly became the city's undisputed ruler. But this city, this little kingdom, was not enough for Pisiris. The daily activities of the city's rising number of Aramaeans, who were of Semitic lineage just like the Assyrians, were a source of concern for Pisiris. He was utterly obsessed with the idea that one of these days the Assyrians would turn the keys of the city over to the Aramaeans. He dreamed of establishing the great Hittite kingdom once again. Yet only an idiot could believe that the Assyrian Empire, under whose rule we lived, would possibly allow such a thing to happen, to say nothing of the sheer difficulty of reassembling the Hittite kingdoms now parceled into small city-states. But blinded by his mad ambition, Pisiris could not see these realities. And because he considered himself to be the possessor of all knowledge, he paid no mind to my father's warnings. My poor father sensed the oncoming disaster, but, unable to deal with the ambition of this young king, he could do nothing but writhe helplessly in despair.

Pisiris thought history to be as simple as the game of checkers that our forefathers had learned from the Egyptians. He therefore held on strongly to the false belief that he would be able to reestablish the great empire with his small acts of cunningness. In checkers, the tokens themselves are motionless; they move only to the square that you push them to. But the kings who surrounded us were at least as smart as Pisiris, and determined and experienced enough to protect their own interests.

Pisiris believed that the Storm God of the Heavens Teshub, his wife the Sun Goddess Hepat, their son Sharruma, and the goddess Kupaba were on our side, because the dreams that he had, and the fortunes that he had read to him, told him so. Yet the Assyrians also had powerful gods, like Asur, Enlil Shamash, and Ishtar, Goddess of the Land and the Sky. But Pisiris, drunk with the exuberance of his own dreams, was forgetting these realities and putting into practice, step by step, the scheme he had conjured up in his mind.

Letters and agreements were being composed under the utmost secrecy. The first letters were written to minor Hittite kings, such as Unki, former King of Hatti, new King of Amk; Pnammu, King of Samal; Tarhulara, King of Gurgum; Allumari, King of Milidia; Kushtashpi, King of Kummuh; Urikki, King of Kue; and Vashshurme, King of Tabal. This was an attempt to gauge how these kingdoms, virtually all of which lived under Assyrian oppression, would respond to the idea. But the responses received were marked by extreme caution. Their soldiers had been slaughtered by the Assyrians like sacrificial lambs, young and old alike had been skinned alive, their heads stuck on the ends of stakes, and their cities had been burned, hence these kings had no intention of throwing themselves into the fire for no good reason.

Pisiris, however, refused to see the hesitancy in these responses and worked with a blind stubbornness to realize his great dream. Letters were also written to Phrygian King Midas and Urartian King Sardur. However, the letters sent to the kings of these two mortal enemies of Assyria were delivered not by messenger, but personally by my father, Araras. My father was ordered by Pisiris to take as gifts two gold goblets embroidered in gold, a sun disc made of gold, a golden bull symbolizing the Storm God, a silver stag symbolizing our patron god, a ceremonial axe of the Mountain God with a two headed lion and djinns on it, and other valuable gifts, and to try and get a sense of the intentions of those kings.

Meanwhile, the Assyrian Empire was not forgotten. In order to give the impression that all was calm in our kingdom, and to keep the cruel Tiglath-Pileser from becoming suspicious and carrying out an untimely attack, taxes were paid on time, and valuable gifts were presented to the Assyrians. However, this would not be enough, for it would be impossible to rescue our small city from falling victim to the tyrannical Tiglath-Pileser's wrath.

I, who was dizzy with love for Ashmunikal, would come to find out all that had happened only much later.

CHAPTER SIXTEEN

Unable to find out exactly what had happened, Esra's mind dwelled on the village, and on the gunfire. She could call up the police station and ask them what had happened, but then what could they possibly tell her at that point? Besides, that would hardly be appropriate with Elif squirming next to her in pain like this. By the time the jeep had made its way through the worn, narrow streets of Antep and up to the stone building of the American Hospital named after Azariah Smith, Elif's convulsions had greatly increased. Thank goodness Timothy had had the good sense to go ahead and call the chief medical officer David. A group met them at the door and immediately transported Elif to the emergency room. It was late, already ten o'clock at night, yet the David had not hesitated to come all the way to the hospital. It was he who carried out the first intervention. Afterwards, seeing Esra and Kemal's faces white with fear, he approached them with an optimistic smile on his face.

"There's nothing to be afraid of," he said. "Scorpion poison in Turkey isn't usually fatal. It's only dangerous if the victim's body is allergic to it. I gave her an anti-allergy shot before putting her on serum. So, as you can see, everything's under control."

"I feel awful," Elif moaned, despite David's soothing words.

Her friends looked at David with expectant eyes.

"Could it be a late allergic reaction?" the doctor said to himself. He smiled when he noticed the anxiety in the eyes of the patient's friends.

"Don't go panicking now, the patient's life is not in any kind of danger. But it's a good idea to keep her under observation for a while. Let her stay here for the night, and maybe tomorrow night as well."

"Do whatever you have to, doctor," said Esra. "Do whatever it takes."

"Don't worry! We've done everything that we can so far. We need to wait for the effect of the toxin to pass now, and that'll take a few hours. You're going to wait here, right?"

"Yes, we couldn't possibly leave her alone like this," said Kemal.

"In that case, let's get you into a three bed room so you can stay with the patient."

Esra's eyes shined gratefully.

"That would be great. Thank you for your help."

"Don't mention it, it's my job."

David's blue eyes resembled Bernd's, except that they lacked the latter's coldness . Although he was the same age as Timothy, David's hair had fallen out early, making his high forehead stand out prominently. The combination of his thin beard so befitting his bony face, his gold-rimmed glasses, and his wise eyes lent him the air of an intellectual.

"I'm sorry, we've been so worried about our friend, we haven't had a chance to introduce ourselves," said Esra, extending her hand. "I'm..."

But the doctor completed her sentence for her.

"You must be Esra. I'm David. Tim mentioned you. But to be honest, I really wasn't expecting such a beautiful woman."

Esra's face turned a shade pinker.

"Thank you. Tim has spoken of you as well."

"And I'm Kemal," said the young archaeologist respectfully, but at the same time thinking to himself, "Ha, right, he's Timothy's friend, so of course he's not going to waste any time hitting on Esra."

"Nice to meet you," said David warmly. "Please, let us go to my office. Let me offer you something to drink."

Kemal wasn't at all enthused by this invitation.

"I'll stay here, in case Elif needs something."

The doctor didn't press him. "So it seems the young fella doesn't want to leave the patient's side," he said. "In that case, shall we?"

There wasn't much happening in the corridor; two patients stood in a doorway chatting, and a nurse carrying a tray of medicines was making her rounds, popping in and out of the rooms.

"So what's Tim up to?" the doctor asked. "We didn't really have a chance to talk on the telephone. He was in quite a panic, just kept asking me to get to the hospital right away... It's been so long since I've seen him. He's doing well, yes?"

"Yes, he's fine," answered Esra, preoccupied with the thought that she really should call up the excavation crew and give them an update. Nevertheless, she was quick to defend Timothy. "He's extremely busy these days. He's working on transcribing and transliterating the Hittite tablets we've uncovered."

"He must be busy, otherwise he wouldn't have fallen out of touch like this. Actually, I should be angry with you for stealing my friend away from me."

"You can get together after Wednesday, our workload will have lightened up a bit by then."

They took the stone steps up to the second floor. David's office was the modest but large room next to the stairway.

"Please, have a seat," the American said, motioning to a chair before proceeding to sit down at his desk.

As Esra sat down in the chair the doctor had indicated, her cell phone began to ring. She answered it immediately.

"Hello... Tim, is that you? We're at the hospital. Mr. David has been very helpful, God bless him. Elif? She's better now, but she's going to spend the night in the hospital, and maybe tomorrow as well. No, no, there's nothing to worry about. We're going to spend tonight with her. Oh, um, I wanted to ask... On our way hear we heard gunfire... Yes... Do you know what happened? Really? I'm dying of curiosity, too. Well, I'll go ahead and give the Captain a call then in a little bit. Maybe he can tell us what's going on... And could I ask you to go to the excavation tomorrow? Actually, everyone knows what to do, but it'd be better if you were with them, too. Thank you. We'll telephone again tomorrow. Greetings to the others. Bye now. Okay, I'll tell him."

"Timothy sends his greetings," Esra said as she placed the phone back in her purse.

A look of curiosity had appeared on David's face.

"What happened, has there been a fight?"

"We heard gunfire on our way here. But we couldn't figure out what was going on."

"There've been two murders in the last two days. I saw it on the news. I wonder who's responsible."

"So do we."

"My father said that a similar string of murders was committed seventy eight years ago."

Esra's weary eyes suddenly became animated.

"What do you mean?"

"My father said that there was a series of murders exactly like this one way back then, and in the same area, too."

"If your father's talking about incidents that occurred seventy eight years ago, he must be quite old now."

"My father Nicholas is ninety five years old. But he still has an excellent memory. He was the chief medical officer at the hospital before me."

"So who committed the murders seventy eight years ago?"

"Unfortunately, I had to dash over to the hospital before we had a chance to discuss the details."

"But this could be very important."

"So," said David, trying to understand what she was getting at, "you think there might be a connection between these murders and the ones committed seventy eight years ago?"

"Maybe. Could I have a talk with your father?"

"Of course. He'd be delighted. The other day, another member of your excavation team, Bernd..." But then he hesitated, uncertain about the name. "It is Bernd, right? The German..."

"Yes, his name is Bernd," said Esra, now staring straight at the doctor, curious to find out what he had to say next.

"Right. Well, he came over. He'd heard about my father from Tim. He asked him questions about the Armenian incidents that occurred at the beginning of the century..."

"That Bernd's lost his senses over this whole Armenian affair," thought Esra. "Everywhere he goes, that's all he talks about. The idiot's going to get himself into big trouble one of these days."

"And so my father told him what he knew," David continued. "Then our old man wandered about with a big ol' smile on his face for a full week afterwards. When you're elderly, knowing that you've been useful is a big boost to your morale. If he puts up a fight, I'm sure I can convince him, but I highly doubt that he will. I'm sure my father will be delighted to chat with a beautiful woman like you."

"Thank you," said Esra. It was unclear if she were thanking him for the compliment, or for trying to set up an appointment for her with his father.

"Well, look at that! We got so wound up in conversation that I haven't even asked you yet what you'd like to drink. That's a big no-no here in Antep. A guest should also be treated like royalty."

"Thank you, perhaps something cold..."

"How about ice tea? The folks in these parts don't care for it much, but I think it's the best way to cool off."

"Sounds good," said Esra. After David ordered the teas, Esra mumbled, like a guilty child hoping for forgiveness, "I hope you won't mind me asking, but, could I smoke here?"

"You can smoke in here, but not in the corridor. Don't worry though, dear, I smoke a pipe after meals myself. That Indian curse is a hard habit to break."

Seeing the uncomprehending look in Esra's eyes, the doctor asked, "You mean you haven't heard the legend? When we took their lands, the Indians cursed us with tobacco. And the curse has persisted ever since."

Esra laughed as she lit her cigarette. "Don't you get bored here?" she asked after taking a puff.

"Why should I? I was born here. It was this city that prepared me for life. I spun tops and played leap-frog on the streets here, went for dips in Alleben Creek—without my father's knowledge of course—armed myself with a slingshot under my belt and went bird hunting in the fields, explored the remains of the old fortresses and the underground caves surrounding the city, tested my courage, and was always on the hunt for all manner of adventure here... Then when I grew up I went to the U.S., to Houston, to study medicine. I saw the metropolises of Europe and America, visited small towns, got to know different cultures. But Antep continued to occupy a unique place in my heart, like that pure, shy excitement of one's first love, something that can never be repeated, never be experienced again. And so as you see, in the end, I came back."

Esra found David's poetic talk to be rather comical, but she didn't show it.

"And your father, doesn't he miss America at all?"

"My father was born here, too. He was the head doctor here before me, and before him, it was my grandfather, Christian. My family's been living in this city for a full three generations. My grandmother, my mother, my brother, they're all buried here."

Esra shook the ash off of her cigarette and onto the marble ashtray on the small table.

"I didn't know the hospital was so old," she said in a surprised voice.

"Perhaps not old enough to be included in your area of expertise, but it is quite old," David explained. "It was founded in 1878 by American missionaries who came to the city."

"The name on the door of the hospital..."

"Azariah Smith, you mean? After finishing his studies at Yale, he came to Antep, and was amongst the first doctors to arrive in Ayıntap, as it was known then."

"He graduated from Yale? You mean the same school that our Tim studied at?"

"Yes, but I think Azariah Smith came in 1847. Unfortunately, he became gravely ill with something like typhoid fever or pneumonia and died. They named the hospital after him to keep his memory alive."

Esra was just getting ready to ask another question when there was a knock on the door. A nurse came in with two ice teas. “Is their anything else I can do for you?” she politely asked after placing their teas before them.

“We have a guest keeping the patient in room number seven company. Why don’t you have a look and see if he wants anything?”

Once the nurse had left, Esra proceeded with her question.

“Excuse my ignorance, but why did the Americans feel the need to establish a hospital here?”

“In order to spread Protestantism,” David explained, after taking a sip of his tea. “Early last century, some clergy in America set out to spread the Protestant religion throughout the world as part of what they called ‘The Great Awakening.’ Their goal was to spread their religion by establishing relations with the people by opening aid institutions and founding educational and health centers. And that was the ultimate goal behind the founding of our hospital as well.”

“You don’t do missionary work anymore though, do you?”

“No, no,” said the doctor, shaking his head. “Now we just provide health care. Just between you and me, I’m not on very good terms with religion anyway. Though I’m not an atheist like Tim, I have serious doubts about the existence of the kind of god described in the Bible.”

“Tim doesn’t have any religious beliefs?”

“No, of course not. He’s never told you? I guess all that debate about the Hittite gods hasn’t left you with much time to talk about your own gods.”

“I guess so,” Esra said as she extinguished her cigarette in the marble ashtray. Then she shook her head and added, “To tell the truth, I’m rather surprised that Tim is an atheist.”

“Why? Does he seem like the religious type to you?”

“No, not at all. But still, I don’t know, it just seems odd to me.”

“You’re right, it is, but Timothy is the world’s most honest pagan. Maybe there are some religious types who are just as honest and as good as he is, I don’t know. My grandfather Christian was that way, too. And I do see a resemblance between Tim and my grandfather. But my grandfather’s honesty and kind-heartedness also had to do with him looking out for his self-interest, because ultimately, he was thinking about the pay-offs in the world hereafter. Though he never admitted it to anyone, he was quietly suspicious of anyone who wasn't Protestant. I've never witnessed such a thing with Tim though. The fact that he has chosen to be honest and upright even though he doesn't believe in god or the hereafter only makes his behavior all that more valuable."

"My father always thought like you do," Esra said, taking a sip from her ice tea. "He used to say that the first steps towards a higher level of civilization will have been taken when people can be good without fear of the torment of hell."

"Wonderfully spoken! And as I see it, Tim is one of the first people to begin building that civilization."

She found this statement to be rather exaggerated, but she didn't object.

"It seems you're very fond of him," she mumbled.

"You may not believe it, but I have never met anyone else like him before, ever, though I certainly have seen my fair share of the world. I lived in America. I stayed in Paris for two years. So as you'll guess, I've been around the block with quite a lot of people. But I've never met anyone else like Tim. He's both a hardcore academic, and gregarious—he's so social that he can spend hours on end chatting with anyone, even farmhands in the village coffeehouse."

Esra thought of the eighty-some year old Infidel Nadide and how Timothy had befriended even her.

"That's the thing that I really admire about him," David continued. "He has something to say about everything, but he's not snobbish."

"Having something to say about everything isn't such a great characteristic," Esra said. She was bored of the praises the doctor was showering upon Tim. Perhaps she was secretly jealous of her colleague, though she had never admitted this. "A person who knows something about everything cannot possess profound knowledge of anything."

"And that's what's so surprising. Tim's not like that. I don't know what it is, if it's because he's seen so much of the world, or because he's read so much, but he has in-depth knowledge about the things that he talks about. He can even explain what appear to be very abstract academic topics in very simple terms. But he does so without making the simplicity of it into something superficial. I've always found depth in whatever it is he has to say. And besides all of this, he's a very loyal friend—a friend whose absence I have felt, and whose presence I have longed for, more than any other recently."

Esra, too, knew that Tim was a talented archaeologist, a determined researcher, and a good person, but the only explanation she could find for doctor's praising him to the high heavens presenting him as some kind of modern day prophet was the doctor's loneliness here in this remote southeast city. She thought Timothy must seem to him like some extraordinary being simply because he hadn't had anyone else to talk with around here.

"Maybe he's stuck around these parts because of his friendship with you," Esra said jokingly.

"I highly doubt that. He's working on a book. That's why he's here. But he truly loves it here. He more than loves it, he's absolutely attached to this region. Last year terrorists stopped Timothy and a second lieutenant while they were on the road in Osmaniye and abducted them."

Esra's eyes opened wide in amazement.

"Are you serious? I haven't heard anything about that."

"Tim doesn't like to talk much about unfortunate events like that."

"So what happened?"

"They shot and killed the lieutenant, but they let Tim go. But it was days before he was finally able to get over it. I saw him weeping like a child. I suggested that he go to a psychologist, but he refused."

Esra tried to imagine Timothy crying, but couldn't. David continued talking.

"He loves this country and these people so much that it perhaps pains him more than any of us to see them killing one another."

"The villagers in the region are also very fond of him," said Esra, who had finally overcome the shock of the preceding revelation. "In the region where we excavate, the locals know him better than any of us."

"Of course they're fond of him. The mister? doesn't only conduct research, but he works for the locals, too. Two years ago he got health surveys conducted in the villages. Our personnel worked on the campaign for a whole month."

"Something in your voice tells me that you weren't too pleased by this activity."

"You work for free, running from village to village like that, who would be pleased," said David, but then he began to laugh. "Oh, don't take me too seriously. It did everybody a lot of good. We experienced the joy that comes with helping others."

"And what's more, you did it without trying to turn them into Protestants."

"Yes, we did it simply out of the goodness of our hearts."

David noticed that Esra was sneaking a glance at her watch.

"If you're tired, don't let me keep you any longer."

"It's probably a good idea if I go check up on Elif,"

Esra's real intention, however, was to gain some privacy and call Eshref. Throughout her conversation with the doctor, the worry she felt for the Captain throbbed in her head like a toothache.

"Thank you for the fine conversation," she said as the stood up.

"It was my pleasure."

Before she reached the door, Esra took a moment to remind the doctor, "You won't forget to talk to your father, will you?"

"Don't you worry, the first thing I'm going to do when I get home is talk with my father about this."

David accompanied her out into the hall and asked, "Will you be able to find the room? Or shall I come with you?"

"Oh no, please don't trouble yourself, I'll find it. Have a good evening."

Esra left the doctor and made her way down the stairs, and then quickly walked to the open window at the end of the corridor before taking her cell phone out and hurriedly dialing the number of the police station. At the other end of the line was the same soldier that had answered her phone call that afternoon. He recognized Esra's voice immediately. He told her that the Captain wasn't in, and that nobody knew exactly when to expect him. "He doesn't want to reveal any information," Esra thought. But she persisted.

"We heard gunfire," she said. "What's going on?"

He didn't know. Just then, someone else interrupted the conversation, and after keeping Esra on hold for a few moments, the soldier told her that he was putting her through to the sergeant.

"Hello Esra Hanım, this is Sergeant Ihsan, how can I help you?"

The man's voice was hearty and cheerful. "He wouldn't speak in this tone of voice if his men had suffered any casualties," thought Esra.

"Hello Sergeant Ihsan. We heard some gunfire and just wondered..."

"There's nothing to be concerned about," the Sergeant [illegible]utting her off.

"[illegible]one of your men were injured or anything?"

"No, thank God," said Sergeant Ihsan. "Everyone's in perfectly good health. Our Captain will be making an official statement tomorrow."

"How is the Captain?"

"Doing very well, very well, everyone's just fine."

"Can't I speak with him?"

"He's out and I don't know when to expect him back."

The Sergeant sounded convincing. There was no point in drawing this out any longer.

"Okay then, can you let him know I called?"

Esra felt a great sense of relief when she hung up the phone. So the Captain was okay. But her relief didn't last long. She hadn't asked if the conflict was over yet or not. "But what if it's still going on..." she thought, deeply worried by the prospect. "Actually, the Sergeant spoke as if it were already over. But still, one can't be sure, I mean, we're talking about armed conflict here, not a football match! And it's dark out. But it's not like this is his first conflict, I mean, the man was off fighting in the mountains for months. He'd know better than I what to do, and how to take the necessary precautions," she thought in an attempt to console herself. But it was in vain, for once that anxiety that she knew all too well began eating away at her guts, there was no stopping it. She could hardly go into Elif's room and wake Kemal up to talk while she was in this chaotic state of mind, and so she began wandering aimlessly up and down the corridor.

TABLET SIXTEEN

After I had become smitten with Ashmunikal, I did everything I could to avoid an encounter with her; not only did I stay away from the palace, but I made certain not to take any routes where I thought I might run into her. The trips to Phrygia and Urartu that my father Araras was preparing to undertake, however, made my presence in the palace imperative. My father asked that I go to the palace and work with his assistant Laimas in his absence. Laimas was a good man, but he was a little naïve. My father believed that an industrious, talented young man like myself would be the ideal complement to his assistant. But my father did not know of my affair with Ashmunikal and I had to act in accordance with my father's wishes.

Every day I went to the palace with a tangled web of feelings. On the one hand, I was desperately yearning to see Ashmunikal, while on the other, I was afraid of seeing her, like a small child scared witless of encountering djinns in the dark. As I helped the good hearted, but thoroughly untalented Laimas, my mind was on that section of the palace where Pisiris' women were kept. A stone stairway led up to this section located on the highest floor of the palace, and it was comprised of two large rooms overlooking the Euphrates. Though I refrained from even looking in the direction of the staircase leading up to that section, I could feel that Ashmunikal was there, and I awaited the moment when I would encounter her with a heart full of fear, impatience, and joy.

On the seventh day of my father's trip to Urartu, one of Pisiris' guards came to my side while I was working in the palace library. He said that the king wanted to see me. I became anxious upon hearing this, and wondered why the king should want to see me. Perhaps he had learned that I was the man that Ashmunikal had made love with at the temple? That was impossible. But what if he had spies at the temple? No, he wouldn't have the nerve to place spies in the temple. He was a king, but he could not violate the privacy of worship carried out for the gods. With these questions running through my head, I went before the king.

Pisiris was seated on the divan next to the window. Next to him sat a woman who was facing the window. I respectfully approached the king. He looked at me, and I knelt down before him, bowing my head low.

"Stand up, young Patasana," Pisiris said, with a compassion that I had never bcfore heard in his voice. "We have an assignment for you. We hear that you have been taking care of the library since your father Araras left for Urartu, as we commanded him."

I had risen to my feet, but continued to focus my eyes upon the floor.

"Yes, your highness," I said, "thanks to you, I am taking care of the palace library together with the scribal assistant Laimas."

"Don't speak to me of that talentless Laimas!" he roared. "And look at me when addressing me."

When he said this, I raised my head and saw next to Pisiris' ugly face the ethereal face of the love of my heart, Ashmunikal. I immediately averted my eyes to the ground once again.

"So it seems all this time with Laimas has muddled your brain as well," Pisiris said in a mocking tone. "Raise your head and look at me."

Helplessly I did as I was told. But I was trying to keep myself from looking at Ashmunikal. I focused my attention entirely upon Pisiris.

"Yes, your highness, I await your command," I mumbled in a shaky voice.

Pisiris smiled. His shapeless lips spread across his face, revealing his small, gaping teeth.

"That's it," he said in a very confident voice. "Be an understanding, talented scribe like your father; like your father, be intelligent, a man whom I can always count on to follow through with my commands."

"Thank you, your highness; thanks to you, I shall be a scribe with all of the characteristics you desire," I said, pandering to Pisiris' hubris. I cannot possibly describe the shame that I felt at that moment. I had been disgraced before the woman that I loved, and it was I who had put myself in this situation. But I suppressed my shame immediately. I was standing before the king. I had to be prepared to make any kind of sacrifice, including that of my own life, at his bidding. He was the representative of the gods here on earth, and the defender of our people. Next to these, how important could the love of a young man, not yet even risen to the position of palace scribe, possibly be? I gathered myself together and repeated:

"Yes, Sir, I am here to do as you bid."

Pisiris's square face was overcome with a deep compassion. A sweet expression welled up in his bloodshot eyes. In the softest tone that he could muster up with his deep voice, he told me what he wanted of me:

"Ashmunikal is my beloved. But she is not like the other women in the palace. Her father was a teacher. She grew up with legends, epics, poems, and songs. We would not want her to grow bored here with us. So, you need to show her a list of all of the legends, epics, poems, and songs in our library. And you need to make sure that she is provided with the tablet of her choice whenever she wants it. I am assigning you with this task. Whatever you do, do not get Laimas mixed up in this."

With great effort I gathered my mind, which was a jumble of surprise, excitement, joy, and fear, and proceeded to speak.

"As you wish, Great Pisiris," I said, my head bowed low before him. "I shall carry out your command without fault. The esteemed Ashmunikal shall make use of the tablets in the library as she wishes."

"That's my boy, young Patasana," said Pisiris. "I've heard very good things about you, and if what I have heard is correct, and if you carry out my commands to perfection, you will have an excellent future awaiting you."

He then turned to look at Ashmunikal, his eyes languorous with love.

"All of us have an excellent future awaiting us," he said. "The future shall restore to us the abundance, mirth, and power of ages past."

As Pisiris spoke, for a moment I imagined his short, fat body between Ashmunikal's legs. My face automatically puckered up in disgust, but thank goodness I was able to collect my wits and put on a respectful, complacent, humble facial expression before Pisiris noticed. Just as I was about to ask for permission to leave, Ashmunikal's voice rang out, filling the room with a lively joy.

"I'd like to come to the library early tomorrow morning and look at the tablets. Will you be there in the morning?"

"Tomorrow morning?" I asked, pausing as I tried to overcome my surprise. "Of course," I said, pulling myself together. "Whenever you like, your highness."

"You heard her," said Pisiris authoritatively. "Wait for Ashmunikal in the library tomorrow morning."

"I shall, Sir," I said, and bowed my head. But my heart, sensing the disaster to come, had already begun beating fast with fear. Before the swift beat of my heart had a chance to spread to the rest of my body, I asked for permission to leave and dashed out of the room. As I walked down the stairs, a merciless sense of foreboding began to weigh heavy on my heart.

CHAPTER SEVENTEEN

Esra woke up distressed. She had had a restless night that kept her half awake and half asleep. She sat up on the bed. Elif, who had spent the night moaning, had finally managed to fall asleep, and Kemal, too, who had fought sleep to keep an eye on Elif, had finally given in to slumber towards morning. Esra got up silently so as not to disturb her friends, went to the washroom, washed and dried her face, and then took her mobile phone and walked out into the corridor.

The corridor wasn't calm like it had been at night, but had been overtaken by the slight flurry of activity that comes with the breakfast hour. The nurses walked slowly down the halls carrying trays of food, which they then turned over to the patients or their caretakers. She would have to go out into the garden to speak comfortably. She found a silent corner behind the door and dialed the number of the police station. The voice of the soldier on duty at the switchboard rang in her ears. Recognizing the caller, he wasted no time with pleasantries.

"I'm putting you through to the Captain," he said.

So there was nothing to be afraid of.

"Hello Esra."

A sense of relief spread through her body as soon as she heard Eshref's voice.

"Yes, it's me. How are you? Are you okay?"

"I'm fine, just fine. Great, really," replied the Captain. His voice was tired but confident. "Praise be to God, none of our men were killed or injured... They told me you called last night, too."

"Yeah, I did. Why didn't you call back?"

"It was three in the morning by the time I got back to the police station. I didn't want to disturb you."

She was about to say, "I wish you had called. I thought about you all night," but then she changed her mind.

"I got worried when I heard the gunfire."

"I was thinking I might stop by the excavation this morning and tell you all about it."

"But I'm not at the excavation right now, I'm at the hospital in Antep."

"At the hospital you say?"

She felt a secret thrill upon hearing the worry in his voice.

"I'm fine. A scorpion bit Elif."

"She's doing all right, I hope."

"She's getting better. Would you please tell me what happened? I'm dying to know."

"I'd rather not tell you about it on the phone. For the time being, suffice it to say that everything's fine. You can carry on with your excavation in peace now."

"So, you mean you caught the murderers?"

"Yes, they won't be bothering you anymore."

"Did they confess?"

"They were dead when we captured them."

There was a pause.

"Are you sure they were the murderers?"

There was another pause before the Captain responded in a troubled voice.

"It's not very opportune to discuss this here on the phone. When are you coming back?"

"I'm not sure, probably this afternoon though."

"Stop by on your way back and I'll fill you in on the details."

Esra would have preferred to have found out all about it right then and there, but she realized there was no use in pushing the Captain.

"Okay. See you this afternoon then."

She'd been worried about nothing. The Captain was perfectly fine. Yet she still wasn't totally relieved. She didn't find his words very reassuring. Time and again she had considered the hypothesis that it was the separatists who were behind the murders, but she just wasn't convinced; it didn't make any sense to her. For them to murder the Head Village Guard Reshat was plausible enough, but there was no reason at all for them to murder Hadji Settar. Besides, if the separatists had committed the murders, then they would have made a public announcement; there was simply no reason for them to hide it. Granted, Reshat Agha had only been murdered the day before, but if the separatists were behind the murders, then surely they would have made a public statement about Hadji Settar's murder by now? Her head full with such questions, she walked back into the hospital and nearly collided with David.

"Good morning," said the doctor cheerfully. "I was just looking for you. You haven't had breakfast yet, have you?"

"No, why?"

"We're going to my place. My father has invited you to breakfast."

"That's nice, but my friends are still asleep."

"The nurses will tell them where we are when they wake up."

Esra couldn't decide. She really wanted to talk with David's father, but Elif hadn't fully recovered yet, and she just couldn't bring herself to leave her alone at this point.

"But Elif..." she said.

"There's nothing to be worried about. The effect of the poison is decreasing with each passing day."

"Okay, well, let's go then," said Esra. "They'll tell the others where we've gone, won't they?"

David put on his confidence inspiring smile.

"Don't you worry one bit. I'm going to tell the head nurse now. I'll be right back."

Esra's cell phone started to ring just as the doctor began to walk away. It was Teoman, wondering how Elif was doing. Esra gave him an update. Everything was going fine at the excavation as well. Tim had come along with them to the site. They were taking a break so that the workers could have their breakfast, and so Teoman was taking advantage of the opportunity to give her a call. The workers were fine, too. Everyone except for Şıhlı had come. Nobody knew why he hadn't shown up, but the others were working hardily. They wanted to call it quits a little early today though because of Hadji Settar's funeral. Teoman and Murat would be taking the workers into the village. The two of them would also be attending the funeral on behalf of the excavation team. Oh yes, and he and Murat had made up. He didn't know what had happened to him the evening before. He apologized. Esra didn't want to talk about it. She told him to pass her greetings along to the others and hung up.

A little worry would do Teoman some good. He needed to learn to be more careful about how he behaved towards his friends.

Actually, Esra, too, had been surprised by the way Teoman had acted the previous night, because he was generally so easy-going. He wasn't a very particular person, and he didn't have any great aspirations, neither in terms of his life nor his career. He had wanted to become an architect, but because he was so laid back in high school, as he was now, he hadn't worked too hard towards that goal. And since he found the idea of taking the university exams a second time simply too overwhelming, he'd just made do with archaeology. Eating, drinking, sleeping, and conversation were the things he enjoyed most in life. In short, he was a carefree guy. But the night before, for some reason, he'd just lost it all of a sudden. Maybe Murat had gone a little too far with him. "No matter what, he had no right to behave that way," Esra thought. And so she'd thought during their telephone conversation that it was still too early to indicate that she had forgiven him.

David's Volkswagen Golf passed through the narrow, black stone-paved streets leading along the zinc plated doors and stone walls of the magnificent houses that comprised the old fabric of the city and onto a broad avenue. This was just like any other ugly avenue that one found in Istanbul, or anywhere in Turkey, with its rows of stores, pedestrians rushing down the sidewalks to their respective destinations, and the cacophony of running motors and honking horns. Thank goodness the journey didn't last long. The Volkswagen entered another avenue, with broad sidewalks lined on either side by mulberry trees. Esra recalled having seen this avenue on her first visit to the city. And so her first impression of Antep had been a positive one. Then this avenue, too, came to an end, and treeless sidewalks and crowded bunches of apartment buildings took over. Thankfully, this didn't last long either, and soon they were surrounded by lush greenery once again. There were fewer houses now, just one or two poking through the overgrown trees here and there.

Esra felt a slight stir of anxiety.

"Are we leaving the city?"

David smiled innocently.

"Don't worry, I'm not abducting you. My father's at our summer house in Sarıgüllük. We're heading out there."

"And where is this Sarıgüllük anyway?" Esra asked jokingly. "Are you sure you're not abducting me?"

"I'm sure," he said, and then a short while later motioned ahead with his hand. "And this is Sarıgüllük. And that's our house."

"It's nice," Esra said upon seeing the stone building. "Looks old."

"It's very old. There wasn't a soul living in this area when this house was built, but recently there's been lots of construction around here."

The two story stone building had been erected directly in the center of a fenced-in grove. A breakfast table had been set in front of the house, beneath a huge walnut tree that extended high up into the sky amidst a bed of colorful roses. Esra saw two old men sitting at the table and a middle aged woman carrying a tray full of breakfast all looking her way.

"The one with the glasses is my father," David explained.

"Does he live alone here?"

"The woman standing there, Gülsüm Bacı, takes care of him. My wife and children stop by now and then, too." He paused, and then gave Esra a flirtatious look. "But they're on vacation now. So as you see, I'm a bachelor during the summers."

"And who's the other man?" Esra asked to show that she had no interest in his grass-widower status.

"Sakıp Amca, a friend of my father's. A well-known personage here in Antep; he's a veteran of the War of Independence, and a retired teacher..."

The Volkswagen had pulled up to the house. It stopped in the shadow of the acacia tree to the left. "I didn't know he was coming," said David as he turned the motor off. "Now they'll get all stubborn with one another, like goats."

"Don't they get along?"

"Not at all, they're complete opposites. My father never used to fall for Sakıp Amca's bickering ways, but as he grew older, he began needling him more and more. An argument inevitably breaks out whenever their paths cross, but still they just can't do without one another. They go way back. They studied together at the American high school. And none of their other friends are living now. If one of them dies, the other is going to be very lonely... But still, it would've been better if Sakıp Amca hadn't come today."

"Maybe he just thought his friend was bored at home, all by himself."

David just shook his head in response.

They passed by the garden and walked up to the table, which was lying in the dark shadow filled with the scent of roses and was decked out with a lavish breakfast. The two old men rose to their feet. Nicholas, his blue eyes twinkling in his wrinkled face like those of a djinn, stepped forward and offered his hand to Esra.

"Hello, I'm Nicholas, retired doctor."

Esra introduced herself as well as she shook the man's hand, with its prominent purples veins.

"And this is my old friend, Sakıp," he said with a mischievous grin that boldly revealed his straight false teeth.

It was only then that Esra noticed that Sakıp was leaning upon a cane to stand up.

"Retired history teacher Sakıp," the old man said, emphasizing each word, as if to fill in the blanks left by his friend, as he extended his shaky hand to the woman.

His head of hair, now white, was just as lush as it had been in the days of his youth, but the brown eyes on his dark face, speckled with small, dark stains, had turned grey, as if a curtain had been draped across them. Feeling that the old man had gotten a little too close for a comfort, Esra took a little step back.

"Forgive me for standing so close," the old man said by way of explanation. Unlike his collapsed body, his voice was still full and deep. "My great grandson broke my glasses. I have to get up real close to see. I hope I haven't made you uncomfortable." He motioned with his head towards Nicholas and added: "This fella and I don't get along very well, but when he told me on the phone that he and Esra Hanım were going to talk about the old days, I couldn't help myself, and so here I am."

"And it's a good thing you are," interjected David. "You can fill in anything that my father might forget."

With a shaky hand Nicholas motioned the guest towards the chair across from him.

"Please, have a seat."

As she sat down, Esra's eyes met those of Gülsüm Baca.

"Welcome," said Gülsüm shyly.

Due in part to Gülsüm's insistence, they immediately sat down to breakfast. She had decorated the table with an array of scrumptious foods, from honey to homemade jam, thick Antep cheese to tulum cheese, and olive salad to haricot bean salad. The two old cronies looked upon the food on their plates longingly, but were unable to stomach too much, and soon they started with the usual questions: Which district of Istanbul did she live in? Where had she studied? How long has she been working as an archaeologist? How long would the excavation by the Euphrates last? Esra gave short, precise answers to their questions as she partook of the breakfast. And so it went throughout the duration of the meal.

They were only able to get down to the real discussion once Gülsüm Bacı had gathered up the remnants of breakfast and the old men had been brought linden tea with lemon, and David and the guest a sugarless Turkish coffee each.

"You told Mr. David that murders similar to the two recently committed here had happened seventy eight years ago, too," Esra said. Everyone's eyes were on the old doctor. "Are you sure about that?"

"Of course I'm sure about it," said Nicholas. "Sakıp surely remembers them, too. It was seventy eight years ago. If I'm not mistaken, that would be 1921."

"In 1339?" asked Sakıp through squinting eyes.

"No, no, that'd 1340 according to the hegira calendar."

"I remember. Antep was under siege. May God never show us days like that again. Oh, what times those were!"

"I'm talking about after the siege," his friend warned.

"Alright, alright. You mean after the siege had been broken, and Captain of the Antep Forces, Özdemir Bey, had broken through the surrounding French forces and out of the city..."

"No, no, I mean after that," Nicholas said, correcting his friend once again. "I'm talking about after the decision was made at the London Conference for the French to withdraw from Antep."

Sakıp was riled up now.

"I get it, dear. You're talking about when the Armenians began to run away."

"There you go... That's the period I'm referring to. Most of the Armenians had begun to fear an exile like the one in 1915, and so they'd sold all their belongings and headed for Syria."

"Of course they did," said Sakıp. "They should've thought about what they had coming when they met the French with marches and flags, and put on their uniforms and pranced about as the French forces entered Antep, just to spite their fellow countrymen."

"How could they know? They thought the French had come to their rescue... Anyway, anyway, moving on," said Nicholas, who then cleared his throat. "Now, where were we? Ah yes, the Armenians had begun to desert the city, but then there were some in the town where you're excavating and its surroundings who didn't run away. There were five or six families who had been left alone during the exile of 1915, and so thinking that nothing would happen to them this time around either, they decided to stay. The church priest, Kirkor, Ohannes Agha, a man who owned much of the land around today's Göven village, and the coppersmith Garo, were among them. And these three men were ruthlessly murdered one week after the French withdrawal. Priest Kirkor was pushed from the bell tower of the church, which is the mosque today. Ohannes Agha was killed on the road into the village, decapitated with his head in his lap. And Garo was hung from a beam in his own store."

"Weird," murmured Esra. "The first two murders are exactly like those of Hadji Settar and Reshat Agha. So, weren't the murderers ever arrested?"

"Arrested? In those days, we were at war. The Armenians were considered to be the enemy. Who were they going to arrest?"

"Who's to know who's guilty and who's innocent in the midst of battle?" interjected Sakıp.

"C'mon now, Sakıp, it's obvious who was guilty. The locals were always talking about a group that got all riled up and slaughtered those men right before everyone's eyes. And everyone saw that it was Kurdish Istendiyar, the grandfather of Reshat Türkoghlu, the man murdered yesterday, who led the pack. And after all, didn't Istendiyar Agha take over Ohannes Agha's land and become Agha himself?"

"I don't know about any of that stuff," the old man rebutted. "It's a world of give and take. You reap what you sow. None of this would've happened if the Armenians had just minded their own business."

Esra didn't take much interest in what Sakıp had to say.

"What happened to the families of the men who were killed?"

"I don't know about the families of Ohannes Agha and coppersmith Garo, but Priest Garo's family ran away to Beirut. The man has a young son, and a younger daughter. When the young man realized that his little sister would only hold them up, he left her with a kind neighbor and ran off to Beirut together with his mother. And from there they went to France..."

"Why do you ask about their families?" David interjected. "Do you think it might be one of them who committed the murders?"

"Don't you all go troubling yourselves about this any longer," said Sakıp, as if they'd asked for his opinion. "It's the terrorists who are responsible for these murders. Those lowlives are trying to divide the country. Everyday a booby trap, everyday a martyr. Those wretched scoundrels, as if our people suffered any less than the Armenians."

"But the Armenians sure suffered plenty at your hands, now didn't they?" said Nicholas, who had no intention of letting his friend get the upper hand. "First them, and then you, you just took turns going for each other's throats."

David seemed upset by his father's words and so he turned towards Esra to see how she would react, but the young woman was still stuck on the similarities between the murders that had been committed seventy eight years ago and those committed just days before.

"Anyone listening to you would think you were speaking the truth," said Sakıp, grabbing on to his cane. "It was they who initially ruined the friendship, the brotherhood. We had accepted them. We were living side by side, like brothers. We interfered neither in their language, nor their religion. The biggest religious building in Antep was the Mother Mary Church, isn't that so?"

"But then you cruelly sent them into exile."

"Because of you," said a now enraged Sakıp, "you incited us to do it. You told them to found their own state. And so those simpletons fell for it and started playing games behind our back."

"Don't get the Americans mixed up in this," said Nicholas. His attitude had that same sweet aggressiveness characteristic of a fan standing up for his own team during a football match. "It was the British, Russians, and French who were behind all of that. We didn't incite anyone to do anything."

Sakıp ferociously pounded his cane into the ground.

"That's a lie! You were mixed up in it, too."

He turned to face Esra and continued.

"He's lying, my dear. What business did these guys have thousands of miles away from America, huh?"

Esra was curious about this point herself.

"Excuse me," said the old man to David. "I'm not referring to you. You're one of us now, please don't be offended by my words." He turned to face Esra again.

"At the beginning of the last century, the Protestants founded something called the American Board."

"American Board of Commissioners for Foreign Missions," Nicholas said, thoroughly enjoying getting his friend all wound up.

"Alright, alright, don't interrupt me," retorted Sakıp. "As you can probably infer, these guys were planning to spread their religion in foreign countries like ours. And as soon as they founded their Board, they made Antep part of the program, as if we'd specially requested their presence or something."

"Not as soon as it was founded," said Nicholas, as if trying to prove that his memory was still as fit as ever. "The Board was founded in 1810, and Antep was included in the program in 1819."

"Alright already, we got it, now just shut up... Anyway, dear, as you might infer, the men were very conniving. When Mehmet Akıf referred to 'The single toothed monster,' the last good tooth of the imperialists that he was talking about was America. And so when our treacherous Ottoman Empire granted America 'most privileged country' status, these fellas began playing their horses as they pleased in our country."

"So, we played our horses and what bad came of it? We opened a school, founded a hospital, and performed acts of good will."

"That's right, but why did you open the schools and hospitals? To divide the country, to take over Ottoman lands."

"Sakıp, you really have gotten to be a grumpy old man," said Nicholas.

"The guilty party sure knows how to lay the blame. C'mon, go ahead, say it, call me a senile old man. But say what you will, you can't stop me from revealing your fraudulent scheme."

Sakıp seemed to be truly enraged now. Esra had begun to blame herself for having started such an argument between two friends. She'd already learned what she needed to find out, and so she began to think that it might be a good idea if she made her escape at the earliest opportunity. But Sakıp Bey wasn't done yet.

"My lovely girl, have you ever heard of Muslims turning Christian en masse?"

"I don't know, I guess not."

"You haven't, you couldn't. But for a Catholic to become Protestant, a Protestant Catholic, or a Gregorian Protestant, now that's not unheard of. No matter how much they quibble, in the end, they all gather together under the Christian flag. What I mean to say is that their objective was not to make Christians out of Muslims, but to make the Gregorian Armenians into Protestants. And so for this reason they supported the Armenians' efforts to establish an independent state."

"Now, stop making stuff up," complained Nicholas.

"I'm not making anything up. Did you not open schools in Antep and Marash to educate Armenians?"

"Esra Hanım, those schools were not opened to educate Armenians, they were opened to educate everyone," Nicholas explained. "This fella here has forgotten because he's so darn old. He himself studied at one of the very schools he's talking about."

"No, I haven't forgotten, and you're right, I did study at one of those schools, but how many Muslim children were there? Most of the students were Armenian."

"What fault is it of the school administration if Muslims didn't enroll their children in those schools?"

"There's no fault about it, they were pleased of course. Why? Because it's more difficult to pull the wool over the eyes of Muslim children. It's easier for you to fool the Armenians. After all, they're already Christian. But you couldn't manage that either. Despite all of the money you spent, and all of that education, you were still only able to make one fourth of the Armenians into Protestants. No? In school, we had an Armenian friend named Masis. Masis was Gregorian, and they enrolled the boy thinking he'd become Protestant.

But he didn't. Most of the Armenians were sharp like Masis, and they didn't change their denomination. Masis..."

The old man suddenly paused, and Esra figured that he was probably trying to recall something, but then Sakıp turned to his friend, as if he had completely forgotten about their argument.

"For real Nicholas, even after so many long years, I sometimes still dream of Masis. What happened to that kid? You never heard from him again either, did you?"

The cheerful gleam in Nicholas' eyes was suddenly extinguished by the sound of Masis' name. Aware of this, Sakıp turned to face their guest.

"If only all of the Armenians were like Masis," he said sadly. "We'd have gotten along perfectly with them and lived in harmony ever after."

"So Masis was your friend?"

"Friend is no word for it; he was our blood brother. We were like three peas in a pod. We were inseparable. This fella here, Masis, and I, we were like the three musketeers back in high school. The only one missing was D'Artagnan."

When Sakip motioned with his head towards Nicholas to indicate that he was "this fella," Esra turned her eyes towards the man sitting across from her. And it was only then that she realized that there was nothing left of Nicholas' earlier cheerful demeanor. Though not to the same degree, a rather gloomy expression had come over David's face as well. Unaware of the effect he was having, Sakıp continued his speech.

"Masis was a few years older than us. He was like our big brother, protecting us from the bigger kids. And seriously, he was a great fighter, and he was very intelligent, too."

"What happened to him?"

"He disappeared," said Sakıp. "He was never found again, neither dead nor alive. We ended up in different camps when Antep was occupied. Masis had joined the French supported Armenian forces; Nicholas had withdrawn to his father's hospital and watched the war from there. And I had joined the resistance movement. Because I was so quick on my feet as a young man, I became Özdemir Bey's own messenger boy. I shuttled coded letters to Captain Selahattin Bey of the

Second Corps, slipping through the French forces that surrounded the city. The enemy had a huge advantage over us in terms of weapons as well as number of men, and the people in the city had gone hungry for months. The locals made bread out of apricot seeds, soup out of dried grass, and quarreled over horse carcasses. Özdemir Bey and Selahattin Bey wrote to one another frequently. Armenians serving in the French army caught me as I left the city on my fifth delivery. I had civilian clothes on. I tried to tell them that I wasn't a soldier. They searched me and failed to find the encoded letter, but they were still suspicious of me. Two soldiers began to strike me with the butts of their bayonets in an attempt to get me to talk. They ruthlessly beat me on the ankle bones, knee caps, and elbows. I collapsed to the ground. I had just begun to think that this was it, that I was going to be killed then and there when I heard a voice say 'Stop!' It was Masis. 'Let him go,' he said. 'He's alright, I'll vouch for him.' In reality, though, he knew that I had joined the resistance forces. Yet at that moment, friendship, our friendship proved stronger than the animosity between the opposing forces. I stood up and hugged him. 'You better get out of here,' he warned me. I stayed there with him for a few minutes and took a short rest, and then I headed out for the Second Corps. So that's how Masis not only saved my life, but helped me to carry out my duty, too."

Esra was looking at Nicholas as she listened to Sakıp Amca. As his friend praised Masis to the high heavens, Nicholas' face had become a little longer, his blue eyes lifeless. Esra thought she had better take advantage of the lull in conversation to make her getaway.

"Thank you for the breakfast and the fine conversation," she said, "but I really should go now."

"Isn't it early yet?" said Nicholas, but he didn't insist.

Sakıp seemed disappointed.

"There's still a lot I have to tell you..."

"Another time," Esra smiled.

"Let's not pressure our guest now, Sakıp Amca," said David in a show of support. "I promise to bring her back another time."

Both Sakıp and Nicholas rose respectfully to their feet as Esra left. However, Nicholas no longer seemed like the same man who had so cheerfully greeted her upon her arrival, so eager to talk.

TABLET SEVENTEEN

Ashmunikal had not changed a bit. That was my first thought when I saw her next to Pisiris. She was exactly as she had been when I saw her at the temple; mesmerizingly beautiful and frighteningly self-confident.

The next morning, I sat on a wooden bench in the library waiting for Ashmunikal, with whom I had first tasted the lusciousness of a woman's lips, first touched the exquisiteness of a woman's body; she whose name I was afraid to speak even unto myself. I could not tell if my fear was greater, or my joy. All I knew was that seeing her made me happy, and frightened me. Beyond this I knew nothing. And I did not want to. The day before, as soon as I had left King Pisiris and Ashmunikal, I had come down to the library, looked over the epics, lined them up in a row, and written their titles on a tablet. When Ashmunikal came, she would be able to look at this tablet and easily learn what literary tablets we possessed.

As I waited for her, I could not help but wonder if she would be coming alone, or accompanied by an official. I hoped that she would come together with an official or one of Pisiris' beloveds. That way I could talk more comfortably and carry out my duty precisely as the king had ordered. But I would not have to wonder long about the answer to this question, for Ashmunikal made her appearance at the library door bright and early, like a morning star.

When I saw her at the door, my mind and body were overcome by a relentless excitement, just as it had been when I first saw her at the temple. She was wearing a honey colored dress with a flower design, and a silver necklace embellished her long neck. Her brown eyes, which made her wheat colored skin look even darker, looked at me with a sweet expression.

I bowed my head to avoid meeting her eyes.

"Welcome, esteemed mistress, welcome, honorable Ashmunikal," I said, in a cold, insincere voice.

And in response she said, in a warm, sincere, loving voice:

"Thank you, Patasana, how nice to be alone with you again after so many months."

Caught off guard, I raised my head, and at that moment was captivated by the fire in her brown eyes. The shy girl in the temple was no more; she had been replaced by a woman whose eyes were full of different meanings. At that moment, I understood that there was no use in defying it; Ashmunikal was my destiny, and escape from her was impossible. Nevertheless, I put up a resistance.

"I made a list for you," I said, pointing to the tablets I had written the previous day. "All of the epics, legends, songs, and poems in our library are written here. You can choose what you like from this list."

Ashmunikal moved closer towards me, as if oblivious to what I had just said.

"Why do you act as if you do not know me, Patasana?" she asked.

The girl standing next to me was the same one who had driven me mad when I woke up to find her missing by my side; the lover, about whose lineage and family I had begged Chief Priest Valvaziti to tell me, had come to me, and was seeking the opportunity to become intimate with me, so that we might complete the holy lovemaking we had left unfinished on that night long ago. Before my eyes her naked body came alive beneath her honey colored dress, but I immediately banished the vision from my mind.

"I know you," I responded. "You are the esteemed Ashmunikal, a beloved of our great king Pisiris. I am a servant whose duty it is to carry out the orders of you and our king."

"You are not my servant," she said. "For me, you are the first man with whom I shared a bed, before Pisiris."

I looked around from the corner of my eye to make sure that there was no one who might hear our conversation, and then I whispered:

"Please don't talk like that, you shall bring the gods' wrath down upon us."

"No, the gods have fated that you and I be together. It is Pisiris himself who has violated the gods' commands. He is a man who is never sated, a man who desires to become the sole possessor of everything on earth. And it is because of this that he alone shall become cursed by the gods."

"You shouldn't speak of our king like that," I warned her. "He loves you."

"He loves himself. He loves ten other women like me," she said. "Soon, he shall find someone younger, and more beautiful than me, and he shall take her into his harem and make her his beloved. Besides, even if he does love me, I do not love him. He is powerful, but ugly, noble, but rude. He does not look at me sweetly like you do, he does not smile beautifully like you do, and there is no melody to his voice, as there is to yours."

As I listened to Ashmunikal's words, which had me turning multiple shades of red, I noticed Laimas at the door. Immediately I changed the subject and said in a loud voice so that Laimas could hear:

"Esteemed Ashuminkal, if you like, let me give you this tablet to take with you so that you may go over the list and make your selections as you like."

Ashmunikal, too, had seen Laimas.

"I'd like the poem that the Sumerian poet Ludingirra wrote for his mother."

"But of course," I said. As I reached towards the shelf holding the tablet upon which Ludingirra's poem lie, a thought occurred to me, and so turning to Ashmunikal I asked:

"Please forgive me for asking, but this poem is in Akkadian. Do you, I wonder, know the Akkadian language?"

A strange twinkle appeared in her eye, and a feigned expression upon her face.

"I know a little," she said.

"Unfortunately, then, you cannot read it," I said, bowing my head in reverence. "You must have an excellent command of Akkadian in order to understand Ludingirra."

At this, Laimas, who by then had made his way over to us, ever so dutifully interjected.

"Look at what you are thinking, Patasana," he said. "Why don't you just translate the poem for the esteemed Ashmunikal? After all, you know the poem by heart, yes?"

"I cannot!" I yelled, recoiling like one whose bare hand has touched fire. "I have other things to do."

Ashmunikal narrowed her beautiful eyes and said to me, "Then I'll tell our king, and he can find someone else to translate it."

Not translating the poem would mean disobeying the commands of Pisiris.

"No, no, there's no need for that," I said, trying to salvage the situation. "I'll translate it within the next few days."

The confident Ashmunikal looked me straight in the eye. "I would like to be with you while you translate," she said. "That way you could help me to improve my Akkadian."

"What a great honor that would be for us," the meddlesome Laimas spoke up yet again.

Cursing the talentless scribe under my breath, I turned to Ashmunikal.

"So long as Pisiris allows it, it would be an honor for me to serve you," I said.

"Don't you worry, Scribe Patasana," Ashmunikal said, the most beautiful smile in the world adorning her lips. "I shall get permission straight away. Be prepared to translate tomorrow."

Then she left the library, taking the list of tablets with her. Old Laimas stood staring after her as she departed.

"She is a girl like no other," he said. "Like the sprout of grass that cracks the stone, the fire that melts the ice, the wind that directs the sea. How wonderful for our king! Anyone who looks at this girl sees gardens more bountiful than those of our Euphrates; anyone who hears her voice finds peace within, as if hearing the sound of divine music; with her, even the most insipid of times are transformed into sweet moments that pass all too quickly."

As Laimas looked on in awe towards the door that Ashmunikal had exited, I could not help but wonder if he would speak in the same way if he knew what had happened between the two of us.

CHAPTER EIGHTEEN

"I learned about all of this much later," David continued. The Volkswagen had left the garden and was making its way along the road lined with mulberry trees. They had slowed down considerably. Anyone looking on from outside would have thought they were out for a pleasant spin. Yet the doctor was telling his guest about the bitter event experienced so long ago, which had left his father so full of sorrow just a short while before.

As soon as they had exited the garden, Esra asked why Nicholas was so upset.

"It's a sad story," David said. His face became heavy with sorrow like his father's. "My father thinks that it was a shameful event for our family, that's why he always hid it from Sakıp Amca."

Although her curiosity had intensified, Esra realized that it was a delicate subject, and so she thought that it wouldn't be right to push him. "Let's forget I asked, if you want," she said. David was silent for several moments, but then he continued.

"Last night I had mentioned the difference between my father and Tim," he started up spontaneously. "Although I never say so in so many words, it's always the example of Masis that I have in mind. Like Sakıp Amca said, the three were very good friends before the war broke out. They say Sakıp and Masis virtually lived at my grandfather's house. Though my grandmother's delicious raisin cake played a part in that, the American magazines and all the 'new world' belongings at home were the bigger part of the appeal. Masis' and Sakıp's families did not oppose this friendship, because they saw each other every day at the bazaar, and they were friendly neighbors to one another. But after the First World War broke out, daily life was poisoned, and the Party of Union and Progress, which had experienced successive defeats, decided to send the Armenians away using the armed Tashnak groups, who were collaborating with the Russians, inciting riots behind the front, attacking the Muslim people, and organizing massacres, and so they ordered for the Armenians to be removed en masse from the regions where they lived and sent them into exile. Massacres and mass executions occurred as these orders were being carried out; hundreds of thousands of Armenians, men, women, and children alike, lost their lives; blood divided these peoples who had lived together in fraternity for 600 years.

"Masis and his family managed to stay in the city in those days, with help from the Halep governor, since Antep was part of Halep at the time. But when the war ended in defeat for the Ottomans and the Antep region was occupied by the British, and then by the French, the Armenians, who had been forced to migrate to various parts of the empire, returned; and as soon as they returned, in order to gain revenge, they began collaborating with the occupying forces and tormenting the locals. While they were able to accept the occupying forces to a degree, the locals could not stand the fact that the Armenians had joined forces with them, and so they took up arms and began resisting. The resistance in Antep lasted no less than eleven months; the besieged city did not surrender until its people were on the verge of starvation. This resistance, which continued without any real help from outside, meant that the French were forced to keep their important forces in the city, and this situation was a source of relief for the national independence army that was fighting against the occupation. The people fell in defeat not to the French gunners, but to hunger, and finally had to abandon the city. It was the Armenians who were happiest about this, because they thought that they would be able to establish their own state, like the Russians, British, and French had promised. But things didn't pan out as they had hoped. Not ten months after the fall of Antep, the French had to end the occupation due to the London Conference and so they withdrew their forces; the Armenians, who had believed in them, saw their dreams shattered once more and got set to make their escape yet again, with children and all in tow, just as they had in 1915.

"Like Sakıp Amca said, Masis was one of the Armenians' most illustrious fighters during the war. He was a great benefit to them during the siege of the city, taking his place in the front lines of the fierce battles that took place around Chınarlı Mosque. And then afterwards, although he had the opportunity to flee, he chose to stay on and become a member of the committee that organized the migration. But when this committee experienced a delay in implementing their plans, the road that they were to take to Halep was blocked off, and so Masis and his friends had to hide in the city. Then Masis' friends were all captured, one by one, until finally, desperate and with no place to go, Masis showed up at my father's house and asked my father to hide him. My father took him in and hid him in the large cave beneath the house that they used as a cellar, and then told my grandfather about the situation when he returned from the hospital that evening. At first my grandfather was angry at my father for having taken his friend in, but then after thinking about it for a while, he decided to go down and talk with Masis. After half an hour downstairs, my grandfather came back upstairs in a rage.

"'That man is to leave this house immediately,' he said.

"When my father asked what had happened, he said, 'That man's a credulous, lost fool. I told him to become a Protestant and we would save him, and he told me that he would rather die than do anything of the sort.'

"My father began to beg, he told my grandfather that with time, Masis would find the true path and become a Protestant. My grandmother also asked him to let Masis stay, but my grandfather wouldn't budge. While they were arguing, the sound of a single shot rang up from the basement.

"'Oh no!' my father cried and ran down to the cave. He found Masis lying on the ground in a puddle of blood, shot in the forehead. Next to him was his gun, smoke still coming out of its barrel. My grandfather had run downstairs after my father, and finding my father standing there in a state of panic, landed two smart smacks on his face.

"'Pull yourself together now,' he said, 'we'll be in big trouble if they find his body here. Let's bury him in our cemetery.'

"Around midnight, they took Masis' body and buried it in the American cemetery. My grandfather didn't erect a stone or anything, so that it wouldn't be obvious. Long after my grandfather's death, my father had a marble stone placed over Masis' grave. But because of the shame he felt about this tragic event, he didn't have Masis' name engraved upon it. For years he kept this secret even from those closest to him. One day I asked him who was buried in that grave. 'Your uncle,' he said to me. As far as I knew, I didn't have any uncles. I went to my grandmother and mentioned the grave, and she just mumbled some gibberish. Once I'd gotten older and begun to come into my own, I asked my father about the grave again. And that's when he sat me down and told me about what had happened. So, it is Masis who lies in that nameless grave."

"How sad," said Esra. "Now I understand better why your father got so upset all of a sudden"

"It's my grandfather's actions that I find most curious of all. I was seven years old when he died. He was retired when I was a kid and he spent most of his time with me playing in our garden, night and day as if he himself were a child, too. We'd play blind man's bluff, and he'd go down into the cave where Masis had killed himself and hide. He'd make noises so that I'd find him. I'd go down and catch him. I remember my grandfather as one of the sweetest men in the world. And those who knew him loved him, too. Even today, everyone speaks so highly of him. But he had pushed a young man who was like his own son to his death, simply because they did not share the same beliefs."

David took a deep breath. He turned and looked at his guest with his watery blue eyes. "How could such a good man commit such an evil deed?" he asked. "I just don't get it."

"Belief," said Esra in a voice that was emotional yet confident. "Sometimes, it blinds you to everything else. It keeps you from tolerating someone who's different. It makes the death, the annihilation of someone different from you into something natural, in fact, necessary."

David shook his head hopelessly and turned his attention back to the road before them.

"I think you're right," he continued. "No matter what the cost, humankind just can't seem to free itself of its passion for killing, for annihilating. And our family ended up paying a heavy price for Masis' death. It did away with that merry atmosphere at home, and there this tension developed between my grandfather and father, both aware of its cause, but about which they never spoke. And it was my grandmother who was most disturbed by this situation. The poor woman was stuck between her husband and her son, and she kept trying to get my father to forget about the past. But as you yourself have seen, my father hasn't been able to forget about his friend's death."

Esra noticed the quiver in David's voice. It was as if the man who had playfully joked around as they went to the garden and smiled at her flirtatiously had disappeared, replaced by a man oppressed by events of the past, for which he somehow felt responsible.

"I'm sorry," said Esra, "if I'd known that was what happened, I never would have broached the topic, or asked you that question."

"I told you because I felt like it," David said. His eyes were on the road, but his mind was elsewhere. "You're the first person outside of the family to learn of this. I don't know why I told you. I guess there's a heavy burden that comes with keeping secrets, and one can only bear that burden for so long."

He turned to look at his guest once again.

"But still, I'd appreciate it if you didn't tell anyone about this," he said.

"Don't worry, no one else will learn of it."

"Thank you," murmured David.

Both of them grew silent. So many things were running through Esra's mind. Most prominent amongst these was the similarity between the murders that had been committed seventy eight years ago and the way that Hadji Settar and Head Village Guard Reshat had been killed. Was it the separatists who were behind this, like Sakıp Amca had said? If that were the case, that is, if it were really the separatists who were behind the murders, then the problem had been solved, because according to the Captain, the murderers had been caught dead. But what if Sakıp Amca was wrong and it wasn't the separatists who had committed the murders, but someone seeking revenge for the murders that had happened seventy eight years before? But who could that someone be? It would have to be someone whose relatives were killed, or someone close to those murdered, someone like Bernd...She shouldn't think such thoughts about a colleague. But she'd already begun to suspect her German colleague as soon as David told her that had discussed the incidents with Bernd. Hadn't Nicholas spoken of the young son of Priest Kirkor who had been pushed off of the church bell tower, about how he'd taken his mother and escaped to Beirut? And hadn't Bernd's stepfather escaped from Turkey to France? Was that just a coincidence? Fearing the conclusions that her thoughts were leading her to, Esra did her best to repress them. No, Bernd couldn't possibly kill anybody. But then again, recalling their talk the day before, she didn't feel quite so sure about this. Hadn't he said that he'd do anything for his wife, even give up his occupation? But giving up one's occupation was one thing, and killing two innocent people was something else... But hadn't he risked fighting with the police for Vartuhi, even though the matter at hand had nothing to do with him? She recalled the German's eyes, that steel blue that bore right into a person. "No, it just can't be," she thought, trying to distance herself from the idea once again. Besides, even if Bernd were lovesick enough to do such a thing, would his wife Vartuhi approve of it? Would she really want a murderer for a husband? She undoubtedly would not, but what if Bernd was committing the murder unbeknownst to his wife, in order to prove the magnitude of his love? If he were to tell her upon his return to Germany, "I got revenge for your grandfather Kirkor"... Was such a thing possible? Why shouldn't it be, hadn't we seen what love had done to our Kemal? And why shouldn't Bernd, who was already strange enough as it was, commit such insane acts? For real, what was the man up to when the murders were being committed? What else, he was in bed asleep like all the other members of the excavation team. Or was he? She tried to recall all that had happened the night of the murders. Bernd couldn't be found in his room the morning that Hadji Settar was murdered. In fact, they had to start the meeting late because they were waiting for him. And he and Timothy had even had a small argument. She seemed to recall that he had said he had gone for a walk along the Euphrates. And what about the night that the Village Guard Reshat was murdered? She strained to recall, and suddenly she envisioned the short discussion he had had with Teoman that morning. Teoman had said that the tires on Bernd's bicycle wheels had gone flat. A strange expression had appeared on Bernd's face and he immediately jumped to his own defense, saying, "But I didn't ride my bicycle last night." What had he gotten so worked up about it? Or could it be that he'd hopped on his bicycle the night before to go to Göven Village and murder the Chief Village Guard Reshat? She got goose bumps as she recalled how the shepherd who had discovered the body had described the scene. Hadn't the shepherd said that he'd seen a man flying in the sky? Could it be that the shepherd, seeing only the broad specter of the rider, the bicycle itself invisible in the moonlight, had thought that what he had seen was a man flying in the sky...?

"What a bunch of nonsense..." she thought, trying to regain her composure. Here she was accusing a colleague without a shred of concrete evidence whatsoever, and what's more, the killers had already been captured. Perhaps it was because of some subconscious hatred she felt towards the man. Bernd had put her through plenty because he himself hadn't been appointed head of the excavation. No, no, her thoughts had nothing to do with that situation. She always had a tendency to be suspicious of everything, almost to the point of paranoia. Hadn't she once accused Orhan of sleeping with Sevim when they attended a symposium together in Berlin? Yet Sevim was her closest friend, and didn't care the least little bit for Orhan. But Esra also knew that hatred could serve as a source of attraction between people. Moreover, they'd stayed together for a week in a foreign country, and in the same hotel. So was it really that impossible that, with a little help from some alcohol and music, they might have ended up spending a night together in the same room? This idea had started out saying to herself as a little joke, but then after a while, she actually began to believe it, until eventually she was playing out scenarios in her head. By the end of the seventh day, she was absolutely certain that her husband had slept with Sevim. She really put Orhan to it when he got back, until it began to get out of hand and Sevim got word of what was going on and proceeded to give Esra an earful herself. It wasn't until she'd broken the hearts of two people she truly loved that Esra finally understood she'd been wrong all along, and so she did everything she could to win their forgiveness. And now what if she was just as wrong about her suspicion of Bernd?

"No, no," she mumbled to herself.

David heard her say this.

"Excuse me, did you say something?"

"Sorry, I guess I was thinking out loud."

They didn't utter another word all the way to the hospital. Once they stepped into the building, David invited Esra to his office for a cup of tea, but Esra politely declined, saying that it was time she got back to the excavation. She wanted to take Elif along as well, if she had recovered by then. The doctor thought it best that she spend another night at the hospital. Esra didn't insist otherwise. She gave David's hand a friendly shake before leaving.

"Thank you for everything. You must stop by the excavation sometime. We'll have a nice long chat then."

The doctor did his best to put on a cheerful face, though it was obviously forced.

"I thank you," he said. "I shan't pass up on that invitation."

When Esra left the doctor to enter the room where her friends were staying, he found Kemal and the Antep Archaeology Museum Director Rüstem whispering amongst themselves. Elif was still lying asleep in her bed. Both of them stood up as soon as they saw Esra. Rüstem shook Esra's hand. Actually, she wasn't particularly fond of the man, and Rüstem knew this. And so he didn't drag out their conversation unnecessarily. After a few pleasantries, he asked for their permission and departed. But he was a good friend of Kemal's. They had worked together at the Yesemek Open Air Museum Project. When Rüstem left, Kemal sat down again by Elif's bedside and worriedly began watching the girl breath, as if her chest would cease to rise and fall if he were to avert his glance for even a second.

"She doesn't look good," he said. "I'm really concerned about her."

Esra took a close look at the girl and realized that she wasn't nearly as pale as before.

"She's fine," she said. "I think you're the one who needs looking after. Your face is whiter than hers."

"I'll be fine. The only thing that matters is that she gets well."

"The doctor says that she needs her rest. He wants to keep Elif in the hospital for one more night. But I need to get back to the excavation. What are you going to do?"

Kemal hung his head low, as if downcast at his predicament.

"The most interesting part of the excavation season..." he mumbled bitterly. "How many times in an archaeologist's life does he come across a find as extraordinary as the Patasana tablets? Maybe once, maybe never. But I can't leave Elif alone. Being with her makes me happy, even if she doesn't want me here."

TABLET EIGHTEEN

Ashmunikal made me happy. She made me feel like no one else could, and this was the sole unchanging reality in my life, despite all of my fears, anxieties, and reservations. She filled my heart with senseless bliss. I realized this undeniable truth when we encountered one another once again. Ashmunikal reentered my life like a raging fire, like an unexpected storm. As I struggled to keep away from her, she devised ways to spend time with me, found the means to realize her plans, and finally got what she wanted. She proved once again that she possessed not only the beauty of the goddesses, but their intelligence and courage as well. If my grandfather Mitannuwa had been alive, he would have congratulated me for loving such a girl and wished for me to experience this love, regardless of the king. My father Araras, however, would most likely reproach me for coveting one of our king's women and warn me against it; he would not refrain from raining curses down upon me should I persist in loving Ashmunikal, and perhaps he would even turn me over to Pisiris with his very own hands.

As for me, I did not know what to do. I'd fallen into Ashmunikal's hand, like a broken winged sparrow. It had been no use forbidding myself. She had long ago captured me and become an intrinsic part of myself, like the blood running through my veins. No matter how much I feared King Pisiris, no matter how much the training I had received compelled me to behave responsibly, I knew that I could not possibly withstand her. By this point, I was thinking about her everywhere, all the time. She was always on my mind—when eating, walking, watching the Euphrates, talking with my mother, singing, reading tablets, writing tablets, sleeping, dreaming, when awake, and when daydreaming.

Ashmunikal did as she had said she would and came to the library the next morning. I no longer shrank from looking at her, or to be frank, I could not take my eyes off of her. She noticed this immediately. And when she did, I became frightened once again and began to avert my glance.

"Good morning, Scribe Patasana," she said, approaching me with a confident smile upon her face.

As she drew closer to me, my nose caught the pleasant scent of the wildflowers that bloom along the Euphrates in the spring. Inhaling this scent deeply, I responded, "To you, too, Esteemed Ashmunikal."

"I spoke with the king, and he said that we could translate together the poem that Ludungirra wrote for his mother."

Seeing my hesitation, she continued in a sarcastic voice: "Or should I have gotten a tablet with the royal seal showing that he has granted permission?"

"Don't talk like that," I responded. "I have complete confidence in your word."

Scanning the library with her beautiful eyes, Ashmunikal changed the subject.

"Where shall we work?"

I gathered myself together again immediately.

"Here you are, Esteemed Ashmunikal," I said, showing her the table where Ludingirra's poem lay. "Let us sit here."

We walked over to the table together. She was a few steps ahead of me. Without fear, without reserve, I feasted my eyes upon her. Once we had sat down across from one another at the table, Ashmunikal down looked at the tablet. "Laimas said that you know this poem by heart," she said. "Before we begin the translation, could you recite it to me?"

This was the first time we had been so close since the night we lay with one another at the temple.

"As you wish, Esteemed Ashmunikal."

"I am listening then, Esteemed Patasana," she said, wryly emphasizing the word "esteemed." I feigned oblivion to her sarcasm and began reciting the poem by the Sumerian master, a poem of which I, too, was very fond.

"Dear Mother,

Messenger of the king,
I am sending you to Nippur; take this news with you.
I have made a very long journey,
My mother is in grief, she cannot sleep,
She, from whose quarters all grievous words are banished,
Asks all of the travelers about me.
Give her my greetings and place this letter in her hand!
If you do not know my mother, let me tell you about her.
Her name is Shatishtar.
She sparkles
With the loveliness of a goddess, she is a sweet bride.
She has been hallowed since her youth.
She, who with great zeal manages her father's-in-law house,
Who serves the god of her husband,
Who knows how to look after the Goddess Inanna,
Who takes care to heed the king's word,
Who is loved, and lives with love,
She is a lamb, fresh cream, sweet honey,
The butter that flows from the heart.

Let me give you a second description of my mother.
My mother is a bright light on the horizon, active in the mountains,
A morning star
A precious carnelian-stone, a topaz from Marhasi,
A magnificent jewel for the prince,
A carnelian-stone generating joy,
A tinned ring, a bracelet of iron,
A dazzling statuette of ivory,
She is an alabaster angel,
Rising from a foundation of blue stone.
Let me give you a third description of my mother.
My mother is the rain in its season,
The water needed for the first seed,
A bountiful garden, full of delicious fruits,

A fir embellished with cocoons,
The harvest of the first month of the new year,
A channel of water nourishing the fields,
She is the sweetest, most desirable of Dilmum dates.

Let me give you a fourth description of my mother.
My mother is a celebration, a joyful sacrifice,
The princess of princesses, a song of plenty,
A loving and beloved heart full of never-ending joy.
She is the good news of a prisoner returning to his mother.

Let me give you a fifth description of my mother.
My mother is a chariot of pine,
A palanquin of boxwood,
A beautiful, perfumed dress,
She is a crown of flowers.

You shall recognize my mother
According to these descriptions that I have given you,
... that fine woman, you see, is my mother.
Cheerfully deliver this news to her
Who is eagerly awaiting news from me,
Say to her, "Your beloved son Ludingirra sends his greetings!"

When the poem was finished, I looked at Ashmunikal. She was crying. I had never seen her cry before, and my heart filled with pain.

"What happened, why are you crying?" I asked.

She continued sobbing, and did not answer my question. Forgetting all about King Pisiris, who we were, what could happen to us if we were caught, I tried to touch her hand. She pulled away. I wasn't expecting this, and so I just stood there, helplessly, across from her. Ashmunikal wept for a little while longer before calming down. She turned her kohl-lined eyes, the beauty of which even her tears had failed to smirch, and looked me in the face.

"Forgive me," she said, "I was thinking about my mother."

"Where is your mother?" I asked.

"Far, far away. Together with my father, who did not hesitate to trade me to Pisiris in return for a rich field by the Euphrates and three slaves."

"Your own father sold you to Pisiris?" I asked, stunned.

"I do not condemn him for it," said Ashmunikal. "He was old, and could no longer teach. He wanted to spend his final days in comfort. And he thought that I would live a life of plenty in the king's palace. But oh how I miss my mother."

She reached out and took my hand.

"And you recited the poem so beautifully," she continued. "I was touched. Otherwise, it is rare for me to cry."

I felt this odd stirring inside when she held my hand.

"I know that you are not one for tears," I said. "You are a very brave girl."

Ashmunikal looked carefully at my face.

"You are in love with me, aren't you Patasana?"

I fearfully withdrew my hand from hers.

"Are you afraid of the king?" she asked.

"I both fear and revere him," I said.

Ashmunikal reached out for my hand once again, but this time I did not withdraw it. Looking me straight in the eye, she asked, "Is the respect you have for the king greater than the love you feel for me?"

I tried to pull my hand away again, but she would not allow it.

"Tell me Patasana, and if it is so, I shall let go of your hand and leave this place, never to return."

I could say nothing, but then she had known that I would not be able to respond. She stood up and walked over next to me. She gently touched my hair, as she had in the temple. I looked at the library door and mumbled uneasily, "Someone will see us..."

"Then let's go to your father's study," she said.

She knew everything, for there really was a small room behind the library which my father used as his study. If we went in their and locked the door behind us, no one would be able to enter.

"But what about King Pisiris..."

"He is not worthy of respect," she said. "He is not a good man, and he is not a good king."

"What if he comes to the library," I said anxiously.

"He can't," she said. "He went deer hunting this morning."

I could no longer resist the allure of Ashmunikal's words, the mesmerizing sight of her that excited me so. We walked to the small room where my father wrote his secret tablets. We sat next to one another in the room. Because of our unsuccessful lovemaking at the temple, I was afraid to touch her, and so I tried to keep my distance from her. She was aware of my nervousness.

"We shall only talk," she said, looking at me with her large, kohl-lined eyes. "We shall talk tirelessly, until we learn not to fear one another. I shall read you poems, and tell you stories and epics from the tablets, until you learn not to be afraid of my body. I shall narrate tirelessly, until you understand that talking itself is a kind of lovemaking, and until that hunger which shall prove that talking is not enough awakes in your skin."

CHAPTER NINETEEN

What Nicholas had told Esra only served to further perplex her already confused mind, turning all of the events of the past couple of days into a real conundrum. As she made her way along the asphalt road that led her through pistachio gardens in red earth, she was still undecided about what to do. Although she was suspicious of Bernd, she was ashamed of her suspicions. She didn't possess a single concrete piece of evidence with which to accuse him, yet there were so many things that pointed to him as a suspect. Was it just a coincidence that the murders had occurred one right after the other, or was it precisely the nature and order of the murders comprising the essential pieces to the puzzle that would reveal the true identity of the murderer? She couldn't be sure, and because she couldn't be sure, her thoughts just wandered about in a vicious circle only to end up right back where they had started.

What if she told the Captain about her suspicions...? He wouldn't believe it. Besides, as far as he was concerned, the murderers had been captured—case solved. But Esra still wasn't convinced that it was the separatists who were behind these murders. Maybe she was wrong, maybe she was just wasting her time suspecting her German colleague. Or maybe the Captain possessed documents proving that the separatists were behind the murders. "If only..." she murmured without much conviction to herself. "Still, it's best to slow down and find out all the details about what happened," she thought. After all, the Captain was more experienced than she when it came to such matters; he'd spent years fighting in the mountains, and he knew the separatists better than she did. At the same time, he was prejudiced; he suspected the separatists for every bad thing that happened in these parts. As if she herself weren't prejudiced! Hadn't she immediately become suspicious of Hadji Settar's nephew Fayat, and claimed that the religious fundamentalists were behind the murders, well before she actually knew anything about what had really happened?

All of these things were still running through her head as she got out of the jeep and walked towards the police station. Of the two soldiers standing at the door, the one from Ankara, greeted her with a bashful expression on his face. "The Captain is expecting you," he said, before she even had a chance to ask, and pointed towards the residential building located downhill between the police station and the river.

"Is he sleeping or something? I don't want to disturb him."

"No, the Captain is not sleeping. He said to invite you to the residential quarters when you arrived because its garden is cooler."

The word "cool" alone was enough to put a happy smile on Esra's face; finding a cool corner in this hellish heat was a true privilege. The soldier from Ankara led the way, heading towards the charming stairway of handmade large stones gathered from the Euphrates shores.

The garden of the residential quarters was neat and well-kempt, just like the police station garden. And just as at the police station, here, too, two soldiers stood on guard in front of the iron door marking the entrance. Immediately behind the guard's hut on the left stood a humungous linden tree that devoured the entire garden in its shadow, swallowing all of the other trees in its midst—plum, pomegranate, mulberry, acacia, and around a dozen poplar. However, it wasn't only the shadows of the trees that made the garden so attractive in this heat. The moist coolness coming up from the Euphrates, which flowed around 20 meters below, also broke the heat, transforming this place into a veritable desert oasis.

The Captain was sitting at a table beneath the plum tree, silently watching the green waters of the Euphrates. "He's waiting for me," thought Esra. This thought alone sent a shiver of excitement through her body. The guard on duty recognized Esra and bid her "Good morning" as she entered through the iron doors. The Captain turned then to look at them.

"Hello," he said in greeting, a tired smile appearing upon his lips.

Esra politely acknowledged the Captain's welcome and then shook the hand that he extended.

"Come, have a seat," said Eshref.

Esra sat down in the chair opposite the Captain and let her gaze linger on the residential building behind the trees.

"It's not very big. How many families live here?"

Eshref gave the building a glance himself.

"My family would have, if they'd come," he said, letting the sentence escape from his mouth. He wasn't in any mood to pursue the topic further though. "Right now, it's just me."

But Esra wasn't going to let him off the hook so easily.

"So your wife didn't want to come here?" she asked.

The Captain tensed up, and instead of answering the question, turned to the soldier from Ankara, who was standing next to the table, and told him that he was free to go.

The soldier gave a crisp salute and headed out the door.

"What would you like to drink?" Eshref said, turning to face Esra once again.

"Is it really so difficult to talk about yourself?" Esra asked. "Whenever we begin talking about you, you immediately change the subject."

The Captain was caught off guard; he wasn't expecting Esra to snap at him like that. He struggled to find the correct response, but just ended up retorting, "As if you talk a lot about yourself!" in an attempt to one up her. Esra, was persistent.

"And which question of yours have I left unanswered?"

Eshref looked into Esra's bold eyes.

"You're right, perhaps I haven't asked. I don't care much for meddling in other people's private lives."

"People?" said Esra. Her hazel eyes looked at the man reproachfully. "I thought we were friends, you and I."

The Captain shook his head in distress.

"I apologize," he said. "I'm talking nonsense. I had a hard night."

"I know you had a hard night," said Esra "but you were like this before last night too."

The Captain sighed and hung his head. Esra was just beginning to wonder if she hadn't gone a little too far there when the Captain finally raised his head.

"Yes, I have a daughter," he said. "Her name is Gülin, she's in elementary school. She lives with her mother in Istanbul."

"Don't you ever go to see her?"

"I'm not able to go very often. I'm pretty much separated from my wife. We're not divorced yet, but you know, we're ... how do you say it... we're pretty detached. It's difficult now for me to go to Istanbul and walk into that house."

"But you shouldn't neglect your daughter," Esra said, and immediately regretted having said such a meaningless thing. She'd forced Eshref to talk, and learned that he and his wife weren't on good terms. So what would happen now? Was she to remind him that she, too, was divorced from her husband? But if she did that, would she be implying that as two free adults they, too, might enter into a relationship themselves? How could she possibly get on with someone like Captain Eshref, whom she didn't even know very well, when she had failed to get along with someone like Orhan, a mild-mannered man from the same professional background? After all, the more she got to know the Captain, the more she came to realize that the two of them certainly weren't made for one another.

"I talk to her on the phone," Eshref continued. "She sends me cards on holidays - drawings that she's done herself, of the Bosphorus, the Maiden's Tower, the Galata Bridge, Sarayburnu, Kuleli Military Academy... There's a different part of Istanbul on each card."

Esra looked curiously into the dark eyes, their lids lowered wearily, of the man sitting across from her.

"So she's talented."

"Yes, she is," he said before adding shyly, "I wasn't bad at drawing myself."

"Maybe you would have become a fine artist, if you hadn't become a soldier."

"Maybe, but I'm happy being a soldier."

Esra's hazel eyes opened up wide in wonder.

"Really?"

"Yes, really! Why are you so surprised?"

"No reason," said Esra, who then thought it best to change the subject.

"So what refreshments do you have to offer?" she asked.

"Cola, soda, tea, *zahter*..."

"*Zahter*? What the heck is that?"

"You mean you've never heard of *zahter*? Everyone around here knows *zahter*. It's an aromatic herb, similar to thyme."

"Interesting. Well, if you're recommending it, then let's give it a try."

The Captain called out to one of the soldiers on duty at the door and gave their order. As the soldier walked away Esra asked, "Well, isn't it about time you told me about what happened last night?"

"We got this call yesterday morning," the Captain began. "It was from an anonymous caller who said that the Genceli tribe's youngest son Mahmut had been staying in his cousin's house in Göveli Village with a friend for the past five days. We began watching the house yesterday, but we were unable to get any leads. We had no other choice but to raid the house, which is exactly what we did last night. They fired at us and so an armed fight broke out. We captured Mahmut and his friend dead. Like I said before, we didn't lose any men."

"God was with you," said Esra, but that questioning look remained in her eyes. "So how do you know that they were responsible for the murders of Hadji Settar and Reshat?"

"From documents we found at the house," the Captain said. "They'd come to this region to do some grassroots organizing for the separatists. As you know, after being defeated in the mountains, the separatists' began shifting their focus to cities and towns and trying to draw attention to the separatists' acts and prove that the state is weak. It says so quite openly in the brochures that we found. So they killed Hadji Settar and Chief Village Guard Reshat to attract the people's attention."

"Does it say, 'That's why we killed Hadji Settar and Head Village Guard Reshat' in the documents that you found?"

"Of course they don't say that in so many words," said the Captain. There was a tense expression in his tired eyes. "But you don't have to be a genius to figure it out."

"It's exactly like I thought," Esra thought to herself. He had no concrete evidence whatsoever. Still, she wanted to be sure that she wasn't mistaken on this point.

"Do the fingerprints found on Hadji Settar and Head Village Guard Reshat match those of the terrorists?"

The Captain gave her a look, as if to ask "What does that have to do with anything?" but proceeded to answer nonetheless.

"There were no fingerprints on Hadji Settar's body. His autopsy report says that there are bruises on his neck, but it was actually the skull fracture that killed him. And it's thought that the skull fracture resulted from his falling from the minaret. They're going to do an autopsy on Reshat today."

There was now a strained sound to the Captain's voice, but Esra paid no mind.

"I don't know, but it seems to me that the men you captured may have been here for other reasons."

"Like what?"

"You said yourself that they came to do regional work for the separatists, but murdering Hadji Settar and Reshat hardly seems necessary for that."

"You should have become a public prosecutor," said the Captain. "I'm sure no stone would have been left unturned, no case would have been left unsolved—and idiots like me would have learned how to catch killers."

When she noticed the spark of anger in Eshref's dark eyes, Esra realized that she had gone too far.

"I'm sorry," she said in a soft voice. "I would never think about insulting the work that you do. I know that you and your officers brushed elbows with death last night."

The Captain didn't seem likely to calm down anytime soon.

"What does any of that matter? What matters is that you sit in your comfy abode and come up with a list of our shortcomings."

"That's not exactly fair. I mean, okay, maybe I wasn't at the scene of the conflict, but I was very worried about you last night. I waited for hours for your call..."

The sparks in the Captain's eyes were slowly extinguished.

"But I can't help it," Esra continued, smiling. "That's just how I am. There's always this voice in my head nagging me with questions, and it just won't stop until it gets an answer."

"But groundless accusations won't get you anywhere," complained the Captain. He was certain of himself, like a teacher in the middle of a lesson. "What happened is much simpler than the scenarios you've cooked up in your head."

"You may be right," she replied with a smile, "but I learned something this morning that I bet would send you for a spin, too."

"Oh yeah? What's that?"

"The former chief medical office of the American Hospital, Nicholas, says that murders similar to those of Hadji Settar and Reshat were committed seventy-eight years ago, too. And a coppersmith was murdered back then as well."

The Captain couldn't immediately grasp what he was being told.

"Who killed whom, and why?"

"Seventy-eight years ago right here in this area, the Priest Kirkor was killed in the same manner as Hadji Settar, pushed off of what was then the bell tower of the church, and Ohannes Agha, who owned most of the land of Göven Village, was found just like Reshat, decapitated with his head in his lap. The only addition is that back then, coppersmith Garo was murdered, too."

"Who told you about this?"

"I told you, the former head doctor of the American Hospital, Nicholas. He was in Antep when the murders happened."

"How old is this guy?"

"Ninety-something."

"Couldn't be that he's senile?"

"No, his mind's in tip-top shape. He remembers everything that happened seventy-eight years ago, dates and all, as if it were yesterday."

The Captain pondered this for a while. Esra thought he was about to admit he was wrong when he started up again.

"What Nicholas said supports my own thoughts as well," he said, starting to defend his theory all over again. "As you know, the separatists were never strong in this region. They take advantage of every opportunity they can to try and gain a foothold here. And so they recruited the Gencelis' son Mahmut into the party in order to do just that. The goal was to infiltrate the Genceli tribe and establish themselves here. But they failed. The information that Nicholas provided shows that the separatists tried a new strategy this time around. Göven and Mucur, where Reshat was killed, are Armenian villages. They don't consider themselves Armenian, but their roots are actually Armenian. In 1915 they chose to become Muslim en masse and renounced their former religion. And nobody stuck their nose into their business. They continued to live as respectable citizens of this country. The separatists though want to show that they've gotten revenge for forgotten incidents that happened seventy eight years ago by repeating those same murders, and thus inciting the populations of those two villages to revolt. In this way they'd be able to gain sympathizers from among those citizens and gain footholds in new areas as well."

As the Captain finished talking, the soldier who had taken their order approached with a tray carrying two tea glasses of a steamy, yellow drink and a small jar of sugar.

The Captain saw the soldier approaching, but continued speaking.

"Can you imagine how sly those guys must be? They go so far as to take advantage of an incident that happened seventy-eight years ago just to get a foothold in the region..."

The soldier walked up closer to the table, but then stopped short. He didn't have the nerve to interrupt the Captain, and so he just stood there waiting. Esra's eyes slid to the soldier and the Captain finally addressed him.

"Have you brought the drinks then? Set them down there."

The soldier approached politely and began to place one of the glasses onto the table when his foot slipped, causing him to lose his balance and pour the entire glass of *zahter* onto Esra's lap. The young woman screamed at the top of her lungs and jumped to her feet. A dark stain covered part of her light green blouse and the top right side of her beige colored linen pants. The Captain, too, had sprung to his feet.

"Look what you've done! Why don't you be more careful?" the Captain snapped at the soldier.

The young soldier was standing at attention, taking the verbal beating from his commander in dead silence. The Captain then walked over to Esra. "Did it burn you badly?" he asked worriedly.

Esra was pulling on her blouse and pants, trying to keep them from touching her skin. The Captain turned to the soldier once again.

"Bring some water," he yelled, "quick!" He looked at Esra, and suddenly changed his mind.

"I think we had better go home."

"There's nothing wrong, I'm fine," Esra said, but her face contorted in pain, belying her brave front.

"Let's go home and you can put some cold water on it. It'll soothe the pain."

Esra didn't put up a fight, and so they walked to the entrance of the residential buildings. Unsure of what to do now, the soldier stood staring after them with fearful eyes.

The Captain's apartment was on the ground floor. It was quite tidy, but then Esra was in no state to notice.

Eshref pointed to the half open door.

"The bathroom's over there," he said hurriedly. "You go ahead and go in. I'll bring you a clean towel."

As soon as she was in the bathroom, Esra took off her shirt and pants. She stepped behind the shower curtain and turned the water on. The water began to flow over the red area on the right side of her stomach and her leg. The water, warm at first, gradually grew cooler. And the cooler the water became, the more it eased Esra's pain. Suddenly she recalled that she had left the door cracked open, and so she turned the water off and quickly went to shut it. The Captain was nowhere to be seen. She approached the door, water running down her body. As she pushed the door close, she heard the Captain's voice.

"I brought you a towel and some dry clothes. I'm putting them next to the door."

She could make out from the sounds that he was hanging the stuff on the door handle. She waited a few moments and then opened the door and took the towel and clothes. She took off her underwear and got under the shower again, and taking care not to get her hair wet, remained there until the pain had largely subsided.

When she got out of the shower, she found that the burn still stung but that it didn't hurt as much as it had before. She took the towel and began to dry off in front of the sink. Once she was dry, she looked over her right leg and stomach again; they were red, but there wasn't any swelling. "Got lucky that time," she thought. She looked at the pants and blouse that she had thrown on top of the washing machine. Perhaps she should go ahead and wash them? She wet down the areas onto which the *zahter* had spilled. They would dry off as soon as she hung them out on the balcony. She put on her underwear, and then pulled the thin cotton pajamas that Eshref had brought up over her legs, and his dried rose colored t-shirt over her back. She got a whiff of a faint, familiar, pleasant scent, which was either coming from the t-shirt or the pajamas. No, it wasn't like the scent of detergent, more like shaving lotion. Suddenly she recalled that it was the perfume that Orhan used. So it seemed that Eshref used the same scent. She looked at her face in the mirror and felt rather odd. There she was, in the bathroom of the man she was attracted to, wearing his clothes. She remembered that she used to wear Orhan's pajamas after they had made love. She used to watch proudly as her husband looked at her, marveling at her breasts, at her legs, visible beneath the unbuttoned pajamas. Really, just how long had it been since she'd made love with a man? She looked up to the face in the mirror again. She must not have been pleased by the faint crimson in her cheeks, and the odd sparkle in her eye, for at that moment she mumbled to herself, "Stop this nonsense, Esra." She shouldn't go doing things that would only complicate things. But it wasn't easy to suppress the stirrings of desire deep within her. She touched the soft fabric of the large t-shirt that hung from her body. She thought of the Captain's dark hands, his long fingers. The warmth in her cheeks began to spread throughout her body. She quickly pulled herself together. What was she thinking? She shouldn't do such a thing. "No, no" she snapped at herself. She didn't even know Eshref all that well yet. Besides, with so many problems for them to worry about already... She turned on the faucet and began to wash her face, as if the water would rinse away the desire arising within her. She was trying to banish any and all thoughts from her mind as she dried off, picked up her wet clothes, and stepped out. She walked towards the living room and suddenly came face to face with the Captain as she turned the corner. They were so close each could feel the warm breath of the other. Although she had encountered those dark eyes so many times before, for the first time she saw an expression there that she did recognize. She dropped the clothes in her hand and embraced him. After a short hesitation the Captain began to hold her as well. For a while they just stood there like that, leaning against one another, becoming familiar with one another's bodies. Esra once again caught the sweat tinged scent of the Captain's perfume. Her heart began beating excitedly, like that of teenager. Seeming to sense this, the Captain moved gently, pulling back until he could see the young woman's face before grabbing her by the shoulders and leaning in to kiss her.

TABLET NINETEEN

I compassionately stroked her hand, looked lovingly at her face, into her eyes, but I tried to keep my body away from hers, because I was afraid—afraid of kissing her, of taking off my clothes, or making love with her, of failing once again. Ashmunikal was aware of all of this. She tried to make me relax, with her sweet words, encouraging glances, small touches. But it was not easy. We constantly talked with one another, touching one another with fairytales, epics, poems. We made love not with our bodies, but with our words. This small room in the library in which I write these tablets was the sole witness of our strange love.

My grandfather Mittanuwa was the first person to bring me to this room. It was in those days that Mitannuwa, then chief palace scribe, showed me how to mix the clay for tablets and write in cuneiform. Then, after Mitannuwa had been removed from his post, I came here with my father, Araras. Oh how many times have I worked until sundown, helping my father to write tablets! In this little room, secret texts were composed to kings and secret pacts arranged, but it would never have occurred to my grandfather Mitannuwa, my father Araras, or to me that the same room would one day host a secret love. A human is not a god, and therefore cannot think of everything or know everything beforehand. And so that which we had not thought of, which we had not predicted, occurred and for Ashmunikal and me, this small room became our room of love.

Ashmunikal came to the library almost every day, and we would make a dash for the small room whenever we managed to escape from Laimas. If it had gone on like this, King Pisiris would have learned of our love very soon. But one day, the Chief Priest Valvaziti saw us during a visit to retrieve a religious text from the library.

Knowing our past, Valvaziti understood what was going on as soon as he saw us. And that night, he came all the way to our house. He asked if Ashmunikal and I were having an affair. I said that we were not. He did not believe me, but he did not say so to my face. He only warned me with the following words:

"Son of Araras, you tell me that you are not having an affair with that girl, who is a member of our king's family, but what I have seen tells me otherwise. Still, I want to believe you, because in the future, you will be one of the people who determines the fate of this country. Your mind, your experience, your knowledge shall be at the king's command and shall be used for the happiness of the people. I am not unwise to the ways of love; I know what a burning, vital emotion it is, how it can drive a man mad with bliss. But love resembles the sun's appearance in full regal mode in winter, or a sweet, sudden downpour in the heat of summer—though it possesses a mad beauty, a kind of passion that takes one's breath away, it is but temporary. Just as the winter sun's life is a short-lived one, just as a summer downpour comes to an end before truly saturating the ground, love, too, comes to an abrupt end. It is senseless to offend your gods, and your king, for such a fleeting emotion. Be yourself, and keep away from this diseased emotion. Do not allow a young woman to provoke you to certain acts. Show that you are different from a wild stallion that becomes lustful at the mere sight of a pretty mare. Do not cast a shadow upon your family and the honor of your father Araras."

For a moment, Valviziti's words struck fear into my heart, but when I thought of Ashmunikal, fear instantly melted away. I looked the priest straight in the eye and continued to lie, thinking that I was successfully deceiving him. But Valvaziti, experienced as he was, did not believe me. When my father returned from his travels a month later, Valvaziti told him all about what was happening. My poor father, already sufficiently burdened by the stress of government affairs, confronted and questioned me, all the while breathing through his nose like a wounded pig. I responded to each of his questions with a lie, denying the love I felt for Ashmunikal and all that we had experienced together. My father did not know whether to believe me or not, but he had no intention of leaving the matter to chance. The tribulations of the state were sufficient; the last thing he needed was for my affairs of the heart to instigate further trouble for him. He forbade my entrance into the palace. From now on, he himself would be teaching Ashmunikal Akkadian. Thus did it become impossible for me to see my one and only love, the beloved of my heart, the most beautiful and most brilliant girl of these lands. Reigning curses down upon my father, I began to ponder ways to reach Ashmunikal and to seek out ways that we might see each other again. But I failed. My father had ruthlessly cast away our love. He was in no mood to withstand even the slightest bit of gossip that may cast a shadow upon the king's honor. Especially when our country had already become embroiled in a dangerous game with the neighboring kings...

But my father Araras' efforts were in vain, for the gods would join our bodies together in that small room of the library, so that we would never again part for all of eternity.

CHAPTER TWENTY

Their naked bodies lay next to each other in the double bed that Eshref had slept in alone for so long. The heavy breathing and deep moans, the shuddering and spasms of pleasure were now at an end, and the gentle, warm wind streaming in through the curtains had begun to dry the beads of sweat on their skin.

Esra felt completely at ease, which was rather odd considering the circumstances. After sleeping with a man for the first time, she'd usually rise from the bed with a troubled feeling—a feeling of alienation, a feeling that she'd been soiled. But now, she lay there with a naked man next to her and felt neither anxiety nor shame, but instead a sense of relaxation and happiness. This must be what Sevim was talking about when she used to say, "Nothing does a woman more good than a fulfilling session of lovemaking," she thought. When she turned her head, she saw that Eshref was watching her from beneath his long eyelashes. She reached up and lovingly stroked his short hair.

"Look at you," said Eshref, "acting as if we've been lovers for half a century."

Esra quickly recoiled from him. "What do you mean by that?" she said with sparks of rage in her eyes.

The Captain reached out and grabbed her by the waist.

"Wait, don't get all upset now. I like it that you're so relaxed."

"I'm not mad," said Esra, her good-humor restored. "But I wouldn't want you to get the wrong idea about me."

The Captain pulled her towards him without saying a word. He began kissing her. Esra thought they were going to begin making love again, but then the Captain relaxed his arms and looked her in the eyes.

"Why me?"

Esra slid out from between his loose embrace.

"What kind of a question is that to ask?"

"I'm just curious," he said. He laid his head upon the young woman's stomach. "What's wrong with that?"

Esra's lips twisted into a naughty grin.

"Maybe it's because of Memduh Abi," she teased.

"And who the heck is Memduh Abi?" Eshref grumbled.

"Memduh Abi was my childhood sweetheart," she said, continuing to spin her tale. "I was seven or eight years old and he was twenty or so. He was a student at the Naval Academy on Heybeliada, and the son of our next door neighbor. I was enamored with his uniform."

"But theirs is white."

"I know. What's the difference, white or khaki, they're all uniforms, aren't they?"

Eshref seemed put out by this.

"So, you mean you're with me because I remind you of someone else?"

"Just kidding..." she said, placing a gentle kiss upon his lips. "I don't know why you. There's something about you that attracts me to you, but I can't put my finger on it."

Eshref was pleased by this answer, and he leaned over and tried to kiss her breasts. "Don't!" Esra cried, covering her breasts with her hands to stop him.

The Captain compliantly withdrew, but his eyes remained fixed upon her.

"Do you realize," he said, "that you have never told me anything about yourself either."

"What do you want to know?"

"Your husband. Why did you leave him?"

"He wasn't sincere," she said. The words just spilled out of her mouth before she even had a chance to really give them any thought. "He was constantly telling me that he loved me. He supposedly doted over me." She went quiet, her eyes staring at the opposite wall.

"But..." said the Captain, touching Esra on the shoulder to indicate that she should continue.

"But he didn't really love me," she said once she'd come to herself. "He just pretended to love me."

"How can you be so sure?"

"I got pregnant," Esra said. Eshref saw that her eyes were welling up with tears, although her tone of voice did not change at all. "We both wanted the child. Orhan was more enthusiastic about it than I was, as if he wanted the child even more than I did. He doted upon me. Whenever I went to pick up anything just a wee bit heavy, he'd immediately stop me. He made sure that I ate well, he prepared my meals himself, and begged me not to smoke. His attitude really got on my nerves sometimes, but I'd be lying if I said I didn't like it most of the time.

"There were times when I was suspicious of his feelings, when I thought there was something fake about his behavior. But my suspicions never lasted long. That's the way Orhan was; he enjoyed taking care of me, spoiling me. Or rather, that's what I thought. During the fifth month of my pregnancy, Orhan had to go to Ankara for an international conference. It was an important step in his career. Renowned archaeologists from all over the world would be there. He'd been preparing his talk for this conference for months. The conference was to last three days, and Orhan's talk was to be on the first day. I was as excited as he was, and curious to see how the others would react to his talk. That evening he called. He was elated. He'd received a giant applause and heaps of praise for his talk. I was so happy for him. I just couldn't sit still, and so I decided to go see Behidje Hodja, who lived just a street below us, to give her the good news. I was so worked up out of excitement though that as I started to make my way down the stairs, my foot slipped and I tumbled all the way down to the next landing. When I opened my eyes, I was at the hospital. My mother was standing next to me. I asked her what had happened. She said I was fine, yet her eyes were full of tears. I immediately thought of the baby. I'd lost the baby. I felt this hole, this emptiness inside, as if a piece of me had been ripped out, a part of me stolen. I wanted to cry, but I held it in. I asked about Orhan.

"'We told him about it,' my mother said. She herself had spoken with her son-in-law. He, too, was very sad about what had happened.

"'When's he coming?' I asked.

"'His conference is very important,' she said. 'When he heard that you were okay, he decided to stay until the end of the conference. He'll be back in two days.'

"I started to laugh, and soon I was laughing hysterically. My mother thought that I'd lost my mind and immediately went to get the doctors. But I was fine. I was just relieving my nervous tension. By the time my mother returned with the doctors, I had begun crying. The doctors gave me a shot to calm me down and told my mother that my reaction was normal. They said that expectant mothers who miscarry sometimes become depressed like that. Orhan called that evening. I asked my mother to tell him that I was asleep. I didn't speak with him at all until he got back from Ankara. He understood that I was upset with him. As soon as he got back, he began begging for forgiveness, with all of those 'my darling,' 'my life,' speeches. The more he tried to win my heart back, the more detached I grew from him. Every word, every action of his began to grate on my nerves. In that hospital, I had not only lost my child, but I had also lost my love for Orhan. And six months later I left him."

Esra was silent for several moments before lifting her head to look at the Captain.

"So that's how it is," she said with a bitter smile.

"Didn't you ever consider giving him another chance?" the Captain asked.

"No. What we lived was so fake. And the worst part of it was that Orhan was fooling himself, too. The man didn't love me, but for some reason, he didn't want to accept this. It was as if the world would come to an end if he accepted the fact that he didn't love me."

"Maybe he really did love you, but at that moment his work outweighed everything else."

"While his beloved wife was in the hospital? Having lost the child that he had doted over so before it was even born?"

The Captain didn't respond, and for a while both of them were silent.

"Maybe," said Esra, "if he hadn't smothered me so, I could have forgiven him. Sometimes people make big mistakes. But Orhan just wasn't sincere. He wasn't admitting his true feelings, neither to me nor to himself. Instead, he preferred to play the good husband. There was nothing I could do for him. I did both him and myself a favor by leaving him."

"I see," said the Captain. "It seems like you did the right thing."

"I know I did the right thing."

The Captain looked at her in awe.

"How wonderful that you're so sure of yourself."

"That's not true," said Esra. She pressed her cheek into the Captain's palm. "Actually, I'm..."

"No," the Captain said, interrupting her. "You're the strongest, most self-confident woman I have ever met."

Esra swallowed, she couldn't hold in her tears any longer. She embraced the Captain and began to weep. Eshref lovingly stroked her rebellious light brown hair until her crying ceased. Then he turned her head towards him and began planting tiny kisses on the corners of her eyes. He moved his mouth down Esra's burning face until he found the young woman's slightly open mouth. They passionately locked lips as their bodies became intertwined once again.

By the time they came to, night had long fallen. Esra's eyes moved to the window. "Ohhh, it's gotten late," she said in a sleepy voice. "I should get going."

Eshref seemed disappointed.

"Are you leaving so soon? I thought we'd have dinner together."

"It's best if I go," she said, even though she didn't really want to go.

"Is the excavation crew expecting you?"

"They aren't, but..."

"But?"

"I've been missing in action all day."

"What's the big deal if you show up a few hours late...?"

It wouldn't be the end of the world if she went back a few hours late, but for some reason that even she herself did not fathom, she proceeded to get out of bed. She looked at the Captain with imploring eyes that seemed to say, "Please understand," and began looking for her clothes. The light of the garden lamps was shining into the room, illuminating Esra's square shoulders, her small but shapely breasts, her taut stomach, her genital hair, her long legs. The Captain felt an unbearable desire to touch her. But he held himself back and instead continued sitting there on the bed with a sullen face. Esra left the room and went to fetch the clothes she'd left in the living room. They were almost dry, and more importantly, the *zahter* hadn't left any stains. She got dressed and went back into the bedroom. When she found the Captain just as she had left him, sitting on the bed with a long face, she realized that there was no way she could go. However, she was in no hurry to tell him about her change of heart. Smiling, she walked up to him. She sat down on the bed and touched his face.

"What's wrong?"

"What do you think?" said Eshref. "You're taking off."

"That's why you're angry?"

"Yes. Wouldn't you be angry?"

"I would," said Esra. She leaned over and planted a big kiss on the Captain's lower lip. "Okay, I'm staying. But how are you going to explain the young woman in your bedroom to the watchmen at the door?"

With great ardor the Captain tried to embrace Esra.

"They left their posts some time ago," he said. "There should be new soldiers on duty now."

Esra masterfully wiggled out of the man's embrace.

"I'll stay, but I have no intention of spending any more time in bed. I'm dying of hunger. I haven't eaten anything since breakfast."

The Captain pulled himself together immediately.

"Let me have some stuff brought in from town."

"No, no, I don't want you to do that. Is the soldiers' mess really all that bad?"

"It's not bad, but wouldn't you like something better..."

"Okay, it's settled, we're eating in the cafeteria," Esra interrupted. "When will it be ready?"

The Captain looked at his watch; it was twenty after five.

"They should have dinner ready already. Let's call and order."

Half an hour later they were eating the soldier's mess—*dalyan* meatballs, salad, and plum compote—on the table out on Eshref's balcony, in the shade of the linden tree. Despite her host's coaxing, Esra refused to drink any alcohol.

"I love *dalyan* meatballs," she said. "I haven't had them in so long."

Eshref was watching Esra with a happy but far-off expression on his face. When Esra's eyes met his, he paused and smiled, before leaning over to touch Esra's hand.

"I can't believe you're here," he said. "It may sound funny to you, but I feel a kind of apprehension inside and I don't know why."

This behavior of the Captain's caught Esra off guard.

"What do you mean 'apprehension'?"

He didn't know quite how to explain it. It was similar to the fear that he had felt when he was laid up at the hospital, a fear that had sent him mentally and spiritually topsy-turvy. And just as he had been unable to explain it to his psychologist, neither could he explain it to Esra, although he very much wanted to. Still, he tried.

"Like that there's going to be a conflict, that news of something is going to arrive, that we're going to become alienated from one another..."

But his explanations did nothing but confuse Esra.

"That's why I didn't want you to go," the Captain continued. "Because we may not be able to see one another again."

"Why wouldn't we see each other again? We're both here."

The Captain let go of her hand.

"I don't know, life's full of traps. Something unexpected happens to you every day, there's always some uproar over something."

He had averted his glance. For a while he just stared at the bread on the table, lost in thought. Esra had stopped eating too. She was confused. Could it be that the Captain knew other developments regarding the murders and was keeping them from her? Was his fit there in the garden when he spoke to her so derisively, was that done intentionally, as some kind of cover up?

"We really are having some hard times these days, but that's all over now, isn't it?" she asked. But what she really wanted to say was, "Or is there something you're not telling me?"

"You're right," said the Captain. He spoke as if he'd just awoken from a long slumber. "It's all over now."

Esra remained silent, studying his face carefully.

"Why aren't you eating?" asked Eshref. "I thought you said you loved *dalyan* meatballs?"

"I am eating," said Esra, but she thought that Eshref was trying to change the subject. Finally, unable to stand the tension any longer, she asked him outright:

"Are you hiding something from me?"

"No, of course not. Why would I hide something from you?"

"You're acting a little weird."

"You're right, I got a little lost in thought there, but it's not what you think. It has nothing to do with the murders."

Esra didn't believe him, but she didn't protest. Instead, she just silently continued to eat her meal. Eshref was silent too. Esra considered his silence evidence of his guilt.

Suddenly she dropped her fork and said, "Shall I admit something to you..." She had narrowed her eyes in anger, and her face was tense, as if to signal that she was ready to do battle. "I don't believe that the separatists are behind the murders."

Eshref didn't say anything, but just looked at her with a bitter smile on his lips.

Esra had begun to feel insulted by his every action, his every mimic.

"What are you laughing at?" she snapped.

"This is exactly what I was afraid of! Look, those damned murders have come between us again."

"This topic is more important than our relationship," said Esra. "We're talking about people's lives. And if the murder or murderers haven't been caught, then that means that all of our lives are in danger."

"But the murderers have been caught," said the Captain, trying to convince her. "They can't harm anyone anymore."

"Do you believe what you're saying right now?"

"I do," he said. "Because it's the truth."

"I don't think it is. The separatists don't carry out murders like these."

"If you knew them, you'd know that they do."

"What does this have to do with knowing the separatists?"

"A lot," said the Captain. "You're underestimating the separatists. To you, they're half ignorant, misled people of a cause that's bound to be defeated. And so you don't think they're smart enough to carry out a series of intricately planned murders in order to gain support of the Armenian villages, like I said."

Seeing the skepticism still there in Esra's eyes, he continued. "There are major countries backing them. The Germans, British, Greeks, Syrians, Iranians. Even the Americans, who appear to be our allies, are secretively supporting them. They have excellently trained forces."

"I don't know what kind of forces they have, but I don't think that they commit murders like these," Esra said without hesitation. "I, too, read the newspapers and watch the news, and not once have I ever heard of the separatists committing murders like these."

The Captain looked at her helplessly. He didn't want to argue, he didn't have the strength for it, but he also knew that he had no other choice now but to talk about it. His throat had gone dry. He reached out to pick up the glass in front of him and noticed then that his hands were trembling. He tightly grasped onto the glass to steady his hand and took a big gulp.

"Don't put too much trust in the news you read in the newspapers," he said with sincerity. "I'm going to tell you about something. It's not news, it's something that actually happened. It's the incident I avoided telling you about the other night."

"Why didn't you tell me that night?"

"Because they're such horrible memories and I didn't want to relive them."

"But won't you relive them now?"

"What other choice do I have?" he said. "There's no other way to convince you."

These words, which Eshref said with his head hung low, touched Esra, and it seemed that her anger had subsided, though she didn't show it. Instead, she just looked at him as if to say, "I'm listening." She knew that they were very different, that they viewed these murder cases from totally different perspectives, and that they would not be able to have a life together. Yet his existence put her at an unfamiliar ease, and made her unusually happy.

TABLET TWENTY

My father had returned from his trip with news that would please Pisiris. Urartian King Sardur and Phrygian King Midas had stated that they were prepared to help Pisiris do battle against their ancient enemies, the Assyrians. Nevertheless, my father still chose his words carefully when telling Pisiris that the kings were prepared to lend their support. "We should still be wary of what the kings say," he cautioned. Pisiris, however, had gone mad with joy upon hearing this news, and, despite warnings from my father and from the elder nobles, had begun sending messengers to the small Hittite kingdoms to tell them the good news that release from the tyranny of the Assyrians was imminent.

Meanwhile, however, the Assyrian's tyrannical king Tiglath-Pileser had murdered his older brother in the palace and successfully suppressed the domestic turmoil in his kingdom and established order once again before founding the most powerful, most ruthless army in Assyrian history. Already he had mounted his swift three-horse war chariot and set out on a campaign to bring those kingdoms revolting against him into line.

Not even the news that Tiglath-Pileser had started his campaign was enough to intimidate Pisiris. Pisiris trusted the Phrygian King Midas and the Urartian King Sardur. The other kingdoms, learning that the Assyrian king was at war, began gathering together like a flock of deer that's caught scent of a lion. The small kingdoms gathered around the Urartian King

Sardur, thinking that in this way, they would be able to stop Tiglath-Pileser. And at the top of the list of these kings came Pisiris, who supported Urartian King Sardur whole-heartedly.

Then the inevitable moment came; the Urartian and Assyrian armies became embroiled in battle. The Assyrian lion devastated the Urartians. Sardur began to make his escape, taking what was left of his army with him. Thus did one of Pisiris' trusted pillars collapse. The Phrygian King Midas meanwhile preferred to watch the war from the comfortable heights of the Anatolian plateau.

For the first time, Pisiris realized his mistake. The Assyrian King Tiglath-Pileser had learned that our country was in cohorts with the Urartians. With fear dark as death descending upon his broad face, Pisiris withdrew to his palace and began contemplating what to do.

The news of the Urartians' defeat fell upon the city like an ominous disaster. News of deaths was coming from the Euphrates shores, from those regions through which Tiglath-Pileser passed en route to Arpad. The Assyrian army was burning, destroying, and pillaging the regions that it defeated; it was carving out the eyes and cutting off the hands of the people of these regions, and sending them into exile from their cities, their villages, their homes. It was only a matter of days before the Assyrian army would be pounding down the gates to our own city. The people, trembling with fear, were waiting for King Pisiris to appear before them and say some comforting words. But the days passed, and the king did not emerge from the palace.

Among those who regarded this situation as very odd was my father Araras. Although it was true that ever since Pisiris had first ascended the throne he had traditionally preferred to do things on his own, in such a dire situation as this involving the fate of the city and all of its people, certainly the proper thing to do would have been to gather together the Council of Nobles, or at the very least consult his closest advisor. But Pisiris did neither of these. He thought, and decided, by himself.

Days later he called for my father to come see him. He said that he had had a secret pact written which he needed to get to Tiglath-Pileser. He explained that he was suggesting they pay twice as much tax as before. However, it was his most trusted man, my father, who would have to deliver this message to Tiglath-Pileser.

Two days later my father, accompanied by twelve palace guards, set off to present Tiglath-Pileser, who was leading the Assyrian army in its siege at Arpad, with the two tablets containing the text of the pact and some valuable gifts. For some unknown reason, Pisiris had told my father not to read the tablets. But then there was no way that he could anyway, for the tablets were being guarded by Pisiris' twelve palace guards.

Before leaving, my father said his goodbyes to us as if he were bidding his final farewell. This behavior of his frightened me. I asked him what was going on. My father's eyes welled up with tears. And he spoke thus:

"The Euphrates brings bountifulness to the land, ears of grain give forth wheat, an apricot tree gives forth apricots; sheep provide us with meat and milk; the king commands this country; soldiers fight; scribes write pacts and advise the king. Everyone has his duty. But sometimes the Euphrates overflows, and it brings forth death instead of bounty; there are droughts and the ears of grain do not give forth grain, the apricot fails to grow on the apricot tree; diseases spread and the sheep die, their milk cannot be drunk; and a time comes when the king cannot command the country, and soldiers cannot fight. These may happen, but a scribe cannot use these as an excuse to turn his back on his duty. For the scribe is the pen of the gods. It is not the king that has given him this duty, but the Storm God of the Skies, Teshub. He must do as he is bid, even if it ultimately means death or betrayal. This is his debt to the gods. And he must pay his debt as it is deemed necessary."

That day, I did not understand what my father was talking about. It would take a long time, and for Laimas, writhing with pangs of consciousness as he lay on his death bed, to tell me the truth before I would come to understand.

My father confidently joined the procession that was setting off to deliver the tablets to Tiglath-Pileser. He held his head higher, and his eyes shone with more dignity than ever.

One month later Pisiris called me to his palace. There was a sorrowful expression upon his face. He greeted me in a friendly manner. He took my hand in to his and spoke as follows:

"Young Patasana, I have some painful news for you. I am sad to say that tyrannical king of the Assyrians, Tiglath-Pileser, brutally killed my advisor, my chief scribe, your father, Araras. And he sent a message stating that he took Araras' life as the price for leaving our city alone. His intent was to intimidate me by taking the man closest to me. Your father's death is a great loss, but even as he died, he did so for the benefit of our kingdom. Even as he died, he protected our country from the plundering and ruthlessness of the Assyrian barbarians. I have great respect for that noble man, who is now at peace with the gods, and command you, as his worthy son, to take over your father's post as chief scribe."

This unexpected news of my father's death devastated me. My mind was in shock, my heart was in pain, and my body shook from head to toe with rage. I recalled the look on my father's face as he left us, and his words rang in my ears, but I did not know how to interpret these events. I held back my tears and listened to Pisiris. Then I asked for permission to leave and ran home, for I thought that I should be the one to tell my mother. My mother collapsed to the ground, wailing in grief, and began clawing at her hair and eyes. I stopped her and told her that she must accept this death maturely, for she was the wife of chief palace scribe Araras, that noble man of the state and advisor to the King Pisiris. I managed to hold back my tears as I said all of this, because from now on I myself was to be the great king Pisiris' advisor and scribe, and I would have to be calm and strong in order to be worthy of this honorable title.

CHAPTER TWENTY-ONE

As the Captain began to tell his story, the expression on his face was calm, but his voice was filled with tension, as if what he told Esra had just happened yesterday.

"As I completed my second year of service in the Southeast, there was only one thing that I was sure of: that in order to defeat the terrorists, I had to be like them. I mean, not by living in an orderly army, or responding when there's an attack, or raiding when there's a report. I mean doing exactly as they do, and that meant forming a group of warriors that lives in the mountains and is constantly on the move. It was Seyithan who taught me this. The secret to his success was hidden in the fact that he had learned to live in difficult conditions, in the mountains, and fight like the terrorists. And I have to admit that I wanted to do things this way not only to achieve success, but for moral reasons as well. I had attended the funerals of some martyred soldiers at which the relatives of the soldiers had made reproaches to the effect that their children had been placed in the front lines while nothing ever happened to the commanders. Their words admittedly weren't all that far from the truth, and they had a great impact upon me. I had been taught that the Armed Forces comprised a whole, from the highest ranking officer to the lowest ranking soldier, and that both commanders as well as soldiers had to make the same sacrifices, that in fact, commanders should be prepared to make even greater sacrifices. And if that weren't the case, Mustafa Kemal's army would degenerate. I believed and implemented this each and every moment of my service. I considered it to be the most important principle validating my honor as a soldier..."

He paused. He looked into Esra's eyes, as if afraid that she may not believe him, then added, "I might have lost my family and my mental health because of this, but I did maintain my self-respect..."

He grew quiet again. He sighed deeply, as if struggling to breathe.

"Anyways, let me not get off track here. Though Seyithan and I may have had our differences in the beginning, he became my teacher. That Kurdish firecracker taught me things that I couldn't possibly learn at the military high school, war school, the academy, or during maneuvers. I had to use his method in order to protect myself and my soldiers and to defeat the enemy. But with one difference—he was alone, while I had to learn to fight alongside my crew. I told Colonel Ridvan, who would later lose his life in a military conflict, about this idea of mine. He approved of my suggestion. The war had been going on for so long, which actually led to a much less strict command hierarchy and showed that establishing moving units just like the terrorists was the right thing to do.

"As soon as I left Colonel Ridvan, I began thinking about who might take part in the team. The most important thing was psychological unity, and so I needed to form the team out of brave, vigilant men talented in the arts of war, but just as importantly, men with whom I could work together in harmony. I put my list together in no time; I'd formed a twenty person crew of the finest soldiers under the commander. First I met individually with each of them. I explained the conditions to them. I told them that participation was voluntary, that anyone who wanted could stay on at the headquarters. Two of the men decided not to take part. I respected their decision. I brought our eighteen member crew together and held our first meeting. After a short stint of training, we headed out to Mount Djudi.

"Though the first days were a little difficult, we gradually grew accustomed to our new living conditions. A week later we spotted a group of terrorists; there were ten of them. They didn't see us, but we could easily monitor their every move from behind the rocks where we had set up our base camp. I can't tell you how gratifying that feeling of superiority was, because usually the opposite was the case. They would hide and follow us and then start firing when they thought the time was right. And so we'd hit the ground, search for cover, and ultimately fall prey to the enemy because we would be too shocked to know what to do. But now the roles were reversed. What's more, we were able to watch them at night, too, thanks to our thermal cameras and night binoculars. When they entered an open field which offered no chance for escape, we called for them to surrender. They responded by instantly opening fire. Because the area of conflict was under the control of our weapons, we captured six of them dead, four of them wounded. Only one of our men was wounded, in the shoulder. This was our first big success.

"Most of the terrorists have plenty of experience being in the heat of conflict, and they're sharp enough shooters to knock out a flying mosquito, as hardy as goats, and as firm in their beliefs as a warrior of the prophet. And so the news of our victory was cause for celebration at headquarters. During those years, the separatists hadn't yet been defeated in the mountains, and so there was a kind of see-saw act going on between our forces. We'd take over the mountains, and then they would, and so on. Under those conditions, even the smallest victory was of the great importance. When we got back to headquarters, Colonel Ridvan greeted me like a hero. The others no longer doubted the abilities of our crew and so we were allowed greater mobility. The following months proved time and time again how right I had been. We entered into countless conflicts and usually ended up capturing the terrorists dead. At the end of the first six months, though several of my men had been wounded, only one had lost his life, and that was because he had stepped on a landmine. The terrorists were no longer able to roam freely about Mount Djudi, which they'd once controlled. They had learned that they had to be much more careful now. Although the terrorists had suffered some major defeats at our hands during this time, we still hadn't been able to capture the group Ironsmith Kava, which got its name from the fairytale hero and which was very active in the region. We'd gotten reports about them several times, and we'd almost trapped them once, but at the very last minute they'd stopped short of stepping into the area that we'd surrounded and were able to make their escape. We just couldn't understand how it was that they'd been able to sense our trap. But then one day, my walkie-talkie began to buzz. It was the frequency we used to communicate with the headquarters. I turned on the switch out of habit, and heard a voice that was completely foreign to me...

"'Hello Captain,' the voice said in pristine Istanbul Turkish. 'This is Djemshid, commander of the Ironsmith Kava group.'

"To tell the truth, I was utterly stunned. But I quickly gathered my wits about me.

"'Hello Djemshid,' I said. 'What's up, you decide to surrender or something?'

"He let out an irritating, confident laugh.

"'No, I'm just calling to welcome you. As you know, you're in our mountains.'

"'These mountains are a part of the homeland. And if you consider yourself to be a child of this homeland, then you should surrender.'

"'You know very well that I'm not going to surrender. And as for these mountains, they're not a part of *your* homeland, but of *ours*. And you want to know a little secret: they're not very nice to strangers. So be careful.'

"His intentions were obvious.

"'I was just about to tell you the same thing,' I said sarcastically. 'These mountains don't tolerate traitors feeding off of Syria and Iraq. So I think it's you who should be careful.'

"But my words didn't anger him in the least.

"'As you like it,' he said calmly. 'But you've been warned.'

"'Wait a minute,' I said, thinking he was about to switch off his walkie-talkie. 'You don't have an accent. You can't be Kurdish.'

"'I am Kurdish, but I don't know Kurdish,' he said. 'I've been assimilated by the Turkish Republic. Just like you have.'

"He'd managed to shock me yet a second time.

"'Don't be silly,' I grumbled. 'I'm not of Kurdish origin.'

"'Wasn't your father born in Van, Captain Eshref?' he said. 'You're an assimilated Kurd, just like me.'

"'My father was born in Van, but we're not Kurdish. My grandfather was a soldier, and my father was born in Van while he was on duty there. You've been misinformed,' I said and switched off my walkie-talkie. But now I became suspicious. He knew everything from my name to my father's birthplace. How could he have acquired so much information? At first I suspected my own team, but it would have been impossible for them to know my father's birthplace. Then I thought that the terrorists must have men at the headquarters. Or maybe I'd just gone running my mouth off somewhere. I knew that we had to be especially careful from then on. I decided that from that point on, we wouldn't inform the headquarters of any ambushes we were planning, or even which direction we were heading. And though I didn't consider it very likely that there were really any conspirators amongst them, I would have to behave cautiously around my own team as well; I'd have to be alert at all times, even while sleeping. Another point that I needed to clear up was the true identity of Djemshid. I needed to find out who this arrogant bastard with the polished Turkish really was.

"As soon as I returned to headquarters, I went to see my friend Djevat, who was an intelligence soldier. I told him about Djemshid. He said he knew him. Informants had provided detailed information about him. His real name was Mehmet Serikan. His grandfather was among the commanders led by Sheikh Said during the revolts of February-April 1925. Once the revolts had been suppressed, his grandfather was executed along with Sheikh Said. So his family was then sent into exile in Konya, where Mehmet was later born. He studied elementary and middle school there and was quite a successful student. He was valedictorian of his class in high school. He began studying psychology at Bosphorus University, but dropped out in his third year to join the terrorists in the mountains. He was intelligent, brave, and believed firmly in his cause.

"When we got back to Djudi, I found out their frequency and got in touch with Djemshid again. 'Ooooh, Captain Eshref,' he said in that same arrogant, sarcastic tone when he heard my voice.

"'Bravo, Mehmet,' I said. 'You recognized me.'

"There was a short silence.

"'And it seems you've recognized me, too,' he said, with no intent of losing face.

"'But we haven't really properly 'met' yet, now have we? I really can't wait to meet with you face to face.'

He was immediately back to his sarcastic self.

"'Don't worry, Captain, that'll happen, too. But I hope you don't end up sad or upset when we do.'

"'We'll see about that when the time comes.'

"We talked on the walkie-talkies like that numerous times, but never managed to have a live encounter. Several more times we tried to ambush him, but he never showed up at the places I expected. It was as if he could smell the ambush, sense the trick, from kilometers away. And so it went for some four months, when in the last week of April, we went down to headquarters. We stayed there until early May before setting off for Mount Djudi again. There's a guard village on the skirts of the mountain. That's where we got our reserves. The village had an agha, Hamit. Hamit had a row of front teeth that were completely gold plated, he was a pleasant conversationalist, and he had four wives. Whenever we stopped by the village, he'd sacrifice sheep to welcome us. He got on well with everyone at headquarters, but he was especially fond of our team. He was friends with all of us. In fact, he'd even made me the godfather of one of his grandchildren. Also, Hamit Agha had a special fondness for prayer beads. Whenever someone from our team was heading out on leave, he'd insist that they bring him back some prayer beads. Sergeant Reshit was from Erzurum, and when he came back from his leave with a beautiful string of prayer beads made of jet for Hamit, the big old agha grew giddy with delight, just like a child. He praised Reshit to the high heavens for those prayer beads.

"Anyways, so after we'd left headquarters, we stopped by the village and were hosted by Hamit Agha for the night.

“The next night, we set off again. We covered our foreheads, cheekbones, and the tips of our chins, I mean, the parts of our face that shine at night, with black paint. There we were silently climbing up a rocky slope, with me thinking about Djemshid and about how I’d do whatever it took to capture that man. It was a warm spring night, and the full moon hung in the sky like a silver flower in bloom. A sweet scented breeze was blowing off from the mountains. We were proceeding cautiously, spaced one meter apart from each other. At the very front were Yorgo of Buyukada and Oruch of Izmit, with about twenty meters between them and me.

“As is obvious from his name, Yorgo was of Greek origin. When he was in boot camp, the other soldiers would humiliate him and call him ‘The Greek.’ That really got Yorgo fired up, and so he started taking a position in the very front lines during conflicts and really proving himself. And that hadn’t escaped my attention. He was a natural choice to include in my team. Yorgo’s a fabulous guitar player, but more importantly, he has an amazing ear. He can discern a slew of sounds in nature. Oruch of Izmit is a very alert soldier, too. And so that’s why they always led the pack at night.

“We’d neared the Boynuz Pass about midnight. The pass was on the other side of a small hill to our right. But about a hundred meters before we got to the hill, I noticed someone approaching. It was Oruch.

“‘Yorgo says something’s wrong here, Sir,” he whispered once he’d reached my side. I stopped the team. My soldiers silently crouched down behind the rocks. I carefully approached Yorgo. He’d thrown himself behind a rock and was looking at the stone outcrop that we called the Boynuz Pass.

“‘What’s going on, Yorgo?” I whispered.

“‘There’s some movement over there, Sir,’ he said, without taking his eyes off the pass. ‘I heard sounds.’

“‘What kind of sounds?’ I said, perking my own ears up.

“‘Like whispers, like the sound of cloth rubbing against stone.’

“‘Are you sure?’ I asked.

“‘I wasn’t at first,’ he said, then motioned toward the low stone about ten meters ahead. ‘So I crawled over to that stone.

I heard the same sounds again. I'm sure there are people over there.'

"The Boynuz Pass was an ideal place to set up an ambush. If you could secure the hills, no one who entered the pass could make it out again alive. Moreover, on this full moon night, the targets would be as clearly visible as in broad daylight. But there was at least forty meters between us and the pass. I have no idea how on earth he had heard the sounds from so far away. I looked at the pass and saw nothing but motionless rocks gleaming under the moonlight.

"'Let's look with the thermal,' I said. The thermal can detect body heat and show living things. We looked, and saw that there really was movement.

"'Maybe it's just wild animals.'

"'But I heard whispering, Sir,' he insisted.

"There was no reason to go putting ourselves at risk.

"'Okay, so let's say there are terrorists over there. Do you think it's possible that they saw you?' I asked.

"'I doubt it,' he said. 'I was very careful.'

"Yorgo and I slithered our way out from among the rocks and went back. Sergeant Reshit had grown anxious waiting and came over to join us.

"'Let's feel the place out with the bazooka,' he said upon hearing about our suspicions, 'that should tell us if there's anybody there or not.'

"I didn't agree with him on this point. If they were planning to ambush us, then it was most likely Djemshid's doing. He'd gotten word that we'd left headquarters and he was eagerly awaiting us on our own route. We could have moved to the left, to a more precipitous cliff, climbed for five or six hours to a wooded hill overlooking the Boynuz Pass, and prepared a nasty surprise for them, making them fall into the very trap they'd set up for us. Of course, there was also the possibility that Djemshid would get bored and take off in the meantime, but I doubted that a determined soldier like him would grow impatient like that. Besides, it was worth the risk.

"'And what if we're wrong?' asked Sergeant Reshit.

"He was right to be concerned. Each of us had at least twenty-five kilos of supplies loaded on our backs, and the bazookas to boot.

"'If we're wrong, then we'll have gotten one heck of a workout,' I said smiling. 'We've been lounging around headquarters long enough as it is.'

"'Then let's inform headquarters.'

"But that I could not do. However, another thing I couldn't do was dampen their morale by telling them that there was an informer at headquarters.

"'We'll let them know once we're certain,' I said. 'I wouldn't want them making fun of my team.'

"The word 'team' did the trick. None of us wanted to cause the team to become a target of taunting back at headquarters. And so we withdrew and began our difficult climb up the steep cliff. After a while, it became obvious that the two bazookas were too much for us. It only took about fifty meters before the soldiers carrying the bazookas were drenched in sweat. We hid the bazookas in some brush and continued climbing. Now we had no other choice but to rely upon our G3's and G1's. I was allowing a break once every hour, otherwise there's no way we could've carried on. Still, by sunrise we were completely drained of strength. But just the thought of capturing Djemshid, and of putting an end to the Ironsmith Kava group, made me forget all about the heat and tiredness.

"It was already sundown that evening before we were able to reach the top of the hill, which was covered in stones, large and small. My men were completely exhausted. They collapsed among the stones to rest. As for me though, my curiosity outweighed my weariness. I held my breath and crept to the tip of the hill. The Boynuz Pass was about ten meters below, but there was nobody in sight. I was just beginning to think that we'd been mistaken when I saw something shiny. I took a careful look and realized that it was the barrel of a Kalishnikov. That meant they must have been hiding in the caves down below. They hadn't marched during daylight to avoid detection by the helicopters flying over the control area; instead, they'd waited for the darkness of night to fall. I silently returned to my men. I signed to the others that the terrorists were below and that we'd have to wait until dark to make a move. My soldiers' weary faces quickly perked up.

We quietly began to get ready for battle. We didn't know how many people there were down there, but we'd heard that Ironsmith Kava's group was somewhere between twenty-five and forty people strong. But there were only seventeen of us. So we were aiming to hit seventeen of them with our first shot, and hoping to obliterate them with the second round of shots, taking advantage of the surprise factor, since they wouldn't have expected to run into us here. After a tense two hours of waiting, after everything had taken on an ash gray hue and then succumbed to the darkness of dusk, we made our way to the top of the hill. The full moon was on the other slope of the mountain and wasn't shining on us yet. This was to our advantage as well, since it gave us the upper hand over the enemy because we were able to see and they weren't. We looked down with our night vision binoculars, and what we saw was certainly impressive enough to give all of us a thrill. The hunters—twenty-four of them as far as we could tell—who were on the prowl for us had deployed along the Boynuz Pass and were patiently eyeing the path below. I told my men to choose their targets, not to shoot at the same people, and to wait for my signal before opening fire. My goal was to determine which one was Djemshid and immobilize him with the first shot so that he couldn't get away. But it was rather difficult for me to pick him out from the group below, which was particularly silent. There was a man standing at the very end of the pass. A few people went over to ask him something and then went back to their places. Hoping that he was Djemshid, I aimed my gun at his kneecap. My men had also taken aim and they all knew very well that the first shot was extremely important. We looked at each other one last time, and then I gave the signal and there was a huge roar. I saw that those below us had fallen and were writhing on the ground. I'd shot the person I believed to be Djemshid, and as I began to take aim at someone else, something unexpected happened, and Hüseyin of Kemah, who was standing right next to me, was shot and fell to the ground. When I raised my head, I saw that a rifle was raining bullets down upon us from the next hill. So it seemed they'd taken their precautions and sent someone on up the way.

"'Watch out, the next hill over,' I yelled as I threw myself to the ground. But it took a while for the soldiers to realize what was going on. I heard another of my soldiers getting shot. When our guns went silent, so did the rifle on the next hill. At first I didn't understand why, but then I realized that he couldn't see us, and that he was firing at the sound of our guns. I began scanning the hill with the night binoculars. Meanwhile, I could hear the terrorists wailing in pain down below. When our weapons went silent, someone from the pass yelled something in Kurdish to the person on the hill. I suspected that he was asking how many of us there were. Then the person who had fired upon us moved, and that's when I spotted his left shoulder. I took aim, and thought to myself that now he was going to try and count us. And I was right. He cautiously stuck out half of his face, but it seemed the poor guy still couldn't see anything, for he stretched out a little bit more. When he did that, I got a clear and perfect aim and so I pulled the trigger. I saw the man fall. Now we could begin to deal with our wounds. Sergeant Reshit, who had carried out the first intervention, said that Abdulkadir of Sinop and Hüseyin of Kemah were injured, and that Hüseyin's situation was serious. I ordered them to ask for help from headquarters. Hoping that Hüseyin would make it, I picked up the night binoculars and began looking through them. When I looked down, I saw that fifteen of their people had been shot, and that the others were missing.

"Sergeant Reshit was in favor of waiting for the forces that were to come in from headquarters, or at least for Chief Village Guard Hamit's men, but I didn't want to miss out on this opportunity. I couldn't let the Ironsmith Kava regroup again. Besides, I thought I'd shot Djemshid, and he wouldn't get far with a shattered kneecap. Leaving two people under Sergeant Reshit's charge to deal with the injured, I took the rest of the men with me and we silently made our way down the stony slope and onto the Boynuz Pass. Our night vision binoculars were our biggest advantage, but if you hold them to your eyes for too long, your vision gets all out of whack. So, the binoculars weren't of help for too long. The only thing for both sides to do in the darkness then was to be silent, alert, and ready. And so we carefully made our way down, all the while doing our best to ignore the pain as the thick brush flourishing there in the rain softened earth roughly scratched our faces and hands. When we got down, we didn't go anywhere near the dead bodies, but headed for a massive rock that had been shaped by the wind and rain into a natural stairway leading down to the lower road. We were moving along so slowly that it took us ten minutes just to go a few meters. Suddenly we heard sounds coming from below, and someone cursed in pain. I saw Yorgo fire in the direction from which the voice had come. Someone screamed in pain, and at the same moment, bullets began raining down upon us. Everyone dropped to the ground. The firing continued for several minutes and then stopped. Thankfully, none of our men were shot. I signaled to the two soldiers closest to the pass that they should throw grenades in the direction from which the firing had come. I could tell from the series of deafening explosions that followed that my command had been carried out. I thought the terrorists would open fire after the grenades, but there was no response. So did that mean they were pulling a number on us, or were they running away? After waiting a little while I signaled to the soldiers who had thrown the grenades that they should open fire. As they began firing Yorgo, Oruch, and I slithered among the rocks like three big lizards. The soldiers continued firing until they had run out of bullets in their clips. Another silence followed. This time the three of us began to open fire. My men seized this opportunity and quickly came to join us. It was dead silence again once we'd quit firing.

"'I think they've run off, Sir,' said Yorgo.

"'Let's not rush things,' I said. I didn't want to act rashly and stupidly get caught in some ambush. So we just waited there for nearly half an hour. The only sound to be heard was the moan of the wind blowing through the brush. In the meantime, the full moon had rushed out from behind the top of the mountain, coating everything with a silvery light. We would have to be more careful now. I commanded my men to slither their way through the rocks and push forward. A little while later we were able to see the road. The area was completely deserted. Then all of a sudden I noticed a foot amongst the rocks. I motioned for the team to stop. The foot wasn't budging. I pointed the foot out to Osman of Of, one of our sharp shooters, and told him to fire at it with a pistol. Osman shot it in the sole, and the foot sprang up and then dropped back down again. But that was it, the foot's owner didn't react at all. It must have been the person Yorgo had shot at just a short while before, which meant he must have shot him dead. We remained cautious as we progressed. The man was just sitting there, leaning against a rock, his eyes staring ahead. I looked down at his kneecap, but it was fine. No, this wasn't the man that I had shot. So it seemed they had taken the man I'd shot with them and made their escape. And that was a good sign, because it meant that they couldn't be moving too quickly. We didn't touch the dead body; there could have been a booby trap waiting there for us. I lowered three people, one meter apart, down onto the road below. We kept watch from above, and it appeared that the coast was clear, so the entire team followed suit and climbed down to the road. Still, we remained alert and proceeded cautiously. We clung to the rocks on the left and right sides of the pass and looked at the footprints. It was difficult to understand anything from the footprints, but the blood stains, each looking like a puddle of mud there in the moonlight, sure said a lot. That blood belonged to the man whom I had shot in the kneecap. The traces of blood led downhill, in the direction that we had gone after we'd left the village. The terrorists obviously couldn't have made it too far with a wounded man. If we acted swiftly, we'd be able to catch up with them. But then again, with it being bright out now, there was also a good chance that we'd be ambushed. We would have to be very careful, and that meant that we'd have to slow down. Thank God at least the traces of blood continued to show us the way, like the most precise compass on earth. But then after about an hour, the traces ceased. We looked all over. We searched the rocks, caves, beneath trees, in the brush, but there were neither traces of blood nor any wounded fighters to be found. You could say maybe the man had died and they'd buried him, but they couldn't possibly have done so in such a short amount of time, and besides, if that were the case, then there would been a mound or signs of excavated earth. The whole affair was really starting to get on my nerves. I told my soldiers to spread out and search all over the area. Meanwhile, I began going in small circles around the area where we'd seen the final trace of blood. We were all investigating the scene like that when we heard voices from below, and so immediately we got into position. A short while later Hamit Agha and his men emerged from the darkness. They were thrilled to see us and started asking if we'd lost any men or had any wounded. And I asked them if they'd run into anybody on the way.

"'No, we sure didn't,' said Hamit Agha, hanging his head low. That meant they were still around there somewhere. We got the village guards involved in the search, too. An hour later, forces from the headquarters came to pitch in, too. I sent our injured men to the hospital, accompanied by Sergeant Reshit and another man from the team. We continued our search. Soon it was sunrise, then noon, and then afternoon; there were nearly a hundred of us going over that terrain with a fine tooth comb, but we came up completely empty. It was as if the earth had just swallowed up the Ironsmith Kava gang. As night fell, my walkie-talkie started buzzing. I turned it on; it was Colonel Ridvan.

"'Give up on the search now, Eshref,' he said. 'Obviously the men got away. Let them go, you've already got sixteen dead anyways. They'll have a hard time recovering from that loss.'

"He was right, but I was so riled up. Right when I thought I had him, I let that damn Djemshid slip through my fingers and get away.

"'Sir,' I said in a pleading voice, 'I ask only that you give me one more day. I'll catch them. They're around here somewhere, I can feel it.'

"'I'm sorry, Eshref,' he said. 'We received a report of a raid on the police station at Tash. I have to withdraw the soldiers and guards that I sent out here.'

"'Take them, I have enough men to work with. But we haven't slept since yesterday night. If you could leave four privates to keep watch while we sleep...'

"'I can only leave the recruits, but I'm warning you; they've never been in a conflict, and when they see a tracer, they think it's a shooting star.'

"'They'll just be keeping watch, that's all,' I said. 'We just need them so that we can have a chance to get some rest, that's all.'

"'The colonel finally agreed. The soldiers and guards from headquarters withdrew. Hamit came to talk to me before leaving.

"'Ya be careful,' he said, placing a hand on my shoulder, 'don't wanna see you go down 'cause of some scoundrel's bullet.'

"'Don't worry, I'll catch him this time.'

Together with my twelve men and the four recruits we withdrew to the Boynuz Pass, where the terrorists had set up their ambush. Our eyelids were heavy from fatigue and lack of sleep. I called all of the recruits together and warned each one of them:

"'We're going to sleep at the top of the pass. Two of you are going to stand on the lower road, one on the left and one on the right, and two of you are going to stand guard at the stairway shaped rock up there. Make sure you're well hidden in the rock's shadow. When you hear a sound, use your night binoculars to see what it is. If you become suspicious of anything, fire a shot and we'll come to your aid immediately.'

"'Yes, Sir,' yelled the recruits eagerly.

"'And don't yell so loud,' I said. 'No more talking from now on.'

"My twelve men and I found a quiet corner amongst the rocks where we'd shot the terrorists down the night before and curled up for some rest. We were so exhausted that we fell asleep as soon as our heads touched the ground.

"I woke up when someone nudged me. I opened my eyes, and across from me stood a tall, thin man. I thought it was one of the watchmen.

"'Is it time?' I asked, rubbing my eyes.

"'Yep, it's finally time,' said a familiar, sarcastic voice. 'Finally, we meet, Captain.'

“It didn’t take long for me to comprehend that it was Djemshid. So the person I’d shot wasn’t him! In a panic I looked around me. Seven people were smugly standing over us with their rifles pointed straight at us. I reached out for my own rifle, but it wasn’t where I’d put it. I felt my waist for my pistol, but they’d taken that, too. One by one they were kicking my soldiers to rouse them. When they woke up, the boys experienced the same shock that I’d gotten just a few minutes before, and with their eyes wide open and questioning they looked around, trying to figure out what was going on.

“‘And the watchmen?” I asked.

“‘Too bad you didn’t teach them that it’s not a good idea to listen to their headphones out in the mountains,’ said Djemshid, shaking his head from side to side. ‘They paid a heavy price for their love of music.’

“‘You bastard, did you kill them?’ I hissed.

“‘Yes,’ he said, ‘just like you killed sixteen of my comrades last night. But enough of that. You’ve been in enough conflicts to know that deaths are considered natural in war. What I’m wondering is what you’re feeling right now.’

“It was only then that it occurred to me that I should be frightened. But the funny thing was, I wasn’t. Djemshid and I had this competition, this kind of race going on between us. The war had turned our courage, talent, alertness, and intelligence into a kind of personal struggle for us. And just when I thought I’d had him beat, he’d come out on top. And it was that feeling which ripped me to shreds inside, and which overpowered everything else, making me forget all about the possibility of death.’

“‘Let me tell you, in case you were wondering,’ I said, looking him straight in the eye. ‘It just makes me sick that I haven’t wiped you off the face of this earth yet.’

“He walked up closer to me. Thinking he was going to shoot, I prepared myself for it, but he didn’t. He came over and knelt next to me.

“‘Why do you want to catch me so badly?’ he asked. That’s when I noticed the prayer beads in his hand.

“‘As if you didn’t want to catch me, too, huh?’ I said, my eyes fixed on his prayer beads. But Djemshid’s body cast a shadow over them and so I couldn’t really see them clearly.

He started to laugh, and then he brought the hand holding the prayer beads to his mouth. And that's when I saw that the prayer beads in his hand were the same ones that Sergeant Reshit had brought for Hamit Agha from Erzurum. And that, that totally did me in. I recalled Hamit's words to me as he left us and smiled bitterly.

"'You're right, Captain,' Djemshid continued, thinking that my smile had something to do with the topic at hand. 'I was just dying to catch you, too. I guess it's a kind of existential thing, about proving one's self. Just like the 'King of the Fortress' game that we used to place as kids. It's an interesting game. First you build up a mound of sand, and then someone gets on top. He shouts out 'This is my fortress.' The other children then try to push him off and get on top of the mound themselves. The strongest one stays on the mound and screams out just like the friend he'd defeated: 'This is my fortress.' So what we're playing is a kind of 'King of the Mountain' game. Just a crueler, bloodier version...'

"'I'm not playing,' I countered, 'I'm trying to stop murderous enemies of the state like you.'

"'Come now Captain,' he said in a bored tone of voice. 'An interesting man like yourself shouldn't speak in such clichés.'

"I found it odd that he found me interesting. And that's the first time I realized that he respected me. And what's even weirder is that deep inside, I felt respect for him, too. But I tried not to show it.

"'It's not a cliché,' I said in a devout tone of voice, 'these are values that I am willing to risk my life for.'

"'Alright then, have it your way,' he said. He came a little closer. 'But still, I don't believe you. Anyway... Are you superstitious, Captain?'

"'No,' I said.

"'I am,' he said. 'For example, your team consists of thirteen men, counting yourself. But I know that it won't do me any good to kill all of you, because thirteen is an unlucky number. It's a number to be wary of.'

"I knew perfectly well that he wasn't superstitious. I curiously waited to see where he was going with this.

"'So, in that case, I need to kill twelve of you.'

"As he talked, my eyes moved to my captured soldiers. Most of them were still standing resolute, only I noticed that Oruch was shaking. I wanted to help him, to hearten him, but there was nothing I could do.

"'But I have another hang-up,' Djemshid continued. 'I don't like to mix things up. For example, when I eat fruit after dinner, I eat either apricots, or plums, or watermelons. I never mix them up.'

"These meaningless words of his had really started to get on my nerves. 'Cut the crap,' I lashed out, partly to give my men courage.

"'What I'm trying to say is, I'd really like to kill you. But here we have privates and then there's you, their commander. So, I can't mix things up here by killing both the privates and you. I either kill you, or the privates.'

"'Then kill me,' I burst out, surprised at my own courage. Djemshid gave me a long, admiring glance.

"'I commend you for your courage," he said, "but you're just a single person, while they're twelve experienced privates.'

"I felt my men getting antsy. And that's when I first realized that this conversation was gradually turning into some kind of torture. Djemshid was going to kill every one of us, that much was for certain, but he also had every intention of having his fun with us before pulling the trigger. I had to put a stop to it, somehow. All of a sudden I leapt to my feet and attacked Djemshid, but he pulled away quickly. I landed flat on my face and in the same instant felt a hard blow to my head.

"When I woke up I had a splitting headache, and the sound of flies buzzing in my ears. I tried to lift my head, but this liquid had my face virtually glued to the rock I was lying upon. In a while I'd realize that the liquid was the blood flowing from my head. I slowly sat up, and saw a cloud of flies take flight away from my body. Those fat flies settled down again a few meters away, their wings shimmering in the sunlight. I looked in the direction of the flies, and that's when I saw my soldiers. Now it was they who lay in puddles of blood in the same spot where we'd killed fifteen terrorists the day before. With a last hope that maybe some of them were still alive I quickly made my way over to them. I looked each of them over, but no, they were all dead. They'd killed all twelve of them. Yorgo, Oruch, Osman, Nasir, Ihsan, Ayhan, Mustafa, Nazmi, Selim, Erkan, Atilla, Mürteza... Their hands had been tied behind their backs, and each of them had been shot through the back of the neck, just below the head. I furiously began beating my fist against the rock, but soon collapsed in exhaustion. I calmed myself down and sat up. I looked for my walkie-talkie, but it was nowhere to be found. They'd taken it, too, along with all our weapons. There was still water in our canteens though. I used the water to wash my face and the wound on my head. Leaning against the rocks for support, I made my way down to the road. I felt miserable. I'd lost a lot of blood, but the rage I felt inside kept me on my feet. But then after about five hundred meters, everything went black and I fell unconscious.

"When I came to, I was in Hamit Agha's guestroom. There were two other people in the room besides myself. I could hear their voices. When I opened my eyes, I saw Colonel Ridvan and Hamit sitting next to one another on the floor cushions. I had the taste of dried blood in my mouth. The taste had been in my mouth ever since I'd come to out there on the rocks, and it had stayed with me even through my bout of unconsciousness.

"'So you've finally come to, my boy,' said Hamit, flashing his gold teeth in a saucy grin. To my droning brain the shine of his golden teeth resembled a rifle barrel glittering in the sun. And just then, when I looked at Hamit's shifty eyes as they tried to avoid my own, I remembered everything.

"I heard Colonel Ridvan say, 'Hope you feel better soon, Eshref,' and saw his face long with grief. I could tell though that he was a little sore at me for what had happened.

"I didn't reply but just sat up and then leaned on my hands and pushed myself out of bed.

"'It's not a good idea for you to get up,' the Colonel said.

"'You need to get some rest, my boy,' said Hamit. Their voices echoed in my ears like the sharp buzzing of the flies that had hovered over the dead bodies of my soldiers. The more they talked, the more the buzzing sound increased, and the more unbearable that taste of blood in my mouth became.

"I walked over to the Colonel. I stuck my hand out, and he stuck his out, too, thinking that I wanted to take his hand. But instead, I swiftly removed his pistol from his belt. It only took a few seconds for me to turn off the safety, put the bullets in the clip, and empty all of them into Hamit's head. In a state of shock the Colonel leapt up and began screaming fearfully, 'Eshref, what have you done!' He thought I'd gone mad, and that I was going to kill him, too. But I turned the pistol around and handed it back to him.

"'He's responsible for the murder of my soldiers,' I said. 'Hamit Agha was the traitor amongst us. Have his house searched, and I bet you'll find a terrorist who's been shot in the kneecap. He'll tell you everything.'

"I passed out again while looking at the Colonel's face, which was contorted into an expression of unbelieving horror.

"When I came to, this time around I found myself in the hospital. I'd been unconscious for two days, and for two nights I'd talked in my sleep, saying 'Hamit's going to kill my soldiers, don't let Djemshid get away.' Colonel Ridvan came to see me that afternoon. They'd found the injured terrorist in Hamit Agha's wives' bedroom. They roughed him up a bit and he admitted that Hamit was working for the separatists. The Colonel said in a sad voice that they still intended to open an investigation about me because I'd shot Hamit without an investigation or questioning him at all. But I didn't care about that one bit. My mind was on Djemshid. Even if I were discharged, I was going to find him and get revenge for my soldiers. I couldn't possibly feel at peace so long as he lived... But it didn't happen, because Djemshid and six of his men were captured dead, killed by fire from a Cobra helicopter on Mount Djudi, before I even got out of the hospital. When I heard about his death, I felt a kind of emptiness inside, as if I'd lost my purpose, my will to live. His voice echoed in my ears.

'So what we're playing is a kind of 'King of the Mountain' game. Just a crueler, bloodier version...'

"And that's when I realized the reason why I felt this kind of emptiness inside, and it was because I'd lost my playing buddy. And that's why he hadn't killed me, because he didn't want to lose his playing buddy either. I kept thinking about him until I was released from the hospital...

"The courts found me innocent. But I'd begun acting strangely. I couldn't sleep. I'd stay awake walking about for days until I'd collapse from exhaustion and then I'd start to relive everything that had happened at the Boynuz Pass. They admitted me to the hospital again, but this time to the psychiatric ward. They gave me pills and stuff so I could get some sleep. And they started making me talk, a lot. Talking did me a lot of good. I stayed in the hospital for about a month. The doctors said that I was back to normal, but my superiors thought that I wouldn't be useful in the front lines anymore. They suggested that they transfer me to Istanbul, but I didn't agree to it. And so I ended up here, not exactly on the front lines, but closer to the war front."

"What about your wife? What did she do?" Esra asked, speaking up for the first time since they'd begun talking.

"Like yours, my marriage was a great misfortune, too" he said. "And Gülin's birth was an even greater misfortune... It just killed my wife when I got transferred to Shirnak. I told her to come with me, but she said that she couldn't put herself and our daughter in danger like that. I agreed with her. So I went to Shirnak by myself. I'd go see them whenever I got the chance. But then when conflict in the region heated up, I wasn't able to go visit anymore. My wife would cry on the phone and tell me to pull some strings and get myself transferred to Istanbul, but I couldn't possibly go to my superiors and ask them to do that. My grandfather was an honorable soldier, and it was his example that I had wanted to follow when I joined the Armed Forces. I couldn't act selfishly while thousands of our country's boys were being martyred. I couldn't, not even if I'd wanted to. But my wife didn't get it. When I was injured, she came to the hospital to see me. She began haranguing me, saying 'See, I told you so, you were nearly killed. As soon as you get out of the hospital, get yourself transferred to Istanbul.' When she said that, I recalled how my martyred privates had ripped up their 'dawn notebooks.' Dawn is what the soldiers call the day they get released from military duty. Every soldier has a dawn notebook in which he places a mark for each day that passes. Everybody knows good and well exactly which day they'll 'see the dawn.' When we were first putting our team together, my soldiers had come to me and said, 'Sir, we've decided to rip up our dawn notebooks.' When I asked them why, they just said, 'They confuse us, sir.'

"And so when I recalled how my soldiers had ripped up their dawn notebooks, my wife's words really started to get on my nerves. I asked my doctor not to let her in to see me anymore. In other words, I politely had her kicked out of the hospital. She understood of course, and we've been on bad terms ever since. I send her money every month, and I go to Istanbul sometimes, just to see my daughter. In practical terms, our marriage is over. Sometimes I have to admit that she's not really all that out of line. I mean, the only thing the poor woman wants is to have a husband by her side, a happy life. But I can't help it, the conditions in my life have kept me from becoming that kind of a man..."

Eshref went quiet. He took two deep puffs off his cigarette and began looking into the darkness. Esra reached out and took hold of his hand.

"You've experienced some dreadful things... But you've held up well. Anyone else would've gone mad."

Eshref fixed his eyes on Esra's, which he couldn't see very well now in the dark.

"I didn't tell you about these things so you'd know what I've been through. I told you so that you'd understand how dangerous, how sly the separatists are. They have connections with the population which should not be underestimated. They have talented commanders and forces who are willing to die and to kill, and who are capable of committing all kinds of cunning acts to achieve their goals. And if they believe that there's a potential for strong support in former Armenian villages, then they wouldn't hesitate to get revenge on murders committed seventy eight years ago, if they think it'll help the cause."

Esra didn't know what to say. What he'd told her was striking, but it certainly didn't put an end to her suspicions. And the worst part of the whole thing was that she couldn't just up and tell Eshref that what he'd told her proved absolutely nothing. Feeling his pain, she continued to compassionately stroke the strong hand of this soldier with the wounded soul.

TABLET TWENTY-ONE

Everyone in the city shared my pain. My father's death not only made me the palace scribe, but it also bestowed upon me an undeserved fame amongst the nobles and the people. Everyone I met on the street knew of me as the son of Araras, the man who had saved the city by giving up his own life, and everywhere people would come up to me and sing my father's praises, and advise me to be a brave and wise man like my father had been. And so it was with this fervor and honor inherited from my father that I began to perform my duties as scribe.

King Pisiris called me to see him on my first day. With the queen in attendance, he spoke as follows:

"Our respect for your father was not the only reason we have appointed you to become palace scribe. And it is not because of your lineage, not because your forefathers have been scribes for so many generations. The reason why we want to have you with us, in our palace, always, is that you are one of this country's most well-educated, well-trained young men. Praising the young spoils them, leads them astray. But we know you. You are as morally upright as you are knowledgeable. Those who raised you taught you well, and correctly. And together with the knowledge they imparted to you, they also taught you how to use that knowledge. It will be a pleasure to have you here with us."

With this talk I began my post as scribe, a post for which I had been preparing since childhood, having been trained first by my grandfather Mittanuwa, and then my father Araras. My father used to tell me that being a scribe requires sacrifice. "To fulfill your duty, you must give up everything that ties you down." I had two great fears when I first began acting as scribe: the first was that my father's assistant Laimas would try to undermine me out of jealousy, and the second was my relationship with Ashmunikal.

My first worry resolved itself. Laimas didn't put on any airs and showed no signs of being offended. Instead, he withdrew and allowed me to demonstrate my knowledge, experience, and talents. He supported me. In fact, he acted more politely and respectfully than necessary. There was undoubtedly a good reason for this behavior on his part, but I, naïve Patasana, just interpreted it as a sign of the respect Laimas had had for my father.

As for my second worry, the passion that I could not do without, my first love, my first woman, the first apple of my eye, Ashmunikal... It didn't take long for word to reach Ashmunikal about my arrival at the palace. One morning I found her sitting on a bench in the library reading the legend of the God Telipinu. She looked at me with those piercing dark eyes of hers. It was not a look of condemnation; it is true that there was condemnation in her eyes, but even more so, there was longing, and compassion. That look made me forget for a moment my duty, who and where I was. I immediately sat down next to her. It was early and there was no one else in the library. She touched my hair, and looked at me carefully, lovingly, affectionately, as if trying to memorize every line, every curve, every hue of my face; as if she would never see my face again. Then suddenly she pulled away, and in a voice heavy with fear she said to me, "You have changed."

Ashmunikal understood my intention, she had sensed the words I was about to say: "We must end this relationship now, I cannot betray my king, I cannot sully, like a rag, the honor bestowed upon me by my father." But I pretended not to understand.

"So much has happened," I said.

Her large brown eyes grew lucid like still waters.

"I'm very sad about your father's death."

"It was the gods' bidding, it could not be helped."

She acted as if she had already accepted what I was about to say, as if she were bowing down to her fate. But still she could not take her eyes, so full of love and longing, away from my face. You know how a doe shot by the bow of an expert hunter makes a last effort to hold itself upright? Such was Ashmunikal at that moment, as she suddenly shook her head gently from side to side and addressed me.

"You've changed so much, Patasana," she said with a deep sigh. "Your face has lost its innocence, the shine in your eyes has been extinguished, you look at me like a dead sheep. Has the fire within you gone out, or is it hidden somewhere there behind that pale white face that looks like the product of a talentless sculptor?

"You've aged, Patasana. The lines on your face have grown deeper and your lips, once so eager to smile, are now ashamed of feeling joy. You seem to bear the burden of a man with the weight of the world on his shoulders. Your sweet shyness has been replaced by an untimely listlessness. Your body, once as spirited as a slim colt, has slowed down to become like that of an old turtle.

"You've forgotten me, Patasana, and my presence no longer excites you. You look at me as you would at a tablet. To you, my voice is no different from the voice of any other woman in this palace. You have ripped me out of your heart, like a villager extracts an unwanted weed, ripping it out by the roots."

I wanted to tell tearful Ashmunikal that it wasn't true, that I still loved her madly, crazily, desperately, that I was writhing with grief. I wanted to address her with these words of my father's: "Just as the Euphrates brings bountifulness to the land, heads of wheat give grain, an apricot tree gives forth apricots; sheep provide us with meat and milk; the king commands this country; soldiers fight; so too do I have a sacred duty that I must fulfill. I, grandson of Mittanuwa, son of Araras, the holy pen of the gods, Patasana, cannot give up this duty for love. But you will always be in my heart, like a wound that does not heal, like the increasingly painful longing of a traveler unable to reach his home, like the unwithering hope of a prisoner dreaming of freedom, but doomed to die." But I could not. I could only listen in silence, allowing a pain more profound than Ashmunikal's sadness to rip my heart to shreds.

I renounced that ethereal bliss, that happiness that could so easily have been mine, in the name of the occupation that my forefathers had carried out for generations, in the name of protecting King Pisiris' honor, in the name of my country and the gods. I betrayed myself. I betrayed the tender moments of my youth, precious moments never to be recaptured. I did that which should not be done. I ended that which should not be ended. Into a vault of darkness did I lock up that fragrant wind of my garden. I removed from my heart that wonderful joy, leaving my body desolate, like an empty wineglass. I was aware of my betrayal, and that's why, looking into Ashmunikal's sad eyes, I could summon forth only two words from my quivering lips.

"Forgive me."

Those two words were all that I could say.

"Forgive me."

Ashmunikal did not say a single word. She left me alone with my desperation, with my holy duty, with my seriousness, with my self-inflicted betrayal and quietly departed. And I did not encounter her again, until two years later, when I would grovel at her feet in this same small room in the library.

CHAPTER TWENTY-TWO

The excavation crew was gathered in the small room in the library. Bernd fondly touched the crumbling pieces of stone in the dirt. "There's no doubt about it," he said. "These are the remains of the wall that camouflaged where Patasana hid his stash of tablets."

The excavation site was divided into a grid of five meter by five meter squares, and in one of these squares, D5, which happened to be the right corner of the small room where Patasana wrote his tablets, they had found evidence of two walls.

"You mean this where Patasana hid his tablets?" asked Murat as he wiped the sweat from his brow.

"Most definitely," said Timothy in response to the young archaeologist's question. "We can tell from the first tablets that Patasana was very afraid because what he was writing contained information that was extremely dangerous under the circumstances at that time. Patasana must have had this secret section built into the library because he was afraid that the tablets would be discovered... And this also explains why we found the tablets en masse."

"And why the tablets didn't disintegrate," added Esra. "These walls here must have protected the tablets not only from people, but from fires and earthquakes, too."

With her hat on her head and her glasses in hand, Esra was kneeling next to the three men and inspecting the remains of the thin wall. She'd gotten back late the night before. Everyone except for Halaf had already been asleep. Actually, she was glad that they were, as this relieved her from having to confront their disparaging looks and respond to their nosy questions with flat out lies. Though she was very curious to find out if Halaf knew anything about the murders that had been committed seventy eight years ago, she was so exhausted that she couldn't even muster up the strength to ask. She hadn't been able to get decent sleep at the hospital the night before, and topped by the exhaustion of her lovemaking with Eshref, her eyes fell shut as soon as she got into bed. Esra, who always woke up well before the others, had a hard time waking up that morning and had no desire whatsoever to rouse herself from her slumber. But after repeated knocks on her door, and Halaf's deep voice calling out twice, "Breakfast is ready, Esra Hanım," it was clear to her that she had no other choice, and so she finally managed to crawl out of bed. She washed her face and smartened herself up a bit before heading to breakfast, but she was still groggy. When she got to the breakfast table to find the entire crew waiting there for her, she felt her heart swell up with an odd feeling that was something between shame and longing. At that moment she realized that, despite all of the meaningless arguments that had passed between them, she had developed a real bond with these people over the long weeks they'd spent together.

As soon as Esra sat down to join them they began asking her about the fight the night before. They were all extremely curious to hear what the Captain had to say about the matter. Esra summarized her conversation with the Captain. Oddly enough, nobody offered up any commentary, except for Teoman.

"I hope the Captain's right," he said in a rebellious tone. "We've had enough of these daily murders!"

Bernd changed the topic by asking about Elif. Esra told them all about how things had gone at the hospital. She'd last talked to Kemal on the phone just the night before. He'd told her that Elif was better, and that David had said she could be released that morning. With Elif as the subject of conversation, Esra found herself directing her eyes at Timothy, but the

American appeared disinterested. It wasn't clear if he was just feigning disinterest, or if he had decided not to continue his close relations with Elif so as to avoid creating any further unpleasantness amongst the crew members. Hoping that the latter was the case, Esra went on to ask about how the excavation had gone the day before. Timothy told her that they hadn't had a very productive day. They'd uncovered just one tablet, but it was different from the rest. The colophon on the back of the tablet contained a summary of Patasana's writing, thus indicating that it was the final tablet. They'd now uncovered twenty tablets, which meant they still had eight tablets to uncover. Bernd couldn't help but add his own two cents worth. He pointed out that the importance of having uncovered the last tablet shouldn't be underestimated, and though eight tablets remained missing, their chances of uncovering the entirety of Patasana's writings were still high. This was the first time that Esra had seen her German colleague so passionate. As she listened, she even began to think that she had been wrong about him. How could someone so devoted to his profession possibly be responsible for such heinous murders? But the things she had learned from Nicholas the day before... Actually, what she had learned didn't indict Bernd. How just would it be to consider the man a killer just because he was so sensitive about the matter of the Armenian massacre? As she was thinking this, Bernd continued to deliver the good news. Professor Krencker had called several times the day before to say that a group of thirty journalists including reporters from the likes of CNN, BBC, and Reuters had confirmed participation in the press conference, and that a three person team led by Krencker's assistant Joachim would be arriving in Antep by plane that night to begin preliminary preparations for the conference. Actually Esra's teacher, Behice Hanım, was supposed to be part of the same team as well, but the poor woman, rather up there in years now, had been hospitalized because of gastric bleeding. That meant that Esra would be the university's sole representative. Esra was saddened to hear about Behice Hanım, but glad to know that the process was picking up speed. They didn't have much time left. They'd have to act quickly. She'd have to sit down with Bernd and Timothy at the earliest opportunity and divide up tasks for the press conference. Then they'd have to talk with the Mayor Edip Bey and make sure that the journalists coming to take a tour of the ancient city would be hosted in the best manner possible. Still she couldn't help but ask what had happened at Hadji Settar's funeral. Teoman and Murat had attended, and so they gave their report. It had been a very crowded ceremony, with everyone in the region who had been fond of Hadji Settar, from the *kaimakam* to the mayor, from tribal leaders to village *muxhtars*, on hand to bid Hadji Settar farewell on his final journey. Even the Türkoghlus and Gencecis attended, although they had their own funerals to attend to as well. Though they tried to maintain distance amongst themselves for the duration of the ceremony, members of the two families had accompanied the coffin all the way to the cemetery. What Esra was really curious about was how those attending the funeral had acted towards Teoman and Murat. But nothing bad had happened in that respect. Everyone had treated them well, including the *kaimakam*, and Hadjı Settar's two sons had shaken their hands and thanked them for coming. Only Abid Hodja and Fayat, who tailed the former the entire time, had given them evil looks, but they hadn't harassed them, verbally or otherwise.

This good news eased Esra's mind a bit regarding the murders. It seemed that everything was getting back on track. Maybe all of this wasn't as bad as she'd thought, but once she'd got something into her head, it stayed there. Maybe Eshref had been right all along, maybe it was Mahmut and his friend who had committed the murders. Or maybe... With these thoughts running through her mind, Esra tried to relax as they made their way to the excavation site.

A few hours of work in the library revealed the existence of not just one thin wall in the right corner of the small room, but two, thereby proving that there had indeed been a secret compartment here. And it was from this secret compartment buried beneath the collapsed library that Patasana's tablets were emerging. The crew, however, hadn't understood this until they'd turned up the thin walls. The discovery of these walls answered a question that had been eating away at the excavation crew for days. It was believed that the ancient city had been captured by the Assyrians in 719 B.C.E., and that the city's new rulers had sent the Hittite population that had been living there for centuries into exile and then proceeded to Assyrianize the city. And that meant that it was at least two thousand seven hundred years since the tablets had been written. The question that the excavation crew had been unable to answer was exactly why Patasana's tablets hadn't been uncovered before. After the Hittites, this site had been occupied by many and varied civilizations, from the Assyrians to the Romans. So why hadn't any of them been able to find Patasana's tablets? The two walls concealing the compartment provided the answer to this very question.

"Man!" exclaimed Murat excitedly. "That means we're the first people to touch these tablets since Patasana himself."

"That's right," said Esra. A proud expression spread across her face. "But would Patasana have written these tablets had he known just how much later they would actually be read? That I don't know."

"He would have," said Timothy with a faraway look in his dark eyes. "The man lived through a great tragedy. The poet within him compelled him to share his experiences with others. And so in a way, it allowed him to overcome what he'd been through, and alienate himself from the things he had suffered. We might call this a kind of 'facing up.' Facing up to himself, I mean, to his fear, his shame, and his mistakes. But at the same time, it was a kind of settling of accounts—a settling of accounts with the brutal kings and the cruel gods who were so much more powerful than him. Only such a stark naked facing up, such a courageous settling of accounts could bring him relief... I think Patasana would have written these tablets even if he had known that no one would read them. Life left him no other choice."

Murat stared at Timothy with a stunned expression, as if he'd just seen the strangest thing...

"You really understand him so well," he murmured in awe.

The American archaeologist couldn't help but ask: "What's wrong, Murat? You look like you've just seen the devil himself."

The young man gave a sudden start, as if he'd been rudely woken from slumber.

"Oh it's nothing," he said, putting on an innocent smile, "Patasana just appeared before my eyes is all."

"Come on, admit it," Timothy replied with a mischievous expression, "you thought that Patasana had taken possession of my soul."

"Why the heck would you think something like that, Tim?" said Murat. He was looking at Esra out of the corner of his eye, fearing the excavation director's wrath. "I didn't think any such thing."

Esra allowed herself a smile. Encouraged by this, the young man gave his luck a try.

"Well, actually, I wasn't thinking that Patasana had captured your soul, but there is this thing called reincarnation..."

"This boy is incorrigible," Esra said. "If he were a little less shy, he'd be calling Tim Patasana outright."

Tim put on a grave face.

"I'd be honored," he said. "Look here, the man's tablets are able to stir up interest a full two thousand seven hundred years after they were written. As for us, we'll just die and be forgotten."

The four of them burst into uproarious laughter.

"Enough bumming around," said Esra as she gave Murat a friendly punch on the shoulder. "Now go on and tell them it's time to get back to work," she added, motioning with her head towards the workers taking a cigarette break beneath the old fig tree ahead.

As Murat made his way to the fig tree, Esra grumbled, "Sometimes he's unbearable."

"He's still very young, one day he'll understand the world better," Timothy said, a look of compassion in his eyes as he watched Murat walk away.

"I doubt it," said Bernd. He'd been following the conversation silently thus far. "Murat doesn't look like he's going to be changing anytime soon. But it's not just Murat, in Germany there are plenty of young people interested in spirits and this realm of the unknown, something they call the fourth dimension."

"Well, they're not entirely out of line," said Timothy. "Is it their fault if the reality of today's world is so bland?"

"I don't care one bit whose fault it is," said Esra. "But if anyone on my excavation goes messing with others' heads with silly talk about spirits, ghosts, and grave curses, they'll find themselves booted off of this excavation in no time."

Timothy had started laughing.

"There you have it," he said, turning to Bernd. "Nothing on the face of this earth is as important as the excavation."

There was such a sweet expression on the American's face that Esra, too, couldn't help but smile.

"Interpret it as you like, sirs, but we only have two days until the press conference and we don't have a second to spare with talk of the world of spirits."

Though they poked fun at Esra's words, they proceeded to give it their all as they toiled away at the excavation. By break time they had removed five more tablets, three of them cracked in various places, which brought them that much closer to solving the mystery of the Hittite chief scribe. Three more tablets and the text would be complete.

They returned to the school tired but happy. There was no one else about except for Halaf, who was busy preparing lunch. Kemal and Elif hadn't returned yet. Esra walked over to the cook, who was waiting for her, as he did every day, to give her an oral report.

"Hi Halaf, how's it going?"

The young man from Barak was as smiley as ever.

"Just fine. I've made you fried fava beans with garlic flavored yoghurt, a delicious combination. Bulgur rice and shepherd's salad on the side. And honey melon for desert."

"Great," said Esra, feeling the grumbling cavity in her stomach. "When will it be ready?"

"I'll have the table set in less than an hour."

Esra was glad they had some time before the meal since it meant she would have time to call the mayor beforehand. She dialed the municipality's phone number before hitting the shower. A young woman with a timid voice who, try as she may, just could not manage to speak politely, said that the mayor was out of the office and that he'd be back in the afternoon. Esra had picked up her towel and was just about to head out when her phone rang. She got this weird feeling again when she heard Eshref's voice. "God forbid you be in love with the man..." she thought to herself. "How are you?" he was asking. He hadn't called in the morning because he hadn't wanted to interrupt her work. He said that he was fine. He was in Antep at the moment. He was submitting his report about the raid two days before. He wanted to know when they could see one another again. Esra was eager to see him, too, she said, but she was extremely busy these days. He could come over to the school for dinner though. The Captain leapt at the opportunity. Esra told him about the press conference. She also told him that she'd called the mayor. Eshref was on excellent terms with the mayor. He said he could call the mayor himself, if she wanted. Esra was pleased to accept the offer.

Lunch didn't last long. They told Halaf to bring their teas into the computer room where they went off to commence their meeting. The first item on the agenda was the talk that Esra, Timothy, and Bernd were going to hold at the press conference. They decided to write a two page text containing information about the ancient city but focusing on the Patasana's period. Esra would write the text, and Timothy would translate it into English. They'd photocopy the text at the municipality building and pass out copies to all of the journalists. Bernd would give a broad overview of Neo-Hittite, Urartu, Phrygian, and Assyrian relations in the region in the 700's B.C.E. As the person translating the tablets, Timothy meanwhile would focus upon the archaeological and historical significance of Patasana's tablets. All of the members of the excavation crew would help out during the journalists' tour of the site; they'd provide the guests with information, and also make sure to maintain the grid plan, and see to it that no one interfered in the areas yet to be excavated.

Murat suggested that they enlarge photos of the excavation and hang them in the room where the conference was to be held. Bernd said that the German Archaeological Institute had had the photographs enlarged, and that the team led by Joachim would be bringing them along. The conference was to be held at eleven o'clock. The journalists would be coming with the 7.15 plane from Istanbul. The morning of the meeting, everyone would get up early just like on any other excavation day, finalize preparations, do a final check, and then head for Antep. Maybe a person or two should go in the evening. They'd make a final decision about that after speaking with Joachim.

There was a knock at the door during the meeting. Everyone turned and looked expectantly at the door. Kemal's stern face appeared at the door, with Elif right behind him. She wasn't smiling either, and her eyes looked red. "She's been crying," Esra thought. Kemal nodded a cold hello to everyone and then headed not to the benches where the meeting was being held, but to his own bed. Elif meanwhile, her spirits lifted upon seeing her friends, had already begun hugging everyone. Her green eyes sparkled with joy upon seeing the American walking towards her. But Timothy had sensed that something was awry. Instead of hugging her, he made do with a handshake. Elif was hurt by this, but tried not to show it. Kemal was sitting on the edge of his bed watching them with ice cold eyes. Esra walked over to him, pretending not to be aware of what was going on.

"Welcome back, how's it going?"

"Shitty," said Kemal.

"Why? What happened?"

"What do you think, look at that," he said. "The sight of him makes her all giddy."

"Don't you think you're exaggerating a bit?"

"Not at all. We talked at the hospital. She admitted to me that she had a crush on that dirty old man."

After a short pause Esra told him, "Forget about it, it's not worth getting all worked up over."

"I can't," Kemal responded with a deep sigh. "I just can't help but get all worked up about it. Maybe if I got away from here..."

"I don't think that's a good idea," said Esra. "The problem's all in your head. You'll take it with you wherever you go. You need to stay here and work through it."

"I can't stand it," said Kemal. He pronounced these words so loudly that the rest of the crew, which was gathered around Elif, turned to look at them. He lowered his voice and repeated:

"I can't stand for Elif to get all giddy when he's around."

The rage in his eyes frightened Esra.

"Come on, let's go for a walk," she said. She thought getting away from here for a bit might help to calm him down.

"No, I'm fine right here," Kemal said.

"Are you sure?"

"Yes. I don't want them to think I'm that pathetic."

"In that case, pull yourself together," she said admonishingly. "Don't just sit here all by yourself, go join your friends."

"All right, all right, don't worry about me."

Teoman and Murat had walked up to them.

"What's all that yelling about, man?" Teoman said teasingly. "The doctor gave you a good swift kick in the ass at the hospital, and now you're taking it out on us, right?"

Kemal forced a smile.

"Leave me alone and take a look at yourself," he said, gently punching Teoman in the gut. "You're going to turn into a barrel soon."

Teoman gave him a brazen-faced grin.

"An archaeologist with a tummy is perfectly acceptable. You gotta store energy to use on the tougher days."

"Like you're so busy burning off energy. I bet you spent the whole day napping under whichever temple column had the best shade to offer..."

Esra was relieved; Kemal was turning back to normal.

"We were just talking about what we're going to do at the press conference," she said, calling for everyone to sit back down on the benches again. Kemal settled down in a far corner, far away from everyone, especially Elif and the American. Elif meanwhile had chosen to sit directly across from Tim just to get his goat. Timothy wasn't very comfortable with the circumstances, but he was helpless to remedy the situation and so stayed put. Esra immediately gave a summary of what they'd been discussing, in order to preclude any more drama. They then continued on to the next item on the agenda. The meeting was nearly over when Halaf came in with a tray full of tea. He deftly began passing out the piping hot glasses.

Elif didn't even notice the glass that Halaf had placed before her. She was busy looking at Timothy.

"I'm so grateful to David, he was a great help to us. And he loves you so much."

"He's a good man," said Timothy. "He's helped me out a lot, too."

Kemal's glaring eyes began to beat down upon them as they talked.

"Oh no," thought Esra, "now an argument's sure to break out.

But Elif was either unaware of the impending storm, or she just didn't care.

"He said he was going to stop by for a visit soon," she said. "Esra invited him."

Timothy wriggled uncomfortably on his bench.

"That'd be great," he said, "I haven't seen him in so long."

"So you can go on a double date," Kemal mumbled from his corner. His voice was full of vitriol. Shaking his head, he went on talking with himself.

"These dudes have it out for our women."

An ice cold wind swept over the table. Neither Timothy nor Esra spoke, but Elif persisted in talking, as if she hadn't heard her former boyfriend.

"So you've known David for a long time?"

"Quite a while," replied Timothy, obviously not pleased with the situation he found himself in at that moment.

"You've made quite an impression on him. He praises you non-stop."

"Timothy makes quite an impression on all of us though, now doesn't he?" interjected Kemal once again. "We're all in such awe of him."

Timothy couldn't ignore this taunting, which was so clearly directed at him.

"Thank you, Kemal, but you're exaggerating a little."

"I'm not exaggerating at all," he said. He placed his glass of tea on the bench and now turned his whole body to face the American. "You've made quite an impression on all of us in just a very short time. In fact, some of us are even in love with you."

"Cut the nonsense," yelled Elif.

"Why, didn't you say so yourself? Didn't you say you had a crush on Tim?"

"Please guys," Esra said, cursing Kemal under her breath.

"Esra, please don't get mixed up in this," said Kemal, who was now breathing heavily in his fit of passion. "Elif cheated on me with this guy, right before my very own eyes..."

Timothy was aghast for a moment, but he quickly gathered himself together.

"You're wrong," he said. "I'm not having any kind of affair with Elif. And this is the first I've heard of her crush." He turned to face Elif. "If this is true, then I am honored, but it's not something I'd like to pursue," he said with a rather abashed look on his face.

The young woman turned beet red, and her lips began to tremble.

"He's... he's making that up..." she stuttered. She couldn't continue, so instead she covered her face with her hand, as the tears streamed down, and dashed out of the room.

"This is all so utterly meaningless," said Timothy. "Why are we hurting one another like this?"

"And you have the nerve to keep talking," said Kemal, "when all of this is your fault."

Timothy stubbornly kept his cool.

"You're wrong," he said. "I treated Elif just like I treated everyone else did."

"No, you made her fall in love with you."

Timothy shook his head with the hurt, offended expression of one who's been misunderstood.

"You don't know me at all. I am not some exemplary specimen of humankind, but neither am I low enough to deny being in love with someone if I really am." He paused. "But I'm not in love. And it's a good thing I'm not. Because love is a nasty affair. It's a feeling evil enough to make someone as polite as yourself act as rudely as you are right now. And as I just said, affairs of the heart really don't interest me much anymore."

A malevolent glint came into Kemal's eyes.

"Why? You get tired of picking up all those young gals?"

A bitter smile crossed Timothy's lips.

"No," he said. His voice was laden with irony. "Because my wife ran off with a young Belgian archaeologist."

Esra's heart had begun beating fast. She thought that at this point, Tim wouldn't be able to control his rage, and that he'd certainly explode at some point. But the American continued his words in a sincere voice, as if he were having an intimate chat with a close friend.

"That's why I understand you so well. It was very painful for me, too. Someone you love, and trust, leaves you for another. But after a while, you get used to it. After spilling buckets of tears, after many a drunken stupor, after wallowing in your own pity, you begin contemplating the whole thing.

Suddenly he began to laugh.

"And the conclusion I have reached is that these lands are guilty when it comes to love."

Everyone, except for Kemal, who looked like he could care less, began listening to him more carefully now.

"Believe me, I'm not kidding. Everything began on these very lands nine thousand years ago... You know about the Mother Goddess—the first female god, a fat woman with a lion on other side and a child between her legs. She was the first god of humankind. Do you know why the ancient people of Anatolia chose her as their god? Because men were not aware of their roles as impregnators. They thought that it was the wind, the rain, rivers, in short, nature, that impregnated women. And this was not at all a strange idea at the time. People viewed themselves as a part of nature. They thought birth was magic, a miracle. The matriarchal system at that time undoubtedly played a role in this line of thought. But what had the greatest impact in this regard was that people were ignorant of how reproduction worked. And it was this lack of knowledge that created the Mother Goddess. This thought was so powerful that even after patriarchy became the dominant system, the goddess cult continued in Anatolia. For example, our patriarchal Hittites had a male god, the Storm God Teshub, but that didn't mean they would ever quit believing in the Sun Goddess Hepat and the Goddess Kupaba.

"And love is exactly like the goddess; I mean, it's a magnificent illusion. First of all, it's the creation of men. And that's man's dilemma. On the one hand he establishes a family so that he can have a woman of his own, while on the other hand he longs for his neighbor's wife. Think of how Paris abducts Helen in the Illiad, or of the love of the knights in the middles ages. But the whole situation's much worse for women. Because women, who had multiple lovers during matriarchy, later found themselves being confined to the home as the property of a single man. What could be more natural than for her to long for her neighbor's husband or son? But such a desire is forbidden, it's sinful, it's shameful. And out of this inaccessibility arises what we call love. To love means to exaggerate the features of someone that you can't have, to imagine that he or she is the ideal person and become passionately bound to them. The greater the obstacles to that person, the more passionate the hallucination becomes. And just as our pre-historical forefathers created a goddess of women because they didn't know how pregnancy worked, so too have we created a kind of devotion that verges on worship when we encounter someone we believe to be indispensable to our very existence. It's my belief that love is the current version of that primitive tendency to exaggerate the attributes of the beloved."

When he first began this talk of his, Esra didn't understand what he was getting at. But when she saw everyone at the table hanging on his every word, she realized that he was trying to sweeten up the bitter argument and smooth everything out. She congratulated him silently on this successful effort, before proceeding to add her own two cents worth.

"But what you've just said only explains things from a man's point of view." Her intention was not to pick on Timothy, but to direct the conversation in another direction. "So you mean to say that women can't fall in love?" she asked.

"Of course they can. It wasn't only men who created the Mother Goddess cult, but the imagination of all humankind. In the end, it doesn't matter whether it's men falling in love with women, or women with men, or homosexual love, I believe that they're all the continuation of the same primitive illusion."

Bernd, who'd been listening intently since the word "love," couldn't help but join in.

"You may be right, but," he said, "even if it is a habit created by thousands of years of a primitive way of thinking, and even if it is considered to be but a foolish hallucination, and even if it gives a person more pain than pleasure, a lifetime lived without love is, in my opinion, a poor life."

"Right," said Timothy. "Anyone who dies without having tasted love has lived an incomplete life, I agree, but that's not true for me. It's like that proverb of yours, 'Neither the sweets of Damascus nor the face of an Arab,' that's what I say now. No thanks, it's not worth it."

Just when it seemed that everyone's anger had subsided and they found themselves embroiled in a far more pleasant conversation, Kemal jumped in once again.

"I don't believe you," he said. "You're saying all of this just to rescue yourself. But I'll make sure that sooner or later, everyone sees you for the liar you are."

As soon as he'd finished with his piece, he exited the room before anyone had a chance to respond, slamming the door behind him, as Timothy looked on helplessly.

TABLET TWENTY-TWO

I had finally succeeded in becoming the palace scribe, but I could not erase the memory of Ashmunikal's eyes as they looked at me, so full of desperation. And that's partially why I engrossed myself in my work so ambitiously—to feel Ashmunikal's absence less, but even more so, to prove how good I was at my job.

In those days, we were not yet free of the Assyrian scourge. The Assyrian army was burning the entire region to the ground, raging about us like a humungous fire. After the Samal, they defeated the kingdoms of Gurgum and Kashka. Once they were done with those foes, they came knocking on our gates once again, with their guard units, four person war chariots, cavalry, and foot soldiers.

They'd increased our tax burden immensely. We accepted this without opposition, but it wasn't enough for Tiglath-Pileser. He'd decided not to take his army and return to his own country. He put our kingdom under the command of something called the Outer Regions Administration. We also had to give soldiers to his army during times of war, if they asked us to.

We'd achieved peace once again with a dishonorable pact. I call it "dishonorable," but it was only the nobles who were ashamed of the pact. The people and the slaves celebrated the peace with a celebration that lasted three days and three nights. Because it is they who die, it is their houses which are burnt, and they who suffer from hunger and who are exiled in times of war. Working in the fields by the Euphrates, carving stone to build buildings, and taking care of housework may be trying tasks, but such toil is still better than war. And so the people and the slaves deemed Pisiris "The Merciful King."

A large portion of our produce, the fattest of our cattle, pigs, and sheep, and the finest of our wines and beer were flowing into Assyria, but it didn't matter, for at least there was peace. The people were happy, the slaves were happy, the women were happy. And what about me, the Palace Scribe Patasana—was I happy?

For months I had avoided asking myself this question. Though I failed to grow accustomed to Ashmunikal's absence, I carried out my duties to perfection. And my efforts were not in vain; I had become the youngest but most heeded member of the Council of Nobles. King Pisiris made me his chief advisor, just like my father. His every action indicated that he held me in high esteem, and that he trusted me. And I trusted him, believed in him, was in awe of him, and prayed to the gods for having given us such an intelligent, such a brave king. All the way up until Laimas, assistant to both my father and myself, landed in his death bed.

Laimas hadn't come to the palace for days. He didn't feel well and wanted to get some rest. But rest didn't heal Laimas, and his condition gradually grew worse. The day before he died, he called me to his house. I accepted his invitation immediately. I walked through his small garden and into his abode. His son met me at the door.

"My father's been waiting for you," he said. "He was afraid he'd die before talking to you."

I was taken aback. What matter of such great importance could Laimas possibly have to tell me? Curious, I walked inside. Old Laimas once large body had shriveled and now seemed to disappear in his large bed. His face was as pale as could be. His son knelt down and whispered into his ear to tell him that I had arrived. Laimas turned his narrow eyes to me, and then gathering all of his strength, called me to his side. I knelt down beside him. He motioned with his hand for his relatives to leave the room, so that we were left there alone. He gathered his breath and began to speak slowly.

"I have sinned, Patasana."

I could barely hear his voice. I leaned to bring my ear closer to his mouth.

"I did something very evil to your father Araras. I betrayed your father, a man who had always helped me, the best friend I ever had in my long life. I did a great evil to you, and to your family."

I tried to object to his words.

"Don't interrupt me, I don't have much time left," he said, bringing me to silence. "You remember the pact that your father took to Tiglath-Pileser? I wrote it. Do you know why? Because in that tablet, Pisiris speaks of his loyalty to the Assyrian king, and says that as proof of this, he was sending his chief scribe, who he had learned was acting as a spy for the Phrygians and Urartians, to the Assyrian king. It was not Tiglath-Pileser who killed your father, but Pisiris' guards who did the deed on the way to Tiglath-Pileser. Your father's head was paid to the Assyrian king as the blood money to save Pisiris' own life."

I was enraged by his words. "You're lying!" I screamed at Laimas, and then I began shaking him, though the poor man was already on his deathbed. Laimas sadly shook his head:

"I wish I were," he said. "How long I have lived with these pangs of conscience! Pisiris threatened to cut my tongue out if I told the truth. I was afraid, and so I have hidden the truth from everyone until today. But now I am dying. I cannot go before the gods bearing this sin."

I recalled the words that my father spoke to us as he bid us farewell, and then I understood that Laimas was telling the truth. The tears that I had kept inside ever since I had gotten word of my father's death began running down my cheeks, with the pain and fury of having been betrayed. The elderly Laimas spoke his final words as I wept:

"Whatever you do, do not let Pisiris know that you know all of this. He would kill you instantly. A man of your intelligence would not be so unwise as to choose a king for an enemy. You should carry on with your life in harmony with Pisiris as always."

When I left Laimas' house, my feet automatically led me to the palace, like a sheep heading for the barn out of habit. When I reached the palace I raised my head and looked. Did I belong to the owners of this palace, the same ones who had caused my grandfather to be sent into exile, me to be separated from the woman I love, my father to be killed? The education that I had received, everything I had learned told me that the answer to this question was "Yes, you belong to the gods and their representative on earth, King Pisiris." But the pain in my heart, the rage that strained my body, the fire that burnt my eyes said "No, you belong to you grandfather Mittanuwa, to your father Araras, and to your beloved, Ashmunikal."

I, Patasana, the perfect chief scribe of the palace, had once again found myself wedged between my mind and my heart.

CHAPTER TWENTY-THREE

Esra wanted to write a perfect text for the press conference, but she just didn't know how to begin. There was no one else left in the classroom but her. Bernd and Timothy had chosen to work in their own rooms; Elif, not wanting to talk to anyone, had gone out for a walk by herself; and Teoman, Kemal, and Murat had gone to the only coffeehouse in town possessing a television so that they could watch the Fenerbahche - Real Madrid friendly match. Esra wasn't at all fond of soccer matches, but this time she wholeheartedly supported the guys' request to go, since she thought that it might help to calm Kemal down.

She was sitting in front of the computer, trying to find the right words. She'd prepared papers for two of the annual Ministry of Culture Excavation Research and Archaeometry Results Conferences, but she wanted this paper to be different, more striking and more encompassing than any she'd written before. And so it was with painstaking effort that she sought to choose just the right words to reflect her thoughts. But with this kind of exertion she simply could not get started writing. She used to have problems writing compositions back in high school, too. Her father would always suggest that she begin with a sentence that in some way summarized the content of the composition, and that the rest of the article would just flow from her pen once she'd found that beginning sentence. At first she hadn't believed in this method, but she changed her mind once she'd actually tried it and seen that it really did work. However, the ordeal of finding that first sentence remained. She thought of Timothy's tablet translations, all of which were saved on the computer. She opened the folder containing the translations, and after reading over them for a while, finally found what she was looking for, there in Patasana's own words:

"When my grandfather looked at the Euphrates, in the shine of its waters he saw the secret of our internal joy, while my father saw in the Euphrates the power that made us stronger than our enemies; he saw the olives, the chickpeas, the wheat, the apricots, and the grapes. If you asked my grandfather, 'What is the Euphrates?' he would respond, 'During the daytime, it is the light shining in your lover's eyes, and during the nighttime, it is the unraveled raven hair of your lover.' And if you asked my father, you were certain to receive the following answer: 'The Euphrates is a bountiful body of water that must be protected from our enemies.'"

Yes, she should begin with this paragraph; silently flowing into the Persian Gulf for thousands of years, delivering bounty and prosperity to humankind, this magnificent river, called Mala by the Hittites, was the source of all of the civilizations that had thrived on these lands, past and present. The text that she would compose should be constructed around this river.

She eagerly began pecking away at the keys. Her father had proven right once again, for once the first paragraph was out of the way, the rest just came to her spontaneously. She read out loud what she had written, struck out some paragraphs that she didn't like and rewrote others, pondered the right word here and there, until within just a few hours, the text was complete. She had typed in the final corrections and was just beginning to print the document out when the door opened and Teoman, Murat, and Kemal, the real owners of the room, came in. Esra gave them a joyous welcome.

"Oooo, so the soccer maniacs made it back."

But her friends weren't the least bit happy.

"We're back," said Teoman, who dragged his feet as he headed straight for his bed. Murat looked equally as devastated.

"What's wrong with you guys?" Esra asked.

"Those wretches," Murat wailed. "They beat the crap out of our boys."

Esra began to laugh.

"Oh my, so you fellas lost your match, did you?"

"C'mon, don't laugh, Esra," said Teoman.

"What's the big deal, it's just a friendly match."

"Okay, that may be so, but the hardest part was watching our own former player score a goal," said Murat. His face grimaced, as if he were in pain. "If he hadn't scored that goal, we would have finished the match two-two."

"The no-good scoundrel," hissed Teoman. "He makes me sick."

"Oh no, no getting sick until after the press conference!"

Teoman paid no heed to Esra's words, but just threw himself onto his bed. Murat followed suit.

"Well now," Esra whined, "who's going to proofread my text?"

"I'll do it," said Kemal. He seemed to have calmed down, and he didn't appear as troubled as his friends were by the outcome of the match. He walked over to the printer from which the latest draft of the paper was emerging.

"This is the talk you're going to give at the press conference?"

"Yes," said Esra. She was pleased that her friend was taking an interest in what she'd written.

"I'd also welcome any criticism about the content."

Kemal took the sheets of paper and plopped down on one of the benches. "I'm sorry for what happened earlier," he said shyly before beginning to read. "I'm really sorry for acting like that on your excavation. I hope you'll forgive me."

"I'm only thinking of you," said Esra. "You're tearing yourself apart... Is it really worth it?"

"I don't want to talk about it," said Kemal, who had tensed up at the sound of her words. "Let's just take care of the task at hand."

Seeing that things with Kemal were getting back on track, Esra didn't push him.

"Okay. I'm going to go for a walk and get some fresh air while you read over those pages. I've been pent up in this room all afternoon."

The sun was setting in the rear garden. Cubed meat, sliced tomatoes, and green peppers were lined up in their skillets next to one another on the table beneath the arbor. Halaf, lost to the world as he masterfully threaded fat pieces of meat onto long skewers, was belting out one of those sad folk songs of the Turkmen tribes who had migrated from Horasan. He was enjoying himself so much that Esra couldn't help but just stand and watch him at his work for several minutes. And she would have continued doing so if Halaf, finally feeling the weight of her eyes upon him, hadn't raised his head and finally seen her.

"Shame on you, Esra Hanım," complained Halaf. "You should've let me know you were there."

"I couldn't bring myself to interrupt," said Esra. She nodded towards the colorful display on the table. "Is this dinner?"

The cook's lips formed a carefree smile, indicating that he wasn't really offended in the least.

"Sure is. Seeing as the Captain's coming tonight, I thought we should make him cubed meat with 'six tomato puree.'"

Esra seemed surprise.

"Is that right?" said Esra. "I thought you didn't care all that much for the Captain. You were saying all that stuff about how everyone thought he was crazy and all..."

"Well, I may have said he was a crazy man, but I didn't say he was a bad one. It's the smart ones that you should really be afraid of. What we call a crazy person is just someone who's depressed because he's under this kind of siege of thieves and Jonahs. A poor soul like that just loses it, he has no other choice. But his anger doesn't hurt anyone. Or if it does, it doesn't hurt anyone but himself... For example, Kemal Bey's not like that. Now he's capable of hurting anyone."

"He's in love," Esra said as she sat down, trying to exonerate her friend. "Love's a kind of madness, too, you know."

"He isn't mad, he's just inconsiderate."

Esra laughed at the analogy while the cook continued to speak.

"If he were mad, he'd try to conceal his hurt from others. He wouldn't make a complete fool of himself, the poor girl, and the other man. Personally, I admire Tim's behavior. He may be an infidel, but he's a real man. And the way he's built, one solid punch and he could knock that Kemal out twice over. But the man's been through a lot; he knew just how to keep his cool and he managed to settle the matter amicably..."

The skewer in his hand was now loaded with meat, and so he propped it up on the skillet with the tomatoes. He took up another skewer and continued.

"Just forget about that Kemal, Esra Hanım. I wasn't very fond of him to begin with, and now I've really lost all respect for him. The girl flat out said she's not interested. What more does he need to hear? No matter how difficult or hard it is for you, at that point you just gotta say 'so long.' That's the right and manly thing to do. Even here in these parts nowadays they give girls to the men of their choice..."

Looking to cut short what otherwise could be an interminable monologue on Halaf's part, Esra reached for the skewers.

"Let me help you."

"Be careful, don't hurt yourself."

"C'mon now," Esra said, with an incredulous twinkle in her eye. "I know a thing or two about skewering meat."

A childish smile spread across Halaf's lips.

"All right then. Put those tomatoes on the skewer."

Esra picked up the skewer like a veteran kabob chef and began sliding the tomatoes on one after the other. Halaf had regained his composure. Worried that he'd revisit the topic of Kemal again though, Esra took the opportunity to change the subject.

"I've heard there are Armenian villages in this area, is that so?"

Halaf's eyes, topped by a single long eyebrow, twitched suspiciously.

"Mahmut and his buddy turned out to be innocent, didn't they?" he asked, instead of responding to Esra's question. Then he went on, as if he already knew the answer.

"I told you so..."

His know-it-all behavior was getting on Esra's nerves.

"How did you come to the conclusion that Mahmut and his friend were innocent? I just asked you a question is all."

Halaf looked at her quizzically. Even her anger hadn't been enough to banish his doubts.

"Tell me the truth, Esra Hanım," he said. "Was it really them who murdered Hadji Settar and Reshat Agha?"

"The Captain thinks that it was. But anyway, quit playing guessing games now and answer my question."

Though dissatisfied with Esra's response, Halaf finally got around to answering her question.

"There are two Armenian villages. Abid Hodja's village, Göven, is one of them."

"Wait... Wait a second," said Esra, suddenly becoming all ears, not sure she had heard Halaf right the first time. "You mean to tell me that Abid Hodja is of Armenian origin?"

"Yeah, of course. He's a former Armenian like everyone else in that village."

Esra was now utterly confused.

"Well then, how did he become a hodja?"

"Why shouldn't he become one?" said Halaf. "They're all Muslim now. None of them say that they're Armenian or Christian. They're a little shy about it. That's why Abid Hodja's father sent him to an imam training school."

A stunned expression spread across Esra's face.

"How interesting!" she said. "So how do the Armenian villages get along with the other villages?"

"Really well. They don't have any problems. There are some who don't speak well of them, but I've never witnessed any wrong behavior on their part or anything like that. What can I say, they're very honest folk."

Esra's thoughts were still stuck on Abid Hodja. So the man was of Armenian descent. The first murder was carried out at the mosque where he worked, the second in his village... Could he be the murderer? Pretending to be a devout Muslim while seeking revenge for his forefathers? She began to probe a little deeper into the matter.

"Murders just like those of Hadji Settar and Reshat Türkoghlu were carried out seventy eight years ago, too."

A gleam appeared in Halaf's eyes. He quit skewering and looked at Esra inquisitively.

"I've never heard that before," he said. "But I can find out. Who were these men?"

"Priest Kirkor was pushed off of the bell tower of the church that's now a mosque; Ohannes Agha was decapitated on the road to the village and his head placed in his lap, and coppersmith Garo was hung from a beam in his store."

"Oh my God," Halaf said in a startled voice. "The murders really are alike."

"You ever hear of any of those people?"

"Well, you know who Priest Kirkor is yourself," said Halaf.

"I do?"

"You remember Infidel Nadide who came to visit..."

"What does Infidel Nadide have to do with any of this?"

"Plenty! Nadide, otherwise known as Nadya, is Priest Kirkor's daughter."

"You're right," said Esra, "now I remember. And what about Ohannes and Garo?"

"I've heard of Ohannes Agha. Reshit Agha's grandfather, Kurdish İsfendiyar, was a bandit in those days. When it became certain that the French were going to withdraw from Antep, he became a hardcore supporter of the Kuvayı Milliyeci, the National Forces, and began harassing the Armenians to no end. He killed Ohannes Agha and then claimed all of his land for himself. But I've never heard of Garo."

"There's something else I was wondering about. Is there any relationship between Abid Hodja and Priest Kirkor?"

"I don't know about that, but I do know that Abid Hodja's line goes back to Ohannes Agha."

This bit of news put a sparkle in Esra's eyes.

"So there are two sound reasons for Abid Hodja to peg Reshat as his enemy," she said. Though she looked at Halaf as she spoke, it was herself that she was trying to convince. "Reshat was the man who not only took his sister as his mistress, but he took his ancestors' property, too."

Halaf smiled with the pride of having been proven right.

"And now you've finally hit upon exactly what I've been saying. It couldn't be otherwise. It couldn't possibly be

Mahmut or those guys who killed Reshat Agha. I'm telling you, the man responsible for those murders is none other than Abid Hodja."

But Esra wasn't so sure.

"Okay, but is there any reason for Abid Hodja to kill Hadji Settar?"

Halaf grimaced

"No," he said, "Abid couldn't be the one behind that. The man responsible for Hadji Settar's murderer is Shehmuz..."

Halaf suddenly grew quiet, for he'd noticed that Timothy and Bernd were approaching. The two foreign archaeologists were discussing the differences between the Syriacs, who were one of the communities descending from the Assyrians, and the Harranians, a group that remained firmly bound to their old traditions. When they saw dinner being prepared, though, they left history behind and were swiftly transported back to the present.

"Oooh, shish kabob," said Timothy, licking his lips hungrily. Apparently he had recovered from the effects of the argument that morning.

"Long live Halaf! You've finally prepared the meal I've been waiting for."

"If I'd known you loved it that much, I would've made it sooner."

"You won't make it too spicy, will you?" interjected Bernd, as he watched Halaf thread the meat on the skewer with utmost interest. "I ate this in Adana once and it sent my whole body up in flames."

"This is not Adana kabob, Herr Bernd," said Halaf. "For one thing, Adana kabob is made with ground beef, whereas this is made from cubed meat."

The German turned a slight shade of red.

"I see that it's not ground beef kabob," he said. "I'm saying it's better if you don't make it too spicy."

"And that's exactly what I'm telling you—that this kabob won't be too spicy."

Esra had surreptitiously been eyeing Bernd ever since the two foreigners joined them. Adding Abid Hodja to the list of murder suspects had given her a sense of relief, but she hadn't completely given up on the possibility that Bernd might be the guilty party. She was wondering if Bernd's step-parents lived in this area. And seeing that this was her opportunity to find out, she pounced on it.

"You know, Bernd," she said, "I've been meaning to ask in what part of Turkey your wife's family lives."

"In Cilicia, or rather, Hatay," Bernd responded innocently, apparently not at all wary of the question posed.

So they didn't live in this area. Esra was pleased to hear that that was the case.

"My step-father's also got a penchant for grilling meat," the German continued. "They say all Southerners have a special knack for it."

"Not just Southerners," Timothy interjected. "Look at Esra, she's from Istanbul but she's loading those skewers as masterfully as any kabob chef... And don't they look delicious. My mouth's watering already." Then he pointed at the grill in front of the kitchen and asked the cook:

"Shall we light it?"

"It's early yet," said Halaf. "The fire will be ready in the blink of an eye. Let's wait until everyone gets here and then we'll light it."

It took a good two hours before everyone had finally gathered for the meal. Everyone except for Elif took their places at the table. Kemal sank into the same spot he'd sat that afternoon and silently listened to the conversation around him. The Captain was the last to arrive. He carried a package in his hand and had changed out of his uniform into a white dress shirt and beige linen pants. It was Esra who met him upon his arrival.

There was a sweet tension now between the two of them. Maybe they would have embraced one another if they'd been alone. But for now, they had to make do with looks full of longing and fleeting touches.

"Pistachio ice cream," Eshref said as he handed Esra the packet. "It held up all the way from Antep, but you better put it in the freezer right away before it melts."

Halaf, who was eavesdropping upon their conversation, couldn't help but butt in.

"That was an excellent idea, Captain," he interjected. "It'll go down well after the kabob."

Esra went to put the ice cream in the refrigerator while Eshref approached the table and began shaking hands with each of the crew members.

"Aren't you looking spiffy," Murat teased. "It's the first time we've ever seen you like this."

The young whip hadn't meant to imply anything by it, but a slight blush overtook the Captain's dark face nevertheless.

"I don't wear my uniform all the time. I like to dress in civilian clothes after work hours."

It befell Timothy to defend the Captain.

"Actually, uniforms are very comfortable. They rescue you from the trouble of having to think about what you're going to wear each morning when you get up."

"Oh come on, Tim!" said Teoman. "No offense Captain, but I think uniforms just make a person so plain and common. They just obliterate any personal attributes, any uniqueness."

The atmosphere at the table became very serious all of a sudden. Everyone was wondering how the Captain would respond, but before he did, Murat interjected to put his two cents worth in.

"Yet there are some attributes that uniforms just don't have the power to change at all."

Teoman turned to face the younger student.

"Like what?" he asked.

"Like eating. Let's take you for example. As if you wouldn't be the number one food consumer on this excavation if you were only wearing a uniform."

Everyone at the table began to join Murat in laughter.

"Ha ha," Teoman said mockingly. "Boy, haven't you gotten tired of these eating jokes yet? Exercise your mind a bit and find something else to joke about so we can all laugh together."

While everyone at the table was joking around, Halaf had lined up the tomato skewers on the pomegranate colored glow of the grill's fire. The crackling sound that emerged quickly diverted everyone's attention to the kabobs.

At one point the Captain leaned over and whispered in Esra's ear to ask why Elif hadn't joined them at the table.

"I don't know," she said. She'd become a bit worried about the girl's absence herself. "She isn't quite back up to par yet, maybe she's fallen asleep. Let's send Murat to get her."

But Murat came back from Elif's room alone. She'd said that she wasn't feeling well and wouldn't be joining them for dinner. Neither Timothy nor Kemal gave signs of any response. At first Esra was upset at Elif and thought about going and scolding the girl, but then she changed her mind. Maybe it was better this way. Maybe a night apart would help to calm them down a bit.

Eshref told them that he'd talked with the mayor. When Edip Bey heard that Turkish and foreign press would be attending, he said that he would be thrilled to help out, saying that all of the municipality's equipment and personnel were at the excavation crew's command for conference purposes.

During the course of this dinner conversation the tomatoes had come off the grill, to be replaced by the meat skewers. A few minutes later a scrumptious scent filled the air.

"How about we have a little to drink, just this one night?" moaned Teoman, who kept fidgeting around in his seat, as if the scent were somehow causing him pain. "You can't eat this meat without alcohol, it's just not possible."

Encouraged by the fact that Esra hadn't immediately interrupted to override him, Teoman then turned to Eshref.

"What do you say Captain, shall we drink tonight?"

"But of course," said Eshref, unaware of previous objections to the crew's drinking. "If I'd known, I'd have brought some *boghma* rakı. I've got two bottles sitting in my refrigerator."

Teoman sat up straight in his chair with a purposeful air. "That's all right, Captain, we've got some ourselves." And then, looking around at the others at the table, he asked, "Everybody's having rakı, right?"

"I'd prefer red wine," said Bernd.

"Okay, red wine for Bernd it is," he said and turned to Murat: "Come on now, my man Murat, fall behind me and let's usher in the drinks!"

Esra could only shake her head as the two buddies headed for the kitchen. Actually she, too, was hankering for a drink herself; they hadn't drunk in such a long time. Besides, maybe a little liquor would help smooth out the rough relationship between Kemal and Timothy. Within a few minutes the glasses were lined up on the table and filled with rakı, and for a short moment the scent of anise wafted more powerfully through the room than the smell of the meat coming from the grill.

"My father believed that the first sip before the meal was the sip of luck," said Esra, reaching for her glass. "So, what do you say, shall we?"

As everyone began to raise their glasses, Timothy interrupted:

"Since Teoman was the leading force that got us all drinking tonight, I propose that he make the toast."

"Okay," said the chubby archaeologist. He feigned no hesitancy, but instead promptly stood up and raised his glass. "May my struggle to find the right words here be the greatest of our worries..."

He was thinking about what to say when Murat began tugging at his shirt.

"C'mon man, the rakı's getting warm."

"Hold on dude, I'm getting' there... Now, I'd like to lift my glass to the two people who have given us the gift of this fine evening. To two masters, both born on these very lands, though two thousand seven hundred and some years apart. The first of these is Patasana, a rare man among dozens of butt-kissing palace scribes, a man who recorded words of truth, or at least the truth insofar as he saw it. And the second is the culinary master Halaf, who for many days now has been so skillfully preparing for us a rich array of foods, to our stomachs' delight. And so I raise my glass to these two great masters."

At that moment Halaf was wiping the sweat from his forehead with the back of his hand, but upon hearing these words of praise he gave a big smile, revealing rows of pearly white teeth. Esra thought he would be supremely humble about the whole affair, but the cook from Barak proved her wrong.

"Giving up words is easy," he said, having no intention of letting them off the hook so easily. "But I don't hear anybody here giving up a drink, asking this brother if he'd like to slake his thirst, too."

"What?" yelled Teoman, who feigning anger then turned to Murat. "Didn't you give Halaf a drink, dude?"

"You didn't tell me to."

"Do I have to tell you everything? Bring the great master a rakı a.s.a.p.!"

There was uproarious laughter and the cling clang of toasting glasses as everyone happily downed their drinks. The meal, which Halaf referred to as "chopped kabob on puree," was delicious. Not only Teoman, but Bernd, who at first approached the meat warily for fear that it might be too spicy, was greedily gulping down bite after bite of the tender meat and mouth-watering sauce in no time. Scanning the table out of the corner of her eye, Esra saw that everyone appeared to be in a good mood, and so she thought that they had put the argument of that afternoon behind them. Though he was still a bit withdrawn, even Kemal was joining in with his friends, listening to them and laughing at their jokes. He had even stopped giving Timothy that evil look. If things continued like this, then they would be in for a very pleasant evening. But that wasn't to be the case. Soon another argument broke out, spoiling their festive dinner.

"Now that was delicious," said the German, joining the thumb and index finger of his right hand together like an Italian. Bernd had downed four shish kabobs and a bottle of red wine all by his lonesome. "But why don't you ever make us *çiğ köfte*?"

"We'll do that Bernd," said Halaf, who was now in an especially relaxed mood thanks to the praise he'd received that evening—so much so that he addressed the German archaeologist informally. "Seeing as you've gotten to know a thing or two about kabob now, if you say it's time for *çiğ köfte*, then we'll make some *çiğ köfte*."

Bernd mistook Halaf's sincerity for ridicule.

"This isn't the first time I've eaten kabob," he said. "I've had it in Adana, and Diyarbakır, too."

"Good for you," said Halaf, as if giving the German a good piece of advice. "And during all your comings and goings to Turkey, I bet you've figured out *çiğ köfte*, too."

Bernd's voice began to take on a harsh tone.

"I didn't learn *çiğ köfte* from you. It was the Armenians who taught me *çiğ köfte*."

Halaf made a face.

"Come on, Bernd," he said. "Armenians don't know much of anything when it comes to *çiğ köfte*."

"And why shouldn't they?" said Bernd. That gleam in his eyes, induced by a merry degree of inebriation, had gone out. "What, so you're the sole, rightful owner of *çiğ köfte*? It's your invention or something now, is it?"

"Of course it's not," Esra said interrupting. She'd sensed that this conversation was headed down the wrong path since the word Armenian had come out of Bernd's mouth. "Anyone with the skill to do it can."

"No, not just anyone," Halaf insisted. "There's nothing simple about *çiğ köfte*, you have to know just how to make it."

"Enough already, Halaf," said Esra as she stared daggers at the cook. "I've seen English people even who can make *çiğ köfte*."

But the cook was in no state to comprehend either Esra's harsh looks or what she was trying to say.

"You're wrong about that, Esra Hanım," he said. "It's our forefathers who discovered *çiğ köfte*, and that's why we make it better than anyone else."

"That's just flat out wrong!" exploded Bernd. "The history of *çiğ köfte* goes back millennia. We see the first *çiğ köfte* on relief paintings discovered at Karatepe, reliefs dating back to the 8th century B.C.E. A full one thousand eight hundred years before the Turks arrived in Anatolia. Get it?"

"I'm not really clever enough to get all that, Bernd my man," said Halaf. By now the alcohol had induced him to abandon polite conversation all together. "As far as I know, Armenians can't make good *çiğ köfte*."

Bernd gave Halaf a malicious look. Seeing the sparks of rage in her German colleague's eyes, Esra knew that it was too late. And to make matters worse, Halaf seemed blatantly unaware of the delicacy of the topic at hand.

"And just why shouldn't they be able to make good *çiğ köfte?*" said the German. "They were living here long before you even set foot on these lands. They were founding civilizations and building great cities while you were busy capturing other countries and taking away people's homelands. And now you say they're incapable of making *çiğ köfte?*"

Halaf clucked his tongue and raised his head in opposition. "Nope, they can't," he said.

Esra was growing increasingly worried as the conversation progressed. "That's enough already, Halaf!" she yelled. But the cook, who'd begun to feel the effects of the alcohol he'd consumed, didn't stop there.

"Oh now, Esra Hanım, why do you say that?" he said. "We're just having a pleasant conversation here with my man Bernd." He placed his right hand upon his chest and turned to face the German. "Okay, you're right, Armenians lived on these lands, too. They also have excellent dishes after their own style, but they cannot make *çiğ köfte.*"

Bernd's face twisted into a disgusted grimace.

"You deride them even when it comes to food. You're all prejudiced to the core."

"Oh, now don't say that, Bernd my man. We live together side by side with the Armenians. We even have Armenian villages here."

"Ha, Armenian villages. The people in those villages don't even call themselves Armenians anymore. Because they're afraid they'll fall victim to the same kind of massacres that befell their forefathers years ago."

The peaceful atmosphere at the table was no more, and now everyone had their ears tuned to Bernd and Halaf. Bernd, however, paid no mind to the attention he was attracting as he continued to berate the cook in a loud voice. Halaf finally understood what a mess he'd gotten himself into, but by that time, it was too late. Bernd was so enraged it seemed he might start lashing out physically at any moment. And Halaf was up for the fight, but at the same time he was afraid he might do something wrong in his inebriated state. Just as he was beginning to think that perhaps he should apologize to Bernd, the Captain joined in the argument.

"I think you've been misinformed about some historical events," he said.

His voice was tense, but even.

Bernd's narrowed eyes moved from Halaf to focus upon the Captain.

"Actually, it's you who's been misinformed," he said, without even giving it a second thought. The fact that Eshref was their guest, and that he had helped them out numerous times, did not cause him to lower his tone of voice. "Your leaders have been pulling the wool over your eyes for years. They're trying to hide the fact that they carried out the world's first genocide."

A faint redness spread over Eshref's dark face.

"The wine has dulled your mind," he said, emphasizing each word. "You're confusing the Turks with the Germans."

Bernd wasn't expecting this response and it angered him even more. He was just about to open his mouth and say something when Timothy interjected:

"Bernd, please calm down. This isn't a good time to discuss these things."

"And why isn't it?" asked the German archaeologist. His face had turned beet red with rage. "I'm a free man, I can talk about whatever I want, whenever I want." He turned to Eshref and continued the discussion. "I am not, Sir, confusing the Turks with the Germans. Yes, we Germans did things that we should be ashamed of; humankind will never forget the massacres that we carried out, but we have accepted responsibility for them. So why don't you accept responsibility for what you did?"

The Captain was on the verge of losing all control, but he managed to maintain his cool thanks to Esra's incessant warnings as she kept hitting his foot beneath the table.

"Look, Bay Bernd, you keep saying 'you, you,' but I'm a soldier of the Turkish Republic, while the incidents you refer to happened during the time of the Ottoman government. I mean, the Turkish Republic destroyed and then replaced the government and the state structure that caused those events."

"I know," Bernd said, breathing heavily, "I, too, know that the new government destroyed the old. But the new government never accepted that the massacre happened either."

"And it never will," the Captain flared, "because people weren't consciously, deliberately massacred en masse like you did during the Second World War. They were forced to emigrate."

Bernd shook his head disdainfully.

"And that's why thousands of people died?"

"There were a lot of people, some unwanted events occurred during the migration..."

"That's all a bunch of crap," Bernd said, cutting him short. "The massacre was planned by the leaders of the Committee for Union and Progress itself and was implemented under the leadership of the *Teshkilatı Mahsusa*, because the leaders of the Committee for Union and Progress had failed to establish national identity and couldn't stand the existence of a Christian nation that might destroy the unity they were striving to forge in Anatolia. And that's why..."

"You're wrong," said the Captain. By now he was no longer paying any heed to Esra and her constant kicks under the table. "You've been misinformed about everything. During that period the Ottomans were fighting the Russians in the East. The Armenians started stirring up trouble. They began to support the Russians, the Ottoman enemy. I mean, they breached the front from behind. And for a front to be punctured from behind means death for an army. Likewise, it was the Armenians who were responsible for the 90,000 soldiers freezing to death in Sarkamısh because they were the ones who informed on them to the Russians. Under such circumstances, what could be more natural than for the Ottomans to try and reinforce their position behind the front?"

"And that's why you killed hundreds of thousands of Armenians?"

"Why do you insist upon not understanding?" the Captain flared. "These things were not wanted. They happened because people were caught up in the furor of the moment. The people who were really responsible for the events that happened back then were the Russians, British, French, and

Americans who incited the Armenians to establish their own independent state in order to break up the Ottoman lands. If it hadn't been for their provocations, the people who'd been living together in peace here for some six hundred years would have continued to do so."

Bernd's blue eyes opened wide with rage:

"I really don't think so, Captain. Whenever the Armenians asked for even the slightest of rights, you drowned them in blood and fire."

"You're very prejudiced," said Eshref in a blatantly reproachful tone. "I thought you a wiser man than that."

Now the argument was becoming personal. Esra was panicking, contemplating a strategy for putting an end to all of this when Bernd's mobile phone came to her rescue. Briefly bewildered by the interruption, Bernd paused before finally answering the call. He was speaking German with his caller, and at first this increased Esra's fears all the more, for she thought perhaps it was Vartuhi who was calling, and that Bernd would get even more fired up after talking with his wife. However, her dread was unfounded, for the caller wasn't Vartuhi, but Joachim from the German Archaeology Institute. They'd arrived in Antep, but apparently there was a problem with the hotel and so they were calling Bernd for help.

"You can't go alone in your state; let Murat go with you," Esra told Bernd, while to herself she was singing Joachim's praises for rescuing her from her predicament.

The German paid no heed.

"There's nothing wrong with me," he said, standing up. "I'm fine. It isn't the wine that got me so upset, but certain nations known to have carried out mass murders."

Of course Eshref was quick to retort:

"Then you better quit looking at yourself, otherwise you're sure to go mad in no time."

"And I was just about to suggest that you take a good hard look at your own history," said Bernd. He'd stood up, but he was swaying as if he might collapse at any moment. "Take a good hard look at your history and you'll be able to solve the Kurdish problem, too. But if you don't, believe me, you'll have a lot of trouble ahead of you." He extended his hand before the Captain had a chance to respond.

"Goodbye. We'll continue the discussion another time."

Eshref shook the hand that was held out to him, though he was distressed at not being allowed the opportunity to express his own thoughts and feelings in response. As Bernd staggered away, Timothy, too, stood up.

"I'm going to go with him. He can't drive in his condition."

"The man's so obsessed with Armenians it's driven him crazy," the Captain mumbled as the two strangers walked away. "It's like he's an Armenian terrorist, not an archaeologist."

"They're all mad," Kemal complained. "I'll never join an excavation with the likes of them ever again."

It once again fell to Esra to calm everybody down.

"As if there are never any problems in crews comprised entirely of Turks!"

"There are, but at least nobody's insulting our country."

"I'll talk with Bernd when he gets back," said Esra. "Let's close the lid on this topic a.s.a.p."

"I wouldn't wait up for him if I were you," muttered Teoman after taking another gulp of rakı. "God only knows when he'll get back."

TABLET TWENTY-THREE

The gods had Laimas tell me what I needed to know at the time most appropriate for themselves. After hearing what Laimas told me, I could not stand to go back to the palace and see Pisiris' face. I walked down to the shore of the Euphrates. I walked by the slaves harvesting in the summer heat and neared the river. I sat down beneath an old fig tree and began thinking about the years that I had lived. My rage had subsided, but the pain stung my heart like the sun that dries out the bright green grass.

What Pisiris said was correct; I had received the best education and training of any man in this country. I was knowledgeable, devoted, hard-working, obedient—but what benefit had I reaped from these traits? My grandfather bore the same characteristics, and my father, too, but how had they benefited? My father said that scribes were the pen of the gods, yet we, whether smart or stupid, brave or cowardly, wise or ignorant, we had done nothing but act as so many checker pieces in the bloody games that kings play amongst themselves. But weren't each of the kings just a toy of the gods, too? Did the gods not reward or punish the kings at their own whim? Ultimately, was it not the gods who decided who would win and who would lose at war?

In that case, it was the gods, and not the kings, who were guilty. Yes, it was the thousand gods of Hatti who were guilty, beginning with the Storm God Teshub, his wife the Sun Goddess Hepat, and their son Sharruma and Goddess Kupaba.

Were they not the true lords of us all? Were they not aware of our every deed, whether good or evil? Most important of all, weren't the kings who waged these bloody wars the representatives of the gods on earth? Did the priests not say so? Did it not say so on the tablets? Did they not warn us to "fear the wrath of the gods"? Our gods were awful, cruel, exactly like the gods of the Assyrians, the Urartians, the Phrygians, all the lands I knew... They could rain lightning down upon us, burn us in eternal fires, break us with illness, discipline us with hunger. They were powerful, and their wrath should be feared... But could there be any greater wrath than war? Could the rage of the gods possibly be more destructive than this war that was bathing the Fertile Crescent in blood? Young warriors ruthlessly strangled, women raped, the elderly and children forced out of their homes, peoples of various tongues wailing in mourning to the high heavens... Could there be a greater wrath, a greater punishment than this?

So what did the gods get out of people suffering, dying, being crippled, being exiled from their homelands? If their servants should die, who would build them magnificent temples, present them with valuable gifts, hold their ceremonies, and entreat and pray to them?

Or could it be that it was not the gods but people who were responsible for this savagery? It was the kings, the representatives of the gods, who carried out the orders to kill, seize, and destroy, but those who massacred, who cut off hands and feet, poked out eyes, and burnt down houses, were the slaves. They would be unable to carry out this savagery if they did not possess a powerful instinct to kill, an urge to destroy, a lust for extermination. Or could it be that savagery was within all of us, kings, nobles, commoners, and slaves, one and all?

I was sitting beneath the fig tree on the shores of the Euphrates, repeatedly posing these sinful questions to myself, but unable to find any answers. Each question compounded my confusion, and each answer that came to my mind heightened my sense of fear. As the inside of my head quaked with this chaos, I heard a sound like the moan of an injured wolf.

When I raised my head, I saw a slave child handing me a jug. His body stood dark black like an olive amongst the blonde wheat. His naked feet were cracked and had already developed calluses, despite his young age. You could count the bones of his thin frame, which his torn clothing failed to conceal. He was repeating himself in a weary voice, trying to get me to hear him:

"Would you like some water, Sir?"

I smiled at this small slave, whom exhaustion had failed to defeat. I took the jug that he held out to me, leaned my head back and began to pour. The sweet coolness of the water wet my dry lips and spread to my mouth. Though only briefly, the yellow heat of the day and the dark sorrow of my heart became things of the past. The holy liquid of the skies spread through my veins and throughout my body, washing and purifying my soul. I got this feeling, an appreciation of just how beautiful breathing, touching, tasting, smelling, seeing, and thinking truly was, in spite of all of the tyranny and cruelty meted out by the gods, the kings, and people. The water that I drank from the jug held out to me by the slave child restored my love of life, and my strength to resist. There were so many signs on this earth showing us that we simply must live; a lingering glance, a compassionate touch, a sincere whisper, a sweet smile, the taste that raw fruit leaves in your mouth, the delicate flowers that bloom on the driest of land. To look only at the tyranny and cruelty of the world and become vexed with it would be nothing less than an injustice to ourselves. "Ashmunikal," my lips whispered of themselves. "Ashmunikal..." Suddenly I realized just how much I missed her. I thanked the slave child as I handed him back the pitcher. The child took the pitcher and silently walked away. And then I stood up myself. I walked to the Euphrates. When I came to the edge of the water, I knelt down and washed my face. I erased the traces of the tears I had shed for my father. I felt the cool water trickle down my face. I saw my own reflection in the still waters of the Euphrates. "Scribe Patasana..." I murmured, looking at my reflection in the water. Then shaking my head I added: "From now on, there is no Scribe Patasana. Now there is Patasana the Lover." Everyone would still address me as "Scribe Patasana," but in truth I would be Patasana the Lover. I had failed to change the course of my people, of my country, but my own course I would not fail to change.

CHAPTER TWENTY-FOUR

He was standing on the road. Though his back was turned to her, Esra could tell that it was Bernd because of his short blonde hair, broad shoulders, and height. She thought about calling out to him, but before she could do so, her colleague had already left the road and entered the poplar grove next to it. Where could he possibly be going? She began to follow him. She left the dirt road that led to the village and made her way into the poplar grove as well. Suddenly she founded herself enveloped in shadows. Try as it may, the sunlight failed to penetrate the canopy of small but dense leaves that crowned the lofty poplars. Esra kept a careful watch on the German archaeologist so as not to lose him in the darkness of the shadows. Seeing Bernd stop, she stopped, too. There was no longer much distance between them. She saw Bernd turn around suddenly, and so she quickly threw herself behind the nearest tree. She stayed in this position for a while before cautiously poking her head out to take a look at her colleague. But he was gone. She came out from behind the tree and began scanning the area with her eyes. No, Bernd was nowhere to be seen. But he couldn't have gotten far. The dense concentration of trees and rough terrain would've made it extremely difficult for him to move very quickly. She began to make her way through the grove, carefully eyeing her surroundings each step of the way. She went a good fifty meters, but still there was no sign of her colleague. The deeper into the orchard she wandered, the darker it became, until it was pitch-black like the darkest of nights. Maybe he'd gotten lost? No, that was impossible. After all, it was a small grove, ending just five hundred meters away on either side. With these thoughts in her head she pressed forward. But the orchard seemed to go on and on interminably. It had grown quite dark and the scent of decayed grass was heavy in the air. She was progressing more slowly now because she could no longer see ahead of her very well. Then suddenly she tripped. She thought she must have tripped over a fallen tree trunk, but when she took a more careful look, she saw that it wasn't a tree trunk at all, but a human body. "Oh my God!... Bernd?..." She anxiously knelt down next to the specter lying face-down on the ground.

"Bernd... What's happened to you, Bernd?"... she said as she tried to turn the heavy man's body over. She felt something on her hand. She looked and saw that it was a dark liquid.

"Are you hurt?"

The man was deathly still. She heard nothing but her own voice echoing in the grove. Finally she succeeded in turning the man over. "Oh my God!... It's Eshref!..." she screamed upon seeing his face.

"Yes, it's Eshref," said a familiar voice. "And Bernd and Tim's bodies are just over there."

Horrified, Esra turned in the direction that the voice was coming from. A man was standing just a few meters away from her. It was too dark for her to make out who he was.

"And who are you?"

"Shame on you, Esra Hanım" the man said as he walked closer to her, "don't you recognize the man who makes you those delicious meals, with whom you chit-chat every day?"

"Halaf, is that... is that you?"

Halaf's insolent voice rang out in the grove.

"It's me, who else could it be?"

"But why would you do a thing like this?"

"I did it in honor of a fellow townsman."

"A fellow townsman?"

"Oh come on, don't tell me that you still don't get it. I'm talking about Patasana. You invaded his privacy, took what wasn't yours."

The poplars suddenly made way for the sunlight to break through, as if they'd somehow been ordered to do so. The light beamed down upon Esra and Halaf, allowing Esra to see the face of the man she was talking to. But it wasn't Halaf. It was a man who had escaped from the depths of history, with his odd cap, his long embroidered robes, and his broad sword in hand.

"Patasana..." Elif stammered, her voice hoarse with fear. "You're Patasana..."

"I warned you," said Patasana, speaking in Halaf's accented Turkish. "You did not do as my tablets ordered. And you're gonna pay."

Esra saw the man's sword swing upwards, but she was in such shock, so stunned with fear that she could neither speak nor move. All she could do was look on silently, as if resigned to her fate. The man raised his sword. Esra saw the raised sword cut through the sunlight. The sliced sunlight fell to the ground, dazzling her eyes on the way, then it disappeared into the darkness of the earth, followed by the sword. It all happened so quickly, in a single blink of Esra's eyes, which then opened to see the gray morning light seeping in through the window. She sat up in bed, all of a sweat. She had a splitting headache and her heart was racing like mad. Leaning her back against the wall she took several deep breaths.

As soon as she understood that it was only a dream, she began to laugh, thinking "That's what you get for eating so much of Halaf's kabob." Laughing made her head hurt that much worse. She tried to get out of bed but noticed that her feet were trembling. "It was just a dream, for goodness sake," she grumbled to herself. Stubbornly she stepped onto the floor with her bare feet. "But what a dream it was!" As if the unpleasant episode of the previous night hadn't been enough, she then had to deal with a nasty nightmare.

An odd sense of unity had developed amongst the Turks, in the wake of Bernd and Timothy's departure. Yet Esra never ever would have thought that Teoman, who had tried every which way to get out of doing his military duty, could share the same thoughts as Eshref. And the same was pretty much true for Kemal as well. And what about Halaf, who because of his Kurdishness was actually rather shy of the Captain, as much as he tried not to show it? Even he'd started spouting off about foreigners. They were so sure they were right that Esra herself, as the director of the excavation, might have shared the same feelings, had she not been aware of how dangerous the formation of such factions amongst the crew members would be. But her duty forced her to behave more responsibly, and so she'd told her friends that they had been much too quick to take offense towards the foreign members of the crew. Though she herself had her suspicions about Bernd, she did her best to defend him, and in doing so angered Eshref, which was by no means her intention, causing a rift between the two of them.

The Captain had gone so far as to reproach her right there in front of the entire crew. "You go so far as to put up with the man's blatant insults just because he's a foreigner, but you're suspicious of anything I have to say just because I wear a uniform," he said.

While Esra tried to return to the Captain's good graces, Kemal started in with more accusations. "That Timothy guy's one of them, too," he said. "Look at the lengths he's gone to help that Armenian woman find her brother."

This was taking it too far.

"Now you're really talking nonsense!" she yelled. "You're about to declare the man an Armenian conspirator just because he's trying to help some poor woman out."

This last argument put a real damper on the night's festivities, making the table grow silent for some time. Hoping to break the silence, Teoman asked Halaf to sing a song, and the young cook responded by piping out two folk songs of Barak. Teoman and Esra tried to join in on the singing, but it just wasn't happening and so that was the end of the folk songs. Eshref had begun to soften up towards the end of the night, and even whispered in Esra's ear, suggesting that they take a stroll along the Euphrates. When Esra had called him to come to dinner that day, she'd thought they would sit on the same rock they'd sat upon a few days earlier and watch the river. But after everything that had happened, she was in no mood to take in the glimmering waters of the river or the enchanting glow of the moon. And so using their drunken state as an excuse, she had declined the Captain's offer. She was sad when she saw his long face after she'd turned him down, but she was a grown woman and knew well enough how to say no to things she didn't want to do.

But after having seen Eshref off that night, Esra lay down in bed and thought that she'd acted unjustly towards him. Was she a harsh, soulless person? No, not really. But she hadn't been able to bring herself to go for a midnight stroll with Eshref when there was so much work to be done, and especially right there in front of the crew. Love had caused enough problems on the excavation as it was already. She certainly didn't want to become yet another troublemaker herself. Especially with those murders that were constantly occupying her mind... She thought she'd done the right thing, but it didn't make her feel any better. Those weren't the real reasons why she hadn't gone off with Eshref. She just hadn't wanted to. If she'd really wanted to, she would have found a way and gone with him, but the truth was, she simply didn't have the urge to. Or was she tired of him already? So quickly? Oh no, c'mon... But she knew very well that this relationship had no future. Every time the two of them met it became more and more obvious just how different they were from one another. Yet she still hadn't hesitated to sleep with him. What's more, she'd really enjoyed it. "Oh, for goodness sake," she said in a perturbed voice, "there's no use dwelling on the matter. The relationship will just have to run its course."

She was late to breakfast the following morning, as she had been the morning before. Halaf had already begun filling up their tea glasses when she arrived at the table. Her eyes were still half-closed as she greeted everyone with a "good morning." Bernd and Timothy were sitting across from her. Elif was sitting at the other end of the table, having decided to keep her distance from the American this time around.

Timothy looked at Esra with a concerned expression upon his face.

"You don't look well. It seems you must have continued drinking after we left."

"We got a little carried away," Esra said with a grimace. "You know how it is, once you get started, you just don't know when to stop."

"Drink coffee instead of tea," Bernd said. His concern seemed sincere, and he appeared to have completely forgotten about the argument the night before. "Take two aspirin after breakfast and you'll be absolutely fine."

Esra was still angry at Bernd, but she wasn't in any mood to argue with him now.

"You're right," she said. Pointing to the tea glass in front of her she turned to Halaf. "Could you take this and bring me a nice, strong cup of coffee?"

She didn't feel like eating anything, but she nevertheless took some cheese and two slices of tomato and put them on her plate.

"Have some of the olive salad, too," said Halaf, "the sour will settle your stomach."

"What does Joachim have to say?" Esra asked Bernd as she reached for the olive salad.

"Nothing important. There was a problem at the hotel. Joachim's Turkish isn't that good. There was a misunderstanding and they tried to give us the small meeting hall. We talked with them and took care of it though. They're going to begin preparations this morning."

"Since you mention preparations, I've written the text to be passed out to the journalists. Kemal proofread it, so it's ready to be translated now."

"Excellent," said Bernd. "I'll translate it into German as soon as I get back."

"Does Kemal have the text?" Timothy asked.

"Yes," said Esra. It was clear to her that the American didn't want to talk with Kemal himself. "Don't worry, I'll get it for you."

"If you can find him, that is," said Murat. "He wasn't in his bed when I woke up this morning."

Esra's half-closed eyes opened wide with surprise. What the heck was this guy saying?

"That's true, I haven't seen Kemal around at all," Teoman chimed in. "Did you send him somewhere?"

"No...," said Esra. "I didn't send him anywhere. He must be around here somewhere."

"He's not around here anywhere. I went all the way to Grandma Hattuch's garden thinking maybe he'd gone for a walk, but he wasn't there either."

Esra felt like her head was going to explode. She didn't want to think about Kemal now.

"Then he's gone down to the river," she said. Speaking was like torture to her just then. "Don't worry, he'll be back soon."

But Kemal didn't return. He was nowhere to be seen during breakfast, or when the crew got into the van and car to go to the excavation. Esra sent Elif and Murat with the van to go pick up the workers, and told Teoman to go down to the Euphrates to look for Kemal. She herself checked Kemal's room, together with Bernd. His bed was unmade, which meant that he had gone to bed the previous night. But it was not at all like Kemal, an utter clean freak, to leave his bed in this state. For the first time Esra began to grow genuinely worried. Her headache, which had partially subsided thanks to the aspirin, began to assert itself once again.

"Could he have quit the excavation?" asked Bernd. "Maybe he didn't want to stay on after what happened between him and Elif."

Would he take off like this without letting anyone know? But really, come on, without telling *anyone*? It was true that he'd said he wanted to leave. But then Esra wouldn't let him... Would he do such a thing? She bent down to look under his bed. She lifted the edge of the bedspread and saw that his brown suitcase was still there.

"So he hasn't gone away!" she said, her voice so full of cheer one would have thought she'd found Kemal himself and not just his suitcase. "He just got carried away with drinking last night, like we all did. He must have gone down to the riverside to try and come to."

When they got back to the arbor they learned that Teoman had come back empty handed. Unfortunately Kemal wasn't down by the Euphrates either. And so they began to worry all over again.

"Where could that boy possibly have gone?" murmured Esra. "Unless something bad has happened to him?"

"Like what?" said Teoman.

Esra gave him a fretful look instead of an answer.

"Maybe," said Timothy, who had remained silent on the issue all morning, "he disappeared on purpose, to upset Elif and draw attention to himself."

Esra looked at the American with eyes that longed to believe his words. It was logical. Kemal wasn't one to just up and abandon the excavation, but he was entirely capable of carrying out such a childish disappearing act. If he were hiding somewhere, then they had no other choice but to wait for him to reappear. They looked to the sky and saw that it was nearly sunrise.

"Then let's go to the excavation," said Esra. "We're not going to be able to work tomorrow, so we best not dally around anymore today."

The American turned to Halaf before boarding the jeep.

"If he comes, please, whatever you do, call me," he said. "My cell phone will be on."

Esra thought about Kemal all along the way to the excavation site. She tried to convince to herself that nothing bad could possibly have happened to him. Timothy's conjecture was the most plausible one. Kemal's goal was to get Elif's attention, perhaps because he believed she still loved him, by disappearing for a while. Though she tried to calm herself down with such thoughts, that suspicious devil in the deep regions of her mind just wouldn't leave well alone, and with its ominous voice kept whispering to her all the worst possible scenarios. Suddenly she found herself considering the possibility that Kemal had been murdered. But that was ridiculous. Whether it was the separatists, as Eshref believed, or someone seeking revenge, as Esra guessed, there was no reason for anyone to kill Kemal. If there was to be another murder, Esra thought that it must be of a coppersmith... But what if the killer had changed his tactic? But even if he'd changed his tactic, why would he target Kemal?

Esra set about her work at the site, her head throbbing relentlessly and a deep anxiety that she tried hard to suppress eating away at her. Everyone, especially Elif and including the rest of the crew, from the worker's foreman Maho to Murat, was doing their best to avoid her. She just kept walking about with a long face and responding to everyone's questions with curt answers. During the midmorning break, as the workers headed over to sit beneath the old fig tree, she called Timothy. No, he told her, Kemal hadn't come back. She wasn't to worry though; Timothy would definitely let her know if he showed up. Easier said than done. Where was that kid? While the rest of the crew got back to work after breakfast, Esra didn't feel like working, and so she continued to sit in the shade of the tree. This was too much. They were all scientists, all academics. What did they want from them? That idiot Bernd kept going on about the Armenians. What's it to us anyway, Armenians, Kurds... She felt better after drinking another cup of strong coffee and taking another aspirin, but she still didn't go to the library. She couldn't stand the thought of going out into that sun with her headache. Half awake and half asleep, leaning against the old fig tree and letting herself be stroked by the cool wind coming up from the Euphrates, she watched the rest of the crew work. Then she started thinking about Kemal again. She looked at her watch; it was going on noon. But Kemal was still nowhere to be seen. She called Elif over to her. The younger woman came, dragging her feet all the way. Yet she was quick to speak, before Esra had a chance to.

"I'm sorry for all of this," she said. She hung her head like a criminal confessing her crime. "If you want, I can quit the excavation right now."

Esra frowned.

"I don't want anyone quitting the excavation," she said. "I'm sick of hearing about you people wanting to leave the excavation. After so much hard work here, we can finally see the light at the end of the tunnel and everyone's talking about quitting... So now tell me, is there anywhere Kemal would go when he wanted to be alone?"

"What do you mean?" Elif stuttered.

Esra's headache grew worse the more she talked, and the more she talked, the more she thought about what a stupid girl Elif was.

"What do you think I mean?" she responded chidingly. "I mean someplace where the two of you would go to be together, for example... A secluded shore of the Euphrates, a quiet garden, a cave..."

"No. We'd just go down to the Euphrates, and Teoman already looked there."

"All right, so did Kemal ever get angry and storm off somewhere?"

"Sometimes," said the young woman. "Whenever we'd have an argument, he'd just take off. He wouldn't call or anything, and when I would call, he wouldn't answer his telephone. I'd ask him where he'd gone off to and he'd always just say, 'Nowhere, just walking around.'"

"I hope he's just out walking around this time, too," mumbled Esra. "But then if that's the case he's gonna be real sorry..." Suddenly she noticed Murat waving at her. "Are they calling for us to come over?"

Elif narrowed her eyes to get a better look.

"Yeah," she said, "I think they've found something."

Esra didn't rush. She drank a glass of water from the terracotta jug. The sweet coolness of the water wet her dry lips and coated her mouth. Refreshed, she stood up straight and put her hat on, then turned to Elif. "Come on," she said, "let's go see what they've turned up."

Murat met up with them before they reached the library. He was ecstatic.

"We've found the last three tablets," he said, jumping up and down for joy. "Not only that, but they're in excellent condition, as if Patasana had penned them just yesterday."

So the entire text of Patasana's twenty eight tablet long personal history was now complete. The excavation crew's efforts had finally born fruit. It was a monumental achievement, a history making success. As a now buoyant Esra gave Elif a celebratory hug, she couldn't help but say, "If only Kemal were here, too...," for he had played a part in this success as well.

TABLET TWENTY-FOUR

This was not my first sin, but it would be my first revolt. I had committed my first sin with Ashmunikal, and my first revolt would I realize with her as well. I had committed my first sin when I touched a woman that the gods and the law had forbidden me. At that time I was a child with a naïve heart, looking at the world in wonder, and I knew that what I was doing was wrong. But now I wasn't so sure that what I had done was wrong. This time, I would ponder, plan, and enjoy the sin that I was about to commit, for I had ceased to believe in the gods. I did not respect them. My worries were no longer due to the gods or to Pisiris. My concern was whether Ashmunikal would forgive this lover, this stupid, treacherous, fame hungry lover who had abandoned his one and only love for the mere sake of his rank.

She had shown me love, had injected a thrill into my life that was previously unknown to me; she had offered me her heart and her skin; she had taught me courage and how to sin; it was she who made me appreciate life. But now, as I thought about going back to her, I was afraid that she might not forgive me. With this fear I sent my new assistant, Eriya, to the harem to see Ashmunikal. I sent her word that the new tablets containing Ludingirra's poems had arrived, and that if the esteemed mistress and admirer of the poet should like, she could come and read them. Then I set about anxiously waiting in the library. When my assistant Eriya returned with the good news that the lady would visit the library the next day, I was so overjoyed I didn't know what to do with myself.

The next day I sent my assistant out of town together with two slaves to go get clay. I began waiting in the library in the early morning hours. As always, Ashmunikal did not keep me waiting long. I welcomed her at the library door. With her doe eyes she looked at me quizzically. And I think that at that moment, she understood what was happening. She walked over to the shelves, and away from me, and began looking at the tablets.

"I've been told that Ludingirra's tablets have come; I'd like to see them," she said.

She was cold, distant, like a total stranger to me. I was losing her, or perhaps I had already lost her. The thought drove me mad; heedless of the fact that someone might come in and see us, I impetuously grabbed her hand and knelt before her. And with the following words I beseeched her:

"Forgive me. Forgive this petty upstart full of false pride for his nobility and training. Forgive this ignorant fool who has been unable to differentiate between good and evil, beautiful and ugly, lover and foe. Forgive this idiot who upon finding gold threw it away as if it were a mere pebble. Forgive this insensible simpleton who was unable to realize that a life without you would become but the driest of deserts. Forgive this rude man who has been unforgivably greedy, ambitious, and disloyal.

"If you do not forgive him, the last piece of stone holding up this poor man already on the brink shall collapse into the depths, and him with it. If you do not forgive him, his weak body shall disappear in the waters of the Euphrates. If you do not forgive him, he shall lose everything about him that is good, beautiful, and innocent, and shall be trapped in the dark world of the djinns. If you do not forgive him..."

I felt Ashmunikal's hand, at first seemingly motionless in my own, begin to stir.

"Stand up," she said in a shaky voice. When I raised my head, I looked to find her face bathed in tears. It was at that moment that I understood that she had not forgotten me, and that she loved me still. I stood up and embraced her delicate body that trembled with her sighs. I felt the warmth of her body on my own. I once again tasted the incomparable deliciousness of her lips, which were coated with the salt of her tears. Once the intoxication of our meeting had subsided, I felt a rush of anxiety. We left the library for the small office, where we sought refuge behind the security of the bolted door.

As I kissed her inside our little shelter I simultaneously expressed with words my gratitude for her forgiveness. She put her hand over my mouth.

"Do not thank me," she said, "because I am not doing you a favor. It's true, I was angry at you; but how could you think that I had stopped loving you? Does the earth stop loving the clouds because it does not rain? Does a mother stop loving her child because it does not smile? Can the seed do without the earth, grain without the sun, bugs without flowers? How could you think that I stopped loving you?"

The more she spoke, the greater did the fiery passion in my heart rage, its heat spreading throughout my veins. This fire had made its way to my groin, swelling my manhood. I was purified of all fear, and thought that she and I were the only two people on earth. I held Ashmunikal tight. And wholly and completely did she open up to me the door to her slender, delicate body. With curiosity and desire did I enter her, as if entering an unknown temple; I explored as if I were in a foreign country for the first time; I smelled and tasted of her holy fruits. I saw that my touch transformed Ashmunikal's face into a wild ethereal flower. The fire that ignited in her eyes with each touch made her beauty that much more divine, and her skin so fresh, like the earth in spring.

Ashmunikal taught me that without this magic spell of touches, this ceremony consecrated with kisses, I would not be able to taste love. I was in a state of blissful bewilderment, that state that a young man experiences when the burning desire that begins as an attraction to beauty turns into a proof of manhood, and then becomes love. Feeling myself the pain of her love wounds, touching her, kissing her, taking in her scent, I could not help but wonder how I could possibly have been able to bear those days without Ashmunikal. And I understood better the emotion that had made my grandfather fall in love as he neared his death. I etched it into my memory, that I might remember it forever.

But there was another truth that I also needed to etch into my memory: Ashmunikal belonged to the king. Even if Pisiris no longer took an interest in her, truth was, she was his property. And those who made love with Pisiris' women were dealt the most severe punishment in the land. The mere thought of it darkened my face with gloom and set my heart trembling with fear.

CHAPTER TWENTY-FIVE

"We have to find Kemal," Esra said fearfully.

She had the full attention of everyone at the table.

"We have to find him," she repeated. "He's been missing for how many hours now? I'm seriously worried."

When they returned from the excavation to learn that there still wasn't any word from Kemal, it had become clear to her that it was time for them to do something. Before talking with the crew she'd tried twice to reach Eshref and met with the same response both times: "The Captain is out of the station." They had neither offered any information as to his whereabouts, nor told her what time he would be back. Nothing else, just those seven words... Could it be that the Captain was hurt by her behavior the other night, and that's why he wasn't taking her calls? "I shouldn't have gotten involved with him," she thought. It was the first time she'd felt regret for having gone to bed with him. Why had she called him anyway? Why else, to tell him that Kemal had gone missing, and to ask for help. Was that really the reason, or was it to take refuge in the comforting words of someone special, right now when she felt so helpless herself? "No," she countered the incessant voice in her head. "I'm not thinking of taking refuge with the Captain or anything of the sort. I have a more important issue to deal with." As she tried to expel the Captain from her mind, she called for the crew members to gather around her. Everyone was in a joyful mood because they'd found the last remaining tablets. And so Esra's words came as a real party pooper. Esra realized this as well, but she didn't have any other choice. One of their friends had gone missing, and what's more, he'd disappeared in the aftermath of two murders.

"We should leave everything and start looking for him," she continued. "This isn't a very big place. Let's form teams, and one group can go into town while another group searches down by the Euphrates..."

The crew, gathered around the table, listened with concern to her words, which were spoken without much thought and with hardly a breath in between. Their minds were occupied with the preparations for the press conference to be held the following day. Timothy had found Esra's text in the computer room and had translated it into English, but it had not yet been photocopied, and the photographs that they were to pass out to the journalists had not yet been developed. Elif had to get to work in the darkroom, and she had no time to lose. It wasn't right for them to be spending their valuable time under these stressful circumstances looking for Kemal, who had perhaps just taken off for a bit to get away because his feelings were hurt. Everyone except for Esra shared this opinion, but nobody had the courage to say so. The task befell Bernd.

"We won't get anywhere with this haste," said the German archaeologist. His voice was soft but resolute. "We don't know if Kemal went off of his own accord, or if something bad has happened to him. I think it's too early to get all scared and worked up about it though. Especially when there's so much work to be done right now..."

Esra frowned and was just getting ready to oppose him when Timothy jumped in.

"I think Bernd's absolutely right," he said. "We all know that Kemal's been very tense these days. He virtually pounced on me yesterday. It's natural for a person in such a mood to take off, to want to get away for a while."

"It's not like him to act so irresponsibly," responded Esra, shaking her head hopelessly. "He should have at least called by now."

Teoman, who was sitting next to Esra, placed a hand on her shoulder.

"I'm just as worried as you are," he said. "But as we were coming back from the match last night, he kept saying, 'This excavation's lost its charm, I'm getting out of here.' So maybe he really did leave."

"But his luggage, all of his stuff is still in his room. If he left, why would he leave his stuff behind?"

Murat interjected, with all good intentions:

"He said that Rüstem, the director of the museum in Antep, was his friend. Maybe he's gone to see him."

Esra had considered this possibility as well. But how could he get to Antep at such an early morning hour?

"How?" she asked.

"By truck," Halaf replied. "Trucks from the villages down the way drive by here on their way to take vegetables to Antep. He must've taken one of those."

"That early?"

"That early. They hit the road extra early so that the vegetables don't soak up all the sun and lose their color."

Was it possible?

"Could be," said Murat hopefully, "I hitchhiked the other day when coming back from town, and the guys gave me a ride without any hassle. And they brought me all the way to the school."

"Let's call the museum," said Elif excitedly, "that way we'll know for sure if he's gone there or not."

The girl was right. Esra immediately whipped out her mobile phone. She dialed. Everyone at the table had gone silent, their eyes riveted upon Esra.

"Hello... may I speak with Rüstem Bey? He's not there? Do you know where he is? He has a guest from Istanbul? Do you know the guest's name? I see. Could you give me his mobile number? This is Esra, the archaeologist. I'm ready to write it down. Okay... Okay... Thank you very much."

"Rüstem's out of the office," Esra said, turning to her friends. "He went to the Yesemek Open Air Museum together with a guest of his. They're going to spend the night there."

Murat smiled proudly at having been proven right.

"Well there you have it, Kemal's with him."

Esra, however, wasn't so quick to jump to conclusions.

"Now we'll find out for sure," she said as she began dialing Rüstem's number. She held the phone to her ear and waited, and waited and waited... With an air of frustration she put the phone down.

"He can't be reached."

"You're getting all worked up over nothing," said Teoman. "I bet Kemal's with him too. You know he was part of the landscaping project at Yesemek two years ago."

Esra, who recalled seeing Rüstem at the hospital speaking in hushed voices with Kemal, was a little relieved, if not convinced. Kemal might be with him.

After a brisk meal, everyone set about getting to work. Elif and Murat withdrew to the darkroom where they developed black and white prints of the tablets, Timothy began transcribing and translating tablet number twenty-eight, Bernd reviewed the text that would be read at the press conference, and Teoman and Esra took their seats in front of the computer and prepared a list of excavation finds besides the Patasana tablets. It didn't take long to complete the latter task. Taking Murat with her, Esra headed off to town to photocopy the text that would be handed out to the journalists.

Murat drove the jeep. The heat coming off of the asphalt that flowed beneath them was so dense that it was visible to the naked eye. There wasn't a single bird in the sky. People, animals, and insects alike had sought out a cool place and taken refuge there. Even the Euphrates, which Esra always enjoyed watching, looked hot and heavy, like molten lead. All of the jeep's windows were open, but the wind that filled it didn't provide the least bit of coolness. She noticed that she no longer had a headache. Her head still felt heavy but she'd finally gotten rid of that damned throb. She picked up the frozen bottle of water that lay next to her feet. It hadn't even been half an hour and the ice had half melted already. She threw her head back for drink. The water overflowed, spilling out of her mouth and down onto her chin, dribbling from there down to her chest. She closed her eyes and tried to feeling of coolness that the cold water had aroused on her skin.

"Isn't that the Captain?" Murat asked, prompting Esra to open her eyes. There was a jeep coming towards them from the opposite direction. She squinted, looking carefully. Yes, that was Eshref sitting next to the soldier who was driving. His movements indicated that he'd noticed them, too. Murat slowed down their jeep, and the jeep coming from the opposite direction pulled over on the right. The Captain was signaling with his hand for them to stop as well. Murat pulled their jeep over and into the shade of a large walnut tree by the roadside. The Captain had already made his way over to them by the time they stepped out of their jeep.

"I was just on my way to see you."

Esra smiled.

"Is that so?" she said. "And what business do you have with us in this heat?"

The Captain didn't return her smile; his tired face maintained its worrisomely grave mien.

"I've got bad news," explained the Captain, "there's been another murder."

Esra felt as if her entire world were collapsing around her.

"Kemal," she stuttered.

The Captain looked at her with a stunned expression.

"What happened to Kemal?" he asked.

"The victim isn't Kemal?"

"No my dear, it's Nahsen from the village of Timil. What does Kemal have to do with anything?"

"He's been missing since this morning," Esra said sadly.

"What do you mean missing?"

"We don't know," said Esra. She was sad about her friend, but her curiosity won out. "We'll talk about later. You go ahead and tell us about the man who was murdered."

"A villager, fifty some years old. He was sleeping under the arbor in his garden to keep watch for thieves. When they went to see him in the morning, they found him hanging from one of the beams of the arbor."

"Was the man a coppersmith?" Esra asked excitedly.

"No, but his father was," said Eshref. For a moment, their eyes met. Both of them were thinking about their conversation at the Captain's lodgings. "Not only that, but he was

Garo Usta's apprentice. But his father passed away five years ago."

"They killed the son in place of the father."

"So it seems. They even put a copper wire around the man's neck."

"They hung him with copper wire?"

"No, they hung the man with the bridle that he used to tie up his horse. But they also tied a copper wire around his neck."

There was an odd sparkle in Esra's eyes.

"It's a message," she murmured, "the murderer wants us to know why he's committed these murders. There were messages in the other murders, too. A monk dressed in black pushed Hadji Settar off the minaret, in a way to remind us of Priest Kirkor. And Chief Guard Reshat was murdered in exactly the same manner as Ohannes Agha..."

"It's obvious now that you were right about these being copycat murders of those committed seventy-eight years ago," said the Captain. He paused, then wiping the sweat off of his forehead with the back of his hand, added: "But I still think it's the separatists who are behind it all."

This time Esra found the Captain's childish tenacity rather endearing. She looked at him fondly. The frowning Captain's thick lips were in a slight pout. Esra thought about those lips grazing along her neck. She recalled how they had made love the other day. She felt the Captain's muscular body on top of her, inside of her, sending a quiver through her body just then. She quickly composed herself and asked, "Would you like some water?" she asked.

"Yes, I would," said the Captain, "we've been withering away under this sun since early this morning."

Murat took the bottle of water and handed it to the Captain.

"Ice cold," murmured the Captain happily when he felt the bottle. Then he threw his head back and with his eyes closed began gulping down the welcome liquid.

"Slow down," said Esra as she watched him, "or you'll make yourself sick."

Having had his own fill, Eshref turned to the soldier sitting in the jeep:

"Erol, look, they have ice cold water."

"Give it to me, I'll take it to him," said Murat.

"Actually, I agree with you that these murders are politically motivated," said Esra, once the young student had begun making his way over to the Captain's jeep with the bottle of water. "It seems really implausible to me, too, that a single person could be behind all of these murders. So I also think it's politically motivated, but unlike you, I don't think it's the Kurds who are behind it, but the radical Islamists."

The Captain's eyes were riveted upon Esra's face.

"You know something?"

"I heard that Abid Hodja was Armenian."

The Captain gave her a look as if to say, "Do you realize what you're saying?"

"Don't look at me like that. The man is of Armenian origin. More importantly, he's a relative of Ohannes Agha's. What's more, he took Head Guard Reshat's sister as his mistress."

The Captain's surprise turned into suspicion.

"Where the hell did you learn all of this?"

"Here and there. With a little research you could've gotten hold of the same information yourself."

"What you say has to be true in order for me to investigate. Is this information from a reliable source? Or is this another jewel from your meddlesome cook?"

"Everyone knows it. Go ask the old folks in town."

The Captain was having a hard time believing what he had just heard. His eyes lingered upon Esra's face for a while as he contemplated her words.

"So," he said, "you mean to say that Abid Hodja killed Reshat?"

Murat, who had just returned to their side, tuned into their conversation when he heard the name Abid Hodja.

"Not just Reshat," Esra said, emphasizing each word, "he killed all three of them."

"That's a pretty big claim to be making," said the Captain. "Let's say that Abid Hodja had a motive for killing Reshat, but what about the others..."

"He wanted to get revenge for the murders that happened seventy-eight years ago. Isn't it possible that his family somehow imbued him with such hatred? How Muslim can you really become when it's forced upon you?"

"Seventy-eight years is a long time to keep hatred like that alive," said the Captain.

Esra was ready with her response:

"Beliefs have long lives, too. They live for centuries. There's a woman known as Infidel Nadide. Even she hasn't completed renounced her beliefs. She believes in both the Kuran and the Bible."

"I don't know," said the Captain, wrinkling his brow, "he's not just anyone, he's a hodja at the mosque."

"Actually, I'm suspicious of Abid Hodja, too," said Murat, putting in his two cents worth. "When we were talking about Hadji Settar's murder, Halaf said that only Abid Hodja had the key to the minaret. I mean, the hodja was there when Hadji Settar was killed."

The Captain was displeased at the fact that Murat, too, felt compelled to put forth his own conjectures about the murders.

"He never hid the fact that he was there," the Captain chided. "I talked with him myself. He opened the door to the minaret so Hadji Settar could go up, and then entered the mosque, just as he does every Friday. It's impossible for him to see or hear what's going on in the minaret while he's in the mosque. He wasn't aware of the murder even after Hadji Settar had hit the ground. The folks who had come to pray told him about it."

"But what if he's lying?" said Esra. "What if he pushed Hadji Settar off the minaret and then entered the mosque?"

"He would have no reason to do so. Okay, let's say that he did. Eyewitnesses say that they saw a man dressed in black fleeing the scene of the crime..."

"Abid Hodja dressed up in black like a monk in order to disguise himself and then entered the mosque. There was nobody inside because the call to prayer hadn't been read yet. So he took off his robe and hid it somewhere and then began to wait for the congregation."

"I just don't know," said the Captain. There was a look of helplessness in his eyes. "For some reason, that just doesn't seem very plausible to me."

Once again there was a brief silence. The only sound to be heard was the rustling of the warm wind as it roamed amongst the branches of the walnut tree. It was Esra who finally broke the silence.

"But you don't have any more suspects. If Abid Hodja didn't do it, then who did?"

The Captain had listened to Esra with narrow eyes. It didn't take long for him to put forth his response:

"What about Bernd? The man talked like a real Armenian fanatic last night. Did you see the rage in his eyes when he looked at me? What if the man is secretly mad? Do we know where he was at the time that the murders happened?"

Esra didn't know what to say. If she told him what she thought about Bernd, Eshref would declare him their number one suspect, right then and there. And he wouldn't exactly be out of line in doing so. Hadn't she herself been ready to believe that Bernd was the killer, before she'd learned that Abid Hodja was of Armenian origin? Everything had changed though once she'd found out about the latter. Abid Hodja had better motives for carrying out the murders.

"No murderer would get tangled up in arguments that would give the underlying motives away," she said. "If Bernd were behind the murders, then he wouldn't defend the Armenians so fanatically. He'd try to hide it."

The Captain knew that she was right.

"I think you should question that Abid Hodja," Esra continued. "If you're afraid of how the congregation would react, then you should do it on the sly. You should at least find out where he was, and who was with him, at the time of the murders, because the guy has plenty of resources. He has people like Fayat who obey him blindly. How do you know he didn't form some kind of organization with them?"

This was enough.

"Oh come on Esra!" the Captain yelled. "Are you trying to tell me that an Islamic organization carried out murders for the Armenian cause?"

Esra didn't have the least bit of doubt about her hypothesis.

"The man's very sharp. He didn't tell his men that the murders were being committed for the Armenian cause. He told him it had to do with the great Islamic awakening or something."

The Captain sighed in distress.

"Are you aware," he asked, "that we're now right back where we began? When Hadji Settar was murdered I was saying that it was the separatists who were behind it, and you were saying that it was the religious fanatics..."

"I don't think we're back where we started. We've come a long way, in fact. If we act wisely then we can catch the killer soon."

The Captain had something else to say, but he was uncertain about whether to tell Esra about it or not. Finally, he decided to spill the beans.

"I don't know if it'll do any good, but we have another clue," said the Captain. "We think the killer was injured."

"How do you know?"

"We found traces of blood near the arbor. Seeing as the victim didn't bleed at all, the blood must belong to the killer. And we also found a sickle with traces of blood on it. We think the victim put up a fight and injured the murderer with the sickle as he was being strangled. We found the same traces of blood in the victim's stolen horse buggy. We think the murderer escaped with the horse buggy after being injured."

"Where'd you find the horse buggy?"

"In the meadow below the village."

"This is great news," said Esra. Her eyes had begun to shine with excitement. "So it means the killer's been injured. So now we just have to check and see if Abid Hodja or any of his men are injured."

"We'll do that, but to be honest, I highly doubt that we'll find anything."

"Yes you will," Esra said. She touched Eshref's hand and smiled confidently. "Believe me, this time we'll figure it all out."

The Captain looked at her as if to say, "I hope you're right," then gently squeezing the young woman's hand added: "Anyway, don't let me keep you. It looks like you're going into town, huh?"

"To the municipality," said Murat, "we have texts that we need to get photocopied."

Esra turned to the Captain before getting back in the jeep: "Stop by this evening, if you want."

A mixed expression appeared on Eshref's face.

"You're always so tired," he said, "I wouldn't want to bother you."

A faint blush rose up in Esra's cheeks.

"I'm sorry about last night. I won't be tired this evening."

They didn't take off until the Captain had gotten in his jeep. As the military jeep disappeared down the asphalt road that seemed to be evaporating beneath them, Murat and Esra headed into town.

"I was watching you while you were talking back there," Murat said, unable to disguise his admiration, "you seemed more like a detective than an archaeologist."

"So?"

"I was impressed. The way you look at things, your ability to solve things, and most importantly, your determination. I thought I'd never be able to learn anything from another woman after my mother. But you changed that. You yell at me more than anyone else on the excavation, but you also teach me more than anyone else."

Esra liked what she was hearing.

"I'm glad you think that way," she said. "You know that I love you. I want you to become a good archaeologist. But you need to get over all those nonsensical beliefs of yours. You know what I'm talking about?"

The young student shook his head.

"Yeah, I do." After looking at the road stretching out in front of him, he began to talk again.

"I want to say something, but promise you won't get mad," he said shyly.

Esra looked at the young man curiously.

"I really liked the way you talked and behaved with the Captain, but it seems to me like you're intervening a bit much. Do you think it's right for you to be trying to influence him like that?"

"I'm not trying to influence him," Esra objected, "I just said what I thought. And you did, too."

"I shared my own thoughts, yes, that's true. But the poor guy got all confused."

At any other time she would have conceded that Murat was right because she knew that she possessed an urge to lead, to direct others. However, it was difficult for her to accept this right now, with the argument being so fresh.

"A little confusion will do him good. He's looking for the murderer in the wrong place. Look at how he tried to defend Abid Hodja," Esra continued.

"Maybe he's afraid of sinning," suggested the young student.

"Oh good, then it was I who committed the first sin by trying to influence him."

TABLET TWENTY-FIVE

Pisiris appeared to have forgotten all about Ashmunikal, as well as his own sins. Throughout the years of peace he had devoted himself to his beloved sport of hunting. He would spend days trailing after a large antelope, a fierce lion, a wounded boar. This passion of his gave Ashmunikal and me numerous opportunities to be together. And we knew very well how to turn those opportunities into moments of bliss without letting on to anyone, or if we did let on, also making sure to muddle the minds of anyone who became suspicious. But ever since I betrayed them, the gods had been fiercely determined to have their revenge upon me. Perhaps they had allowed me to taste those moments of happiness with Ashmunikal so that I would later suffer all that much more. As always, they would have the last word. Like a tree poisoned by its own flower, our love, too, would come to an end because of the very fruit that it bore.

Pisiris was unable to bear children. However, thc avaricious king did not hold himself responsible for this; instead, he blamed the queen and the other women in his harem. Yet no matter how many women he took into his harem, the result was always the same; none of them bore him any children. Pisiris did not weary though; he continued to wait for the woman that the soothsayers had told him was destined to bear him an heir. But it was a lie. The truth was that Pisiris was as infertile as a rock. Unfortunately, the mischievous gods left it to me to prove this truth. It is perhaps one of the cruelest ways to get revenge upon your enemy. And though I did despise Pisiris, this was not a kind of revenge I desired, because I knew what a tremendous disaster would befall us as a result of it.

The love that we hid from evil eyes, gossipy women, sycophants, palace officials, would be revealed by my sperm that took root in Ashmunikal's fertile earth.

While Pisiris was out on another long hunting trip, Ashmunikal came to the library. It wasn't the day when we usually met. Her beautiful face was overcome with sorrow.

"I'm pregnant," she said in a single, quick breath.

I didn't fully comprehend what was happening at first.

"By Pisiris?" I asked.

Her eyes overshadowed by a deep anxiety she shook her head.

"No, by you. I haven't been with Pisiris for months."

Oddly enough, at first a feeling much like pride welled up within me, but it didn't take long for me to comprehend the dire trouble that we were in.

"What are we going to do?" I whispered.

"I don't know," she said. She hung her head and thought for a while. "I have to be intimate with Pisiris," she said finally. "I have to sleep with him."

She was right, it was the only solution, but nevertheless I could not soothe the tortuous ache in my heart, or keep a dark jealousy from overtaking me. Writhing with jealousy, with pain, with hope, we began to wait for Pisiris' return from his hunting trip. Unfortunately, things did not go as expected. A new beloved had arrived at the king's palace before he got back from hunting. Burning with the expectation of an heir, there was no way that Pisiris would even look at Ashmunikal with a new girl in his bed. And that's exactly what happened. Knowing that she had no other choice, Ashmunikal decided to wait for him to forget about the new beloved. But her stomach grew larger, and she was afraid that the women in the harem would realize that she was pregnant. And alas, it did not take long for her fear to become reality. Puduha, the first woman to be taken into the harem, understood Ashmunikal's nervousness and began keeping a watch on her. Upon confirming her suspicion that Ashmunikal's stomach was indeed growing larger, she ran to Pisiris to deliver the good news.

Upon hearing that Ashmunikal was pregnant, Pisiris' initial reaction was one of shock, followed by rage. Foaming at the mouth, he stormed into the harem. With a slap he knocked Ashmunikal, the woman I could hardly bare to besmirch with my own kisses, to the ground, saying that if she did not tell him who was responsible for her pregnancy, he would cauterize her sexual organ and kill her. The delicate Ashmunikal passed out with the second blow and was placed in confinement in a room overlooking the Euphrates in the top floor of the harem.

Dreadfully ashamed of this unexpected act of betrayal, Pisiris tried to conceal the incident from everyone. And so he gave strict orders that it was not to go beyond the harem walls, and threatened the women with dire consequences if it did so.

After commanding that he be informed when Ashmunikal woke up, Pisiris set out to investigate who was responsible for this act. As Pisiris conducted his questioning to find out who had met with Ashmunikal, I was still ignorant of what was going on. Some officials from the palace had told him that the sinful woman sometimes visited the library, but Pisiris did not suspect me, and chose to focus his attentions upon a visit that Ashmunikal had made to her parents three months before. He thought that whatever had happened, had happened there. And so he had Ashmunikal's parents brought to the palace.

At that time Puduha noticed that Ashmunikal had come to, and so she told her that the king was having her parents brought to the palace, and told her to reveal the name of her lover, otherwise the king would torture her parents. Ashmunikal pondered this for a while before telling Puduha: "I shall reveal the name of my lover. Call for the king." Once Puduha had left the room, Ashmunikal threw herself from the open harem window upon the stone outcrop below, like a broken-winged female eagle.

Upon getting word of Puduha's message, Pisiris returned to the harem, but when he failed to find Ashmunikal, he went mad with rage and began beating the woman next to him. Just then guards looking down from the window saw the red blood of Ashmunikal, and so Pisiris went down to the stone outcrop below, where he found Ashmunikal's lifeless body. The courage of this young woman, who challenged him even in death, sent Pisiris into a frenzy; he immediately assigned his closest men to find Ashmunikal's lover.

It was my assistant Eriya who brought the painful news. I was sitting in the library composing a letter to the new Assyrian King Shalmaneser, celebrating his recent ascendance to the throne and expressing our fidelity to him, when Eriya came in.

"Sir," he said, "admirer or Ludigirra, the Esteemed Ashmunikal jumped out of the harem window. Her body was found on the rock outcrop below."

Yes, Eriya stood there at the library door and said precisely these words. And as soon as he did, I understood the truth of the matter. I wasn't surprised, for though I hadn't actually admitted it to myself, I was expecting such an ending. She exhibited the courage that I had not possessed. She had deserted this cruel, deceitful, treacherous world.

The pleasure of my bed, the sweet longing of my nights, the nervous excitement of my days, the beauty that besieged my loneliness, the warmth that embraced my shadow, the madness that pushed my mind to the edge of sanity, no longer were. The sweet-smelling, night-eyed, rain-haired beloved, the sovereign of my very veins, had left me alone with my fears, and my vileness, never to return.

And though I had learned the truth of this, I did not go mad, I did not rip out my hair. I did not scream out to my assistant Eriya, who delivered news of this disaster, "No, she did not love Ludingirra, she loved me!" And I did not conceal a sharp dagger beneath my gowns and try to shred Pisiris' cruel heart. I just stood there, frozen, in the middle of the library. Then the scoundrel in me rose to the surface, suppressing my fear, surprise, and grief. I began to think that Pisiris would capture me, and torture me. I hid my sorrow, I held back my tears, and I even suppressed my anger. I failed to do so much as go and see the shattered body of the woman I loved, just for the sake of my own miserable soul.

But my fear was in vain. Ashmunikal had given her life to protect mine. It wasn't until the following day that I understood this. Yet I still could not rid myself of that feeling of apprehension. I thought that surely Pisiris would not let the matter rest just like that. The only person who knew of my relationship with Ashmunikal was the chief priest Valvaziti, and he had passed away the previous year. It would be quite difficult for him to prove that I was the father of the child in Ashmunikal's womb. Everything came to pass just as I had thought it would. I began to free myself of that petrifying fear that had once controlled me, but alas, for me there was no longer any peace on this earth.

King Pisiris, representative of the gods here on earth, had caused the death of the woman I loved, and my own child, and I, the spineless Patasana, did not confront him, did not spit in his face. Fear befell my mind, my heart, overtaking my entire body, like a dark night that strangles the light. Yes, I was a coward, but cowards, too, seek their revenge. In fact, perhaps it is cowards who reap vengeance best. Without letting on, waiting there furtively, until the moment when it is least expected...

CHAPTER TWENTY-SIX

He had waited furtively, committing the insidious murders at the moment it was least expected. Only a series of murders so masterfully planned and carried out would suffice to quell seventy-eight years of hostility and rage. Yes, yes, the murderer couldn't possibly be anyone other than Abid Hodja. Such were the thoughts that ran through Esra's head en route to City Hall.

When they reached City Hall, an official standing at the door bowed deeply to welcome them. They were told that Mayor Edip himself would have been there to meet with them if he hadn't been called out on some business that had to do with the canal construction. But what could he do about it—duty necessarily came first. They were told that he would, however, be there the following day when the reporters came. They weren't to worry though, for the City Hall was at their service and would provide whatever they needed. Esra was pleased that she hadn't had to see the Mayor, as it meant she wouldn't have to go through all that phony polite conversation. She told the official that they didn't have much time, and that they wanted to use the photocopying machine right away. The official, whose smile never waned, immediately fulfilled Esra's wish. He led them down to the floor where the photocopying machine was. He asked if they would like anything to drink before finally leaving them there to do their work. As Murat began photocopying, Esra took out her cell phone and dialed. But Rüstem's telephone still couldn't be reached. Or perhaps Kemal had asked him to turn off his phone? But then there was no need to exaggerate... Surely he wouldn't go that far.

It didn't take long for them to complete their task at the City Hall. Murat had finished all of the photocopying before Esra was even done drinking her soda. As they exited the City Hall, they saw Abid Hodja entering the mosque. Esra stood and watched him, carefully, as Murat got into the jeep. She wanted to see if he was suffering any injuries, had any scars. To the contrary, he looked extremely fit. "Maybe it's only a small wound and his shirt's covering it up," Esra thought.

Abid Hodja was walking with his head down, as if he were afraid that his eyes would give his secret away. If she weren't so afraid of stirring up trouble, Esra would have gone over and stopped the man for a closer look and seen what info she could coax out of him. But she knew that it if she did so, it would only perturb the Captain. After watching with helpless eyes as Abid Hodja entered the mosque, she proceeded to join Murat in the jeep. Seeing Abid Hodja walking like that with his eyes to the ground only convinced her further that he must be the killer. She was a big believer in body language. It was body language, she thought, that most often gave away the emotions, weaknesses, and lies that people tried to conceal. She recalled that there was a shifty look in Abid Hodja's eyes when she first ran into him. That's right, this time she was certain; this man had to be the killer. It was because he couldn't bear the weight of his deeds that he was all hunchbacked, slinking along and hiding his face. But there was still one point that she just couldn't figure out. She could understand how he might have gotten rid of old Hadji Settar, but how could he have killed such a sure-footed man as Reshat? The poor guy murdered the previous night must have been caught completely off guard; he'd tried to defend himself, and even wounded the murderer, but he'd failed to escape. He must have made sure they were unconscious before killing him. But none of the victims suspected him because he was a hodja. It must have been so easy for him sneak up on them. Who would ever think that a hodja could be a killer?

When she got back to the school and saw the gathering of people at the arbor, she assumed that Kemal must have come back and so she leapt joyfully from the jeep without even waiting for Murat to park. But her joy was in vain. Kemal wasn't anywhere to be seen amongst the group that had assembled there. The first person she recognized was Joachim from the Istanbul office of the German Archaeological Institute, and then she recalled also having seen the other two Germans talking with Bernd before as well. She thought that they must be the crew that was to have arrived from Istanbul the previous day. As soon as he caught sight of Esra, Joachim stood up with a smile.

"Frau Esra, how are you?"

Esra forced a smile in return. "Thank you very much, and how are you?"

She shook hands with each of the guests and welcomed them. Timothy, Teoman, and Elif were nowhere to be seen. "They must be working in their rooms," she thought. "What a time to be welcoming guests, when there's so much work to do."

"Congratulations," said Joachim. He'd begun speaking English. Though he spoke English with an accent, it was certainly easier to understand than his poor Turkish. "You have achieved something truly extraordinary here. To uncover a find like that on this site, a site that's been excavated for so many years, is nothing less than miraculous. Archaeological circles are showing a keen interest in your work here. E-mail is pouring into us from all over the world. There are a dozen scholars wanting to come to Turkey from America, England, and Germany just to see the tablets and the site. It's really something."

Esra tried her best to be courteous.

"This achievement belongs to all of us, and your own contribution was hardly a small one. Speaking of which, how are preparations going in Antep?"

Joachim was all ears trying to keep up with Esra's fast paced English.

"Everything's ready," he finally answered. "There was a small problem yesterday, but thanks to Tim and Bernd, we took care of that. I talked with Herrn Krencker an hour ago. He says everything's ready in Istanbul. They'll be here tomorrow."

"We're ready, too," Bernd interjected, unable to keep quiet any longer. Then he turned to Esra and added: "I'm going to take our guests to the excavation site in a little bit. It would be good for them to see it before the journalists do."

"Good idea," said Esra. Even as she said this her eyes remained focused on Joachim. "Of course you'll be staying for dinner then."

"Unfortunately we have to be back at the hotel this evening. The journalists arriving from Ankara may try to reach us."

Secretly pleased with this piece of news, Esra nevertheless insisted: "Oh, c'mon now, certainly you can go back a little late."

There was a hint of condescension in Joachim's eyes, who found so much insistence rather *alaturka.* "Thank you," he said, "but really, we can't."

Esra appeared to be saddened by, but accepting of, his decision. She politely asked for leave to go and get the photocopies in order. All of the men rose to their feet. They bid her farewell until the next day, when they would see each other at the hotel.

She noticed as she walked down the hall in the school building that Timothy's door was open. She walked towards it, but then seeing that Infidel Nadide and her grandchild were inside, took a step back. She had no time to squander away with them. She headed for the classroom with the computers.

She found Teoman sitting in front of a computer, just as she had left him.

"Any word from Kemal?" she asked as soon as she stepped into the classroom.

Teoman's eyes were exhausted from staring at the screen. "Nope," he said, squinting, "he still hasn't called. Did you have a chance to talk to Rüstem?"

"No."

Esra laid the folder in her hand down on the school desk and then pulled out her telephone and started dialing. The result was the same. *"The number you have dialed cannot be reached."*

"Doesn't that open-air museum have a telephone?" Teoman grumbled.

"Apparently not, or at least the person I talked with didn't know about it." Esra's eyes landed on the computer screen. She saw that Teoman was writing something about the tablets.

"What are you doing?"

"Tim translated the colophons on the backs of the tablets. In other words, he came up with a summary of the tablets. I'm typing them up and saving them on the computer. He said we might need them at the press conference."

"That's smart of him. We're sure to get questions about the contents of the tablets."

Esra headed for the door. "I'm going to take a shower," she said. "I'm all sticky with sweat."

She'd taken a few steps but then turned back around and walked over to Teoman to give him her cell phone.

"I'll leave this with you, in case Kemal calls."

For several minutes Esra just let herself be washed over by the cold water. It was as if the drops raining down upon her forehead were washing away all of the thoughts that kept eating away at her brain, as if they were infusing her soul with a profound calmness. The drowsiness hit her as soon as she emerged from the shower. With quick steps she walked to her room in an effort to avoid the others. She was lucky, for she made it to her room without running into Halaf or Timothy. She lay down in bed and slept for about an hour. By the time she woke up she was drenched in sweat once again. She got up and left her room.

Timothy was seated beneath the arbor, and Halaf was pealing dried onions and fresh garlic in front of the kitchen in preparation for the evening meal. Esra walked over next to Timothy.

"Hi. So it seems your guests have left."

"Hi," said Timothy, gathering himself together. "Yes, they've left."

"You don't seem to be in a very good mood."

"Unfortunately I didn't have any good news for the old woman," said Timothy. He looked so distraught that, if she didn't know him better, Esra would have sworn he'd been crying.

"So were you able to find out anything about her older brother?"

Timothy sighed.

"Yes. Like I mentioned before, I have had this student who lives in New York. So I sent him an e-mail with the address on the letter and asked him to see what he could find out about this Dikran Papazyan. Yesterday I heard back from him."

"So quickly?"

"I was lucky. I caught him when he had plenty of free time, so he went to the address that very same day. The building was still there, but there was nobody there who knew the man. Apparently though there's a man named Bill who's worked at the bar on the corner for years. Everybody told my student that if anyone knew anything about the man he was looking for, he would be the one, and so they sent him to ask Bill. As it turns out, old Bill actually did recognize the name Dikran Papazyan straight away. Dikran Papazyan was a friend of his. He'd known him ever since he'd moved into this neighborhood. Dikran had managed to make his way, together with his mother, to Halep, and from there to Beirut, after leaving his sister Nadya behind in Turkey. But his mother, who was already ill, died in Beirut. Dikran stayed on in Beirut for a while before heading off for the New World at the insistence of his relatives who had escaped long before. His relatives found him a home and a job. It was back then that Bill got to know Dikran. He said Dikran was a quiet man, a gentleman. In fact, he said he was a little too quiet. He also said that when he drank, he'd lose it and start crying, and then he'd start attacking everyone. And being quite a strapping fellow, he wasn't easy to restrain either. So that's why Bill stopped serving him liquor. He was aware of this affliction of his and so he tried to keep his distance from others, especially women. But Dikran was an extremely handsome man and the women just wouldn't leave him alone. Finally, he was captivated by this woman named Nancy Wilkinson.

Nancy pushed and prodded until he finally agreed to marry her. For the first year of their marriage, everything was fine. They had a son, and they were both perfectly happy. Dikran named the child Armenak. But as the child grew, so did Dikran's fears. He'd have nightmares and wake in the middle of the night and run to his son's bed, crying out, 'They're going to kill my son...' This fear of his gradually turned into paranoia. He'd tell everyone he saw that they were after his son, and when the child caught the slightest illness, he'd beat his wife, claiming that she'd poisoned the boy. The poor woman could only take the abuse and beatings for a few months before she left the house in a panic one night in the middle of the night, afraid that her husband was going to kill her. Left alone then with his son, Dikran really truly started to lose it. The doctors who examined him didn't have any trouble coming up with a diagnosis: he was a paranoid schizophrenic. And so they immediately locked him up in a mental hospital. It was then that Nadide stopped receiving letters. The man died in the hospital twenty years ago."

Esra was shaken up by what she'd heard.

"So what happened to little Armenak?"

"Dikran's family searched all over but failed to find his mother. A middle class American family adopted the kid. But because there's so much secrecy about these kinds of things in America, it would be impossible for us to find him now. Besides, I doubt Aunt Nadide will go to too much trouble to find him anyway."

"What did Aunt Nadide do when she found out what had happened to her brother?"

"What could she do? At first she sighed and wept, and then once she'd calmed down, she motioned towards the sky and said, '*Mukadderat.* Such are the ways of fate, everything that comes to pass, does so according to his will.' So in short, she used a defense mechanism that the people of Anatolia have been using for thousands of years to try and console herself. She tried, but this time it was no use. Not the words of Jesus, or Mohammed, or the Bible, or the Koran were able to comfort her. I looked carefully into her dark eyes and saw that it was no use, she was just as sorrowful as before. And when I saw her like that I said to myself, 'Timothy, you idiot, why did you go and tell her the truth?'"

"None of this is your fault," said Esra. "Don't do yourself any injustice. You helped the woman."

"I don't think I was any help," said Timothy. Esra had never seen him so desperate. "The best way to help her would have been to lie. That way she could have gone on living thinking that she had a brother somewhere out there, even if he was a disloyal one. By telling her the truth though, I took away any hope she had. So you tell me, was the truth really so necessary?"

"Come on, Tim, you know that it's wrong for you to think that way. If it weren't for truth, there'd be nothing. Look at us, thrilled at having found the Patasana tablets because they'll bring us closer to the truth."

"You're right, but in the end, it's all meaningless."

Esra looked at Timothy uncomprehendingly. Actually, there were times when Esra thought that Timothy didn't really attach much importance to what was going on, and that he observed everything that went on at the excavation with a sense of indifference. Now she saw that she was right about this, but still she couldn't help but be surprised.

"Tell me please, dear Esra," the American continued, "Exactly which previously unknown truth will the Patasana tablets reveal to us?"

"How the Neo-Hittite period came to..." Esra started to say.

"No, no, I mean which truth, which fundamental, universal truth will they teach us?"

Esra didn't understand what he was getting at. Timothy finally had to answer his own question.

"The cruelty of humankind, right? The Patasana tablets tell this truth. But is this something you didn't know already?"

He raised his voice, repeating the question: "Tell me, is this something you didn't already know?"

He stared at Esra with insistent eyes. After a few short moments of silence he continued:

"The history of humankind has been telling this story from the very beginning anyway. Some idiots who go on about how 'people are good, people are beautiful, people are noble' are not going to change this truth..."

He grew quiet, taking deep breaths as if it were a struggle now for him to speak.

"Do you know why I didn't take part on any excavations for so long?"

Esra lowered her head, indicating that she didn't.

"Because of that truth we were just talking about," he said, "my experiences in Vietnam made me ill. I received psychological treatment at a clinic for months."

Timothy spoke these words as if they were just insignificant details, but to Esra they came as a great shock. So the American had received psychological treatment. That was the reason why he seemed so sure of himself when he spoke of Eshref's war syndrome. He had experienced the same feeling, and so he was able to understand the Captain. So just why, Esra wondered, hadn't he told her about this before today? But then, who would? It's not that easy to tell someone you've undergone psychological treatment. Yet she would have thought that a man like Timothy, apparently so at peace with himself, wouldn't have a problem revealing such a thing. But then, well, he *had* told her. But why had he waited so long to do so?

"There was this hefty psychologist with pointy red hair whose real name I don't know, but whom we called Jerry," Timothy continued. "He was really different from all the others. He used to tell me that war was natural. 'You're not the only person in the world to have killed people,' he'd tell me. 'Millions of people killed other people before you. I mean, what you've done is normal. Don't blame yourself.' And so with his encouragement I managed to gather myself back together again. It was from him that I first learned that this feeling of savageness, this impulse to kill, was not an illness unique to our age. And so that's how I managed to forget all about my buddies, the ones who'd died right next to me, who'd had their arms and legs blown off, who'd moaned in pain and trembled with fear, and the charred bodies in the villages we burnt, and the screams of the Vietcong soldiers, men and women alike, that we shot to death. I was only able to go back to work after the war thanks to Jerry's rehab sessions.

"I devoted myself utterly and completely to archaeology as soon as I got back to work so that I could forget about the dreadful things I'd experienced. The time for killing was over, and the time for creation had begun. I was a scholar; I was supposed to uncover the past so that people could establish a better, more advanced future. I thought that there must be so much that unknown civilizations would teach us. And so in order to learn those things, as soon as I'd completed my master's degree at Yale, I headed straight for Mesopotamia. Full of hope, and belief, and determination, I dug into the earth. But unfortunately every mound, every tumulus, every ancient city, every temple, every library, every grave revealed nothing different from what Jerry had said; not only in our age, but since the beginning of its existence humankind had always been but an incorrigible scoundrel deriving pleasure from causing bloodshed and making others suffer. But still, I did not give up. I persistently continued digging away at the earth, thinking that I would find some tablet, some inscription, some relief, some sign that would tell me otherwise. But each time I found myself writhing in pain and shame, like a detective trying to prove the innocence of his convicted father, only to be devastated by each clue, each piece of evidence, each witness proving that his father was nothing but a monster. And that's why I ran away and came here five years ago. Here, in this relatively backwards existence I tried to find new friendships, simple beauties that would help me reestablish a bond with life. And I was partially successful; I made friends in Antep, in its towns and villages, and they generously made room for me in their lives. I discovered how beguiling the red of the pomegranate flower was, the sweet tartness of the plum, the exquisite taste of the grape, the miracle in every folk song. But I also found that that truth that hounded me existed side by side with all of these. The same savagery that exists in America, and in Vietnam, exists here as well. I stopped listening to the news or reading the newspapers so I wouldn't hear about all the deaths. I tried to escape from humanity, from myself. But I couldn't; it's impossible to escape your own self... That's why I hesitated before accepting when you invited me to join this excavation. I was afraid of reaching that same damned conclusion. And it happened, just as I had feared. I found myself face to face with that same horrendous truth once again, not only in Patasana's tablets, but with that old woman's migrations, the ethnic hostilities, a life ravaged by religious fanaticism."

As Timothy talked, Esra recalled the incident that Eshref had told her about. She thought of how news of armed conflict had become such a banal part of their daily lives. Images of the corpses of the young Kurds, their shattered bodies lying in the rock cavities, and of the funerals of soldiers, their caskets wrapped in flags, and the tears and wails of the mourners who surrounded them as they are seen off into the afterlife passed one by one before her eyes. She understood where Timothy was coming from, and she shared his sentiments, for she could feel the same pain in her own heart. But she could not stand for a man like this, who was so good at what he did, to become so embittered toward archaeology, and become so estranged from his occupation.

"You're right, but still we must do our duty," she said. Her voice lacked the resolve she was hoping for, but she continued nevertheless. "At least we will have shown people this truth..."

"My dear Esra, even if we uncover thousands of documents like the Patasana tablets, it's no use. Man is a creature of stupidity."

"So what are we to do then?" Esra grumbled. She'd started to become perturbed by the pessimism of this colleague who before had always given her his support, and hope.

"Are we just going to do nothing because humankind is cruel, because murder is in its nature?"

"Of course we'll do what we have to do," said Timothy. He was just about to say something else when Teoman came running up to them with Esra's cell phone in hand.

"They're calling you," he said, "from the museum in Antep."

Esra excitedly grabbed the phone. She assumed it must be Rüstem who was calling. She was finally going to receive news of Kemal's whereabouts. But it wasn't what she had expected. The person calling was the secretary with whom she had spoken that morning. The secretary had spoken with Rüstem and told him that Esra had called. And Rüstem Bey had replied that there was something wrong with his cell phone, and that he would talk with Esra at the press conference the next day. That was it.

"That blockhead must be with Rüstem," said Teoman, "otherwise how would Rüstem know about the press conference? We certainly didn't tell him about it."

Esra's face lit up hopefully.

"You're right," she said, "we forgot to tell him about it. He must've heard about the press conference from Kemal. So it seems his highness isn't planning on making any public appearances until tomorrow morning. I'm really going to give it to him tomorrow, press conference or not."

None of this talk relieved Timothy's pessimism. He just stood there, silently, with his head hung low. Sensing from the discussion that there had been some news of Kemal, Halaf put down his onions and garlic and walked over to them. Esra saw the curiosity in his eyes.

"Nope, no new developments," she said. "We're just running through the possibilities, is all."

"I hope to God he shows up safe and sound," said Halaf.

"I hope so, too."

Seeing that Halaf continued to stand there in front of her, Esra asked him, "Is there something you want to ask?"

"Not me, but you should..." he said, smiling shyly.

"Oh yeah? And just what should I be asking?"

"What I've cooked for dinner. You know, you ask at noon."

Esra started to laugh.

"God bless you, Halaf, and I thought it was something important."

"You call that unimportant?" said Teoman. "What on this earth is more important than food?"

"Alright, alright... So what are we having for dinner this evening?"

"Şiveydiz," replied Halaf.

This was the first time that Esra and Teoman had ever heard of such a thing, and they looked at one another before posing the same question:

"What's that?"

"It's a wonderful dish."

Esra felt suspicious and gave the cook a wary look.

"Ask Tim," Halaf said. He was offended by their wariness. "He knows very well just what kind of meal it is."

Absent-minded Timothy came back to life.

"What?" he asked.

"Şiveydiz," said Halaf.

The American did his best to smile.

"A scrumptious dish," he said, "very different, very unique..."

Halaf looked at the others as if to say, "See, I told you so."

"Good then, let's see how we like it," said Esra. "Oh, and while we're on the topic, make a little extra, the Captain might stop by."

A lewd grin spread across Teoman's broad face.

"You're a man of greatness, Halaf," he said. "Anyone who's eaten your food never ever forgets it. The Captain was here last night, and now I'll be darned if he isn't coming again tonight."

Esra was aware that her friend was needling her, but she ignored it.

"Anyway, I'm going to open a restaurant in town after the excavation," said Halaf before heading off to the kitchen.

"That's a good idea, and you should call it Hittite Restaurant. And your first customer's already lined up: Captain Eshref."

Now Teoman was getting carried away. It was about time someone gave that boy a slap on the wrist and let him know what's what. "Let's just hope he doesn't continue to be so tactless tonight at dinner with the Captain here," thought Esra. But Teoman wouldn't have the opportunity to do so, for the Captain phoned an hour before dinner to say that he wouldn't be able to make it. There were some important developments, he said. But then she could already tell that from the excitement in his voice. He couldn't explain it on the phone, but he could tell her this much: they'd called Hadji Abid to the station for questioning. He was going to speak with him in a little bit.

Esra was thrilled that Abid was going to be questioned. Though she expressed her regrets that he'd be unable to make it to dinner, Esra was actually pleased at the Captain's absence. There were two reasons for this: first of all, they'd begun to see a lot of one another, and this had piqued the excavation crew's interest to a disturbing degree; secondly there was her fear that the Armenian argument of the night before would fire up again tonight. Then again, Bernd hadn't touched upon the topic all day. But then how could she possibly trust him?

Halaf's oddly named dish was truly delicious. Not only the voracious Teoman, but even Elif, who wasn't usually on such good terms with food, asked Halaf for the recipe to *shiveydiz*. Feigning no reluctance, the cook from Barak eagerly began explaining it to them:

"First you place the chunks of meat in a pan, and then you add chickpeas and leave it to cook. You add the onions and garlic, chopped the size of the second knot of your thumb, later. You place sieved yoghurt in another container, and then add an egg and mix it in, then bring it to a boil. After the yoghurt's come to a boil, you add it to the first pan and mix it in. Once it's done cooking, you sprinkle on some mint, *haspir*, and black pepper, and then serve."

Teoman, who was listening ever so carefully, was the first to speak up:

"And what the heck is *haspir*?"

"You know, those red herbs on top of the dish, those are *haspir*. They give flavor to the dish, and strength to the body."

While drinking their teas they went over the preparations one last time. The Turkish and English texts to be passed out to the journalists were ready, Timothy and Bernd had finished composing their speeches, and Elif had begun developing her photos. Teoman had written the summary of the tablets on the computer and printed out two copies. It seemed that they were good and ready for the next day's event. Esra felt a sweet sense of relief. It seemed that the nightmarish anxiety that had overcome her when Kemal disappeared was finally wearing off. She looked at each of her colleagues affectionately.

"In that case, we all deserve a good night's rest," she said. Her voice was tired, but not gloomy. "Don't forget, we have to get up early tomorrow."

Despite the warning, nobody headed off to bed. Teoman helped with the dishes and continued chattering about food for a while. Bernd went over his talk for the next day again; he wasn't satisfied with the ending and so he revised it twice. Timothy and Murat went for a walk by the river and got wrapped up in a discussion about the tradition of human sacrifice amongst the Aztec. And Elif called Esra into her room to help her pick out her clothes for the next day. But the younger woman was so picky about the matter that she kept Esra captive in her room until Halaf came to tell Esra that the Captain was waiting for her at the arbor.

What, the Captain was there? She looked at her watch; it was eleven o'clock. Something major must have happened or he wouldn't have shown up at that hour. She rushed out of the room, ignoring Elif's question: "So do you think the cream colored blouse matches?"

The Captain was standing under the arbor by himself, with the jeep that had brought him waiting out on the road with the headlights on. The Captain seemed to be tense, but when he saw Esra, he tried to smile.

"Good evening," he said.

"So what brings you out here?" Esra asked. "Nothing bad I hope?"

"Nothing to be afraid of." But as he said it, he averted his eyes. "Some hunters found a deserted shelter. There's a dead terrorist inside. We were headed over there. Since your place was on the way, I just thought I'd stop by."

"It's nothing dangerous, is it?"

"I doubt it. It must be the hideout that Mahmut and his buddies used. They would have stayed there when they weren't in the village."

"And what about the dead terrorist?"

"Maybe he was injured in the conflict last week and got away, but only made it as far as the shelter and died there."

The Captain couldn't have come here just to say this. That sheepish expression on his face, the fearful averting of the eyes, the tense movement of his arms... All of a sudden, Esra understood.

"What happened with Abid Hodja?" she asked, a hint of taunting in her voice.

"He's innocent," said the Captain. The two words quickly poured out of his mouth.

"He's hiding something from me," Esra thought.

"He's innocent," the Captain repeated. This time, the words came out of his mouth more slowly. He turned his bashful eyes to face the young woman and explained:

"He was somewhere else when the murder happened; there are witnesses."

"When the last murder happened?"

"Yes."

"And what about during Reshat's murder?"

"Look Esra," said Eshref, "Abid Hodja is innocent. I spoke with the witnesses. We have absolutely no evidence that points to him."

"So then why did you feel the need to question him?"

"I wanted to be sure."

"And so he said, 'I'm innocent,' and then you were sure, is that it?"

"It's not that simple. If I'm telling you that he's innocent, then that means he's innocent. Trust me."

Esra looked at Eshref, her eyes full of anger. She was certain that he was hiding something, but she also knew that he wasn't underhanded enough to go covering up for a murderer.

"You're not protecting him, are you?" she asked bluntly.

"What are you trying to say?"

When she saw how her words set the Captain's eyes aflame with rage, Esra was reassured; no, Eshref wasn't protecting Abid Hodja.

"You're hiding something from me," she said. Her voice had softened. "And so that makes me suspicious."

She was right. He was concealing from her the fact that Abid Hodja worked for intelligence. Abid Hodja was seen in his sister's village the night that Reshat was murdered. And that's why the Captain felt the need to question him at the station. He'd asked Abid Hodja where he was around the time of Reshat's murder.

"I was at home," Abid Hodja had responded. "I got back late from the village."

But he lived alone, so there was nobody to confirm what he said.

But when he asked, "And so where were you yesterday?" Abid had responded that he was in Antep, that he'd gone there to visit a friend.

The Captain asked for the friend's address and telephone number. When the Hodja hesitated to give it to the Captain, the latter cautioned him: "Remember, you're here as a suspect for three murders."

The word murder made Abid Hodja visibly nervous, and he said that he wanted to make a phone call, but the Captain wouldn't let him.

"Either you give me the name and address of the person you saw in Antep or we'll just have to try another means of communicating with you," he said.

Abid Hodja was beginning to worry now, and so he decided to cooperate, saying that he wanted to talk with the Captain alone. Once the other soldiers had exited the room, Abid Hodja told the Captain that the person he'd met with in Antep was none other than Head Commander Yılmaz of the Terrorism Unit. The Captain could call to find out for himself. At first Commander Yılmaz was taken aback by the Captain's unexpected phone call, but once the Captain had explained to him he was quick to respond. "Yes," he said, "Abid Hodja was with me last night. You can trust him, he's a devoted citizen."

Still, the Captain couldn't be sure. He called Colonel Nedim from gendarme intelligence and asked him about Commander Yılmaz. He was told that Commander Yılmaz was one hundred percent reliable. And so the Captain apologized to Abid Hodja and told him he was free to go.

"I hope this stays between us," the Hodja said before departing.

Of course it would remain between them, because it was a state secret. And that's why he couldn't tell Esra either.

Esra believed him, even though she knew that he was hiding something. This belief was not founded on any concrete evidence, or the trust built up over years of companionship, or a reliable promise; rather, it was based on a relationship that was called love, but which was characteristically fickle, and the course of which remained dubious. Moreover, Esra's believing the Captain resolved nothing; it laid wide open once again that disturbing, momentous question that had been waiting to be answered ever since the murder of Hadji Settar: If Abid was innocent, then who was the killer? The Captain didn't have the answer either. And right now, he didn't want to think about it. He left Esra alone with puzzling questions and departed; the only thing on his mind was that body in the rock cavity.

TABLET TWENTY-SIX

Ashmunikal's body disappeared. Pisiris did not give her shattered and broken body to her family; he did not place her in an earthenware jar and give her a proper burial like he had done for his other deceased beloved; he did not tell anyone what he had done with her body. He obliterated, destroyed the body of Ashmunikal, a body so beautiful it was the envy of the goddesses.

Pisiris was angrier at the fact that his sterility had been revealed, than he was at Ashmunikal's infidelity. Now those at the palace were also in on the secret he had known for many years. Fearing that news of this embarrassing incident would leak out of the palace, the king cut the investigation short. A fabricated scenario about how Ashmunikal accidentally fell out of the harem window was spread amongst the people. Meanwhile, Ashmunikal's parents were released, but only after they had been thoroughly intimidated with threats. Pisiris talked with me just one time about Ashmunikal. He asked me when I had last seen her, which tablet she had read, and whether or not she had been sad. My responses were even and cool-headed. He shook his head solemnly as he listened. And then he changed the subject.

Pisiris was experiencing the worst years of his life. His dreams of re-establishing the Great Hittite Kingdom were left incomplete due to the Assyrian attack, his sterility had been revealed, and he had understood that there would be no one to carry on his family line. It was extremely difficult for someone like him to accept these facts. Pisiris threw himself into the one activity that had been his passion since childhood, hunting. Every opportunity he got he would leave behind the thick city fortress walls and not return for days on end. As he sought to forget his years of failure, and to heal his wounded honor, through the joy of his hunting parties, I was nurturing inside of me a hatred that would put him in his grave.

At home, at the palace, in the library, along the Euphrates, I constantly thought about how I would take my revenge. It should not be a short-lived vengeance; rather, I should take my time to prepare the perfect trap for him. Pisiris should have no inkling of what I did, and it would be much too late by the time he realized that he had fallen into my trap. What my revenge required more than anything was patience. Like a blind snake I began to wait, motionless, for the right opportunity to capture my prey.

In the meantime, I put an end to my bachelorhood, which had become a topic of gossip, and thus deflected unwanted attention from myself. I married Pishshuvatti, a daughter of a nobleman. My mother was happy, the girl I married was happy, Pisiris was happy, but there was still some time before I would be happy.

It was an era of peace. The Assyrians were busy with their own affairs. Salmanasar's reign was short-lived. His successor Sargon found himself taking over an empire fraught with chaos. And once he had proven his sovereignty by shedding the blood of so many in his own kingdom, he began to focus his attentions on other lands.

The new Urartian king, Rusa, was yearning to get even for the defeats his people at suffered at the hands of the Assyrians. And he did not hide his intentions, did not refrain from speaking openly of them in his tablets to and talks with us. When I read to Pisiris the tablets that came from Rusa, I saw a sparkle, similar to that of yore, in Pisiris' aging eyes. In order to take my revenge, I needed the courageous but utterly ignorant ideas that underlay that sparkle. But Pisiris, remembering the defeats of years passed, was cautious. He maintained good relations with the Urartians, all the while refraining to openly support their endeavors.

I would have to wait—wait until time had clouded Pisiris' memory, until he had forgotten the lessons of the past, and the scars of past atrocities had faded away. And so I waited. For days, months, years, I waited. My wife became pregnant and had our first son, and I waited. The hair on my head turned gray, wrinkles appeared on my forehead, and I waited. My mother died, my wife gave birth to a second son, and I waited. The Urartians continued to send congenial letters, the Assyrians to increase taxes, and I waited.

Once Pisiris began spewing angry words about the Assyrians in public, I realized that I was done waiting. I skillfully wormed my way into Pisiris' mind. Though he was enraged at the Assyrians, he was still afraid of taking sides with the Urartians. Realizing this, I suggested another path that was sure to destroy him. I mentioned fostering relations with the Phrygians who, though they weren't openly at war with the Assyrians, were seeking an opportunity to defeat them. War between Assyrian King Sargon and Urartian King Rusa was imminent. No matter who emerged victorious, both of the kings would be exhausted by the effort. And so in such a situation, we could act in alliance with the Phrygians and their rested, intact army to free ourselves from the Assyrians. Pisiris was intrigued by my suggestion. And so the ambitious but foolish Pisiris, ignorant of my plans, accepted this apparently harmless recommendation of mine. He immediately dictated a tablet expressing his goodwill to the Phrygians' wise king Midas, who was elated to receive Pisiris' tidings. And which king in his position wouldn't? A kingdom under the administration of his arch enemy, the Assyrians, was trying to endear itself to him. The Phrygian king immediately responded with a tablet expressing his delight at our message. Pisiris, now grown recklessly daring thanks in part to my own prodding, this time dictated a tablet openly expressing his intentions. He explained that the Assyrians were nothing but barbarians who exploited the Hittite Kingdoms like a parasite, and he described Midas as a savior. Midas' response was even more munificent. He informed Pisiris that he was prepared to offer assistance of any kind.

In the course of this correspondence, I, the man Pisiris trusted more than any other, had already gotten in touch with a commander in the Assyrians' Foreign Regions Administration. I informed the Assyrian commander that Pisiris was preparing to drag us into a bloody venture, and I began providing him with copies of each letter that we sent to Midas, so that he could forward them to King Sargon.

It was around that time that Sargon, having completed his exploits in Syria and Egypt, turned his armies north towards the Euphrates. Coming first to Tabal, Sargon appointed to that country a king loyal to himself, and then came pounding at our door before engaging in battle with the Urartians. Now was my time to settle scores with Pisiris. Finally, I would get revenge for my father, Ashmunikal, and my unborn child.

CHAPTER TWENTY-SEVEN

Finally, the moment had arrived. Like all archaeologists, Esra, too, had a burning desire to uncover evidence, documents, signs that would illuminate the dark pages of history. Like everyone who shares her occupation, she also dreamed of being one of those legendary individuals to discover important finds that would reveal the true portrait of those lost civilizations, the remains of which ruthless time attempted to erase with earthquakes, wars, fires, migrations, and epidemics. And now, she had finally achieved it: she'd made a dream come true that hundreds of archaeologists couldn't even come close to, despite dedicating their entire lives to the effort, and at such a young age to boot.

She got out of bed in a chipper mood, with no intention of letting anything cast a shadow upon her excitement that morning. Yet she'd spent most of the night anxiously tossing and turning in bed. When the Captain said that Abid Hodja wasn't the killer, she'd begun to think of Bernd again. But then the killer must be injured, right? Yet Bernd couldn't be in better shape. Or at least he looked like he couldn't. But what the heck is that supposed to mean, "he looked like it"? He was perfectly fit. He could hardly be hiding any serious wounds under that thin t-shirt. And that meant that he wasn't the one responsible for the murders. But would the Captain believe it? After the argument the other night, he'd begun to view Bernd as a potential enemy. So what if he took him into custody, too? If that happened, it would totally dampen the mood of the excavation crew, which was already upset enough as it is by Kemal's absence. She should talk with the Captain at the first opportunity and explain that Bernd couldn't possibly be guilty. But what if Bernd really was the murderer? What if his wife's family didn't migrate from Hatay like he'd said, but from here? And if he still had relatives here? What if he committed the murders with the help of one of them? The string of questions kept her wide awake. But what a bunch of nonsense! She'd never seen Bernd even talk with one of the locals. Clearly her incurable paranoia had kicked in yet again, and so there she was again exaggerating everything. It was about time she rid her mind of these matters. The effort they'd put forth for so many long days had finally borne fruit; they'd achieved a great success on the excavation. What could be more important than that? But while she could be enjoying her success, instead Esra obsessed about unsolved murders and possible suspects, like some kind of amateur sleuth. She once again recalled her father and how he always referred to "right thinking." And it truly was time now that she discipline her mind. Though Kemal's disappearance did worry her, and though the person responsible for the recent murders was yet to be found, she needed to focus all of her attention upon the press conference, and think of nothing else. She could go back to pondering the murders once she'd successfully passed this test. Pleased with this resolution, she closed her eyes tightly and fell asleep within minutes; whether this was due to her strong will power or because of exhaustion, who knows. When she awoke, she felt as if she had slept off all the worries that had nagged at her the previous day. She got up and took a shower and then got dressed. She tamed her wavy, rebellious hair into something presentable. She looked at herself in the mirror, trying to imagine how she would look at the press conference. Pleased by the image that appeared in her mind's eye, she left the room.

The other members of the excavation team, who were gathered at the breakfast table, were in a similar mood. This was the first morning that there was nobody who failed to wake up, who was running late, or who came to the table with drowsy eyes. There was an endearing tension visible in their faces, and the pride of success gleamed in their eyes. Everyone had done away with ripped jeans, stained pants, and sun-faded t-shirts and replaced them with ironed slacks, skirts, blouses, and dress shirts.

With the exception of a few of the photographs that Elif had developed turning out badly, all preparations had been flawlessly completed according to plan. The excavation crew was ready to face off with the army of journalists.

Seeing them there, so sweet and jittery and all decked out like kids on a national holiday, Halaf got carried away himself and asked: "Can I come along to the press conference?"

"Unfortunately not," said Esra, "somebody has to stay here. The journalists are going to come here, too. Everything thing should be perfectly in order. Everyone's already straightened up their rooms, but it'd be a good idea for you to double check everything once we're gone."

Halaf didn't push. He'd done his military duty as a commando and knew the importance of discipline. He, too, was a part of the crew. And if they told him to stay put, he would stay put.

There was no trace of Bernd's famous cool-headedness this morning. He finished his breakfast before everyone else and kept reminding the others over and over that they shouldn't be late.

"Calm down now, Bernd," said Teoman, who was busy enjoying his breakfast, "it's only five a.m. still."

"But we have a long trip ahead of us," said the German, "and there's work to be done in Antep."

"We'll make it on time, don't you worry."

But it wasn't only Bernd who was in a hurry, for Timothy quickly stepped up to second Bernd. "The earlier we get moving the better," he said. He was looking a bit tense himself this morning. "I know a bit about press conferences, and believe me, there's always some problem or other that holds things up."

It was Esra who had the final say.

"I agree with Bernd as well," she said. "We shouldn't leave Joachim to take care of everything all by himself."

Teoman hemmed and hawed, but he couldn't just disregard the other's cautionary remarks, and so he began shoveling away his food faster. Esra watched on with a smile as her gluttonous friend struggled to swiftly devour each bite, and felt sorry for having pushed him to speed up the process. If only they'd gotten up a little earlier. But then even if they had, would things really be any different? After all, their minds were already consumed with thoughts of the press conference. And they wouldn't get back to normal until they'd reached the meeting hall and made their appearance before the journalists. The best thing to do would be to hurry up and hit the road as soon as possible. But they were stopped in their tracks, for just as they were getting ready to leave the breakfast table, the Captain's jeep emerged from out of the ash gray, early morning light and parked just a few yards away. Everyone turned to look at the approaching jeep as soon as they heard the purr of its engine.

"It seems the Captain's confused dinner with breakfast" Teoman said jokingly, but nobody laughed. They waited anxiously, seeming to sense already that the Captain had come to deliver some bad news.

"Maybe he's coming with us," said Teoman, to break the silence. "We've become so chummy with the guy. I mean, he's virtually a member of excavation crew himself."

Esra paid no heed to Teoman's words, which were in part a taunt directed at her. She had her eyes fixed on the jeep and watched as Eshref emerged from it and approached the table.

It was Halaf who gave voice to everyone's thoughts at that moment.

"It's not a good sign for the Captain to be stopping by so early," he said. "I hope nothing bad has happened."

Esra noticed that as he walked up to the table, Eshref was slouching and dragging his feet, just like he'd done on Friday when he came to give them news of Hadji Settar's death. Something bad has happened, she thought. And seeing the pessimism on his face, and how he averted his weary eyes, she mumbled, "Something really awful has happened." And she was right. The Captain didn't greet them; no hello, no good morning. For several moments he just stood there at the end of the table, a guilty look upon his face as if he himself were responsible for the bad news he was about to impart. All eyes were upon him, which only served to trouble him even more, and so he just stood there, unable to bring himself to say what it was he had to say. When he raised his head and came eye to eye with Esra, he finally spit it out, in a single breath: "The bodies in the rock cavity weren't terrorists." Nobody except for Esra had any idea what he was talking about. The young woman was all ears. "The hunters were wrong," continued the Captain. Esra understood what the Captain was about to say, but still she tried to convince herself she was wrong, and waited for the Captain to say the words himself. But when he didn't, she could no longer endure his hesitation and finally she blurted out: "Is it Kemal?"

"Yes," said the Captain, "unfortunately the body found in the cave belongs to Kemal."

"Oh, my God! Kemal, no!" wailed Esra. Her body began to shake and tears began to stream down her cheeks. At the same moment, there was a shriek at the table. It was Elif.

"No, it can't be true!" the young woman cried out.

Esra forgot about her own sorrow and embraced Elif. The two young women began to cry. The men at the table were looking at the Captain, their eyes full of horror and trepidation. Three people had been murdered before, but none of them were members of the excavation crew. This time, the victim was one of their own.

"Why?" grumbled Teoman angrily, his hands in tight fists. "Why would they kill Kemal?"

"Why else?" said Murat. "Because he witnessed another murder. And so the murderer killed Kemal, too, because he was afraid of getting caught."

Timothy and Halaf's mouths were sealed shut. They hung their heads sorrowfully and appeared to be grappling with the reality of this terrible incident.

Bernd, who directed his frightened blue eyes at the Captain, had his own theory.

"Someone's trying to stop the excavation," he said. "So they killed three people outside of the excavation to scare us off, and when that failed, they went straight for our own crew. Why else would they choose the day before the press conference to murder Kemal?"

"I'm afraid the situation's a little more complicated than that," the Captain said. He still seemed agitated, as if he hadn't yet gotten around to what it was he really had to say. His eyes moved to Esra, who was crying. "If you can gather yourselves together, I'd like to tell you what it is I'm thinking," he said. He'd raised his voice so that Esra would be sure to hear him. However, the first response to his words came not from her, but from Bernd.

"We'd love to hear all about it and help you out, but right now we've got a press conference to get ready for."

That familiar coldness had replaced the look of trepidation in Bernd's steel blue eyes. For a brief moment uncertainty reigned over the table, until Esra interceded.

"No!" she roared, ripping herself away from the other young woman. Ignoring the tears running down her cheeks, she continued: "To hell with the press conference. I'm not budging one inch until I find out what happened to Kemal."

Her red eyes gleamed stubbornly in the morning twilight, making it clear that she would be making no concessions.

"But..." Bernd began to object.

"There are no buts about it," said Esra. "I will not go to the press conference until I've found out what happened to Kemal."

"Then I will," said Bernd, his blond eyebrows knit into a frown.

"You can't go either," Esra said. She spoke the words assertively. "You will stay here and you will listen to what the Captain has to say."

"And why is that?"

"Why do you think?!" Esra exclaimed. "Four people we know personally have been murdered. So perhaps the murderer is amongst us."

These final words both shocked and frightened the crew members. Again Bernd was the first to respond.

"So you mean to say that one of us is the murderer?"

"I'm saying it's possible. So far we've searched for the killer out there, outside of us. But isn't it possible that one of us is actually the killer?"

After saying these words, she picked up a napkin from the table and dried her tears. She was wiping her petite nose when Teoman spoke up.

"Esra, are you alright?"

He couldn't fathom that Esra was actually accusing the crew members of murder.

"No, I'm not!" Esra yelled. "I'm sad, I'm angry, I'm full of suspicions, I'm worried, I'm afraid. But I'm in my right mind. And I will not let any one of you leave until we've listened to what the Captain has to say."

"Then let me get right to it," the Captain said before anyone else had a chance to object. "It's a very complex situation. What you're about to hear from me may be most upsetting of all. And you might think that I'm out of my mind." He became silent, and then turned to look at Esra. "Maybe you most of all will think that I've completely lost it," he continued, "but I need to know what all of you think in order to carry out an effective investigation."

Esra was perplexed by these words which reeked of uncertainty. What was this guy trying to say? She wouldn't have to wait long to find out.

"Last night after I left here, I went to the cave where the hunters reported they had found the body," the Captain explained. "It's a small cave carved out by the waters on the shore of the Euphrates, about three kilometers from here. There's a huge stone in front of the entrance, so it's pretty well hidden, which is why it took so long for the hunters to notice it, too. They only found it when their dogs, having caught the scent of blood, lead them there. When they entered it they found the dead body lying on the ground, and then some equipment lying in a cavity, and so they notified us, thinking that it was a hide-out for terrorists. When I reached the cave, the first thing I did was use my flashlight to get a better look at the body on the floor. It was the clothing that first caught my attention. I knew that I recognized the clothes from somewhere. But whether from shock or excitement, at first it just didn't occur to me that the clothes belonged to Kemal. You can imagine my surprise when I turned the body over and saw his face. His head was injured, and there was a deep wound, about two and a half centimeters wide, on his right temple, but there wasn't much blood on the ground. Once I'd gotten over the initial shock, I began to look around the inside of the cave. There were blood-stained clothes, a pair of boots, two commando knives, a sharp hand axe, six pairs of thin gloves, three flashlights of various sizes, two bottles of fainting spray, a 9 mm Beretta pistol, first aid equipment, and a black monk's uniform..."

"So you mean the murderer was using the cave?" asked Esra.

"Exactly. So now we know why there were no weapons, fingerprints, or evidence of any kind at the crime scene. He was coming to the cave after he'd committed the murders and hiding his weapons there, then changing and going back out into public."

"Poor Kemal, man," Murat moaned, "he found the murderer's hide-out and was killed for it."

The Captain kept his poise.

"That's what I thought at first, too," he said, "but we were unable to find the weapon used to kill Kemal in the cave."

"You mentioned an axe?" Esra conjectured.

"There weren't any traces of blood on the axe. Besides, the axe would have left a scar wider than two centimeters. Kemal was killed with something pointy, but not a knife, more like a sickle." He fixed his eyes upon Esra and added: "Notice I said 'sickle.'"

Seeing the uncomprehending Esra looking at him with puzzled eyes, the Captain went on.

"I mentioned before that at the scene of the last murder we found a sickle with traces of blood on it."

"Yes," Esra said, recalling. "You said that the victim had injured the murderer with a sickle..." And then she stopped. She now understood the meaning of the Captain's pause. "Wait a second... Wait a second..." she said in a tense voice. "You don't think that Kemal was the murderer?"

The Captain looked at her like a child expecting her to be understanding, but seeing the glints of rage in Esra's eyes, he took a step back.

"We need to analyze the hair and fingerprints on the clothing before we can say anything for certain. But the boots we found in the cave were Kemal's size..."

"This is nonsense," said Esra. "Kemal can't possibly be a murderer."

"We're not sure that it was him. But I think we shouldn't rule out the possibility."

The Captain's efforts at placating Esra were of no use. She was no longer listening to him.

"Well you're wrong about that," she fumed. "Kemal could not possibly be a murderer! Say what you will, find any evidence you like, you cannot convince me of it."

"I wasn't expecting anything like this either, but it implicates him, and if the evidence is there, then we have no choice but to follow up on it. It wouldn't matter if it were my own best friend in question, that's just the way it is, the way it has to be."

"Well that's all good and well," interjected Teoman, "but there's no reason for Kemal to have murdered those three people."

"We've sent what we found to Antep. The technical investigation is still underway. I hope that it turns out not to be Kemal, but you have to understand where I'm coming from. We can't solve this investigation with our emotions."

"I'm not talking about emotions," said Teoman. He seemed at least as calm as the Captain. "I'm talking about the motive. If the murderer isn't mad or psychotic, then he must have a reason for committing these murders. Kemal never even knew the Chief Village Guard Reshat, or the poor victim of the last murder. As for Hadji Settar, Kemal was at least as fond of him as any of us were, maybe more. So why would he up and kill him?"

"That's what I'm hoping to learn from you," said the Captain. "Did you ever see Kemal acting suspiciously? Did he ever behave in an odd manner?"

"You're looking in the wrong place," said Esra in a cold, almost antagonistic voice. "We're not the sort of people who would go so low as to slander our own friend."

A fragile expression appeared in the Captain's dark eyes. "There's no reason to be so harsh. I'm not an enemy of yours or of Kemal's. I'm trying to track down a murderer who is endangering your lives. If I'm wrong, then help me out, set the record straight, but there's no reason for you to be on the defensive."

Timothy, who had been oddly silent from the very beginning, spoke up. "The Captain's right, guys," he said. "Even if we don't like what he has to say, we need to help him. We are obligated to do so, and not only because he's a policeman, but just think of how much he's done to help us out. It's true that one of our own was murdered. He was our friend, but we have to answer the Captain's questions if he is to conduct a proper investigation."

Her eyes bloodshot from crying, Elif raised her hand like a student asking her teacher for permission to speak. "I want to say something," she said, sniffling, her voice still quivering. "Kemal couldn't possibly kill anyone." Then she went quiet, afraid that she would break out in tears once again. She composed herself once again and continued. "He's jealous, he's got a temper, he's vindictive, but he wouldn't kill anyone." She couldn't go on any further. She lowered her head and began crying again.

Timothy spoke up once again. "I speak for myself when I say that I never saw Kemal do anything suspicious. Yes, he was a little jealous. He did yell at people from time to time, but I never saw him act in any way that would indicate he was capable of murder. I have no idea why his body was in that cave, or what the wound on his temple might mean, but I agree with the others; I don't think he could have committed those murders. Maybe it was the murderer who killed him, and then placed his body in the cave because he didn't want it to be found."

Timothy's hypothesis invigorated the discussion.

"That's what I was thinking, too," said Murat. "It's a more likely scenario than Kemal going to the cave after he was injured. Kemal saw the murderer in the act. He tried to stop him. They fought. The murderer struck Kemal with the sickle. And Kemal died. Then the murderer carried his body to the cave so that it wouldn't be found."

"Okay, so why wouldn't the murderer want the body to be found?" asked the Captain, who had been listening silently all this time. "Why would he take that risk of loading the body onto a horse-drawn cart and transporting it kilometers away to that cave? He must have had a good reason for doing so. I thought about it all night and I just couldn't think of a reason. Believe me, I would be thrilled if any one of you could explain this to me."

Nobody had a good answer to the Captain's questions. Several theories were put forth, but none of them was convincing.

"I understand you all, really," the Captain continued. "You can't accept that your murdered friend might be declared a killer. But don't worry, if he isn't, the fingerprints will tell us so right away. In the meantime, we need to carry on with this investigation before we lose any more time."

He took a deep breath. Averting his glance from Esra's glaring eyes, he posed a question to the group: "Did anyone ever hear Kemal say anything about Armenians, or ever talk with him about them?"

His eyes settled upon Timothy.

"No, not all," said the American, thinking that the question was directed at him. "We never spoke about the topic."

"What do the Armenians have to do with any of this?" asked Bernd, his eyes blinking suspiciously.

Bernd's reaction did not escape Esra's attention.

"I'm just asking," said the Captain. He didn't appear to be particularly concerned about the topic. "Did he ever speak with you about it?"

"It was more like we discussed it as a group," replied Bernd. "We only talked about it amongst ourselves once. I criticized the Turkish stance on the issue, and he agreed with me. He agreed that there was an Armenian genocide."

"You're lying!" screamed Esra. "Kemal never said any such thing."

Everyone looked at Esra fearfully. They had never before seen her so angry.

"Please calm down, Esra," said Teoman. But the cat was already out of the bag.

"Stay out of this, Teoman. The man is lying."

"No, I'm not," said Bernd. Esra's reaction had surprised him, and even more so, had shamed him. "I'm not lying," he repeated, his face beet red.

"Yes, you are." Esra's eyes were burning with rage. She slammed a fist down on the table and screamed, "And now you're going to tell us why you are lying... What are you hiding? Or are you the murderer?"

"Esra, what do you think you're doing?" This time it was Timothy who interjected. "Just calm down a bit."

"Tim's right," said the Captain, in an attempt to pacify Esra. "We won't get anywhere by directing accusations at one another."

It didn't take long though before the Captain was again on the receiving end of Esra's rage.

"But you got somewhere by accusing poor Kemal, didn't you? Because he's dead, because he can't possibly defend himself, isn't that right?"

She turned to face the others sitting at the table. "Friends," she continued, "I want to tell you something. The Captain knows all about it already, but you don't. These murders are copycat murders of ones that happened seventy eight years ago. One or more madmen are repeating these murders in order to get revenge for three Armenians who were killed seventy eight years ago. But as you, too, know very well, there's no reason why Kemal would do such a thing."

Again she turned to face the German.

"But you, Sir, may very well have a reason. You've been ranting about an Armenian genocide since the day you arrived. You've caused unrest numerous times by bringing up the topic. You very well may have committed these murders, and then killed Kemal so you could lay the blame on him..."

Bernd, who was trying to appear strong, gave a nervous smile. "You've lost your mind," he said. "You're calling me a murderer because I've defended a fact of history?"

"Not just because of that. I know how much you love your wife. Didn't you tell me that you would do anything for her? So if one of those people who was murdered seventy eight years ago was a relative of your wife's, for example, her grandfather..."

"But my wife isn't from this region."

"That's what you say."

"If you don't believe me, I'll give you my stepfather's name and surname and you can do your own research. Then you'll see that I'm telling the truth."

His self-assured attitude as he spoke these words was aggravating. Esra was still trying to come up with a response when the Captain intervened.

"That's a great idea," he said. "I would appreciate it if you could write down here his name, surname or title, nickname, any forefathers you know of, and the name of the city or town he lived in."

Bernd was visibly upset by this response.

"I thought you suspected Kemal," he said in an offended voice.

"Unfortunately I have to suspect everyone. Would you please write down the information for me?"

Bernd wasn't at all pleased by this request, but he wasted no time drawing out a small pad of paper and writing down all of the information requested of him.

As the sun made its ascent, faces grew more tense, eyes harsher, and the discussion went on inconclusively. It was Timothy who intervened to put a stop to this vicious circle.

"Eshref, Sir," he said, speaking gently, "perhaps you've noticed that we're going on and on about the same things. And the more we talk, the more we offend and hurt one another. It is not at all a pleasant situation for a group of people like us who live all together here, and especially since we have a press conference in just a few hours time. I kindly ask that you put an end to your questioning for today. We'll have plenty of time after the press conference. And perhaps the killer's trail will become clearer by then. But please, for now, just let us get on with our work." He motioned toward the reddening sky and added: "The sun is about to rise. We should get to Antep before it gets any later."

"Alright," said the Captain with a bashful look on his face. "I'm sorry if I have caused you any suffering, but I'm just doing my job. Thank you for your time."

The Captain focused his eyes upon Esra, but the young woman was indifferent to his attention, and so dispirited, that he just turned and began making his way back to his jeep.

With a sense of relief Timothy addressed his friends: "With the permission of the head of our excavation, I'd like to make a proposal," he said. "Let's forget all about this unpleasant conversation until the press conference is over. Let's pretend that none of us has accused or hurt anyone else. The Captain did not come here this morning and we're still those jolly scholars getting ready to hop in their cars and go tell the world about their discoveries..."

"I'm prepared to forget about everything," said Bernd, looking at the other members of the crew from above the rim of his glasses. "I simply won't allow a few moments of anger to overshadow a day as important as this one."

"I'm not forgetting about anything," said Esra. She was still quaking with rage. "But I do agree with the idea of putting this behind us until after the press conference." Turning her eyes towards Bernd, she continued: "Kemal was not a murderer, of that I am certain. And the real murderer can be sure of this much: I will catch him, even if it costs me my own life."

Bernd remained silent to these words, which were spoken directly at his face. He got up together with Timothy and headed for the jeep. The others followed after them. They were about to announce to the world their enormous success, yet in the heart of each weighed that same sense of foreboding.

TABLET TWENTY-SEVEN

King Pisiris, the Panku Council, the people, the slaves, everyone in the city was nervous, but nobody, myself included, could foresee the true enormity of the disaster about to befall us. When Sargon's forces showed up at our city gates, it was assumed that the Assyrian army had come to get supplies. Neither King Pisiris, nor the nobles or the people suspected otherwise. Everyone, all those who had escaped massacre by Tiglath-Pileser's forces, an escape for which my father Araras had paid his life was at ease about the Assyrian king's arrival. Only I alone was excited, ebullient, in fact, with joy. The day when I would wreak vengeance upon King Pisiris had arrived. I watched Pisiris as he stood in a corner, unaware that he was to be sacrificed, preparing to fawn over Sargon like a sheep following his owner. I cannot possibly describe the joy I felt at seeing this. It was at that moment that I first understood how the gods, who hold the fate of humankind in their hands, felt. It was I who had prepared this bitter end for Pisiris, I who had determined his fate. Yet there he was, his body fattened by many long years of peace, raining down commands and fluttering about in an effort to welcome his guests. Cattle, pigs, sheep were being slaughtered, the finest wines were being taken out of the cellar, and white bread was being baked from pure wheat.

Finally, the moment came. Sargon's battle chariots pulled up to our city walls, and the Assyrians sauntered into our city as if entering their own home. The palace gates were open wide. All of the members of the Council, especially the king and queen, were dressed in their finest clothing as if for a holiday celebration. It wasn't long before Sargon, with his imposing body and dark face, made his appearance in the palace. Pisiris walked over to Sargon, accompanied by his wife. But when he saw the guards storming into the palace after Sargon like an army of pillagers, he was taken aback and grew fearful. The queen began to cry. Yet Pisiris managed to quickly regain his composure, and with skill that would have put even the grandest of palace sycophants to shame, smiling from ear to ear he respectfully bowed down before the Assyrian king.

"Oh mighty sovereign, hero king Sargon, it is a great honor for us to have you here in our palace."

But Sargon paid no attention to him. Instead, he looked at the palace staff, which was standing right behind Pisiris, and asked:

"Which of you is the Scribe Patasana?"

Everything in the palace grew utterly still. I could feel upon me the shocked, frightful, and hateful eyes of Pisiris, his face frozen in fear; the nobles whom I worked with in the Council, the palace guards, I could feel their eyes riveted upon me.

However, I paid no heed to their stares, for I was finally going to get the revenge that I had secretly thirsted after for so many years.

"I am Patasana, almighty sir," I said, taking a step forward.

Sargon walked over to me and put his hand on my shoulder.

"So you are Patasana. You have done us a great favor, and I thank you. You shall be compensated for your deeds."

Then he turned to face Pisiris.

"And as for you, king, you shall be punished for your deeds."

Dumbstruck, Pisiris looked at me, and then at Sargon, and then in a panic, he threw himself at Sargon's feet in a pathetic display, begging and pleading with him like a mere slave. Before my eyes appeared the dignified face of my father Araras who, even in the face of death maintained his honor, and the brave body of Ashmunikal, shattered on the rocks ... Once again I felt my hatred for Pisiris well up inside me.

Sargon completely disregarded Pisiris' desperate entreaties; he did not even turn around to look as his guards dragged Pisiris into the palace garden to sever his ugly head from his fat body. Once Pisiris had been taken from the room, Sargon cast a hasty glance at the terrified palace officials still standing before him.

"Separate the queen and the harem concubines," he ordered his guards, "and behead the rest."

The guards drew their swords and attacked the palace officials. I looked on as the people I worked with every day, struggled to escape, screaming. I had not expected anything like this to happen. I thought Sargon would punish the king alone, as he had done in Tabal, but it turned out that his intention was to eradicate the Hittites and turn this place into an Assyrian city. While my friends and fellow countrymen tried to run for their lives, I threw myself at Sargon's feet and beseeched him:

"Please, almighty Sargon. All of them, they are innocent."

Sargon's eyes shone bright with madness, like those of an animal of prey intoxicated by the scent of blood, and with those eyes he looked at me and said:

"Don't worry. You and your family will be safe."

My begging was useless; Sargon was determined to Assyrianize this city. A massacre even bloodier than the one happening inside the palace was taking place outside. Homes were being burnt, people were being slaughtered, women and girls were being raped, temples were being looted. Those who resisted were skinned alive, set on fire, had their eyes plucked out. Meanwhile I, pathetic, ignorant Patasana, who believed that he could take on the gods themselves, retreated to a corner and frightfully looked on as my people were exterminated.

The gods had made me pay dearly for my vanity. The Assyrians' massacre continued for no less than seven days and seven nights. For seven days and seven nights I listened to the wailing, screaming, and moaning of my people. On the seventh day all of the survivors walked past the decapitated heads of Pisiris and the palace elite which were displayed on spears at the King's Gate, and gathered before the city walls.

Young and old, women and children, the injured and the ill, everyone was made to step into line; they were then forced to set off on their march to Assyria, with the guards, looking like ravenous dogs, accompanying them in front, rear, and at the sides. If I had known that I would be able to withstand the look in their eyes and their bitter words, then I, too, would have taken my place amongst the pitiful procession as it made its way, shedding tears and emitting woeful cries. But I, a man whom these people knew to be a scholar, a nobleman, a skilled bureaucrat, I could not stand to join them. Not out of fear that they would kill me, but out of shame.

After that day, for me there was no longer any sunlight; after that day, I could no longer touch my wife, or look my children in the face. The air I breathed, the water I drank, the food I ate was all poison to me. The Euphrates, which had been my companion when I took leisurely walks to calm down, became my enemy. The river no longer gladdened my spirits or allayed my worries. I could no longer face the sunlight, and the sweet sleep that had once given me peace of mind deserted me. My hands forgot what it was to touch, my voice forgot what it was to speak, my lips forgot what it was to smile, my eyes forgot what it was to see. Ever so slowly the river of life that had flowed through my veins dried up. But I resisted; I struggled to stay on my feet, and to escape the lightning of the Storm God, which in a single strike was capable of felling huge trees to the ground. I resisted because I wanted my life, which had been so full of villainy, betrayal, and fear, and which I did not believe would last much longer, to end in a meaningful way; I wanted to tell everyone about all I had done, and about the murders I had caused.

CHAPTER TWENTY-EIGHT

"We're going to have to stop the excavation now," said Teoman, speaking in a whispering voice so that the others wouldn't hear.

He was walking alongside Esra in the treeless garden of the hotel where the press conference was to be held. They were a good two meters behind the rest of the crew.

"None of us is safe," Teoman reiterated. "We can't risk having someone else murdered."

The sunlight that had begun to beam down upon them as they were en route to Antep was growing harsher by the minute.

"Fine, but what about Kemal's murderer?" Esra asked, with a tense, even accusatory expression on her face. "Should he just be allowed to get away with murder?"

"No, but tracking down the murderer is not our job! We're not the police, we're scholars."

Esra stopped. "But the person who was killed was our friend," she said, looking Teoman in the eye. "And the murderer may be amongst us."

"We can't possibly know that for sure," said Teoman. He had stopped as well. "If we try to figure this out I just know we'll make a mess of it. And maybe a few more of us will end up dead in the process. I think we need to give it a rest for a while. Let's just postpone the excavation, that's all we have to do."

"I can't, not yet."

They'd begun walking again. Teoman, who was trailing after Esra, emitted a deep sigh and asked: "Okay, so when then?"

"I don't know," she replied curtly. There was a weary expression on her face now. "I don't know. And I really don't want to talk about the matter anymore."

"But we have to talk about it. You're taking this matter personally when it's not. I respect your sense of responsibility, but these murders are not an attack directed at the excavation. We're not the murderer's real targets. As for Kemal, he was killed because he was at the wrong place at the wrong time, that's all."

"I'm not taking it personally, I'm just thinking about the welfare of everyone on this excavation," Esra objected, albeit in a softer tone of voice. She knew that Teoman was right. She had no right to endanger the life of anyone. They had uncovered all of Patasana's tablets, and so it was the perfect opportunity to take a break. The ancient Hittite city had been more than generous to them and given them much more than they ever could have wished for. And now it was time to call it quits. Any other excavation director would have done just that. Like Teoman had said, their job was to illuminate the past, not to catch killers. They should leave it up to Eshref to catch the murderer. All of this was perfectly correct, yet Esra could not get that intractable ambition or that stubborn rage of hers to listen. The murderer had challenged them; he had taken the life of one of their own and turned their lives upside down. She couldn't stand to think that he still hadn't been caught, and that he might possibly continue murdering even after they had gone. She thought that it would be cowardly, like running away, if she were to call off the excavation at this point and return to the university like the successful scholar that she was.

"If you're thinking about everyone's well-being then you should stop the excavation," Teoman persisted. "That's the right thing to do."

By now they had almost arrived at the hotel door, where Joachim and two others awaited them. Esra realized that this was her chance to escape any further questioning by Teoman.

"We'll talk after the conference," she said, heading for the door. Joachim's head of red hair made him immediately apparent amongst the small crowd gathered there at the entrance.

"Did you have a restless night or something?" he asked in his heavily accented English upon seeing Esra's eyes which were red and puffy from crying.

"You could say that," Esra said, doing her best to evade the topic. "I mean, I worked some last night..."

"You shouldn't have done that. You should avoid doing anything that might cast a shadow on your beauty on a day like this."

Esra quickly grew bored with Joachim's conversation.

"Are the journalists here yet?" she asked, changing the subject.

"No, not yet; it's still too early. Their plane's probably just taken off."

They left behind the dry heat of the morning to take refuge in the coolness of the hotel. Under the curious eyes of the hotel workers they passed by the huge plastic flowers and walked down a red carpet to the conference hall downstairs. It was a small but endearing space looking onto the Alleben Stream, which was lined with old plane trees, one of the symbols of Gaziantep, on either side. The long, narrow table where the speakers would sit had been placed next to the window. Nearly fifty empty chairs were lined up in front of the tables, awaiting the journalists who had yet to arrive. On the table were four cardboard signs with the names and titles of the speakers written in large letters. The sign with Esra's name was second from the right. Prof. Krencker would sit on one side of her, and Timothy on the other, while Bernd would be sitting at the farthest end next to the wall. "I hope I don't lose it and break down in tears while I'm talking," Esra thought as she watched the hotel workers checking the microphone one last time. Actually, she was feeling better now; that ruthless knot that had welled up from deep within her breast to clog her throat seemed to have disappeared. Seeing Murat and Teoman already hard at work also helped to alleviate her worries. They had begun to pass out the photocopies and Elif's photographs, leaving one large envelope on each chair for the journalists. Bernd was standing at the hall entrance holding out the text for his talk and asking Joachim something. He seemed to have forgotten all about Kemal's death and their unpleasant argument that morning. How could someone be so relaxed after such a tense discussion? Bernd's attitude made Esra all that much more suspicious of him. Timothy was standing in front of the window, looking out at the old plane trees. As soon as she saw him, she felt herself grow all warm inside and her heart well up with trust. She automatically began making her way to the window when she noticed Elif and stopped in her tracks. The young woman was sitting on the edge of one of the chairs in the back row with her chin propped upon her hand, brooding. Within only a few hours time what was once a healthy and happy girl had turned into the most bereft person on the fact of the earth. Esra felt just awful for her. She decided against talking with Timothy and walked over to Elif instead.

She held out her hand to the younger woman. "Come on now," she said with a heartfelt smile.

"Where to?" Elif asked, the pain on her face still palpable.

"Just come on," Esra persisted, grabbing Elif by the hand and almost literally dragging her out of the conference hall. She asked the guard at the door where the bathroom was. He motioned towards the end of the corridor. There was nobody else in the bathroom. Esra took Elif's face in her hands and looked lovingly into her eyes.

"Now we're going to make you the world's most beautiful photographer. The journalists who see you are going to forget all about the Patasana tablets."

The girl's green eyes grew moist and her body began to shake.

"He died because of me," she said in a hoarse voice. "If I hadn't left him, he'd be alive now."

"No," said Esra, wiping the tears from the girl's cheeks. "He didn't die because of you."

"I keep seeing him with that scathing look in his eyes... The way he'd look at you from beneath those eyebrows, his eyes full of reproach..."

"You are not to blame for anything that happened."

"But he blamed me. He died while he was mad at me. He'll enter my dreams. He won't ever leave me alone."

"It'll be alright, Elif. This will all pass. He wouldn't have wanted anything bad to happen to you. And you wouldn't have wanted anything bad to happen to him either."

"I wouldn't, and if I'd known it was going to end like this, I never would have broken up with him."

"I know," said Esra. She embraced Elif to hide her own tears. In comforting Elif she was actually trying to calm herself down and ameliorate her own fears, doubts, and anxieties.

By the time that the twenty-five journalists arrived at the hotel, all preparations had been completed. Esra had done Elif's make-up, and while she may not have turned Elif into the world's most beautiful journalist, she did manage to lighten up the pessimistic air that surrounded her and give her the appearance of a dignified young woman. The full bearded, smiling president of the Istanbul Branch of the German Archaeological Institute, Professor Krencker, arrived at the hotel together with the journalists and congratulated the excavation crew members one by one. He rained down praises upon Esra, paying no mind to Bernd's jealous looks their way. He even went so far as to announce to the journalists next to him that "The real hero of this dig is the young woman right here." Noticing Kemal's absence, he asked where Kemal was. There was a distressful silence until Timothy finally intervened to tell him that Kemal was ill. He hadn't wanted to tell the older archaeologist, whose reaction he had no way of predicting, about what had happened and risk having the press conference, which was just about to start, cancelled or postponed. After about an hour of conversation and refreshments, the speakers and journalists took their places in the conference hall.

Esra, who now sat surrounded by the three men at the table, was irritated by the flashing of the cameras. She had to squint to look at the journalists gathered all around her. Teoman, Murat, and Elif stood at the right end of the table, the joy on their faces overshadowed by their sorrow. As for Joachim and his two men, they were standing close to the door.

Professor Krencker was the first to speak. After thanking the journalists for coming so far to join them, he spoke of the German Archaeological Institute's successful work in Turkey over the past seventy years during which the country had been the site of one of the Institute's ten branches established in principle centers of archaeological importance throughout the world. He talked about the discoveries that had been made by Institute sponsored excavations. Finally, he ended his brief talk by saying that the uncovering of the Patasana tablets marked another great feat in the history of archaeology.

Esra was next to talk. She looked a little nervous; her voice was shaking and at first she had a hard time getting the words out. But this only served to make her speech seem all that more sincere, and the journalists were soon infected by her excitement. She provided information about the history of the ancient city. Though she had her talk written out in front of her, she tried not to look at it, thinking that it would only confuse her. She talked about the Neo-Hittite period in which Patasana had lived in a simple yet detailed speech. By the time she had reached the end of her talk, she had calmed down enough to look the journalists in the eye. That's when she saw the Captain. He stood out like a sore thumb in his uniform there amongst the civilians. "I wonder why he's here," Esra thought. Presumably he was there to win her heart back. Esra had been very angry with him that morning, but when their eyes met there in the conference room, she couldn't help but break out in a little smile.

Next up was Bernd. He explained the geopolitics of the states in the region in the 700's B.C.E. In academic language he told the crowd about relations amongst the city-states of the Neo-Hittites, Urartu, Phrygia, and Assyria; his speech was a bit bland here and there, and he certainly didn't skip any details. Using examples he explained how the peoples back then interacted, the relationship between the Hatti, which was a tribe indigenous to Anatolia, and the Hittites, who were of Indo-European origin, and the influence of the Aramaeans, a Semitic tribe, on the region, frequently pushing his glasses back up his nose throughout his talk.

Timothy was the last to speak. Like Bernd, he started off in an academic tone. He explained that the tablets had been written some two thousand and seven hundred years ago, that they were composed in the Akkadian language in cuneiform script on clay tablets, and that they had been baked to make them durable. He had brought the first tablet along with him, and this he proceeded to show to the journalists, who promptly aimed their cameras to photograph and film the important artifact. Timothy then began explaining the significance of the Patasana tablets.

It was at that moment that Esra noticed how the American's voice got louder, and how the words rolled so harmonically off of his tongue like a poem or an elegy. He spoke with anger, fear, passion, his very soul afire, as if it were he and not Patasana who had written the tablets, as if he had witnessed the massacre that had happened two thousand and seven hundred years ago with his own eyes, as if he had heard the screams of the people slaughtered by the soldiers with his own ears, as if he had smelt the scent of blood spilled onto the city's stone streets with his own nose. His talk, reminiscent of the furious screams of a wounded animal, touched everyone in the conference hall, including Esra. She looked at her colleague from out of the corner of her eye. Seeing Timothy's strong chin trembling beneath his red beard, she wondered to herself, "What the heck's going on with this guy?"

"Maybe some archaeologists will try to debate the truth of the matter by writing these tablets off as epics or fairytales," the American continued. "But as the person who translated these tablets, I swear to you that Patasana wrote these words with the very light of his mind and spirit. His was a sincere attempt to convey the reality as his mind and spirit understood it onto these clay tablets. On the first tablet, the one that I showed you, he wrote as follows:

"'You can be certain that what I have written contains not a single word of untruth. My words that were not true I had carved onto the wall of the Water Gate in praise of the King Pisiris, and it was with these words that I furnished letters to the Phrygian King Midas to fool him; I strung such words together to confound the Urartian King Rusa and I expended them to provoke the Assyrian King Sargon. I used exaggerated, fancy, lying words to set kings, whose names were large but their selves small, and who swelled with pride the more they were flattered, quarreling with one another. Not even one of those lying words has made its way into the tablets you will read.'

"I believe him. Patasana was a forerunner of today's intellectuals. This state official who experienced the trials and tribulations of his age in the worst way, successfully managed to think independently of the king and wanted to relate his own experiences to subsequent generations so that the massacres, mass murders, and tyranny of his age would never be repeated in the future; and he did so while serving up the harshest criticism for himself and defying the gods. Patasana was one of the earliest authors to discover the monster that resides within mankind. His tablets are full of sentences warning us against ourselves. The Patasana tablets are therefore an extremely important archaeological find. However, they are important not only for archaeology, but for history, sociology, politics, and ethics, in short, for humanity as well."

Timothy grew silent and looked the crowd over, his velvety black eyes ablaze. "It's important," he said, extending his arms out, palms up, in despair, "but unfortunately, it won't do any good."

A rush of murmuring rose from the crowd as the journalists looked at one another, seeking reassurance that their ears weren't playing tricks on them. The rest of the excavation crew meanwhile just assumed that the experienced archaeologist was trying to turn a striking phrase to make his speech more compelling.

"You heard right," Timothy roared. "Just as Homer's Illiad, Moses' Torah, Jesus' New Testament, Mohammed's Kuran, and the thousands of pages composed by hundreds of philosophers, Patasana's tablets will not be enough to put a stop to the savagery in the hearts of men."

Esra's curiosity had by this point turned into a troubling sense of bewilderment. She couldn't take her eyes off of him. There was something extraordinary about her colleague at that moment. The veins in his neck were swelled, his face was taut with excitement, his chin was trembling even more than before, and he spoke in a quarrelsome tone. No, this was not the Timothy that she knew. That reasonable, dignified, sophisticated archaeologist had been replaced by a sentimental, ragingly mad man consumed by his passion. Krencker and Bernd also turned their curious eyes upon the American archaeologist, trying to figure out what was going on. Timothy, though, paid no attention to his colleagues' puzzled looks or the cameras flashing and beaming in his face, but simply continued to speak.

"Man continued, in fact multiplied his atrocious acts after all of these texts were written. The 20th century will go down in history as the age of atrocities. Never before in history had humankind experienced anything like the genocide carried out by the Nazis, or the instantaneous obliteration of a hundred thousand people like at Hiroshima..."

Krencker was uncomfortable with the current content of the American archaeologist's speech, and so he wrote down the words, "You're getting off track, please return to topic" on a piece of paper and placed it in front of him. Timothy read the note and turned to Krencker, self-confident and resolute.

"I'm not getting off-track," he said. "To the contrary, I'm getting right to the heart of the matter. Patasana never would have written these tablets if he hadn't have maintained a hope that humankind would change. He wrote these so that people would quit killing one another. And the other great texts were written for this reason as well."

He then suddenly turned to the crowd of journalists in the conference hall and asked them, as if in casual conversation with another individual. "Tell me, what good would it have done?" he asked. "Aren't people in most of the world today cutting each others' throats, using linguistic, religious, and racial differences as an excuse to take over land, profits, markets? It has been a full two thousand and seven hundred years since Patasana wrote those tablets, and in that time humans have solved the mystery of the earth, the sea, and the sky, but, mind you, they have not put a stop to their habit of killing one another. So now are Patasana's tablets going to achieve what holy books holding sway over millions have failed to do? Are you naïve enough to believe such a thing?"

A waved of whispers and laughter surged through the crowd.

"Then why did you invite us here?" a female journalist asked. "If, as you say, the Patasana tablets are so useless, then why have all of us come all this way?"

Professor Krencker started to offer up an explanation, but Timothy cut him short.

"Please, Professor. Right now it's my turn to speak. You can talk as long as you want once I'm through."

He said this so emphatically that the old man did not insist any further. Timothy turned to look at the journalist who had posed the question.

"You will not be sorry that you came here, little lady," he said. An enigmatic expression appeared upon his face. "None of the journalists here today will be sorry they came. You're all going to go back to Istanbul with some headline news, you'll just have to be a little patient."

Two more journalists wanted to ask Timothy questions, but he quieted them, asking them to be patient, before continuing his talk from where he'd left off.

"Patasana felt the darkness of the human heart, but he had no idea how to define it. Holding on to the hope that future generations would prove better than his own, he tried to wriggle his way out of the mess by laying the blame upon the gods. Patasana was an intellectual, and like many naïve intellectuals, he was seized by the illusion that what he wrote would influence people, and change them. But the truth of the matter is that expecting people to change for the better thanks to the influence of religion, science, art, or philosophy is nothing but a pipe dream. Neither religion, nor art, nor science really has any sway over man. Death is the only phenomenon that really truly holds any influence over man."

He grew quiet once again. The whispering and laughter in the conference hall had stopped. Everyone's eyes and ears were directed at Timothy.

"Man is the most intelligent of selfish creatures," his voice rang out in the small conference room. "For him, maintaining his existence comes before everything else, all other values. This is true not only today; that's the way it's always been. And the opposite of existence is death. And the more impressive, striking, and unusual the form of death, the more afraid, the more impressed, and at the same time, the more excited by it man is. To feel death, to be close to it, to touch it, to watch it; there is nothing more exciting. That's why death is one of the most powerful words in all the languages of the world. At the mention of death everyone grows silent with fear, respect, and anxiety, just like they did in this conference hall a couple of minutes ago. Death lures us in, one and all. That's why the best way to convince people not to kill is, unfortunately, by killing. Just like the Turkish proverb says, 'One nail drives out another.'"

There was a flutter of activity in the conference hall and the journalists could be heard talking under their breaths. All of the blood drained from her face, Esra looked at Timothy in a state of anxious dread, her worry about what she was about to hear greater than her shock at what she'd just heard.

"So, you mean to say that murder is a good method for preventing murder?" asked the same young journalist who had spoken up a while before.

"Yes," said Timothy as naturally as possible, "there's no better method than death for getting your message across."

"But," the young journalist said, raising her pen, "as you yourself said, there have been hundreds of wars throughout history and millions of people have died, but man still hasn't learnt his lesson. So, I mean, killing hasn't done any good."

An ice cold smile spread across Timothy's red hot face in an expression to which his friends were entirely unaccustomed.

"The great French philosopher and founder of sadism, Marquis de Sade, said: 'A single murder may pang the conscience. But when the number of murders increases, when they are repeated by the tens, by the thousands, the conscience grows quiet.' That's why war makes murder seem so banal. Yet the truth is that cleverly planned murders both rescue murder from banality and attract attention. And that's the piece of news I wanted to give you. I'm going to tell you about tree cleverly planned and masterfully executed murders. I'm going to convey to you a message of great import for humankind, a message sent by a realistic intellectual who refuses to waste his time with pipe dreams."

The journalists were all ears now that Timothy had moved on from the topic of death to the topic of murder.

"What murders? What are you talking about?" Professor Krencker interjected. The old archaeologist no longer had any patience for this nonsense, and his right eyelid had begun to twitch nervously. "Please wrap up your talk immediately."

There was a devil-may-care expression on Timothy's face, and his lips were still molded in that same cold smile. "Let's ask them," Timothy said. "If they don't want to hear my statement about the murders that happened here, then I'll stop talking."

The crowd of journalists broke out into a loud commotion. They all wanted to hear what Timothy had to say.

"You see," Timothy said, looking scornfully at his elder colleague. "They want to hear about the murders."

He turned to face the journalists. With cold but grateful eyes he looked over the group gathered there and began to speak.

"I was sure you'd be more interested in the murders than you would be in Patasana. I thank each and every one of you for proving me right. Yes, friends, you have heard correctly; three major murders have been committed in this region since last Friday. A prominent figure in the village, Hadji Settar, was thrown from a minaret; Chief Guard Reshat was decapitated; and lastly, the son of a coppersmith was hung and killed in his garden. The planning of these murders took about year, but their actual execution was squeezed into a mere five days so that they would be on schedule for this press conference. These murders were designed and executed to draw attention to three people who were murdered in the same way seventy-eight years ago. Seventy-eight years ago, in this same region, Priest Kirkor was thrown from the bell tower of what was then the village church, and is now the village mosque, Ohannes Agha's head was cut off and placed in his lap, and Garo the Coppersmith was hung from a beam in his store. As is obvious from their names, all three of these men were Armenian, but the more recent murders were not carried out in revenge for their deaths."

"How do you know that?" asked the piercing voice of a tall television journalist.

"Because I committed the murders," replied Timothy, who was still smiling.

A deep wave of murmurs resounded in the conference room. Esra gave Eshref a brief glance. He was in a state of utter shock, just like herself. He was frowning and struggling to understand exactly what was going on. And in this respect he was exactly like the rest of the excavation crew members. These words that so easily spilled out of Timothy's mouth explained the God damned unknown that had been messing with their minds and eating away at their hearts for days. But they did not want to believe what they had just heard; their minds were not prepared to apprehend this truth that they were forced to confront so unexpectedly. They just remained frozen, their eyes riveted upon Timothy, not knowing what to do or say. There was still a bit of hope in their eyes. They were waiting for him to retract his words, or offer an explanation about why he was talking like this. But instead, Timothy remained silent, as if to savor the impact his words were having. Esra was the first to recover enough from the shock to speak up.

"What are you trying to say, Timothy?" she asked in a tense and resonant voice.

"Not Timothy," the American replied. "My name is Armenak Papazyan. Dikran Papzyan, who was the grandson of the murdered Priest Kirkor and would go on to lose his mind, dropped me off at an orphanage as a small child, where I was later adopted by the Hurley family. That's right, I'm Armenak Papazyan, the nephew of the old woman known as the Infidel Nadide, the little Nadya of long ago."

There was a flurry of clicking shutters as every member of the excavation crew, as well as Captain Eshref, felt themselves being overwhelmed by this second wave of shock. It was Bernd, his blue eyes agape in wonderment, who directed the next question at Timothy.

"You mean you're the one who committed those murders?"

"Yes, that's exactly what I mean." The expression on his face was so blatant as to leave no doubt to the truth of his words. "I committed each and every one of them."

Like Bernd, the rest of the crew was struggling to fathom just what was happening.

"So," Bernd said, "you came to this region to kill those people?"

"No. When I first came here five years ago, it wouldn't have occurred to me in a million years that I would have been capable of such murders, though they certainly did teach me the fine points of killing back in Vietnam. There, I was always on the front lines, proving just how skilled I was in the arts of death. I would dance with death, over and over, before withdrawing to the trenches, where I would lay side by side with it; I breathed the same air, ate the same dirt as death. There was hardly any space left between us. I was so sure that death would capture me one day that I just stopped fearing it. But death loves surprises, and so it took my family, not me. My adopted parents, the Hurleys, died in a plane crash. It was in part due to the death of those good people I called mom and dad that I ended up seeking psychological treatment after the war. It was as if some power was punishing me for the things I'd done during the war.

"When I got out of the clinic, I found myself completely alone once again, just like when I'd been at the orphanage. I was thinking about going to get my masters at Yale and pursuing a real career in archaeology, but I didn't have the money. Around that time, I started working at a museum for a small salary. It was at the end of the second year that the miracle that would make me return to my original career happened. My mother, who had left our home so long ago when my father went mad, found me. She told me all about my father. She told me that he was from Turkey, from this town on the shores of the Euphrates. From that point on I was determined to visit Turkey. But that was about twenty years ago, when I was still a young archaeologist with a burning desire to practice my profession. And so with some help from my mother, I completed my studies. For fifteen years I was happily occupied with my career in archaeology. During that time, upon several occasions I crossed over into Turkey while excavating in Iraq. I had the opportunity to visit up-close the places where my father had lived. And what I saw I found fascinating. I was touched at how warm the people here were, despite the backwardness of the region, and I was impressed at how the old culture still persisted to a certain degree. I came and stayed here for about a month. I met David, the chief physician at the American Hospital, and his father, Nicholas. I concealed my identity and tried to collect information about my family. What I learned was horrendous, but I didn't feel any animosity towards the people here, and the idea of murder never occurred to me at the time. I knew history very well. I'd seen with my own eyes on digs just how cruel peoples could be towards one another. I decided to forget what had happened and search for the traces of that ancient culture in my father's homeland. I should add that my ex-wife played a part in this as well. Once she'd deserted me, I had no more ties with America, and so my father's country provided the opportunity for a brand new life.

"I settled here temporarily. The more I got to know the people in these parts, the more I liked them, and the more I warmed up to them. In the meantime, I'd also tracked down my aunt Nadide. I began meeting and talking with her, concealing my identity the entire time. I looked into her wrinkly old face and tried to imagine my father, whom I'd never seen in my life. Believe me, I didn't have even the slightest thirst for revenge, not at all. That is, until the day a bus I was on got pulled over by Kurdish guerillas in Osmaniye en route to Antep. A young second-lieutenant named Ömer was sitting next to me. He was traveling with his wife and five year old daughter. He had only recently been stationed in Antep; he was an upbeat kid, and he knew some English. When he found out I was American, he kept speaking to me in English. He was asleep when the guerillas stopped our bus, but then awoke in a fright when he heard their voice. A guerilla got on the bus and asked to see everyone's ID's, and then he made the two of us get off the bus. Ömer's wife cried and pleaded with the guerillas, and I told them I was an American citizen and asked them to let me go, but they didn't listen to either one of us. The last thing I saw when I looked at the bus before it disappeared into the darkness of the night were the large, frightened eyes of that little girl wiping the mist off of the window, looking for her dad.

"They tied our hands up and dragged us into the mountains. We walked all night long before they finally stopped and put us in a cave. They untied our hands and put an armed guard on duty to watch over us. They didn't treat us badly. They shared their food and drink with us; whatever they had, we had, too. We remained there for two days, not knowing what, for whom, or why we were waiting. Ömer totally fell to pieces; he was shaking like a leaf, and he kept saying over and over how they were going to kill us. I tried to calm him down, telling him that I wasn't going to let them do that. I asked to speak to the guerillas' leader, but they wouldn't let me, claiming that I was a spy. Towards evening a group of three people came and started to take Ömer away without explanation. Ömer clung to me in fear, and I grabbed onto his feet and tried to hang on to him, but they struck my arms with the butts of their rifles and ripped us apart. Then they dragged him away.

"I'd seen and experienced many similar incidents in Vietnam. I even participated in some executions. Back then I'd consoled myself by telling myself that we were at war, that everything would go back to normal once I'd returned to civilian life. But in that case, how to explain what was happening now?

"The next day, they took me to the highway down the mountain and set me free, again without explanation. But by that point, I couldn't have cared less if they had killed me. I wandered around for a month, completely numb, completely devoid of emotion. Then I started to think. I started thinking about my grandfather, who was thrown from the church, about my father, who lost his mind, about the young second-lieutenant who'd been murdered right beside me, about his doe-eyed little girl, and about me. All the people I'd killed in battle appeared before my eyes; I recalled all the signs of savagery I'd seen on excavations; I reviewed everything that I knew. The conclusion I reached was no different from what my doctor Jerry had told me when I was being treated at the clinic: Man is a cruel create that enjoys savagery.

"I didn't consider myself to be any different. I had taken part in a war and killed people for the sake of a few ideals, like defending democracy and defeating communism. I was just as responsible for this state of affairs as anyone else was. These thoughts comprised the first step towards my murder project. I decided that I should draw people's attention to themselves, to that dark place in their hearts that constantly generates aggression and savagery, because that very real darkness within us was a topic that everyone inevitably avoided. We enjoy hearing about what good, beautiful, wholesome, wonderful creatures we are. Nobody wants to point out our monstrosities, our cruelty, our selfishness, our narrow-mindedness, our love affair with death. Instead it's this constant lie about what exalted beings we are, as if none of the massacres, none of the wars, none of the savagery had every happened.

"Yes, there were some, like Patasana, who tried to explain this savagery, but their method was flawed. That's why nothing they wrote did any good. I, however, did want for my message to fall victim to the same fate. So I chose the most effective method of getting it across—death. But the deaths in question would have to be cleverly planned, awe-inspiring murders reminiscent of the past. That's why I used those three murders of seventy-eight years ago, one of the victims of which was my grandfather. In no way did these murders stem from a desire for revenge. It is true that the Armenians were victims of mass murder, but if it had been the Armenians or the Kurds or the Arabs in the Turks' situation, I'm sure they wouldn't have hesitated to do the same thing that the Turks did. I haven't done this as some sort of ethnic retribution. What I'm trying to do is hold a mirror up to people via the murders I have committed. I want people to see their horrendous faces in that mirror and put forth some effort to break free of the disgusting sight therein..."

At this point in his talk, an abashed expression appeared on Timothy's face. With sheepish eyes he looked at Esra.

"Back then Esra—who, I know, no matter how many times I apologize, will never ever forgive me—invited me to join her excavation. They were excavating in the region where the murders that I was planning on copying had actually happened. Though I'd decided not to practice archaeology any longer, I feigned reluctance before quickly accepting her offer. After we started working something incredible happened—we uncovered an extremely important archaeological find, Patasana's tablets, from the city library. As soon as the talk about a press conference came up, I realized that it was time for me to carry out my historical mission. And so I murdered those three people, in a manner similar to the murders that happened seventy-eight years ago, just in time so that the news of their killings could make the press conference..."

He spoke of the murder with the same ease with which he spoke of translating Patasana's tablets. Esra stood there listening, her face as white as a ghost, her body shaking. Her hands, which she held clasped before her, were trembling like mad, but she didn't even realize it. Finally she was able to gather the words that had been flying about her head.

"How can you be so calm?" she asked in a voice thick with disdain. "How can you step up here and talk to us so calmly after killing so many people?"

Timothy turned to look at the young woman with a meek expression of true regret.

"I'm so sorry about Kemal," he said. "I didn't want to kill him, but he just went into this jealous rage. He thought I was having an affair with Elif and so he followed me. When he saw me committing the third murder, he attacked me. I had to protect myself. And so when he died I carried him to that cave, so that the press conference wouldn't be postponed."

"The problem isn't just Kemal!" Esra screamed. She hesitated, uncertain what to do next, and then looking at the American, continued her sorrowful wails. "My God, Timothy, can't you see what you've done?"

The crestfallen archaeologist's velvety eyes were lowered in a doleful expression.

"Didn't you hear what I said?" he said in a surprised voice. "It was my duty. I couldn't just fold my arms and wait any longer while people kept repeating that awful, ancient wrong. Don't you understand? I had to do it." He shook his head in disappointment. "What a pity. And here I thought you of all people would understand where I was coming from."

"Just what was I supposed to understand?!" Esra yelled, raising her voice even louder. "How you trapped people and treacherously killed them one by one?" Caught in a flurry of pain and pity, she cried out, "What have you done, Timothy? What have you done..."

"I did the right thing," Timothy said. That stubborn gleam had reappeared in his dark eyes once again. "Even if you don't understand, what I did was the right thing."

Esra was struggling to breathe; it was as if the words were getting stuck and clogging up her throat. Still she managed to speak, though only in spurts:

"And what about those who died? What were they guilty of? What did Hadji Settar do to deserve this? And Kemal, and that poor villager?"

She paused once again. She couldn't find the right words to express her shock and disappointment. "Don't you see? You're a murderer!" was all she could say.

Timothy seemed taken aback by the intensity of her reaction, but he quickly gathered himself back together.

"Yes, I'm a murderer," he said, his posture, the look in his eyes, his voice all saturated with irony. "But I am a murderer who kills to prevent murders."

The look of pity in Esra's eyes vanished. Ignoring the tears streaming down her face and the whispering of the journalists, "That doesn't change the fact that you're a murderer!" she yelled out, emphasizing each syllable. Her voice shook violently. "Do you understand Timothy, you're a murderer... But not just a murderer, you're a monster, too... A... A..." She paused yet again. She was almost too enraged to speak. "You," she said finally, "you're a scoundrel with no qualms about deceiving your very own friends to achieve your goal!"

For several moments Timothy stared at the young woman with a profound sense of sorrow.

"You're right," he said, hanging his head low. "I'm a scoundrel living in the age of tyrants."

TABLET TWENTY-EIGHT

O patient reader, who knows my villainy, and who has seen the awful results of my thoughtlessness. I challenged the gods. I tried to change the destiny that they had designed for me. I caused the death of a king, their representative on earth. And they rewarded me with the most horrendous of punishments. They sentenced me to burn in the fire of my guilty conscience.

The thousand gods of Hatti, Storm God of the Heavens Teshup and his wife, the Sun Goddess Hepat, their son Sharruma and our Mother Goddess Kupaba... Yes, they are the owners of you and me, of the earth and the sky, and the Euphrates, but they are not good. They are horrible creatures lacking any sense of pity who derive pleasure from playing with humans.

Yes, we are evil, but it is the gods who have instilled us with that dark emotion. It is they who have allowed these disasters to happen; it is at their command that kings have declared war; and it is at their command that people kill, torture, plunder.

I'm a coward, I know that, and I also know that the gods will not forgive me after my death. I opposed them and I was defeated. I shall not ask them for forgiveness any longer. Once I have transferred my words to these tablets, neither shall I throw myself down upon the rocks where Ashmunikal came to her death. That would be a much too heroic action for a contemptible man like me. I am not a hero. I am neither a lover willing to do anything for the woman he loved, like my grandfather Mittanuwa, nor am I a noble state official willing to give up his life to protect his country, like my father Araras; I am the most treacherous traitor that the land of the Hittites have ever seen, a scoundrel who has brought the greatest evil upon his people. I shall suffer the punishment that the gods deem fitting for me, and I shall live with the heaviest burden there is on this earth, the weight of my conscience, until the moment that I die.

But I want people to read these tablets. Not so that they will oppose the gods. I would not want for anyone to suffer the pain that I have suffered, but I want for people to know themselves, the kings, the gods. That's why I have written these tablets. So that perhaps people will be able to better cope with their destinies. So that perhaps the kings and the gods will no longer be able to goad them on as they please. So that they will sow this bountiful land between the two rivers not with the blood of their siblings, but with love. So perhaps they will grow wiser and live in happiness, making their lives one long celebration. So that perhaps they will pass down to future generations joy instead of pain, smiles instead of tears, love instead of resentment, and life instead of death. Perhaps...